MW01252646

"If nothing happens in the sky"

T. Stellini

Cielo Publishing

For information, address the publisher:
Cielo Publishing, 7098 Locklin, W. Bloomfield, MI 48324
fax: (810) 366-9025

Library of Congress Catalog Card Number: 95-071615

ISBN 9649272-3-3

Manufactured in the United States of America
Recycled paper

Cover design and illustration by Lightbourne Images,
Copyright 1995

FIRST EDITION

To
BIG JOHN
John, Joe, Theresa, Jimmy and Emily
to
Babe and Theresa, Pete and Fran,
Tom and Rose, Larry and Cynthia,
Sal and Debbie, Robert and Diane,
Danny and Irene, Larry and Sandy,
Jim and Lori

also
Judy Bisogni and Judy Trahey
They made FLORA their friend which made me
believe in the magic of this story...and the
special things that are always
happening in the sky.

"If the stars should appear one night in a thousand years, how would men believe and adore; and preserve for many generations the remembrance of the city of God which had been shown! But every night come out these envoys of beauty, and light the universe with their admonishing smile."

R.W. EMERSON

Chapter
one

Blue Moons

Flora began proofreading a letter she had just written to her good friend Bill. She always wrote to Fr. Bill Pinzanni. Flora shared the good, the bad and the ugly with her Italian friend from the old neighborhood. Bill was like her brother. He was a good friend.

Bill was good looking and had a heart of gold. She sometimes wondered about their relationship...each of them being such a beacon of hope and joy to the other. It reminded her of the movie WHEN HARRY MET SALLY. Harry couldn't believe that a man and a woman could be just friends. And, while others agreed with Harry...she knew, at least where she and Bill were concerned, that being friends was the best thing two people could share. Especially if one was a priest and the other was a married woman.

There were many things in Flora's life that she couldn't explain, completely. Especially, her relationship with her husband, Jack. She tried to work things out for herself always giving Jack the benefit of her doubt. He was a great father...a good provider...a patient man...a pretty good gentleman farmer...and good looking. He even had a sense of humor but, Jack did not love Flora the way she needed to be loved. She needed to be loved even when the driveway was full of bikes without kickstands...she needed to be

1

loved even on the days when Jack walked into a kitchen filled with neighbor women *cackling* and a sink full of dish-es. Flora wanted to be loved without the thousand and one conditions Jack began placing in their marriage contract, one by one.

Flora's broken heart was becoming as obvious as the sun's seasonal position in the sky. Her patience was waning slowly, like the minutes of daylight in the diminishing summer solstice. With her head more in the clouds those days, she, like the earth, was experiencing a different tilt toward the sun. Through some quirky twist of fate...or a simple *miracle* as Flora described it, she began to see things the way they really were, the way they should have been seen. Through a huge misdirection of her emotions toward Fr. Bill, Flora came to understand many of the little changes happening in her life...in the world...in her heart.

"Dear Bill,

It's the last day of July and the sky and the green leaves on the birch trees confirm that date on the calendar. I thought I heard some whispers in the wind this evening. I know why the tall pines rustled from it's gentle stir. Every needle smiled with delight at it's message. I smiled too...not at it's message...I'm not exactly what the old wind blew in their ears...but more from the carefree way it rolled from tree to tree...like juicy gossip from one anxious ear to the next

Bill, it seems I've once again succumbed...(I had to look up that word for Emily yesterday so I thought I'd use it) to the power of the north...like a case of *northern exposure!* It takes over my soul and my better judgement. I expect it though every year like a dose of everything that is good for me. Only this year it's taken an even more odd effect on my being.

Everything up here makes me think of God. He makes me think of love...and that makes me wonder about time and how so much of it is spent in the search for love. So our main goal is to find love...not about time. Time is just a stupid measure that we seem to get all too much caught up in. So it's the journey that's important. Bill, I think I'm going through the change, or I am just changing. Something is telling me to wake up."

Flora jumped when Jimmy's voice pierced through her ear. She got up from the kitchen table and looked out the window where Jimmy's head was peeking in at her.

"The moon is coming up," Jimmy said out of breath. "Hurry, Mom...it's coming up fast and it's so big." Jimmy looked right into Flora's eyes as he took charge of gaining her undivided attention. His big white teeth that didn't quite fit his thirteen year old mouth stole some of his seriousness. Flora smiled hard at her anxious son.

Flora stuffed her letter to Bill in the already addressed envelope. She hoped it wasn't going to sound too far fetched. Flora only wanted him to feel the change that lately seemed to haunt her more and more. She tossed the letter on the sink where she would see it in the morning. Flora ran out of the house like a buckshot rabbit.

"Is this the *new moon* mama," Emily asked half out of breath from running up the sand dune. She stood on the tallest mound looking to the east at a spectacular view of the huge rising moon. She was very excited.

"Not the *new* moon, Emily, it's a *blue* moon." Flora corrected Emily's query as she herself gazed in the direction the wisemen once came. "Can you believe how beautiful?"

One by one the exclamatories echoed back into the cottage living room. They made the others, who at first seemed disinterested in catching the moon rise, wonder what all the commotion was about. One by one they all ran to see what was up.

"I don't know why it's called a *blue moon*..it looks more like a pinky moon...and it's so dang big", Jimmy commented with as much exhilaration and awe as an eighth grader could without being *uncool.*

"I think they call it a *blue* moon because...," Flora hesitated a moment because she wasn't sure what to say next. She had a bunch of scrunched noses looking at her for a simple answer. Flora went on, hoping to be enlightened.

"Ummmm...there is an old saying, *'once in a blue*

moon'...people say it when they want to refer to something that doesn't happen too often. Like this month...we had a full moon on July second...and now today on the thirty-first...I think we only have two moons in a month about every two or three years." Flora looked around at all the little bewildered faces and continued, a bit exasperated.

"You kind of understand?" Flora looked around at all of their faces. "When we get back home I'll go to the library and find out more about *blue moons*...for now we'll just enjoy the big thing, okay?...OKAY!"

Mary Dacy, Flora's delightful and sometimes outspoken summer neighbor, and Sandy, Flora's wild and crazy sister-in law, laughed at Flora and her attempt at explaining *blue moons*. They knew she could satisfy all of them...if not with the right answers...at least with something that would make sense to them. Flora could get down on their level...the kid in her never grew up. She knew that keeping her childlike perspective on things was her greatest source of true wisdom.

"Okay...okay...let's see how many questions we can answer. How many days are there in the lunar cycle?" Flora looked directly into Jimmy's eyes. He smiled at his mother's infantile query.

"TWENTY-NINE days...," Jimmy answered shaking his head back and forth in preadolescent disgust. "Is this question for real or what?"

"I knew that...," Emily quickly added, "...that's a cinchy question, any *moron* would know that!" Emily's announcement took some of the pugness from her brother's cocky grin.

"Yeah, sure...," Jimmy said trying to defend his image of the big and wise brother. "I *bet* you knew that...well why did you call this moon a *new* moon if you're so smart...any jerk would know that a *new* moon means that there is NO moon in the sky."

"Hey...we all get confused...I used to think the same

thing myself...," Flora said in a semi-reprimandal tone, first looking at Jimmy and then quickly turning to Emily. She made sure her eyes connected with all the other kids as she continued.

"It makes sense...a new moon seems like it would be big and bright like a shiny penny...but it's practically the opposite...a new moon can't be seen...like NO moon, so *new* and *no* both start with the letter N, that's how I remember the difference...I don't think Emily will ever mistake the new moon with a full moon again....huh, Emily?" Flora didn't want such a nice wonder to turn sour with arguing. Emily appreciated her mother's kind intervention.

"*New moon and no moon*...simple...but NEW AND BLUE sound so much alike!" Emily shook her shoulders up and down as she responded to her mother's question. Then she smiled at Flora knowing she would never ever forget the distinction or the secret of keeping them straight in her head.

"Hey," Mary said, hoping to get off the subject of moons, "...what's with all the talk about the moon...I smell *marshmallows* roasting...my mouth is even watering." She took Emily's arm and walked toward the top of the dune. Sandy just stared at the rising moon. While holding her son Stephen's hand she vocalized her evening sentiments.

"I'm really turning into a *moon* person more and more...I love the moon...I look for it every night...really, Flora, the dang moon got to me and now I go crazy when I see it...like now...or when it looks like a tiny fingernail in the sky...or when it plays peek-a-boo between the clouds."

"Or peek-a-boo between the branches of the tree outside our bedroom window in the winter...remember like last Christmas Mom?" Stephen said, pleasantly interrupting his mother's discourse.

"You know," Mary said shaking her head, "...all of you are cracked...no...I take that back, you are all *luny*...did Grama put too much *basil* in the Spaghetti sauce tonight?"

Mary walked back toward Stephen. She grabbed him and threw his wiry body in the air as if to send him to the moon. Flora loved Mary's sense of humor and appreciated her friendship to all of her family.

"Let's head down to the beach for the bon-fire...the moon will follow us...and Mary...I brought some extra basil for the marshmallows." Flora said laughingly, hoping Mary knew she was only kidding.

"*She* could use a little basil," Sandy said, knowing she'd make Flora laugh, "...a little oregano...and a *ton* of sweet and low." Flora laughed out loud at Sandy's wisecrack. Sandy had a quick mind and a heart of gold. Sandy was the life of any party and added the special spark to every summer's northern adventure.

Jack was sitting across the campfire joking around with the younger kids. He looked in Flora's direction but didn't see her or the space she had saved for him. Flora stretched her hands in front of the fire where she hoped the heat would take the chilliness from her fingers...from her heart. The campfire circle grew every year.

The kids were growing up and attracted many residents on their beach walks. The beach was the place to be at night. There was something for everyone. Lake lullabies for the musically inclined, shooting stars for the science minded, not to forget the romantically involved, and lots of talk...lots of friendly gossip...and lots of thoughts about love.

"Just saw another one...," Matt said looking over Flora's shoulder.

"Where...?" Flora quickly said turning around and hoping to see what Matt had seen. She turned around knowing she missed another little miracle in the heavens.

"Another one...," Matt said almost in disbelief, "...over there!"

"OH MY GOSH...I see a streak...but it's lasting so long...is it a meteor...or a comet...?" Flora couldn't believe she finally witnessed a falling star. She kept looking in the same direction.

"We saw a miracle, Matt.."

"We did," Matt said not completely sure of what to make with Flora's amazement. He continued watching Flora's face, not the night sky.

"Flora...it was the longest falling star I ever saw...," Matt said now feeling the magic reflected from Flora's expression. "I'd say it lasted about seven seconds...what do you think, Flora?"

"At least...maybe even eight seconds...it took me a couple seconds to look where you were looking and then it seemed I stared at it for another five or six seconds till it totally disappeared...I guess we were lucky to see it...huh Matt?"

"See what?" Sandy asked overhearing Flora's comments. "What lasted eight seconds?"

"A falling star," Matt said, "...we saw it over there." Matt pointed over the black lake.

"God, you guys are lucky...I haven't seen one the whole trip...but I've got the big dipper in mosquito bites on my leg...see... ." Sandy pulled up her pant leg and showed the kids her constellation. "Pretty neat, huh?"

"Yeah...that's the big dipper Sandy, Mary said sarcastically, "...maybe the way Picasso would have painted it...or like the way Matt saw the eight second falling star...and Flora can't count either...maybe you guys are sitting too close to the fire...the heat is affecting your vision...or maybe you saw a vision." Mary chuckled the humorous dig across the fire.

"Believe what you want...I know...rather *we* know what we saw...huh, Flora?" Matt looked to Flora for support.

"We saw it!" Flora said with much affirmation." "I guess Matt and I were pretty lucky...or maybe it was some kind of vision or message."Flora looked at Matt and smiled into his young face. The low flames made his blue eyes sparkle even more.

"I wish I were a poet...I'd stay up all night writing a poem about my first falling star...," Flora said softly exuding her total pleasure from the gift in the sky. "Really...think of it...we wish on stars...we try to catch them so we can put them in our pockets for starless nights. "

"Put them in our pockets? That's poetic," Matt said sincerely while looking admiringly at Flora. "Where did that come from, Flora?"

"I can't take the credit for that line...it's from an old song that Perry Como sang... ."

"Perry Como?...is he new...like Harry Connick?"

"No, not quite...," Flora said with a big smile, "...he's *old*...like Frank Sinatra...and he's a good singer still...let me think of the whole line...'catch a falling star and put it in your pocket...save it for a rainy day...catch a falling star and put it in your pocket...never let it fade away...for love might come and tap you on the shoulder one starless night'...let me try to sing it again in my head...I can't believe I forgot that one line...da da da da da da well anyway, it ends up like, 'you'll have a pocket full of starlight'...I wish I could remember the whole thing."

Flora looked at Matt who was looking at her like the forgotten line of the song. She couldn't quite place either one in her heart though she desperately wished she could.

No one wanted to call it a night. The last bonfire should last forever, at least that was what they had wished for. The moon was high in the sky. It borrowed some luster from the stars and tossed it back into the lake creating a shimmery trail of glistening ripples. The night was beautiful. Even the boisterous waves calmed and rippled a soft, sensitive farewell. Flora crossed the dune and said a prayer. She couldn't ask for anything in particular with words. God knew what she needed and Flora believed with all of her heart that He would always take care of her.

"Flora...wait up... ." Matt yelled to Flora as he ran down

the dune. Out of breath and with a sense of urgency he continued.

"I want to say good-bye...I mean...I really don't want to say good-bye...I wish we didn't have to say good-bye...I wish you didn't have to leave tomorrow, the summer goes so fast when you're up here...and when you leave...it seems like something seems missing...and I miss you...and all the gang." Matt sounded like an over anxious kid trying to make a last ditch plea for a delayed bedtime. Flora smiled with Matt's honest words. She knew exactly how he felt. She felt the same way.

Flora tried not to be the bearer of false hope in her next statement but she wanted Matt to know he wasn't the only one wishing for an extended vacation.

"Matt...I wish we could all stay... ." Flora looked into his eyes that seemed to have heard her desires. Flora went on guarding her expression.

"Hey...time marches on...and before we know it we'll all be back into the swing of September things...like school and getting ready for the holidays... ."

Matt barged into Flora's well intentioned but half-hearted words, "Everyday is a holiday...but look how many we just let go by...in the wind...in the sky."

"Matt...this good-bye thing happens every summer, this place just doesn't want us to say good-bye, the stars don't help things either...I blame those innocent sparkles in the sky for most of the havoc they bring out of our summer souls...those crazy stars." Flora raised her hand to the heavens and turned around as if not to miss accusing one single star for their part in planting the seasonal romantic feelings in her heart.

When Flora turned to face Matt, she found him standing very close. She looked up into his face for what seemed forever. She fell into his deep blue eyes that matched the color of the big lake on a clear day. She kept still as Matt carefully lowered his face placing his lips on hers. He kissed her tenderly. Flora kissed him back.

"I'm sorry Flora...I didn't mean to do that...,"Matt said very calmly. Flora felt foolish for not initiating the end of their kiss, and she was far from feeling calm.

Flora didn't know what to say. She couldn't say she was sorry...she wasn't. That scared her more than the stolen kiss. Then, Flora squeezed Matt's hand as if nothing had happened, as if the sudden earthquake in her heart hadn't budged her romantic foundations. She ran up the cottage steps. She quickly walked inside. Flora slammed the door hoping Matt would just go away. He did.

She leaned against the door heavily, wondering what to do next. Her heart was pounding out of her chest while replays of the moments before whizzed through her mind. She stayed in that position till she gained composure...until the tears she tried to hold desperately back finally over-flowed. As the tears rolled down her cheeks the thought of Matt's kiss thundered in her mind. Flora went to bed feeling very confused and ashamed.

Flora didn't sleep well and the clock's ticking was more of a nuisance than the usual comfort. The noise kept perfect time with the sentence she kept repeating in her head, "*You kissed him back, you kissed him back...why?*"

It was no use trying to ignore her rhythmic con-science...the answer to that query was somewhere inside her heart...but Flora had other things pressing her mind for attention. Flora got up from bed and made coffee.

With the morning sun minutes from rising and the col-ors of pink and blue dominating the horizon, Flora scanned the property in search of forgotten beach towels, tennis shoes and anything else that happened to escape the kids *final check*. She walked down into the gully and swept the patio bricks with affection. She made it her good-bye to them. Flora propped the broom against the woodpile and wished for another week in the north, another week to set things straight with Matt. It would be difficult going home with so much unresolved. Yet so much of her life was.

"We're ready Mom...Dad says 'let's go'."

Jimmy's exclamation snapped Flora out of her good-bye stupor. She grabbed the bag of garbage and walked back to the car reminiscing in every step about the night before. As she approached the open van door she made a quick dash up the porch and looked through the kitchen window one last time.

Flora thought the fireplace looked so inviting...so patriotic. The foil stars she hung across the mantle in honor of the whole month of July were the big decorating hit of the summer...along with her FROM THE GULLY sweatshirt design. They made her realize the importance of outwardly displaying excitement...no matter how simple or extravagant. Flora remembered how everyone that visited her commented on the red, white and blue tinseled garland. She sighed a deep breath and walked toward the car. Flora closed the door halfheartedly. She looked toward the Dacy's cottage and hoped Matt was deep asleep. His kiss came back to her.

"Bye summer home...bye little cottage...see you next year...we love you...," Emily said ceremoniously. Flora looked back at Emily and Jimmy and smiled. She promised them an even longer stay the next summer. When they reached the top of the pine lined driveway she opened her door and slammed it hard. It was time to get on the road, to get on with life.

Flora played her Beethoven tape figuring it would bring them up to the great Mackinac Bridge. As they drove into the direction of the sun it's rays closed her eyes like warm fingers. She thought Beethoven must have had a night under the stars with a heart like hers. A heart so full of love. She imagined his ODE TO JOY had been written from the melody her own heart had heard.

Flora's heart was like the sun, beaming and ready to warm anyone who needed it, even some who didn't need it. That was Flora. Her name made people smile...it meant flower in Italian. If anything affected her early personality development, that bit of knowledge did the absolute most. It established her destiny and became her philosophy way back in the third grade.

Flora was ordained a giver in life and graciously accepted the role she was sure God bestowed upon her. The years had been kind to Flora and she wasn't afraid to blurt them out in praise. "I'm forty-two years and as many pounds overweight", she'd often say proudly. There was nothing to hide on the outside. Everyone could see the external picture and despite the numbers in both directions...she was an attractive woman. But there were things on the inside that she kept hidden from most people...there were things she even tried to hide from herself.

Flora was a missionary of sorts, planting little seeds in the most peculiar places, sometimes causing love to grow in the most foreign soils. "Even dandelions are pretty...and on gray days they're more beautiful...brilliant yellow pieces of gold scattered around the earth reflecting the hidden sun."

Flora shared her precious gift of seeing the best in things with everyone. There was always so much beauty! And if Flora was around, you couldn't help feeling it. You couldn't help seeing it. Flora was a good person...not perfect, though she really tried to be. Perfect in the sense of kindness. She never wanted to hurt anyone intentionally. Not a speck of false humility or pretension was in her bones. But, her will was strong. Her desire in *doing the right thing* sometimes created an impenetrable wall of righteousness for those who knew her well. That wall was intimidating even to those who loved Flora. Their apprehension and Flora's determination allowed much space for loneliness in her life.

It was the end of July. Hot sun, lots of sand and warm bonfires; talk around campfires and millions of stars. Secret wishes and not so secret glances that bare a person's heart and soul...at least for the few seconds it's caught. Then August: morning skies reminding everyone of the short season of summer, good things pass so quickly. They don't last forever.

Her heart felt sad as she gazed into the clouded sky. The six hour trip back home was melancholy. Two weeks in the sand and sparkling waters of Lake Michigan did that to a person; fourteen days of being a part of the natural and wonderful always made Flora sad when the journey back home began.

That was Flora's twenty-second summer up north and it wasn't totally what she had expected it to be. She was twenty years old when her parents built the cottage on the great lake, the same year she married Jack and began her own family. Young Jack was born the following summer and Joe the summer after that...little Flora the year the fireplace was built and Jimmy the summer of the deck raising...and then finally Emily, born on the tenth anniversary of the cottage's completion.

There were so many memories and good times...great times at the cottage. The kids loved Grandpa for their summer place and   Flora knew there was no better gift in the world anyone could have given them. The years were busy and the summer rendezvous' seemed to come more quickly with each passing year. The kids were growing and things were changing for everyone. Especially Flora, especially that year.

Flora could barely keep her eyes open that trip home and the landscape was melting into a monotonous blur. Then *he* came into her mind once again. Flora tried to nip that thought before it carried her back to the northern woods. But, the sweetness of his recollection made ignoring it almost impossible.

The past five years had been difficult for Flora and the awareness of being able to feel special captivated her imag-

ination.Those few precious seconds were heavenly, maybe
even silly...but they were okay. Matt's kiss was pure and
simple...and good. Flora convinced herself that it wasn't a
matter of time or age or place...it was a matter of love...a
smile, an affection, a warm moment bonding two loving
souls.

Their moment wasn't premeditated, she was sure of
that. Flora never made any advancements toward Matt. He
was just a big kid who couldn't contrive anything awkward. It was one little kiss...and that's how Flora was going
to deal with it. She thought they had both been victims of
circumstance. For a few teetering moments the northern
night played with their innocent intentions. Flora tried to
be as open about the situation as she possibly could. Flora
kept telling herself the kiss was over. Flora told herself alot
of things.

Flora realized something she didn't want to, and then it
stared at her in her mind. She didn't want to think about
Jack and his lack of affection for her; his chilled heart made
her into the desperate woman who could accept a kiss from
a man half her age...without saying the word *BOO*. Flora
didn't want to admit to herself that her relationship to Jack
had disintegrated beyond anything that resembled love.
She sat close to the car door...tempted to open it up and run
in the opposite direction, maybe running into Matt...no,
maybe someone who might really understand her.

"Any apples...?" Jack asked not taking his eyes off the
highway. Flora reached into the mini cooler on the floor
between them and pulled out a golden delicious apple. She
handed it to him carefully hoping he'd look at her with a
kind smile and a pinch of genuine gratitude. He didn't. His
stern face made her feel like a sad and helpless soul.

Jack's tanned face stared at the road in a way very
familiar to her. She wondered if he saw dividing lines
down her face. The highway was leading her home. She
wanted to think only of the pine trees and the coming of

Fall.

It was good that Flora's sister, Irene, planned a surprise welcome home dinner for the big gang. Flora and Jack brought up Irene's twin boys who loved up north more than even their witty and totally inexhaustible vocabulary so often expressed. Flora knew some things weren't meant to be explained in words. At least that's what she told the boys. They were Jimmy's age and great company for one another. The trip wouldn't have been the same without Danny and Donny.

Tracey and Christina also came along, as they had for the past six summers. They were seventeen, almost eighteen, a year younger than little Flora, who wasn't very little but was adjectived as such to keep a good order in things. She was given the name in honor of her Great Grandmother(who was deceased) and Grandmother Flora. Flora swore she didn't name little Flora after herself. Although little Flora knew that wasn't completely true. So if the word *little* managed to keep some clarity in family introductions, she would bear with it.

Since the age of two Tracey, Christina and little Flora had been inseparable cousins; therefore given the group title, *three musketeers.*

Joe and young Jack, Flora's twenty and twenty-one year old son's, and all their buddies made the trip every summer, too. The kids would tease Joe's best friend Bud about being like the mosquito's; some days he was pesky and other days almost non existent! Now the joke was, he ate twice his weight in mosquito's each day and triple his weight in groceries. Flora wondered about the mosquito part of the dig, but definitely knew the grocery side of the tale was no exaggeration.

Irene, Flora's sister and Tracey's mother, and Rose, Flora's sister-in-law and Christina's mother, had dinner all prepared for the coming homer's. Everyone sighed a breath of complete satisfaction after the bar-b-qued Italian sausage. The meal was delicious and greatly appreciated by Flora.

Their summer trip had already become a distant memory. They had only been home hours and adventures were growing in every telling. How sweet those tales of midnight fun would become in icy February. All the anxious hearts of summer would thaw with warm stories of summer's past. Magical days of July once again would be dreamt about and longed for.

Flora had daydreams of her own. She wasn't an escapist but she found herself taking mind trips back to the very recent days before. She knew there had to be some innocent explanation for the constant flights back...but she wasn't ready to go into it, not then anyway. Never would she jeopardize what she truly believed in. She always wanted to do the right thing and believed with all her soul that GOD would help her to see the proper light. Now was what mattered most...and...*now* it was time to help with dessert.

She knew herself well. Or, she thought she knew herself well. Flora was very busy the past twenty years and didn't take the time needed to figure out the unsolved puzzle that began two decades earlier. That puzzle affected every day of her life in one way or another. When a piece turned up every now and then...or when fragments of that mysterious haunt surfaced, she'd gallantly turn away.

Like when Jack didn't come home on their fifteenth wedding anniversary because he knew the family was there waiting to celebrate. Or the time he didn't go to the church ceremony for young Jack's choir debut because Flora didn't brown the chicken enough. It was easier for Flora to look in a hundred other directions. Her life was full...and very busy...and Jack was *Jack*, a guy enjoyed going in every direction but the one Flora was in.

Other directions had run out for Flora who tried to keep up with all the snaggled turns of Jack's. She ran smack into Matt, and his tender lips. She realized, at that precious moment, that something bigger than all of Jack's little disappointments had been growing inside of her. The tremendous void from not being loved, grew like the Grinch's heart with Christmas. It swallowed her grand mound of resentment toward Jack and left an ache that could no longer be denied.

A quick farewell broke the lazy pace of the day. Flora gathered up the kids and headed for home. The night was warm and very clear and the stars weren't as bright as they had been up north but they still made Flora smile. The whole day was very pleasant and the clouds up north had vanished in her mind. That was good.

Flora began sorting laundry when suddenly the raspberry stains and sticky marshmallow sweatshirts reminded her about Jim and Emily who were waiting for her upstairs. Emily wanted to say prayers, and Jimmy needed his *side - burns* shaved. By the time Flora made it up to their rooms, the kids were fast asleep. She gently placed her hand on Emily's head and whispered a quick prayer inside her heart. Jimmy mumbled something that sounded like "let's do them in the morning." Good idea, Flora thought. It was all she could do to flop in her own bed and pull the sheet over her exhausted body. Jack had already fallen asleep with his copy of Mark Twain's, INNOCENTS ABROAD.

The sun the next morning shone through Flora's bedroom window. The fresh breeze was crisp and thin and made her feel fortunate that there were two more weeks before school would start. The long easy mornings had been a kind of catching up from the hectic school days last spring. Everyone was taking advantage of the peace, even the cats. They all knew those mornings weren't going to last forever.

Flora noticed the grass was unusually green for that time of year. Her neighbor next door mentioned to her how he hoped they had better weather up north than what they had left behind in Union Lake. It rained every other day for the whole two weeks! That's why everything had looked so green and new, like spring. The weather up north had been excellent. Everyday was good.

The green grass didn't fool Flora. She knew it was August by the deep shadows of the early morning shade. Mornings in May shadows weren't as distinct. That morning, the shade through the old oaks practically shouted August with their refined lines and exaggerated shapes. They left no doubt in her mind that summer days were winding down. Flora wasn't a scientist and couldn't explain, in a scientific manner, the logical reasons for the definite change in the shade. But that didn't matter. Like many things in her life that was just one more thing she understood in her own way. Besides, her readings by Thoreau made her aware of neat things like August shade. Flora often mentioned to the kids bits of wisdom that she knew were so important to every person's soul. "He could give you the time of day within seconds of accuracy by simply observing all of nature around him." Things like that impressed Flora.

Chapter
two

Piper Cubs and Gutsy Things

Flora always got excited in September about her creative pastimes. Her favorites were water color painting and getting the house ready for *nestling* in. Autumn was her favorite season.

Now that the kids were back in school and there was some kind of routine Flora had more time to work on some of the unfinished household projects she began in the springtime with her mother. The ones they both decided to tuck away till Fall.

Flora's mother was her inspiration...her mentor. Flora had four brothers and three sisters and thanked God every day for her family. Grandma Flora was five feet one half inch tall. Her spirit couldn't be measured; it was felt through her motherhood and influenced everything she touched. Everyone who had the pleasure of her acquaintance was never quite the same. She was one of those souls who came around once in ten lifetimes. That's what Flora thought; that's what everyone thought.

Flora was amazed at the adventure in her Mother's bones. Not that Flora wasn't adventurous herself, but daring things like nose-dives and stalling an engine at the age of seventeen was beyond her level of guts. When Flora knew her Mom needed a lift, *tales* from the sky would be told. Flora loved to make her Mother's heart snicker. She

19

loved that shy but proud look her Mom's face would beam when she would take everyone back a few years and set the scene full of dear happenings that grew more exciting as the years went by. Her tough little Mother knew what Flora was doing. They were good friends.

Since the move from the old neighborhood Flora felt a kind of strain in their relationship. That was natural. Flora promised to keep a proper perspective of the situation and not let the odds get the best of them...what did numbers know anyhow? Jack and Flora agreed that the move would be okay and that it would even be an adventure! No one thought it would work and that really peeved Flora. The move made her see how cynical some of her close friends and some family members were. She tried to make the best of things and almost made it a secret resolution never to let insignificant matters louse up the relationship she had with her Mother. When things started getting real crazy she'd take a few steps back and say a prayer that little differences would be resolved. And most of the time they were. Nothing was impossible for Flora. There were times when she really wondered if moving in with her parents had been the best road to take. But, when she looked around at the big picture, she knew the decision that was made, was the best one for everyone involved.

Just four summers ago Flora had a family of her own and parents who thoroughly enjoyed her company. They would come to visit almost every evening when supper was done. They'd all enjoy a fresh brewed cup of coffee and a slice of some new recipe from Flora's kitchen. They'd talk about little things going on in the family, like Larry working two full time jobs, the twins playing basketball in the eighth grade like pros and Cynthia planting another three thousand pine trees on the farm. Night-time coffee was a re-cap of familial happenings. Those nights were very special.

Flora's parents were forced to leave their home of thirty-seven years because it was getting more dangerous to live in that area of the city everyday. In fact, Flora's Father was accidentally shot in the back when some drunk nutbar decided to blast out all the parked car windows in honor of the New Year. Little did the crazed celebrant know that Flora's father was sitting in one of the supposedly empty driver's seats! That phone call at three o'clock in the morning numbed Flora yet made her realize her parents would have to move.

Larry, Flora's younger brother, and Danny, Irene's husband, purchased a lot near their homes, down the same street from them, and sub-contracted a home. It was going to be a little house, enough for their parents. At least they would be safe. But, sometimes plans have a funny way of growing and a rather big house sprouted out of that scenic lot in the woods and made all of them wonder how things, financially, would work out.

The summer before the big move was really hectic for Flora. She entertained, for one month, an exchange student from Spain and became midwife for her cat Polla. Her kids were great about both; Anna from Barcelona and kittens from out of nowhere. Flora's relationship, because of the kids, company and cats, with one of the priests at her parish, was turning into something she didn't completely understand. But it still happened and that threw her for a loop. Flora never thought she would ever get caught up in something so prevalent. She heard of women who fell prey to their emotions but never thought she would be one more statistic. No one ever imagines themselves a victim to common things, especially when someone is as basically happy and righteous as Flora. At least, she always tried to be.

No one had an inkling about Flora's feelings for Fr. Bill. It came upon her so quickly and it was so sweet that it just seemed to fit right in and, it was so nice. Flora didn't even know the how or why of it. Father Bill for sure had no idea what his innocent visits were doing to Flora. Like the time he came to see the kittens and held them with such delight. He couldn't get over their tiny, furry bodies and how he marveled at their eyes when he saw them open for the first time. Flora's heart went out to him and in her mind she felt sad for him...if he was so amazed at that miracle how would he feel looking into a newborn baby's eyes...what a terrible sacrifice men like him had to make...what love they must have for their God. All these things would go through Flora's mind...she felt too much with her own aching heart. She saw too much in his eyes; too much she wanted to see.

Flora was hurt and confused and felt a great solace in Fr. Bill's company. No one would blame her for that, but then again, no one knew. She felt her secret was safe and thanked God for that wonderful ray of goodness in her life. Flora didn't want to look to close or understand too much...it felt good thinking someone really cared about her, secretly. Flora felt more special than she had in a long, time. And, that was good.

That same summer Fr. Bill visited the cottage up north. He spent one jam packed day of swimming, football, poker and Philadelphia sticky buns. He enjoyed the marathon completely and made Flora feel like she was filling that void she thought he must always carry. When he backed out of the driveway and headed down the dirt road for home, a piece of her heart went with him and would remain with him for many months to come. She saw a sad sky that night even though the moon was full. The dancing stars seemed uncomfortably still.

When Flora came home from that summer's vacation and after she realized she was getting too close to Fr. Bill, she thought about her brother's suggestion of moving in with Mama and Dad. She talked it over with Jack and they both decided that moving in with her Mom and Dad that coming winter would be the best thing. They could help with the bills, help in whatever way she, Jack and the kids, could.

Jack and Flora knew if they didn't make the move, financially, things would be very difficult for themselves, too. The tuition payments were taking every nickel from Jack's second job and next year little Flora would be entering high school which would make things totally impossible. If they moved in with Mom and Dad the kids could attend public schools and Jack could leave his teaching job at St. Rita's and have more time at home...even though he would have no home.

Jack loved teaching but the pay was one fourth his earnings at the newspaper. So he promised himself that after the kids were grown he'd go back to school and earn his teaching certification. That thought kept him going and made his life seem better. He knew that it was good to have dreams...dreams got him through more than a couple of hard times. Jack and Flora made the big move...their decision was a desperate attempt to rectify whatever was going wrong in their marriage...whatever was missing between them maybe would be there...in Union Lake. It had to be.

The horrors of moving and all the tales of woe were greeted and taken care of. Flora wouldn't allow anything to spoil their new life. It wasn't easy and most of the prophets of doom were proven wrong. Love conquers all. Flora believed that and kept it nestled deep in her heart.

Their home was beautiful and full of potential. The locality was from a storybook setting. The oak trees Flora counted as her greatest blessing. She never thought she'd live in a neighborhood like the old one which had trees lining the streets. That was as good as being paved in gold in Flora's eyes. She knew God had placed her there in Union Lake...in a home cradled in the arms of Guardian Angel oak trees. It was not her imagination, it was her heart that knew these little things.

Flora wrote once a week to Fr. Bill and looked forward to a reply which came at a much slower pace. Flora began to understand her relationship to Fr. Bill. She knew he understood alot more than she did.

Fr. Bill was always the perfect gentleman. He was a kind of make-believe, semi real hero, that lived far away. Writing to him made her understand alot of things about herself. Over the next couple of years, she grew in *wisdom, age* and *grace*. In retrospect, she found a kind of peace. Flora came a long way from Three Mile Dr. She had an even longer way to go. Through Fr. Bill's disinfected correspondences Flora came to understand the way things really were. She was a lover in a loveless marriage who needed to be loved...who needed to love. Flora felt embarrassed about her persistence and apologized for her blunt and forward writings to Fr. Bill. He understood a lonely person's heart. Flora realized her writing to Bill somewhat compensated for Jack's lack of interest in her life.

Flora's letters were a source of joy for Bill who was going through changes of his own. She wrote about things Bill loved to hear, like what the kids were up to and the latest gossip from the old neighborhood. By consoling him and not expecting anything in return, Flora pulled herself up from her slump and began to understand her life. She began to understand Bill's way...and the sometimes fickle way of life. At first she felt deserted by the man who would very seldom write back. Later she came to accept his *way*. It was the only thing left for Flora to do. Then, she began to mend some of her broken fences at home.

That night came. Flora looked outside her bedroom window and noticed the rocking chair moon which hung low in the dark summer sky. It gave her a super abundance of courage. Enough courage to finally confront Jack with the stolen kiss saga from just a few short weeks before. She got into bed and looked at Jack's eyes that were heavy with sleep but still open with good intentions of reading the newspaper. Before her nerve left her she quickly removed her well rehearsed line from her chest.

"He kissed me the night before we left... ."

"What missed me...are you talking to me, Flora?" Jack continued reading the paper.

"Matt kissed me the night before we came home."

"So what," Jack said with more than a pinch of indifference in his voice. "He always greets you with a hug and says good-bye with a kiss...big deal."

Flora was tempted to forget her confession. But Matt's kissing her wasn't the real big part of her remorse. She had to let Jack know what really bothered her about that night.

"I kissed him back... ." Flora put her hand on Jack's knee that was acting as his reading stand. Jack looked at Flora's hand and then quickly took his attention back to his newspaper.

"Isn't that the way it's suppose to go...boy kiss girl...girl kiss back... ." Jack still hadn't taken his eyes off the paper. His teasing voice and lighthearted manner made Flora believe she had made a big mistake trying to confide her broken conscience to Jack. She almost dropped the whole thing. For a few moments longer, Flora looked Jack's way. Jack felt Flora's eyes on him. He turned and gave Flora his famous glance. The one when he opens his eyes as wide as he can and looks somewhere into hers. Not into the part that says *I'm listening, tell me more*, but into her eyes where it says *enough is enough*. But it wasn't enough.

"Jack...*I kissed him back*...and a part of me enjoyed it...what do you think?" Jack turned away from Flora and put the paper down. He turned out his reading lamp and yawned.

"Whatever you think Flora", Jack said as he yawned again.

Flora hated when Jack ended a discussion with a roll over and lights out. That wasn't how it was going to end that night. She continued talking in the dark, she knew Jack was listening. Flora looked out from her window where her words came with some relief, some surprise and some sadness.

"I guess we ask for alot of our own grief...huh, Jack...I think our love is not our love anymore. Maybe it never was an *our* thing afterall...I was just too busy and too blind to see it. I didn't want to see it. I know I loved you with all my heart and soul...but you slowly broke my heart by throwing it all back at me...and you didn't care...you don't care now...you have a thousand and one excuses for your incompetence and you might even believe they're true...and maybe they are justified...but that isn't what love is all about...that never gave you the right to conditionally dole out your affections as reward packets...as something I earned. Love is something that's just there...and the most natural response of love is giving...freely and unconditionally. I never thought love could die...maybe it can...maybe we let it happen..... ."

Flora paused for a moment and looked at Jack's big bump in the covers. He was sleeping. She looked straight ahead in the dark. The lyrics from the song *ALFIE* suddenly popped into her head. She kept going over one line. *"Without true love we just exist."* Tears filled Flora's eyes. Sadness filled her heart. Sleep finally rescued her from both.

Chapter three

Replenishing

"...I'm glad you decided on going back to school, Flora. You have talent and a style all your own. Even if you feel your intentions are muddled, taking this giant step is in the right direction. I'll be looking forward to a masterpiece of a Christmas card!

"You and your family are in my prayers, love, Bill"

Flora enrolled in a oil painting class up at the community college. She was excited about the class and even more excited to be back to school with her two oldest sons. They were proud of her. Flora was overjoyed that young Jack and Joe had finally made up their minds to go back to school. They were bright guys who only needed a little more time to find their direction. That Fall was exciting for all of them.

The smell of Autumn brought back many fond memories to Flora. She thought it was strange that the season, when so many things came to an end, would always make her feel like something new was beginning. Maybe it was the association with school that brought the awareness of new horizons...new adventures.

Flora had an extraordinary sense of feeling change...in herself and in the world around her. She knew life was simple and it was to be lived in the spirit of true joy. Flora always put so much love into everything she touched. It was natural and it was real. Not everyone felt those things in the exact amount or depth...but felt them just the same...or at least began to feel them when Flora was around. And that was all that mattered to Flora.

Flora's entire family headed to their north country cottage for a week-end. The kids were happy to be together again for a few nights under the stars. The grown-ups were content just to soak up some awesome beauty of the upper peninsula. The kids were in their glory...the trees were in their glory...Flora was in one of her favorite settings.

Flora entered the cottage and before she even set down her carry all bag, her hands were busy undressing the fireplace mantle of it's summer decoration. Red, white and blue flags, shiny foil stars were fine in July and August. But, September was the season of colorful changing leaves and low hanging clouds and warm candle light.

As everyone settled their things in drawers and closets, Flora transformed the mantle into an Autumn visual feast. Persimmon paper pumpkins laced with tiny orange lights stretched across the seven foot mantle. Flora called for attention and ceremoniously plugged in the light cord. When the lights came on everyone's face beamed with a special glow. Their weekend was wonderful.

Her spirit that Autumn needed replenishing. How could she be any good to anyone, especially herself if the spark had gone out of her soul. That's how she was beginning to feel and that's what compelled her to action. It practically pushed her into the watercolor painting class.

The school was only blocks away...a nice walk in good weather. One day while jaunting up the hill with the pine trees in the background she thought of the cottage...she thought about Matt. Maybe it was the pines...maybe it was the clear sky...but something clicked in her mind and brought her back to lazy summer days in the north.

Her easel was set up outside that brisk morning along

with the other eighteen artists in her class. Flora wore her bright white sweatshirt with Michigan's map scrawled all over the front of it. Last year, Flora painted the shirt and pinpointed all the points of interest on the map which made it a fun thing.

Bubba's musical talent was fantastic and the sounds that emerged from the little basement on Teppert street when the kids were young, could not be described. Flora recalled that time of her life as heavenly. Glen Miller and Tommy Dorsey, Stan Kenton and Cole Porter would have grooved to the beat jammed in Bubba's band. Those notes were sweet. Flora's memories were very sweet.

When Flora was in the second grade she asked her teacher to come over one night for a rehearsal. Her teacher accepted. It was Miss Fehaff's first year teaching. Flora didn't know, but Miss Fehaff payed her way to college by singing on the weekends at a local bar. What a thrill it was to see her favorite teacher singing with the *swingingest* band in the Detroit area.

Memories always flowed from her mind to her heart and then through her life. Flora tried to keep things in perspective because she realized how quickly things could get of order, especially if she allowed her mind to dwell on things that could be...or should be. Her painting class would put things back in order. And, October was coming fast. Flora could smell it in the air that day. She saw it in the faded green grass on the soccer field in the distance.

Flora painted the sky and stared at the soft wash of color...lost for a moment in the clouds; the ones on her rice paper and the ones in the sky. Matt was there. What was she thinking of? No! Flora would not make the same mistake with him as she did Fr. Bill. She was older and wiser, if not happier. She did not want to become a desperate woman again, even if that meant building a wall around her own desires and becoming a liar to her self. That used to be her biggest fear; lying to herself to make things seem better. No matter how she tried to make Matt's kiss something past...it became something more present. Flora had confidence that she would eventually straighten her northern fling out. Eventually, she thought.

Flora had control of the situation. She blocked out those sweet but unrealistic thoughts by working herself tired.

Then one day a letter arrived from the Dacys, Matt's parents. It was addressed to the entire family. Jack opened the letter and then began to read it out loud, impersonating Bruno Dacys.

Bruno was six feet five inches tall, and had a walk that everyone could imitate...which made him the brunt of many *northern charades*. He had a thick Lithuanian accent and a peculiar voice that really didn't seem to fit his stature. It would even crack when he got excited...and that, too, was something a few of the truly talented ones in the family had fun with. Bruno was like a sign of the north...a beacon of summer. To see an impersonation of his unique gait or to hear a rendition of his gurgled voice yelling for his dog, Flopsey, warmed everyone's heart and made many anxious minds go back to the very pleasant days of the summer before.

Everyone at home scurried around the table and listened to the words from their summer friends. Jack had more fun reading that letter but kept his composure which made his one-act reading more fun:

"To the GANG at 7098 Lochmoor...We have a volleyball match coming up on the twenty-eighth of October. Matt will be playing against the Oakland U. team that Friday and Saturday and needs a place to stay. Would you mind if he hung out for the night at your place? Mary and I will try to scoot up for the finals on Sunday. Keep in touch. Let's have dinner together that Sunday. See you soon, the Dacys. P.S. The waves were great today! You guys should have stayed!"

The kids were excited to hear from them. Everyone agreed that it would be great to have Matt spend the weekend. And, it would be a treat to watch the great athlete play. He always told them how fantastic he was, at any sport. The kids wanted to show him around the greatest big city, too. Chicago would be chicken feed in comparison! Ready or not the Dacys would be there the next weekend. For sure, Matt would be there.

Flora was scared then brushed that silly feeling away. How juvenile she thought she was behaving. Like, what did she think really happened during their one-hundred second conversation, and their two second kiss? She knew she was overreacting and laughed at her absurd and ridiculous feelings. Flora put all her crazy daydreams to rest.

The plans were set and in a few days he'd be there...she had to make herself believe everything would go very smooth. No big deal. She would just have to get by thirty-nine hours. She could handle that. She had to handle that! Bruno and Mary were the best neighbors and friends Flora had up north. Matt was like another son. She talked herself into a semi-calm and hoped the impending storm would blow over.

Little Flora gathered the gang and made the proper arrangements for Friday night. If anything, they would be very busy. And, hopefully, Matt would be content with the gang. If he lost early in the tournament little Flora wanted to show him Detroit. She visited Chicago and wanted Matt to see that Detroit was a pretty nice place to live, too. She made that thought known many times by singing a tune from CALAMITY JANE. She wasn't a Doris Day, but the point still managed to get across to Matt about her town..."*the windy city is mighty pretty...but it ain't got what we got...!*" Matt heard that ditty all summer from the MOTOR CITY TRIO: Christina, Tracey and little Flora. Thank heaven he had a great sense of humor. Flora thought it was extremely funny and remembered how crazy she was at their age.

Flora didn't want to think too much about anything. Distortion always seemed to set in after an absence...she learned that lesson well enough. Last summer she enjoyed a few moments of feeling *special*, that's all. And, in a small way, Flora would always be thankful for that spontaneous and unexpected flurry of emotions. Matt's innocent kiss caused her to feel alot of things. Like realizing she was still alive.

Flora began to understand a few different things about herself. Things she conveniently kept simmering on the far back burner of life's big stove.

Chapter four

Explanations

October, no matter what the weather, was the most beautiful month on earth, Flora thought, especially in Michigan. It very basically put together life and all it's winter, spring and summer pieces. It was the frosting on the cake of summer...it was the sweet beginning of the season of *nestling* in. How could so much be going on with the earth and nature and not be noticed, if only in the smallest way. Flora had much going on inside her heart. Autumn must have been the time most planted in her soul. She used to often think that *without the Fall of the year...nothing could ever make sense.* Especially, love.

Flora needed Jack to take her in his arms and tell her that he loved her. But, too many things were in the way for him. Things he couldn't overlook seemed to take the best from him, leaving crumbs of goodness to share with Flora.

"What the heck are you doing now...the *homecoming* isn't suppose to be such a big deal...you make too much out of things...I'm going to work early...do what you want." Jack started the day with comments that were meant to place a damper on things. A few unkind words from Jack or a convenient rotten mood wrecked many a festive mood for Flora. But, she was becoming immune to his somewhat diseased temperament.

The excitement over the homecoming was putting everyone in a dither. Dan came down from college to take Little Flora. Christina and Tracey rented a limo. Christina was going with a good friend and Tracey asked her summer beau, Dave. All the young kids, Danny, Donny, Jim, Tim and Emily, Angelo and Tommy and Alicia, decorated Flora's garage with crepe paper and balloons. She helped them set out the snacks and reminisced her high school days as they waited for the limo to arrive. The homecoming *guests* were surprised with the wild decor and the fresh batch of apple squares. The hot homemade cider hit the spot. Everyone had a ball! That day was special for everyone. Celebrations filled the void Flora's heart was carrying.

The following week Flora had to get ready for the Dacys' weekend visit. Her painting class and the fantastic weather that week made all the preparations go nice and easy. She had the older boys gather some wood for a bonfire and then stored some hotdogs in the freezer for the anticipated ravenous midnight snacking. Good food was always the way to a kid's heart. Gathering around a fire with good food on a stick made even the shyest soul bare some of it's secrets...or at least an old camp song from sweet days gone by.

Flora didn't bother to take her easel down. She thought her paints would serve as the fall centerpiece for the dining room table. She hot glued some rusty colored oak leaves to the tubes and jars of paint. A few scattered scarlet and yellow maple leaves underneath them served as a natural placemat. Whenever Flora passed her creative centerpiece, she smiled and thought how much *Martha Stewart* would like her ingenuity.

Quite a few of Flora's newest watercolors were placed on consignment. Many of them sold for decent money. Flora managed to catch up on some overdue bills. That relieved Jack of a lot of pressure, and Flora too. Money didn't make the world go around, but it sure made the ride easier.

Things were going pretty well. Flora was busy and hadn't even thought of Matt or his kiss that much. Her watercolors were her saving grace. She more than enjoyed painting them and now, she was even getting *paid* for it. That was success. For Flora it was the greatest success. A *miracle* that she hoped one day would happen, did.

Miracles weren't an uncommon occurrence in Flora's life. She could recall at least three major ones. She knew there had to be a hundred more she forgot about. Flora remembered the big *three* because they happened within hours of her asking.

The *first* miracle occurred when Flora was thirteen. It was February and the midwinter blahs had begun to slink their way inside the best of everyone. Flora stayed up late and was working on a term paper, watching the cold drizzle hit her window and dribble down. All of a sudden one of her ears tuned into the news that was blaring from the television set in the living room. *Sonny Elliot,* the weatherman declared a *sunshiny day for the morrow.* Flora said a quick prayer for snow...for a snowstorm...no...a giant blizzard! What do weathermen know anyway? Flora went to bed confident the snow would come. It had to, God knew she didn't finish her paper on the *French Revolution*...and she didn't even begin to read chapter seventeen in *Biology.*

Flora tossed and turned all night. She dreamt about snow. Every time she turned or rolled over in bed, her mind sent a prayer up to the heavens...*snow, snow, snow.* Then, all of a sudden, the night was quiet. The rain stopped hitting the window. Flora stopped tossing. It was quiet...peaceful. Time to sleep and dream...there'd be time for term papers and biology. Snow *snuck* into town that night, unannounced...but very welcomed. All *13* inches of it.

The *third* miracle happened just a year after Flora's big move to Union lake. One morning in late November as she was going over her holiday list and budget, she sighed, then she asked God for a *little* financial help. Flora didn't beg for it, but felt God had really heard her. The next day, Flora won twenty-seven hundred dollars in the Michigan state lottery. Flora loved God's sense of humor and His perfect timing. Taxes were due and it was Christmas time! Because of that third miracle everyone enjoyed a happier holiday.

Then, there was the *second* miracle. It happened in 1968. It was the second day of the Spring term. Flora was feeling a bit overwhelmed in her Italian 101 class after realizing the other nine students spoke fluent Italian! Why not...they were from Italy! Then, Jack, one day and ten minutes late for class, strolled in. He was tall, dark, handsome. He told Mr. Modigliani that he didn't have a book yet. Immediately Flora's heart sang Dean Martin's "WHEN THE MOON HITS YOUR EYE LIKE A BIG PIZZA PIE, THAT'S AMORE." That's *amore*. Then, Mr. M asked if Flora would share her book with the new student. "Why, yes," Flora said with vivacious politeness. Jack smiled and sat next to her.

Jack had kind eyes, even though Flora could barely make them out. He was severely nearsighted and his correction distorted the actual size of his big brown eyes. But, that made him more attractive. Flora knew little hindrances in a person's life made make them stronger. Strength came from weaknesses weathered. Like, only people with impaired vision understood the real meaning of perfect vision. Except for Flora. She had perfect vision and still understood what a wonderful gift that was. She saw imperfections as roads leading to a greater perfection. And the greatest perfection being the realization that perfection in anything, is a matter of seeing with one's heart.

Back to the *second* miracle.

It was on Holy Saturday, the day before Easter. Flora had worked that morning at HUDSON'S and decided to walk the last mile home, instead of using her bus transfer; it was only a mile and a half. As Flora breathed the mild spring air, her mind was anxiously coloring eggs and hiding her little brother Jimmy's basket. As Flora approached the front of her Church she decided to stop inside and say a prayer. Lent was officially over. Flora all of a sudden felt guilty for not doing or giving up anything that Lent. She did nothing to prepare her heart for the wonderful feast of Jesus' resurrection. He died on the cross for her.

The sky was gray, a pleasant early April gray. The smell of spring and her heavy shopping bag filled with *Easter Joy* instantly overcame her spirit and overflowed her mind with the best of recollections from years past. With those thoughts she entered OUR LADY OF GOOD COUNSEL church.

It was dark and quiet in the church, almost gloomy. Flora quietly tip-toed to the front of the church. How completely different it would be the next day when everything would change. Like night and day, from black and purple to white and yellow. From winter to spring. How could just a few hours transform so much.

Flora figured that *time* was broken on Holy Saturday night. Like Jesus' resurrection was truly placed in our hearts and all of us *rose*, for at least that one day, from the regular scheme of things...from the predictable. Flora thought that Easter Sunday was more than a day from Holy Saturday. A jillion years out of eternity are planted in our souls during that holy eve. Then we wake up with a muddled fleck of something wonderful. Something that makes us want more. That was Easter.

Flora said a quick prayer to St.Theresa as she passed the life-sized statue of her favorite saint. Then, Flora headed for the votive candles by the SACRED HEART. She knelt down and prayed for her Grandpa who passed away just two short years before. She thanked her Grandpa for all the wonderful holiday celebrations he had given the entire family. His whole life had been a celebration. Flora loved him alot. She wished he was still on earth...he was too young to leave them...they were too young to see him go.

Flora hesitated for a moment. Her eyes caught the candle's reflection in the glass eyes of the Sacred Heart statue. She wanted to say so many things. Jesus seemed to really be there, she wanted to be honest with Him. It was just a statue but she knew there was really someone listening...asking her to talk to Him. Like a trusting child, she did.

"Dear Jesus, I like college...and I know one day if the right guy doesn't come along, I'll probably end up teaching...but my greatest aspiration is to be like my mother. I want to get married and have a bunch of kids and make them happy and fill them with the love I was given. I don't mind school... but *you* know what's in my heart. A Bachelor's degree in liberal arts isn't my main goal. A MRS. is really what would make me happy. You must know that there is this really neat guy in my Italian class...I wonder if he's the one...I'm ready to begin my life...please think about this...I really think that this guy is the real thing...and, dear Lord...I love You very much...I know whatever I ask of You, You will do...and I also know that if You feel this isn't the best thing for me, I know it won't happen...but, just in case You feel this might not be the right time or the right guy...think again, and make it happen anyway...I'm sorry for being so pushy...but I believe everything will be okay. "

Flora whispered a sincere *thank you* in her heart and excitedly headed for home. God *answered* her prayer.

The Dacys came and went. The weekend was great. The kids had a ball at the volleyball tournament. They sat up till all hours of the morning talking about school and last summer's adventures and how next summer would be even better. They all promised to take the last week of July and head up north to the cottage...no matter what! Flora tried to bow out a little after mid-night, but the kids, being so grateful for her late night menu forced her to sit out a while longer...and enjoy the stars. So, she did.

Flora enjoyed the stars and the full moon at the bonfire until Matt took her attention away. She listened to the chatter and dreams, and then...the relaxed silence of the night. The humongous logs turned into small, brilliant embers. A contented exhaustion was reflected in everyone's face. So many thoughts had been put into words, as best as heart thoughts can be. Flora kept hers to herself.

Flora avoided looking at Matt. She felt his eyes following her all evening. Flora realized that not facing her little problem was only going to make his suspicions seem genuine. His quirky little grin and forced coughs made her feel like forgetting the whole dumb situation. It was over, but maybe not over enough for Matt. He was a nice guy and deserved a decent explanation concerning the *up north good-bye* incident. Flora hoped she could give him one. One day.

Chapter
five

An Angel With a Paintbrush

Halloween. October thirty-first marked the end of summer and the beginning of great family gatherings. Halloween was one of Flora's favorite days of the year. Everyday was meant to be a celebration. Halloween was extra special.

Her way of celebrating *the eve of all saints* had always been a treat. Every day, Flora would bring one more decoration down from the attic...even if it was just a skeleton head candle holder. Flora knew the kids would notice them; they looked for them.

There was the pumpkin valance that hung in the kitchen window over the sink. That started the decoration fest on October first. The warm glow reflected from the orange fabric made the kitchen seem like you were inside Halloween itself. Skeleton lights were strung across the mantle, usually around the tenth of October along with the ghost candle strategically placed on the dining room table next to Grandma's flying witch doll that looked as if it had been zapped in mid-flight. Paper plates and napkins with Halloween motifs were strewn wherever there was a doubt about it looking like Halloween.

Then, on the afternoon of the thirty-first, the last decoration would come down from the attic: the Halloween *tablecloth*. The aged black cotton background with jack-o-lantern faces in bright florescent orange could and would be only tolerated on the thirty-first of October. All was fair in love and war...and on Halloween; that's what Flora would tell herself. She cringed while smoothing the wrinkles from that gaudy cloth every time she put in on the table. Then she'd smile knowing how much the kids enjoyed the tablecloth. That was reason enough to dress the table with the almost ugly and really hideous table dressing. Flora loved Jimmy's response, "...it looks beautiful...in a creepy, spooky kind of way."

That night before Halloween while the kids and Flora were carving the pumpkins, the phone rang. No one wanted to answer it and get pumpkin guts all over the receiver, but finally Flora two-fingeredly picked up the phone.

"Hello," Flora said while her eyes admired her half faced squash masterpiece. The voice on the other lined sounded familiar but she couldn't quite place it.

"It's me...Flora...Dolly Langworth, do you have a minute?" Even if Flora didn't have one, she would give anyone ten minutes out of politeness.

"Sure, Dolly...we're carving up the pumpkins...and I'm sure they can wait... ."

Mrs. Dolly Langworth became fast friends with Flora. She was a little older than Flora's mother and reminded Flora of her mother and her beloved Grandmother; except Dolly never married. She was engaged to an Army drill sergeant named Peter Sabatini until the horrible day he was killed in a basic training maneuver while preparing other young men for the war, World War II. Dolly never got over that completely. How could anyone get over something like that, Flora thought.

When Dolly lost her true love...her painting became her life...her new love. And she was an excellent teacher. Dolly was more than a teacher to Flora that Fall. She became a friend, a good friend.

Immediately Dolly took Flora under her wing and shared many fascinating stories. Dolly believed in Flora and Flora knew Dolly's life was a total submission to a love that was lost...but not forgotten. Her paintings were exuberant. Her style was her own yet reflected at times much from the impressionists. Maybe there was comfort in a style and a technique that made so many see the importance and beauty of earth's constantly changing light.

Flora wondered why Dolly would be calling her at such an odd hour. Her voice was full of excitement and made Flora anxious to hear more.

"You are going to think I'm totally crazy, Flora, but I had a long distance call from a dear friend of mine...a dear friend of Peter's...*Vincenzo Viviano*...he lives in beautiful Florence...and we talked about so many things...he brought so many fond memories back...oh, that's another story...so back to the point...he made me an offer I couldn't refuse! He commissioned me to redecorate an old and worn pensione...six bedrooms with a formal dining room and a veranda! There's so much more to this...but I'm waiting for him to call back with more of the details...I'll talk to you tomorrow during class...say hello to the rest of the clan...toodooloo!" Dolly hung up the phone hard in Flora's ear.

Flora looked into her receiver before she hung it up. Flora wondered how she ever got involved with such a crazy woman. Flora liked Dolly's whimsical ways and her stories from long ago. The stories made Flora really understand what Dolly was all about. Dolly was a good woman. There was more to her than successful art career could explain. And, for some strange reason, Flora felt as if Dolly had been sent to her. Like an angel from heaven who was going to help Flora develop all of her talents.

The kids loved Dolly. So did Grandma Flora and Bubba. Everyone was surprised how quickly Bubba took to such a personality, Dolly being so flamboyant and sometimes pushy. She became part of the family...not just a friendly visitor. Dolly was like an old lost Aunt who finally found her way back home. Even the cats took to Dolly. She would take off her sweater and sit by the fire and in two seconds Tom or Polly would be on her lap as if she'd been their favorite niche forever; Dolly would always smile and go right on talking as if it were no big deal...as if she and the cats knew something the others didn't.

Flora knew that Dolly was a heaven send that Fall, not just to the cats, but to her entire family.

Flora and the kids finished their jack-o-lanterns and couldn't wait to see them lit. Jack placed all five of them on the dining room table. Emily flicked all the light switches off, even the ones upstairs. Not not one speck of light could there be anywhere in the near proximity. That would severely dim the enchantment of the glow.

Jimmy had the honor of lighting up the fresh carved faces. Everyone stepped back, taking a deep sigh after each pumpkin revealed it's unique face...after each one came to life with that tiny flame of fire. Then, pleased with their skill, the kids just stood and stared...mesmerized by the atmosphere of the night before Halloween. For a few seconds, Flora allowed the traditional trance to well in her soul. *This is what life is all about,* Flora thought.

She also thought about Jack and how she wished she could light his inner candle. The spark had gone out of his eyes, and his heart. That's what he was missing. The glow from his inner being had been doused...and maybe by Flora. How she hoped that wasn't true. And with those thoughts in her heart she put the little ones to bed.

Dolly talked with Flora the next day after class. Flora was confused after their conversation. The giant news was like an earthquake and it didn't totally sink in Flora's mind. Talk about passports and shots and luggage. Flora was preoccupied thinking about her preparations for Halloween dinner. She stayed after class for an hour, constantly looking at the huge school clock on the wall. She was excited for Dolly and remembered bits and pieces of their conversation. Dolly's big blue eyes and her overlipped lipsticked lips made everything she'd say seem important. Dolly was going to Flora's for dinner and would repeat her *big* news once again. Then, Flora would be able to make more sense out of it. They would all have a glass of wine and enjoy the evening.

The hotdogs were grilled to perfection. Some were cooked golden brown...others till they looked like charred cigars. That's the way Jack liked his. He was the chef that night so everyone had their hotdog grilled *their* way. The kids were too excited to eat but Flora made them eat at least one dog and a few french fries. You had to have "something decent in your belly before all that candy goes down into it." Bad enough the next morning breakfast would be garnished with milky way bars and chocolate covered raisins! But, that was part of the holiday...and that was the way it was suppose to be. That was Halloween.

Dolly kept right up with Jack; she gobbled five hotdogs. Her hearty appetite made everyone feel good...it was like she was part of the gang. She didn't look like she could eat that much and that's what made it even more fun. She kept up with everyone in every way...she even jumped rope one hundred times...she beat Emily!

Dolly could type ninety-five words a minute on the word processor. That topped young Jack's record of ninety...and she could recite Emily Dickinson's poetry, which totally impressed little Flora. Dolly did everything well.

"Did you give Jack the good news?" Dolly asked with a quizzical half smile. Flora didn't have a chance to talk with Jack that day and she really wanted to hear the whole story again. How could she give Jack the good news when the news wasn't straight in her own mind. Dolly began the story all over again...but Flora asked her to wait until the kids were on their way for *trick or treating*...then things would be calmer and Jack and Flora could really listen. So, Dolly patiently waited.

The night was a perfect Halloween night. There was just enough haze on the horizon to put the *magic* in the night...and there was a crescent moon. The trees were bare and the temperature was comfortable with a sweater. The kids were tickled as they dashed off to the first house yelling *help the poor*. Simple times made a person what they were. Flora knew with all her heart that those special times were the ones never lost...they would always be there, ready to explain in their own way what life was all about.

Irene came and dropped off her kids. They caught up with Em and Jim and then met Rose's clan a couple blocks down the way. Bubba poured Irene a glass of cider. As everyone picked on the roasted pumpkin seeds, Dolly tried again to repeat her story...one by one, everyone listened. The night was young and the kids were happy, Flora could finally listen and hear what Dolly was saying.

"First of all I *feel* like a crazy lady...or I've been acting like one. I'm just overwhelmed and too much is happening too fast...where should I begin?" Dolly was feeling good and the grape *cider* she had been drinking took the edge off her hyped exhilaration.

"I'll start at the beginning." She paused, took another sip of her special brew and then sang the next line as if she were auditioning for a part in a Broadway musical. "That's a very good place to start." Then she stopped...looked around ...and continued in her *Dolly* way.

"Before Peter joined the service, he lived in Florence. His uncle operated a *pensione*...that's an Italian word for a boarding house type place to stay...like a bed and breakfast inn. Peter was the handyman...and part time cook, maid, baby-sitter and tour guide during the tourist season. When his uncle died, the pensione Belloni died too. Not because it lacked for boarders...but because the war took away all it's young help, including Peter. Peter went back to the States and enlisted in the army. He left his portion of the estate under the supervision of his favorite cousin, Vince, and promised to return after the war...but he never made it back there... ." Dolly took a deep breath and a five or six second intermission. She wiped a tear that was rolling down her cheek, shook her head and sniffed her nose, and then looked into the sky. Dolly more soberly went on with her tale.

"Well, anyway, Vince called me last night to tell me of his good fortune. When Peter died, Vince didn't want any part of the pensione. He gave it to another cousin on a handshake, never legalizing the deal properly. After all these years, and the pensione just gathering dust, so to say, it has come back to him. Vince went to visit it and became obsessed with the idea of fixing it up and running the old place again. He couldn't imagine himself giving up the pensione in the first place; it was known to have the best views of Florence, from the back three rooms at least. Tons of refurbishing will be needed, but the structure itself is strong. Vince told me that he sat in the kitchen and so many memories popped into his head...he could smell the espresso and wanted to mix up a batch of bread. Vince and Peter would always save a piece of raw dough in the ice-box and late at night, when the chief cook went to bed, they'd heat up the bread oven and roll out the dough and put anything and everything on the crust and then feast...and dream...a bottle of red table wine made even their oddest concoctions taste like heaven, and it made their dreams seem almost real." Dolly poured herself another glass of the potent cider and continued.

"So...Vince felt almost obligated to call me, since Peter and I were going to run the pensione after the war...in fact, Peter would tell Vince how good everything was going to be after he and I were married. He was so proud of my fine arts degree and what better place could there be on this whole earth for an art lover than Florence? How good those words were to hear again. That's what made this crazy old lady say yes to Vince's proposition. I told him I'd be there for Christmas...and my crew, after the first of the year."

"Wow...," Flora said as she looked at Dolly sadly.

It was wonderful news but bittersweet. Everyone else was happy for Dolly. Jack teased Dolly about his going with the *crew*.

"You're darn right you are". All of a sudden everyone was quiet. Flora wondered what Dolly had really said. What was she really asking? Jack wondered, too.

"I'm just teasing you Dolly, but if you ever do need someone down the road a bit...like in a few years...I'll be glad to come and do whatever you need me to do." Jack looked at Flora and shrugged his shoulders.

Jack was sincere and really meant what he told Dolly. He was a fine arts major, too, but never realized his full potential as *artist,* with a capital A. Most artists starve, and he had six other people to think about...so he shoved his art in the closet and put on an accountants robe. Jack was a very responsible guy. Maybe too responsible when it came to putting off those precious matters of the soul. Jack's ambitions had been stifled, denied, in the name of survival. It was easy for him to hide behind the wall of responsibilities. He blamed Flora for much of his grief. Flora felt his anger but tried to tell herself things would get better. And some days it seemed like they were.

"No, I'm not kidding! All of you are invited to come and spend a few months with me and Vince...why not? Everything will be paid for and the kids could be tutored there...Vince will take care of everything...I mean *every - thing!* Flora, I need you...and Jack, too...plus, it's like a job...you'll even be paid."

"A few months...that's crazy," Flora thought as she looked around at everyone's disbelief. Flora couldn't believe what she just heard. Sure, it was crazy, but it was also wild and kind of...miraculous...it was like her favorite dream came true! Now that it was in her lap, Flora won-

dered if she could handle that *come to life* fantasy? She did-
n't know.

Flora went to make up her bed saying yes, yes, yes, to
her heart. But, her mind didn't hear what her lips were saying. She hoped, with every grain of courage she had in her
bones, in her mother's *piper cub* day bones...in her grandmother's *fight the Great Depression* day's bones, that somehow Dolly's proposition would become more than just
words. It was going to be a long night for Flora. More was
hanging on that proposal than Flora could ever imagine.

"What do you think, Jack...," Flora asked Jack as she
tucked the flat sheet under the mattress. "I can smell the
leaves...in the sheets...don't they smell neat?" Jack looked
up from the paper and took a deep sniff into the air.

"I was wondering what that smell was...it is pretty
neat...what do I think about what?" Jack sniffed the air
again and then continued reading the evening paper.

"About Dolly's proposal...about our going to *ITALY*...to
Florence?" Flora was anxious to hear how Jack really felt
about Dolly's proposition.

"She is wild," Jack said as he continued to leaf through
the paper, "...but if she's half serious...I'd go if I were
you...it's a chance of a lifetime...find out more about it."

"I will tomorrow...can you imagine us going to Florence
for a couple of months renovating a *pensione*?" Flora was
excited to hear Jack's enthusiasm about the project.

"Flora...get real...I didn't mean *us*...I could never get
that much time off from work," Jack peeked up from the
business section of the paper and caught Flora's eyes for
one second. He quickly returned to the paper. "But, it
would be great for you and the kids...and maybe I could
swing some time off and meet you there for the last couple
of weeks...find out more of the details...but you'd be a fool
not to take her up on it...and the kids...what a great thing
for them...think about it Flora... ." Jack was very serious and
Flora felt that maybe she *would* be a fool to turn down such

an opportunity.

"I will...I'll find out more...like Dolly will even let me forget."

Flora finished shaking her pillow into the last pillow-case. She fluffed it and tossed it at Jack. She smiled at her bull's-eye of a shot and at Jack's perturbed expression for the mess she made of his paper.

"It was a good night...good night, Jack... ."

"It was a good night...good night, Flora."

Chapter
six

No Simple Answers

"I can't believe you are doing this...you can't stand the thought of flying...and it's a nine and a half hour flight from New York to Rome...but, I'm so thrilled for you...and I'm happy for you, Flora," Fr. Bill said in his annual day before Thanksgiving phone call.

"I can't believe it either...the chicken of all chickens...the woman who hasn't been west of Holland, Michigan and south of Toledo...is actually going to Florence...I'm excited...I try not to think too much about it...one day and ten errands at a time...I just picked up our passports yesterday...I can't believe it, Bill...do you think I'm crazy?"

"NO WAY...it's about time you started using your talents...Dolly must be one pretty smart gal...I've got to meet her one day...do you think she might need a confessor...I'll fly to Florence...Flora really...I'll keep you in my prayers...and keep me in yours...and *please*...you have to promise to visit Montefalco...you will love it...write to me and tell me all about it...I'll be looking forward to your letters."

"Sure I'll write...and Bill...thanks for all the encouragement, I couldn't have done this without you...CIAO my friend."

"Ciao...Flora...and don't eat too much turkey tomorrow."

Flora waited to hear the click in the receiver before she hung up the phone. Bill made everything seem so natural...she envied his faith sometimes and the calm and easy way he accepted everything that came into his life. He was a great example for her...he was a good friend.

The day before Thanksgiving Flora had a billion things to do to prepare for the big family gathering. The excitement of the near weeks before sort of put the holiday schedule behind...but no one minded. Flora wanted everything to be beautiful for their Thursday dinner...it had to be special. Her thoughts of leaving her country in just a few short weeks made her realize even more the importance of family and tradition. The kids pitched in with the last minute cleaning and the turkey was thawing in the refrigerator...waiting to be stuffed and baked.

Little Flora made the cranberry orange relish and Em and Jim decorated the turkey sugar cookies. Grama Flora made the dough for her pumpkin pie tart crusts that she'd bake on Thanksgiving morning in the garage oven. The tarts had to be warm when they were served.

Jack and Bubba set up the extra tables in the celebration room...which was really the garage. They never used it for cars. Why waste all that good space on cars? And, it made a very pleasant kitchen, enough room for thirty or more people to sit and eat.

Flora also plugged in the heaters just in case the temps dipped a little too low, which they all knew wouldn't. A record breaking Indian summer spell had begun a few days earlier. It was suppose to last up to the weekend. That was great news for most of the adults but the kids took it as a major bummer.

"It's suppose to snow on Thanksgiving , at least a little bit." Emily expressed that tidbit to Flora more than once that past week.

Flora knew Emily's sentiments exactly...her own memories of Thanksgiving almost always included snow, and sometimes, lots of it. The sixty-five degrees seemed a little too off season, but for Aunt Cynthia and Uncle Larry...the weatherman's prediction seemed to good to be true. Their ride from the farm would be pleasant...not like the year before when it was an "over the river and through the woods" and through six inches freshly fallen snow! So, there was a bright side to the unseasonably warm weather...there was always a bright side...if a person looked hard enough for it.

At noon Flora headed out to the grocery store for the last minute necessities, like the turkey napkins she saw the week before; the sales lady told her that they would be half the cost if she waited a week. Flora had to pick up the fresh mums and the fruit, the evaporated milk for the pumpkin custard...and something for dinner that night. Things were pretty much under control.

Then, a strange car pulled up into the driveway. Flora didn't recognize the driver. She thought it was someone just turning around. She walked toward her car and then stopped when she heard someone call her name.

"Hey, Flora...," Matt yelled out from the car window. It took Flora a couple of seconds to believe the surprise of the guest visitor. He was on his way home for the holiday. Since the weather was so beautiful, Matt decided he and Josh should make a *little* detour and visit the gang in Union Lake. A kind of day before Thanksgiving surprise! And, it was just that.

Little Flora yelled out the front door for the guys to come in and have some lunch with her and Grama Flora. Flora was happy to see Matt and his friend but she knew if she didn't get going with her errands she'd never be ready for the next day. She walked the boys inside and asked them to stay for supper. Matt graciously accepted her invitation. Little Flora suggested a bonfire...and burgers. That sounded great to all of them. Flora excused herself and headed for the grocery store. As she fastened her seatbelt she thought there should be more hours in the day...and then thought a little more and decided that might not be such a good idea. There would be more to do.

The day flew. The list of "things to be done today" was totally crossed off...except for *set Emily's hair*. Flora reminded Emily about her bath and suggested that it was time for that dreaded ritual. Emily hated taking a bath...it was the second most worst thing she had to do. The worst thing was picking acorns up from the grass everyday after school. Flora told Emily if she didn't doodle...she could sit for a while at the big kids bonfire. Emily ran upstairs to run the bath water.

The temps broke another record. It reached sixty-seven degrees and the night was beautiful. Everyone in the neighborhood took advantage of the weather and raked the straggler leaves that had blown down with the past week's wind and rain. Flora thought burning leaves had to be one of the best smells in the Fall, next to apple pie.

The moon was a perfect half moon, hanging completely perpendicular through the tall straight oaks. The purple haze in the sky set the wonderful stage for a pow-wow. Stories of old Indians and tales of the *first* Thanksgiving kept everyone's imagination going. The more said, the better the stories grew. It was good for all of them to be together. Matt's arrival was perfectly timed. The holiday was already a special one. It was like they were up North. No one wanted to leave the fire.

Emily dozed off on Flora's lap. Her wide eyes during the night fright talk turned heavy and finally closed. Flora carried her up to her room and then told the young kids to *head for the hills*...which meant *bedtime* in kids language. Jimmy went home with the twins. Josh laughed himself tired and bowed out early,too. Little Flora was almost asleep on Dan's shoulder. Christina and Tracey followed Josh inside...to show him to his room...they were being politely nosy.

Young Jack and Matt set up their sleeping bags by the fire...they wanted to rough it. Bubba placed a few more logs on the thick bed of embers before he went inside to watch the Wednesday night movie with Grama Flora. He told the guys to watch out for animals...especially the raccoons. Young Jack and Matt laughed at Bubba's humor...then wondered if he was trying to be funny...or maybe there really were RACCOONS that roamed all over your face at night?

Flora went down to the kitchen to check the turkey. It hadn't thawed as much as she thought, so she placed the twenty-two pound hunk of bird in the *Sunday* salad bowl and submersed it in cold water. She wanted to make sure it wouldn't thaw too fast. There were the gruesome stories of spoiled turkey's and Flora didn't want any belly aching Indians after the big meal on Thanksgiving.

The load of dish towels in the dryer were ready. Flora heard the dryer *buzz*. She went into the utility room to fold them. Flora peeked out the laundry room door at the fire. Little Flora was still resting her head on Dan's shoulder...while the rest of the guys jabbered on about school, football, tennis...and girls. Big Jack went to bed after eating his fourth burnt like charcoal burger. He had to get up early and go to work for a few hours Thanksgiving morning. Joe and Bud left the fire to see if Christina and Tracey were talking Josh's ear off. Their nickname...*blabber duo*, told it like it was. Although they knew Josh couldn't be in that much pain, Christina and Tracey were two of the most beautiful girls in Union Lake.

Dan came in and helped Flora fold the last few towels. He was very considerate that way. When they finished, he grabbed a sweatshirt off the coat rack and threw it over Flora's shoulders and dragged her out to the fire. Flora loved sitting with the kids but she wanted to go to bed early...she had alot to do the next morning. But, the kids were persistent and Flora gave in. She pushed tomorrow's chores from her mind and enjoyed the fire and the company of good friends. It was a beautiful night.

The maple trees were completely bare and the moon was playing peek-a-boo through the branches. Flora's eyes every now and then would catch Matt's. She didn't want to look too long...or too deep.

The anticipation of the upcoming journey to Florence made thinking about some things almost impossible. Flora's final decision to make the trip was based upon the feelings she experienced last summer up at the cottage. Even though her feelings never formulated into anything real, the mental fantasies were enough to make her stop...and think. Flora had to come to terms with the loneliness in her heart. One beautiful falling star...an unexpected kiss flipped her world upside down. Then, one dear and eccentric professor offers her a chance in a lifetime to right side it back in orbit...the way it should be going.

About an hour had passed. It was ten o'clock. Little Flora went inside to get some snacks. She also knew there was a tray of *turkey* cookies the kids could munch on. In the meantime, Tracey and Christina came back outside with Josh. Joe and Bud brought out more pop and some leftover pizza.

"They must have a built in radar for food," Dan jokingly said as the girls sat down in front of the fire. The guys laughed and grabbed a handful of goodies while the girls rolled their eyes and shook their heads in disgust of the male sense of humor.

They all had gotten a second wind...then someone suggested a walk, "to stretch the legs." Flora wanted to sneak inside and go to bed but Matt saw her sly maneuver and asked her to come along. He left no time for saying *no*.

Matt wanted to talk to Flora...she sensed that. She kept her pace with his and before she knew it, they were tagging behind a short distance. Flora thought Matt was a nice guy...a great young guy. She tried for five years to fix him up with little Flora, Christina...or Tracey...things just never worked out. "If I were twenty years younger...I'd go out with him...," Flora said that more than a dozen times to the girls. Flora loved his company and he was very kind to the younger brood. Matt was mature for his age and advanced in his awareness of what really counted in life. Flora looked at him in a special way...a good way. But, since last summer's kiss, Flora knew she had to keep a *guarded* distance.

Last summer was a fluke. It was too close for comfort. Flora should have known where Matt was coming from. All her talk about love...what was she thinking of? Flora blamed herself for Matt's forwardness. No more looking at life through a broken heart either. No more talk about love with the love-starved. She wouldn't use her tipsy relationship with Jack as an excuse for being irresponsible or just plain *stupid*.

Flora tried to imagine Matt like he was another son. But, he didn't treat her like a mother. Flora tried not to hear his words that seemed more like music to her sensitive ears. Walking with him made her snicker inside at her foolishness. She felt the sting of reality...Flora saw herself in the *movie* of the week. FLORA FINDS LOVE IN KINDER-GARTEN.Or, MRS. ROBINSON RETURNS! Matt's voice kindly interrupted her *walkmare*.

"My friend's brother who is a little older than I am, is seeing his chemistry professor...she's quite a bit older than he is...and Josh is having the hardest time dealing with that...he can't believe his brother is that desperate for a girl...or rather, a *woman*...I never figured Josh being the narrow-minded type...he's so open about everything else...I can't see anything wrong with a situation like that...can you?" Matt looked at Flora very seriously.

"It would depend on the two involved, " Flora said cautiously, "...and the years difference in their ages...age has alot to do with the success of a relationship." Flora smiled at Matt. Matt smiled back.

"I never figured you to be rigid Flora...I always pictured you with an open mind about things...especially when it concerns love." Matt tried to ruffle Flora's feminine feathers.

"I don't think telling someone the *truth* about what I believe, is being *rigid*...and I do have a pretty open mind...*especially* when it concerns love."

"Then what's the matter with Josh's brother falling in love with an older woman?"

"There is nothing the matter...if it's a few years and his brother is very mature and the woman really loves him back...there are so many *if's* in that situation... ." Flora wanted to be fair with Matt.

"You know Matt, there are no simple answers, every situation is unique...everyone has to follow his own heart. In a situation like Josh's brother, there will definitely be some tough going...age is a big factor in a relationship...the one thing I know for sure is that if two people genuinely love each other for all the right reasons...they will be able to handle anything that comes their way...'that love is all there is, is all we know of love'...Emily Dickinson said that." Flora took Matt's hand and shook it...making sure he saw her face. They saw in each others eyes their need to love.

"What about last summer," Matt asked defensively.

"You mean...about the kiss?"

"Yeah...the kiss... ." Matt was anxious to hear what Flora had to say.

"It was special...and in a way...a kind of eye opener for me." Flora hoped Matt would understand what she was trying to say.

"*Eye opener*, tell me your eyes weren't open...were they?" Matt was trying to be a joker...Flora appreciated his humor.

"No...they weren't open...but your kiss made me see alot of things I tried not to see for a long time...and for that I will always be grateful." Flora was surprised at the ease her words were coming. She wanted Matt to understand exactly what she was feeling...that was important to her.

"It sounds like I didn't score on the Richter scale...you made the earth move under my feet, Flora... ."

"Matt...trust me...it wasn't a matter of the earth moving or not moving...it was more than that to me...and...in a very special way...I'll always love you for that kiss." Flora took Matt's hand and squeezed it hard.

"I'll always love you, Flora." Matt squeezed Flora's hand back.

"I believe you will."

For a while they were both quiet, increasing their step to catch up to the rest of the gang. There were no summer frogs or autumn crickets to drown the silence of the truth that touched both their souls. There were no crashing waves on the seashore to confuse their hearts song that night. There were no gentle winds in towering pines to make them hear things...feel things they wished or hoped were there.

Chapter
seven

Snow on Turkey Day

Flora was up at five o'clock to stuff the turkey and slide it in the oven. That took about an hour then she went back to bed for a fast five or six winks. She looked out into the early morning darkness and thought about the night before. It was a good night and she felt as if a few things had been resolved.

Flora couldn't fall back to sleep but rested comfortably in her cozy bed. The baseboard heaters, clinking and hissing, kept her company. Their familiar noises were always very soothing. Finally, at seven forty-five, Flora smelled delicious turkey. *What a great alarm clock,* Flora thought as she jumped out of bed! The coffee was ready and some cinnamon buns were on the table ready for the first shift of early birds.

Matt and Josh had to head back to Chicago around nine. Flora sat with the guys for a while and before she knew it, they were on their way back to Chicago. Flora walked with them to their car and tucked a few apples and cookies in the front seat for the ride home. As Josh backed the car out, Matt rolled down his window and called to Flora.

"Thanks again for everything...I had a great time," Matt said as he motioned to Josh to stop the car. He jumped out and gave Flora a big hug. Flora hugged him back with as much feeling.

"Let's blame that night on the moon...," Matt said with a big smile, "...that old devil moon."

"Sounds good...," Flora said as she squeezed his hands. "The moon gets blamed for alot of things...but he can take it." Flora looked at her watch and told Josh to get going. That broke the grip Matt had on her hand. Matt was finally on his way, Flora thought as she sighed a sigh of pleasant relief. Flora waved to the boys as she walked back to the house. She noticed how beautiful her purple and rust mums had bloomed around the oak tree by the porch steps. They looked so much like *Thanksgiving*.

Her attention the next few hours was focused on the basting the turkey, peeling potatoes, Christina, Tracey and little Flora. Between preparing the pumpkin custard for the pies and setting out the china for the big dinner...Flora listened and laughed with the girl's rendition of the night before. The biggest news...which wasn't really news to Flora, was that Tracey fell hopelessly in love with Josh. That was the good news. Josh was hopelessly in love with a girl from Wisconsin...that was the bad news. He still asked Tracey for her address and phone...so maybe there was a chance. That's what Tracey hoped for, anyway.

Dinner was at two o'clock and everyone pitched in with desserts. There was enough food for all the pilgrims at the first Thanksgiving, the second Thanksgiving and the third Thanksgiving. Everything turned out wonderful. The turkey and the gravy and the thirty pounds of mashed potatoes. Flora thanked Heaven for the mixer that mashed the potatoes, for Little Flora's cranberries, for Emily and Jim's *turkey* sugar cookies, for Aunt Cynthia's fresh apple pie, for Grandma's famous pumpkin pie tarts, Aunt Irene's sweet potatoes, Aunt Sandy's super chocolate cookies, Aunt Rose's almond Italian cookies, Aunt Diane's luscious banana muffins, and last but not least, Flora thanked God for Aunt Suzanne's famous raspberry marshmallow jello.

The jello was always a treat and was the family joke. It became Suzanne's trademark...when the kids thought of Aunt Suzanne, they thought of...jello...and chocolate bars. The kids could never eat a candy bar in front of Aunt Suzanne without giving up the first bite to her...and maybe the second. She was their Aunt...they had to respect her...even if it meant giving her their whole chocolate bar. Dolly brought the wine...Italian red table wine, a Chianti sent to her *special delivery* from her dear friend Vince.

Everyone was brushing up on Italian...Dolly was anxious for the trip and already had some sketches made up for the pensione. She made them from memory...and the drawing of the veranda was especially beautiful. Flora thought if the veranda had a view half that spectacular, it would be a part of heaven!

The phone rang half way through dishes. It was Matt. He wanted everyone to know that he made it home okay and wanted to thank everyone again for the nice time. Christina answered the phone and relayed that message to the rest of the gang. Before she hung up everyone wished Matt a Happy Thanksgiving. Flora was happy to hear he made it home safely.

The next half of the dish clean-up was spent analyzing Matt. Flora listened. The synopsis of that roast type discussion was that "he changed since he went away to college" and that "he looked better last year with his braces." The girls were a little resentful from the years before. At one time or another, all three girls had a big crush on Matt. But, "he was too cool to look at us...like he was almost conceited." That was the gist of the conversation during Thanksgiving clean-up, which was sometime before Thanksgiving dessert and after football game number two.

Grandma's baking hutch looked like it was out of COUNTRY LIVING magazine. She made a paper mache turkey and dressed him up in a tuxedo jacket and black bow tie. He had white shirt cuffs and all! Grama Flora

called the skinny sculpted turkey,TOM. Bubba called him
SINATRA. The kids called him BIG BIRD.

Flora liked Bubba's name and even more than the
name, she loved the story behind it.

Bubba had a pet chicken when he was in high school.
A bony bird, named SINATRA. It was too skinny to kill.
What would there be to eat when all the feathers came off?
He was just a bony bird, the kind you would keep for a pet.

Sinatra walked around Bubba's backyard like he was a
struttin' peacock. Coopmates came and went. *Sinatra* never
wondered where his old bird buddies went...or why they
left the cozy coop. He never thought to wake up and smell
the chicken!

Bubba also had a band in high school. He played for
most of the high school dances in the area. Bands back then
usually had a singer...male or female...that didn't matter,
just so they could carry a tune and swoon love's tune.
Frank Sinatra was popular at that time. Bubba played alot
of his songs. Grama Flora enjoyed those tunes a lot.

When friends would come to pick up Bubba for a *gig,*
Sinatra would come out of his coop and nose around. It was
a long walk from the coop to the side door where Bubba
lived...and *Sinatra's* long skinny neck and protruding
adams apple made everyone laugh.

Once, Bubba pulled out his saxophone and started to
play as *Sinatra* began his catwalk from the coop.
Immediately Art, the singer in the band, took his cue and
began singing "*I'm in the mood for love...simply because you're
near me...funny but when your near me...I'm in the mood for
love.*" *Sinatra* seemed to be in perfect beat with the tune and
he resembled FRANK...as much as a chicken could resemble Mr. Sinatra. Bubba swore to that.

All the attention must have made *Sinatra* too content...he started eating more and looking bigger...fatter!
Great-Grama Flora was just as sensitive as the next person...maybe more...but...a good cook knows a good bird

when she sees one. So, one day *Sinatra* must have looked pretty darn delicious. *Sinatra* was about to face his *final cur - tain.*

That night Great-Grandma Flora outdid herself. The meal was great. Fresh broccoli with garlic and olive oil, homemade bread and fried chicken! No one knew *Sinatra* was the main entree, until the next day when Bubba missed his company. While practicing his sax, it dawned on him like the bright summer sun...he ate *Sinatra* the night before! *Sinatra* was one or two of the...three or four of the pieces of chicken he ate for dinner. How could his mother have killed their pet...their friend?

Flora could only imagine the hullabaloo her Grandma suffered for that! Flora's Grandpa was a tough guy...real tough. Through the years and the story's retelling...each time adding one more personal note...it finally was made known that the big guy who could carry four fifty pound sacks of potatoes over his shoulders shed more than a few tears over the skinny bird who became content and then looked too good for Great-Grandma to ignore. So ends the tale of *Sinatra.*

All the kids prayed hard that week for snow. Flora did, too, at least for a few flakes, for the kids, for the holiday. Right before the family started breaking up for the day each heading in their own direction...little Diane and Eugenia caught a glimpse of some snowflakes. Stephanie, running to the grown ups who were chatting around the piano, said she saw some *tiny ones,* too. The kids all scrambled to the window and looked up to the streetlamp...that's where you could see if it was really snowing. Uncle Larry and Uncle Robert came to verify...to clarify...to judge the whole picture. They definitely viewed snowflakes falling...not many, but it was most assuredly *snowing!*

The kids looked at each other and all the adults knew what those young hearts were feeling. The fourth Thursday of November came every year...but not always with snow. Their holiday had been very special.

Chapter
eight

The Goose Is Getting Fat

Dolly walked toward the airport terminal with all the spunk she could muster. She was tough and full of determination. Silly old good-byes had no place in her heart, not now. It was full of happy things and brimmed with hope for bright tomorrows.

Dolly said good-bye once in her life, many years ago. That one time was all she would ever bare. From then on, it was *see you soon, see you later, or ciao*...but never *good-bye*. Besides, now, she was leaving part of her heart with Flora and her *new* family...what reason was there to say anything, when the best part of her remained in the hands of those who came to love her so dearly. And...she was off on a new adventure.

Flora knew Dolly well and sympathized with her philosophy on good-byes. Maybe that's why Flora cried; by herself, in the car, double parked.

She watched her dear professor gallantly walk away. For a tiny second a horrid thought passed through Flora's mind. It made her shiver. The excitement Flora had felt in her bones since Halloween, suddenly turned inside out. A cold, empty panic entered and overwhelmed her high spirit. It made her feel out of control and totally helpless. She wanted *out* of her commitment to Dolly...she wondered what on earth she had done. That black thought left as her welled vision caught Dolly's luggage standing by the curb. The tattered but sturdy tapestry bags made Flora smile. They reminded her of Dolly...kind of worn, but very capable. That simple thought perked Flora up. It even made her giggle inside, then she laughed out loud! The thought of Dolly's reaction to that association totally relieved Flora of the tangled emotions she was harboring inside. She knew her time was coming, and that she would have to be brave...and have faith...like Dolly's luggage that was left standing all alone by the curbside.

As she headed for home, Flora was grateful that no one had come with her to the airport. She was able to shed her tears and not have to worry about keeping a stiff upper lip. The ride home was ironically cheery. The dark, gray, snow ladened clouds excited Flora and made her think of Christmas which was only a week away.

Dolly should have been with Flora and her family for Christmas but Vince convinced her to come to Florence for the holiday. Dolly didn't need *too* much coaxing...she felt honored by Vince's pleasant persistence. That was another reason for Flora to feel good...Dolly was excited to go back to the renaissance land and begin again.

Flora pulled into her driveway, stopped the car, turned off the engine. She sighed a deep sigh of contentment. Flora was happy to be home. The neighborhood looked like a fairyland and she hoped Christmas would take it's time coming. Flora thought Christmas should always be just a few days away.

Flora tried to keep Christmas in it's proper perspective. The birthday of Jesus. Jesus who was born in a stable...and had a manger for his bed and cows breath to keep him warm. Christmas, for Flora was a time to bring into the lives of the people she loved a little more of life's greatest treasure.

Like the pleasure Flora had when she popped in on her sister Irene one snowy afternoon in December. She knew

Irene would be home alone with the kids because Danny was out of town. Irene had told her earlier that day that she was just going to order pizza for supper. So, Flora and the kids walked to Irene's each one carrying something for the chicken and rice stirfry. Flora brought candles and wine, too. Irene and the kids were surprised...Flora and her kids were tickled with their secret plan. All of them toasted the easy falling snow...the lights on the house across the street...and Lady, the Dalmatian...for all her spots. That was what the Christmas season was all about.

Flora broke out of her trance and went inside. The drive to and from the airport knocked Flora out. There must have been a snow storm coming from somewhere because she had the worst change-of-weather headache. She knew aspirin wouldn't cure it...but a snowfall would.

Flora hoped for snow. The winter, up until then, had been too mild and a thick blanket of snow would make things look alot more like Christmas, especially for the kids.

Jimmy had the twins over that late afternoon and Emily was practicing the piano. Little Flora was putting together some cookie dough and Dan was watching T.V. with Bubba and Jack. Grandma and Aunt Irene were shopping. As soon as Flora opened the door all activity stopped. The thousand questions on Dolly's departure began.

Flora called for pizza. She sat down, put her feet on the ottoman and began answering everyone's questions about Dolly's flight. The pizza boy came with the six large pepperoni, mushroom, bacon, green pepper and onion pizzas. Everyone was starved so communications shut down. That was all right. The quiet was even more delicious to Flora than pizza.

After dinner, Jack drove the twins home. It was late. The kids had school the next morning and Flora had to pick up Jimmy's passport. It was lost somewhere in the mail. She had to bring Emily in for her flu shot. Christmas shopping was almost complete. The physical agenda of things to do, had been well taken care of. The mental list needed a little attention. Flora felt like something big was missing in her preparation for the big trip. It had to have been the fact that Jack wasn't going with them...not until February anyway.

Things always seemed better in the morning. Flora was anxious for Dolly's call...she needed to get excited again for the trip; she needed some encouragement. Saying good-bye to Dolly dampened Flora's enthusiasm about her trip to Florence. It brought the whole far-away thing too close. And that was scaring Flora. She went to bed thanking God for getting her through that day. The trip to Florence and the kids being able to go with her, were the second and third blessings she thanked Him for. Flora fell asleep with a questioning mind. Did Jack really care that she was going without him...did he truly care at all? Flora knew whatever was to be, would be for the best. *Please keep Dolly safe, dear God, and deliver her safely to Florence...to Vince.* After Flora whispered her little prayer, she thought of Dolly flying over the great ocean and how in a few hours she would be in Florence.

The next morning was exciting. Snow had *finally* come. Everything was too beautiful.

The kids woke Flora up with a mug of hot chocolate and two really burnt toast. She was very surprised with the breakfast treat. The snow outside her window only made her smile, because she knew *it* was coming.

Emily and Jimmy, the burnt toast and snow made that morning special. Flora thought Christmas had come a few days early.

Little Flora asked to go to the mall. That snapped the three early morning celebrators out of their first snow stupor. Flora declared an early holiday...an unofficial snow-day. She announced a trip to the mall was definitely in order...a kind of early Christmas present. The kids were in total agreement and couldn't have been given anything better. And then...there was the phone call from Dolly. That made all of them realize there were still some things to do...before Christmas...and much to accomplish before the first of the year.

"Dolly...you sound great...," Flora said as the kids watched her face for expressions.

"Flora...I'm in *heaven*...I wish you were here to *pinch* me...you know...I forgot how beautiful this place is...even the empty rooms have so many memories...and Vince...he is too much...he had the wallpaper book on my bed and made me pick it out my room's pattern as soon as I got here...almost before I could say BUON GIORNO, I was ordering the paper for my room...the painter is here right now...wait a minute," Dolly said, now in a muffled whisper, "this guy moves fast."

"The painter or VINCE...". Flora laughed at her pat insinuation.

"Flora...you *behave* now."

"Dolly...*you* behave now."

"Hey...we'll all behave until you get here...so no cold feet...we have lots to do...got it, my nervous little ravioli?"

"We'll be there...say CIAO to Vince for me...bye Dolly." Flora smiled at the kids whose faces looked like lights on the Christmas tree.

Flora went over the phone conversation in her head as the kids piled in the car. Dolly sounded great...maybe a little tired. Dolly had forgotten how wonderful Florence was and how much she enjoyed her life there. Vince was more than kind with his accommodations for Dolly. Arrangements for Flora and the kids had been made...everything had been taken care of. Flora felt as if a ton had been lifted from her shoulders and some of the lost excitement that departed with Dolly at the airport, came back again.

Driving to the mall was a quiet adventure. Flora didn't

know if it was the slick roads and her cautious driving that kept the kids in an unusual state of silence or if they were daydreaming about the big trip to Florence. It was just days away.

Whenever Flora mentioned the trip to the kids or when she'd ask if they had any thoughts or wonders about it, they'd respond with, "no way."

Jimmy was sure of the trip. Emily confessed feeling a *little* nervous. The big girls were anxious one day and teary eyed the next...but always made Flora feel that they were absolutely *positive* about the whole adventure.

But, Flora knew there was more going on in their little heads. She didn't want their visions of sugarplums to *prune* up. If she had been feeling the pre-Florence pangs of an uncertain reality, they must have had them, too. So, after shopping, Flora drove to Irene's house.

Tracey and Christina were there waiting for little Flora. A big pot of herbal tea was on the table. Irene poured all of them a cup. Their nervous bellies warmed. The chilled conversation turned comfortable, even exciting.

The overnight snow meant more to them than being a nice effect for Christmas. The lake had just frozen over and they knew their winter would have to wait for them another year. This season they would be in Italy...and no one was sure of what to expect. Not even Flora.

They talked of snowmobiles and ice-skates and lazy Saturday afternoons with good movies on the television and afghans wrapped around their chilly knees. They knew what they were going to miss that season.

"You know," Flora said, "...this isn't just a pleasure trip, although I know we're going to have a great time." Flora paused for a moment and sipped her tea. She continued with more vitality.

"It's a job for me...a once in a lifetime opportunity...I'm finally going to make some cash...with my artwork...maybe enough cash to buy a little *Boston Whaler* for next summer."

"Honest Mom...a *whaler* for fishing...?" Jimmy looked over to Emily. "Hear that Em-an-em?" Emily smiled back at her brother as she sportingly took the knuckle rub that always accompanied fantastic news, "I know...I know...I'm a good *knucklehead,* too!" Emily was a good sport.

Flora brightened their outlook with some of the brochures Dolly left for them to read while Irene placed a giant platter of holiday cookies on the dining room table. Going to Florence was going to be one huge adventure, that's what Dolly told them. That's what Flora kept telling herself. With departure only days away and Christmas hours from celebrating Flora had no time for last minute jitters. She had to take the next few days an hour at a time.

That afternoon the cold grey sky enveloped her mind like a huge protective canopy. The security of that gentle blanket covering her Union Lake, and the warmth the homefire radiated to her heart, made thinking about sunny Italy bittersweet. It seemed like she was going to go a million miles away from home...a thousand years away from so many of the people she loved.

Chapter
nine

To The Land Of Love

"I'm going to miss all of you...," Flora said as she tried to be brave."You big guys...be good for Grandma...take her and Bubba out for dinner every now and then." Flora wanted to make sure young Jack and Joe got her message. She looked into their eyes, each face for a couple of silent seconds. She didn't say anything. No more last minute instructions. Enough were taped to the kitchen wall above the telephone. No gentle words of wisdom...or wise philosophical phrases. Flora wanted only a picture of them in her mind. That would be worth ten thousand words for her...and them.

Flora hugged her mother and father with everything she had in her heart. She couldn't look at them too long. With mixed emotion, she picked up her purse...grabbed her carry-on...and was finally off. The sniffles Flora heard behind her tempted her to turn around and hug everyone again. She couldn't indulge herself with that sweet temptation.

The drive to the airport was quiet. Jack had been brave for all of them. His corny jokes were welcomed...even appreciated with enthusiasm. Flora thanked him for his light-hearted disposition and his wise gallantry. She kissed him on his cheek and hugged him very hard. For a few seconds she even wondered why she was going away.

Flora boarded the plane as if she was walking into a grocery store. All her fears and anxieties left her. It was as if she was dreaming...a good dream, that wasn't making quite the right sense, but kept on going anyway. She was supposed to feel *petrified* about this time into her adventure. But she was calm. Emily's excursion to the plane's lavatory took Flora's mind off her lack of pre-flight jitters. God answered my prayers, she thought. *Now, if this three thousand ton bird will stay in the air...everything will be okay.*

Emily's fascination with the plane's bathroom set up made Flora relax even more. Emily had the bladder like the stomach of a camel, so, with that visit, she was set for the trip. Her next rendezvous with a bathroom would be in a foreign country. That thought made Flora snicker inside. When Emily asked why she was laughing...Flora told her. Emily began laughing, too. The whole idea flabbergasted Emily but just grossed Jimmy out. To have given such thought to that most basic of mandatory rituals convinced Jimmy that people, even immediate family members, did the strangest things under stress. He didn't want to laugh but Flora's laugh was contagious and Emily being compared to a camel gave Jimmy much fuel for future doggings.

Her entire life Flora vowed she'd never fly. The afternoon before her flight she promised God that she would be mature and not let the awesome fear that was deep in her heart surface. But He had to help her. *He* did.

The anticipation everyone felt on the way to the airport brimmed which left no room in their anxious bones for fear or second thoughts, third thoughts. That made the dreaded departure seem like nothing to Flora. It happened so neat and fast. Timing was everything.

Flora was disappointed that young Jack and Joe couldn't make it to the airport to see her off, but she thought it would be easier if things went on as normal. She didn't want any hullabaloo...she didn't want anything to happen that might give her an excuse to call the whole thing off. She was that unsure of herself. She was that unsure of the whole situation.

Flora was a dreamer...but hadn't the courage to ever really act on her mind's flirtations. Even this trip was something she had always thought about, but probably would have never gotten around to doing. She thought there was enough adventure in her life already. Her family and her marriage were big adventures. She was challenged with situations beyond any mountain climbers imagination; beyond any ballerina's fantasy. Flora's family was her HOPE DIAMOND. Her marriage had always been her PLYMOUTH ROCK.

Jack tried to keep the whole farewell scene on a high note. He knew Flora and how much she would need him to be strong. He kept his good-bye sweet and light...almost to the point of making Flora feel like he was rushing them all off! Flora knew Jack was excited for them and for his own departure in a couple of months, if all went well. He didn't want any sad good-byes. She knew he was doing that for her and the kids, too. That thought kept Flora's mind content and her heart from being totally broken.

Flora was leaving half her family behind and going further in miles than her whole lifetime of travels put together. She was on a nine hour flight to a land she had always dreamt about...a land that was the most beautiful and full of so many things she wanted to see and do...and feel.

Flora thought it was a good idea to travel late at night. In the dark she wouldn't have to hear the kids comments when they'd look out of the airplane's window at the spectacular view! She knew the views were breathtaking...she didn't have to see them to know how really beautiful they were. Flora could feel many things without having the experience first. Every now and again, she'd think herself cowardly. Reading about an adventure or listening to exciting tales from a daring soul was always enough for her. She

was confident in her own heart that if there had been anything she really wanted to do she would have done it no
matter how afraid she was. Flora didn't have to see a sunset to realize the beauty of the sun and sky, the beauty of
the night. Sunsets were in her soul like a hundred other
things that made her realize how precious everything in
her life was. Flora was ready for this big adventure to
Florence.

They were off into the wild blue. The young girls sat
behind Flora, Emily and Jimmy. During take off, even their
stimulating conversations subsided and a gentle calm united all of their hearts. Flora made that *quiet* her prayer.

Flora tried to maneuver her position enough to catch a
glimpse of the girls behind her. She wanted to see their
faces. She wanted to be reassured that all was going well
for them.

"MOM...*put your seatbelt back on!*" Jimmy barked in a
shocked voice as he pulled on her sweatered elbow. "The
plane hasn't leveled off yet...and that's dangerous...if we
crash...you'll go flying...!" Jimmy laughed at his wise pun.
Flora did too. Little Flora, Tracey and Christina were
always grateful for Flora's attention. They looked forward
to her expressions of reassurance, and excitement. They
saw in Flora's eyes that everything on this trip was going to
be fine. They were really, finally on their way.

Flora twisted back into her seat, Jimmy had her seatbelt
ready to fasten. Emily looked at Flora, and then Flora
winked and smiled. They held hands. Their meditative
trance broke with the announcement reminding them that
their seatbelts could be removed. Immediately the kids
slipped off their belts of safety and quickly resumed their
chatter. That was music to Flora's ears and she sat still for a
while longer relishing the security she was feeling at thirty
some thousand feet in the air.

Emily tapped Flora's shoulder. "Anybody home?"
Emily asked in her KNOCK-KNOCK joke tone of voice.

Flora was smiling the whole time with her eyes closed. It was almost that same feeling of euphoria she felt after each one of her children was born.

"You can take off your seatbelt now, Mama. See, it was a snap...just like Daddy told us it would be! They are going to serve some snacks...I hope they have *nachos*...I hate peanuts." Emily rattled on like a possessed talking toy. Then, Jimmy interrupted.

"Okay ENERGIZER...take a break," Jimmy said while he covered Emily's mouth with his hand, "Mom...it's nine-thirty-five...we should be there right in time for breakfast, or rather lunch. Italy is six hours ahead of our time...I wonder what time it will be when the sun comes up?...I've got to write Dad about this...he wanted to know on mv watch that's set for our time, when I first see the sun."

Flora was excited for Jimmy and she knew the double watch set-up would work out very well as a kind of buffer between Florence and home. His old watch was set for Union lake and his new one for Florence. He was designated official time keeper for the next three months. Jimmy loved that title and appreciated the air of importance it bestowed upon him. On this adventure he was the *man* of the house.

"The stewardess is going to start the movie HOME ALONE and after that GODFATHER III," Jimmy could hardly contain his excitement, "...this is going to be great...I'm not even tired! It's nine fifty-seven at home...and...HOLY MACKEREL!...three fifty-seven in the morning in Florence...Emily...we've already stayed up half the night and didn't know it!"

"I'm not even tired," Emily said as if surprised with herself. "I'll watch HOME ALONE but after that I'll read...GODFATHER III was really weird...it's too grown up for me...Mama can I go visit Flora and Tracey...I want to see Christina." Emily turned in her aisle seat to see the girls. Christina popped up and grabbed Emily's whole body and sat her down on little Flora's lap. They were Emily's little mother hens.

Jimmy adjusted his earphones and immediately got into the movie. He had seen it three or four times already, but still got quite a kick out of it. His laughing made Flora giggle. Knowing he didn't realize he was being heard made it all the better. Flora didn't watch the movie. Instead she watched Jimmy's reflection from her dark window which served as a private viewing screen for all the things going on beside her. That was a comforting view for Flora, she liked what was playing.

Flora and the kids had been bombarded with everything for the world traveler Christmas morning. It had been the most unusual Christmas for gifts since Bubba's return from Europe in 65', when German toy airplanes that really could fly and necklaces from Spain and perfume from France were under the tree in surprised abundance.

Flora wore the pendant Bubba gave her that Christmas of long ago for sentimental reasons. That was the most beautiful necklace anyone had ever given her. That would keep her heart close to those she loved. The *love* it represented made her world go around. And, the tiny streak of superstition Flora never admitted to having, would be taken cared of, too. Flora could have never left her pendant behind.

Irene and Rose had given all the girls luggage for Christmas. Jimmy borrowed Joe's travel bags and Grandma and Grandpa surprised him with a camera and a mini-tape recorder. Young Jack and Joe pitched in and bought Jimmy a couple neat outfits for his European stay. They also donated the last third of their bottle of OBSESSION...it would make the Italian girls go wild. Jimmy graciously accepted the cloths but humbly declined their generous gesture for the cologne. He left it back home on his dresser.

Big Jack gave all the kids stationery. There would be no

excuse for them not to write. He also gave each one of them a fifty dollar traveller's check, for fun things, souvenirs...and *postage*. The world travellers were more than touched by everyone's kindness that Christmas.

Flora thought of all the worry she had waisted in regards to her first flight. That night while she was literally in the clouds, she realized how silly she had been about things like flying...and loving, and...for her lack of faith in both.

No matter what was going to happen, Flora felt she'd be able to accept it. She was going to the land of love and miracles. She had been afraid of so many things in her life. No more fear, Flora thought. Only looking at things honestly and courageously. Ready or not, Flora thought, it was time to go after the things that had always lived so courageously in her heart.

Chapter
ten

Old Trains And Gray Skies

"Flora! I'm here!...over here!" Dolly's face beamed with excitement as she waved her arm frantically. Flora met Dolly's *benevenuto Filippi's* sign seconds before she heard her warm familiar voice.

Flora was so happy the flight was smooth and they all made it on the ground again. If she didn't have so many packages in her arms she would have dropped them all and kissed the ground! She thought, *maybe that's why the Pope did it every time he landed safely on the ground.*

Seeing Dolly at the airport was the pot of gold at the end of Flora's surprise rainbow. Dolly insisted she was really somewhere in the *middle*. They quickly shuffled to the baggage depot to claim all of their luggage. Dolly rushed them along and then into two cabs, directing both drivers to the *treno stazione....andiamo!*

"Vince took care of everything," Dolly said as she picked up the last bag from the taxi trunk. She tipped the drivers and then rolled her eyes at Flora. "If you don't know what your doing...*they'll* take advantage of you...*big time*...but that *one* was pretty *dang good looking*... ."Dolly winked at Flora. "We are suppose to be heading for *binario otto*...that's GATE EIGHT...so all of you follow me." They did, anxiously.

"Since it's the middle of the week, and between holidays, the trains are very comfortably situated with passengers...I think *all* of you have a treat in store on this train ride." Dolly squeezed Flora's hand and grabbed Jimmy around the neck with an elbow lock...she was in her glory.

"You didn't have to go through all this trouble Dolly," Flora said sincerely, "...but, I'm glad you did...the flight was wonderful and the kids...as much as they tried to fight it, slept most of the way. Poor Jimmy slept through his *sun watch*."

"Yeah," Jimmy added quickly, "...but the stewardess asked the captain for the time and that's even better than me *waiting* for it...the captain said that I wouldn't have seen too much anyway because of the thick cloud cover...even now it's so grey...is it like this alot Dolly?"

"Not for long...the sky sometimes clears in minutes...especially this time of year. So, don't fret...the sun will be here. Italy didn't earn the adjective *sunny* for nothing...even though this time of year is the most dreary if it is going to be dreary at all." Dolly tried to explain the weather conditions. Then, the train's headlights shone from the distance and completely grabbed everyone's attention. Dolly looked at Emily and winked. Dolly began singing as the train's noise grew louder.

"Who cares about the weather...la la la...as long as we're *together*."

"OH-MY-GOSH...look at the train...it's gotta be a hundred years old...it's like we're in the movie ROOM WITH A VIEW...," Little Flora romantically exclaimed.

Flora saw the huge grey hunk of metal approach them hissing a tune from days gone by. How exciting it all was for all of them. Flora watched little Flora who was probably thinking about Dan. Tears of excitement rolled down Christina's cheek as she hugged Jimmy who was just as overwhelmed. Flora knew she could have never made the trip without them. At least, it wouldn't have been half as much fun.

"Little Flora...it's over a hundred years old...and *almost* as in good a shape as I am...wouldn't you say...," Dolly said teasingly.

"Dolly...as great as the train looks...you put the train to shame...," little Flora said as she hugged Dolly.

"You put all of us to shame Dolly...*you* are my inspiration...when I'm sixty-five, I hope I look *half* as good as you do...," Tracey chimed in with sincere flattery. "I love you Dolly."

Were they dreaming? Dolly kept assuring them that the whole trip was real. Emily clung tightly to Flora's arm and could only shiver with delight at the whole adventure. She marveled at everything she saw. Her purple rimmed glasses framed every step of the way. Every step created an exciting scenario for eleven year old Emily.

Back home, Emily hand-painted sweatshirts for everyone. She painted the word FIRENZE boldly in a deep green. Balanced on the right was the Italian flag and on the left, was the American flag. They brought one for Dolly. As soon as Emily gave it to her, Dolly anxiously put it on. Emily was proud of her artistic design and Dolly was elated with such a kind gesture. There would be no mistaking them for tourists.

Dolly explained to them, after they all had been seated, that the train was one of the oldest but one of the loveliest in the Italian railway system. The seats were plush and comfortable and the decor brought the passengers back to earlier times which gave them a view of an older Italy, maybe the Italy that was in their minds. Immediately, they were taken back to a more romantic time. Ivory lampshades and antiquated photographs tempted little Flora, Christina and Tracey with romantic flirtations. The old train drew them into Victorian plots keeping their sensitive young soul anxious for love. Flora couldn't have hoped for a more wonderful experience. She saw in all of their faces familiar hopes and dreams.

Dolly treated them to a cup of *espresso*. Even Jimmy liked the Italian beverage. More than the taste, Flora knew he was enjoying the whole big scene. They were all enjoying the trip!

Dolly looked at Flora with a big smile and a raised eyebrow, then blurted out what her anxious expression was saying.

"Flora...we'll be there in about forty more minutes...you don't have to say a word...I can see by the huge grin on your face that you are thrilled to be here...and you have to know how happy I am too...really, I've been such a nervous wreck waiting for all of you to get here...and now you *are* here...I can't wait for all of you to meet Vince."

"Dolly...it's going to be wonderful...and I can't wait to meet Vince...," Flora said as she squeezed her friend's hand with a gentle yet firm conviction. "So many things have changed since August...going back to school and meeting you has been such a blessing...actually...a *miracle*...thank you so much for everything Dolly." Flora looked at her friend who could only smile. Dolly sat back into her seat and breathed a heavy sigh. With her face still smiling, she softly closed her eyes and tapped Flora's hand with a suggestion that she do the same.

Flora sat back into her seat and sighed a deep breath. A million thoughts raced through her mind. She couldn't keep her eyes closed like Dolly who had already fallen asleep. But sitting next to her gracious friend and the sound of the train on the tracks relaxed her.

The Italian countryside changed it's garb from suburban Roman flat to country Tuscan hilly. It reminded Flora of the stretch of highway on I-75 from Detroit to Gaylord. That thought travelled Flora's mind back to August...to August night skies and Matt's innocent good-bye kiss. His kiss made her realize something very wonderful was missing in her life. The kiss that made her go back to school and take up painting again. His kiss brought her to room 223,

Professor Dolly Langworth's water color class. And, now,
she was in Florence.

No one greeted them at the pensione. Flora was grateful for that. Now, everyone would have time to investigate
their new home. Flora immediately saw the potential of
every room and could hardly wait to begin. The kids definitely loved it.

Dolly showed them to their rooms. Little Flora, Tracey
and Christina shared one room. The next room down the
hall, was for Flora, Emily and Jimmy. There was a huge
double bed next to a small fireplace and a daybed under
the window for Jimmy. All the rooms were large. Flora was
completely satisfied with the accommodations Vince and
Dolly had made for them.

The girls were ecstatic! Dolly informed them that *they*
were going to decorate their room...or at least make the
final decisions regarding the pattern of wallpaper and
choice of window treatments...and the type of floorcover-
ing. Dolly told them that there were wallpaper books, mag-
azines and paint color charts in the room adjoining theirs.
She told the girls to look them over whenever they got a
chance.

Jimmy just remembered that he hadn't had lunch...or
was it dinner time, he couldn't keep it straight. All he knew
was that his stomach was growling...and he was starved.
He looked at his watch. *Nine a.m. in Union Lake...three p.m.
in Florence.*

"Hey...I'm not on any diet like you chicks who can live
on rabbit food...I'm fourteen and I'm always starving...I'm a
growing boy...no...I'm a growing *man*...and my tank is
empty!" He reminded all of the gang that it was time to eat.
He politely yelled to the girls in their room that *dinner was
on.* Unpacking could wait. They all journeyed down to the
kitchen, stomachs empty but minds full of questions and
wonder.

Dolly met everyone at the bottom the stairs and then

led them to the kitchen which housed an overstocked refrigerator with a sign taped on the door reading, "WEL-COME, now EAT! SEE YOU SOON! Vincenzo and Brutus."

"Vince will be here later on tonight. He apologizes for not being here to greet you...but he is a very busy man this time of year...you will all love him...he reminds me alot of Bubba...you'll see what I mean when you meet him...and Jimmy...you'll get a kick out of Brutus... ."

Dolly talked fast. She set a table...even quicker...especially when she was excited. They were all very excited.

"Go ahead Jims, open the door and take what you want...you too," Dolly said excitedly as she motioned to everyone to do the same. "Whatever you do, don't be shy about the refrigerator or this kitchen...this is your home for the next couple of months and we want want you to feel comfortable...eating and anything else you want to do here...like one day you might want to bake a batch of choco-chip cookies," Dolly smiled at the girls. "Vince can hardly wait to taste them...I brag about you *up and coming* gourmet chef's all the time...so feel at home...I'm just aching for a good home baked treat without *anise* or *almond*...not that there's anything wrong with those extracts, but...a person can get a bit tired of it...and don't even get me started on *nutmeg*, they put it in everything here...even in their *ravioli!*"

Dolly pointed out every flaw in the kitchen. It needed buckets of fresh paint and some minor repair work on the tile floor and the sink counter tops. Flora saw beyond the minor fix-ups and immediately fell in love with the set-up. The kitchen was fantastic. Almost as perfect as her sister Irene's. To Flora,perfection meant being full of family and lots of good food on the burners cooking. So, eventually it would be perfect; something Flora would definitely write home about.

There was a giant cookstove that took up almost one complete side of the wall. It had twelve burners. At the other end of the kitchen there was an old woodburning oven. It belonged to Vince's grandmother. He told Dolly it was going to be the center of the new kitchen. Flora saw *one huge flaw* in that perspective; the grand *fireplace* that was smack in the *middle* of the room. Who could ever see beyond that focal point. It would be like someone ignoring the Statue of Liberty when sailing down the Hudson river!

All the talk of redecorating and warmth made Dolly and Jimmy immediately start a fire in the grand heater, they were hoping to knock the chill out of the damp December day.

"Let's see if the old thing works...," Dolly said with a twinge of the dickens in her voice.

"I'm pretty good at starting fires, Dolly...I do it all the time up north at my Grandpa's cottage." Jimmy didn't want to brag but he was the man of the situation at hand...so he rolled up his sweatshirt sleeves and started.

The mantle on the fireplace was an old beam. On top of the mantle was a gigantic ceramic clock. Dolly said she could hear the *dang* thing ticking all night. And from her tone of voice...she didn't seem to be too pleased with the beat the old clock TICK-TOCKED. The ticking in the wee hours of the morning made Dolly almost forget it was an heirloom. She told the kids, "Thank God it isn't a CUCK-COO clock...I would have strangled the dumb bird a long time ago." Emily and Jimmy laughed till they were hysterical. Dolly loved to make them laugh.

Jimmy's fire was burning hard. Huge flames caught every dry oak log on fire and filled the room with a pleasant scent and a reassuring crackling sound; like the fires back home. The fresh fruit and lunchmeats filled everyone's belly. The homemade wine Dolly *forced* everyone to toast with, mellowed all of their spirits and made Jimmy's *Italian time watch* seem more real with each glance. When it said seven o'clock, it felt like it was. The zinfandel made the six hours they lost during their flight...comeback. Now they knew what jetlag was.

As much as they all wanted to investigate some more, Flora thought it would be best for all of them to finish settling their things . No one fought the suggestion...the girls couldn't wait to get back to *their* room. They cleaned up the kitchen and then exuberantly headed up the ornate wooden staircase. Flora stayed down with Dolly for a while to enjoy the soothing fire and to talk about ideas for the kitchen.

Later on in the afternoon, Flora called Jack to let him know they were all safe and at the pensione. Jack was very excited to hear about the trip and everyone's reaction to the long flight. He thought they were supposed to take the bus to Florence and was surprised to hear about the *old* train excursion from Rome. Not to waste money, Jack insisted Flora hang up the phone and write a nice long letter...or just write and let him know all the details. He reminded her to remind Jimmy to write and Emily to scribble a few lines, too. There wouldn't be any excuse for lazy writers or for a lack of subject matter. They traveled practically around the world from Union lake and he wanted to hear about it in their own words. Kids had a neat kind of vision that Jack appreciated alot.

After a second glass of wine Flora pushed herself from the kitchen table and the glowing embers of their wonderful dinner fire. Flora had to nudge Dolly who dozed off halfway through her refill, so she could say *goodnight*. Dolly sleepily bid Flora a *buona notte* and then went woozily to her room.

While Flora climbed the stairs she thanked God for her wonderful day, and again, for their safe flight.

There was a window at the top of the stairs. Flora peeked out from it and noticed the sky was still gray. There were no stars shining in the ancient sky. It looked alot like Michigan did in December. She was anxious to see the view from every window in the morning. Flora also hoped the sun would be shining, too. Even though their first day was staged with a deep gray sky...nothing would she have changed. It had all been too wonderful!

Flora passed through a vapor cloud of *Obsession* ...no, it was *Polo*. That was a sure tell-tale sign that she was heading in the right direction. The girls had just finished spraying the room...not because it reminded them of young Jack or Joe...but because they often used colognes as *air freshen - ers* which exasperated Flora every time they did it. That night it only made her think of home and what her big boys might be up to. She thought about Grandma Flora and Bubba and Jack. They were probably watching the *WHEEL OF FORTUNE.*

Flora found Emily and Jimmy in the girls room. All five of the kids were sprawled across the two big double beds. In one hour they had managed to transform the stale, empty room into something familiar. Posters and photographs of all those left behind colored the walls. Little Flora brought her portable stereo and pounds of extra batteries and CD's and cassettes. That was the second most important thing on her list of *musts* to bring. The first was Dan's football jersey. That would be her pillowcase for the next couple months. Dan felt good about little Flora's attachment to his high school relic and hoped that it would remind her of their attachment. He loved little Flora very much.

Christina brought her jewelry box filled with silver and gold and other precious things she had tucked away for almost eighteen years. Memento's of great times and letters from good friends and family took up most of the space in the floral treasure chest. Christina left enough room though for *future* treasures, too. Maybe *not so future in the future* treasures. At least that's what she hoped, anyway. "Like a love note from some star struck Florentine who goes *gaga* eyed over me and my sophisticated American way...," Christina said more than one time teasingly. Yet everyone knew she absolutely meant every word of it!

Tracey smuggled her favorite afghan and *borrowed* her mother's expensive handmade, from the ALPS, winter sweater. Flora smiled when she saw her sister Irene's favorite sweater in Tracey's suitcase. But Tracey figured by the time Irene noticed it was gone, she wouldn't be furious, she'd be missing Tracey, her oldest child and only daughter, too much to be angry. And it would probably trigger a welcomed phone call, at least. Tracey had it all figured out. Flora liked the way Tracey had things figured.

All of their clothes were neatly hung and drawers had been divided up. Flora looked around at their labors and smiled. The girls smiled back. Jimmy wondered what the private joke was...then all of a sudden blurted out, "Oh, I get it...Mama's smiling at you guys because she knows the room will never look this good again...and you guys are smiling back because you know it's true." Tracey tickled Jimmy as she gave him a piece of her mind.

"I'm gonna tickle you till you beg for mercy. That's what you get for being such a wise guy!"

Flora stayed with the kids for a while longer as they said their prayers. They thanked God for their safe arrival and then asked Him to take care of all the family back home. Christina added the last petition.

"And dear Lord...,"Christina said sheepishly, "...direct the step of a couple...or even a *few* eligible good looking *sig - nore* to this humble pensione... and we wouldn't mind if they had a few zillion lira either...*thank you*...I mean *gratzie!*" Christina winked at all of them.

While they were saying their prayers Flora had looked into each of their faces. She noticed that Tracey was wearing her scapular from St. Mary's and Emily had worn her rosary bracelet from Grandpa Pete. Christina's Sacred Heart medal sparkled on the chain her father had given her for her sixteenth birthday. Little Flora brought the family Bible from home and had placed it on their dressing table.

Flora was proud of all of them.

Flora went into her room and placed her cherished belongings out where she could see them. She brought the group shot of the family from last summer and her Grandma Flora's crocheted wedding coverlet. She hung it over the rocker next to the window. She looked out into the quiet sky. It was difficult for her to imagine that she was in Florence. She knew her Grandmother would have loved it there. Her mother, too.

Chapter
eleven

Vince And Tall Tales

It rained the next three days. No, it poured the next seventy-two hours. It didn't seem to matter though. Being from Michigan, Flora and the kids were accustomed to gray, dreary and wet weather. Especially in the winter months. Flora and the kids knew the sun was going to come out, eventually. They didn't waste anytime worrying about the weather. The past couple of days were filled with too many neat people and too many neat things to do; museums and statues and rivers and bridges carried them to times past. They were treated like royalty. Flora was pleasantly surprised at all of her *munchkins* and how they handled that matter of hospitality. They seemed to shine in their unpolished roles as celebrities. Everyone was having alot of fun.

They met Vince their first morning in Florence. He was everything Dolly said he was, and more. He did remind all of them of Bubba in alot of different ways. Vince wasn't as handsome but there was something about his face that kept everyone's attention. Christina thought it was his grey-green eyes.

Vince liked to talk and told the best stories of a time not that long ago. His emotion invited every listener to go back with him and live it. He enjoyed cooking for them and appreciated garlic as the *secret* ingredient of every successful chef. He wore his jacket around the house and had a different hat for every day of the week.Vince also loved dogs. Especially his dog, Brutus.

People were walking in and out of the pensione. Some with ladders, some with fabric bolts...some with their dogs! Not all of them were there to *help* with the renovation work either. Many of them were distant relatives of Vince's or relatives of the distant relatives, who heard through the grapevine, which run long and thick in Italy, about the American family. Like, *three beautiful young girls were going to spend the winter with Vince and Dolly.* News like that travelled fast, especially among the eligible bachelor crowd.

Flora and the kids went under the inspection and approval of many inquisitive visitors. Vince called them the *big noses* of the family. In Italian it sounded very funny. But, no matter what the language, they were the gossip spreaders. And, that was the way it was suppose to be.

Vince had quite a few good looking nephews in his family. Some he hadn't seen himself for a few years. Christina and Tracey picked a couple winners from the endless caravan of well-wisher's. Little Flora had to agree with the expertise of her cousins; *there was much temptation.* Little Flora told herself to be good...she wanted to remain true to her man.

The day ended up being a kind of family reunion. Vince invited many of them back for the feast of the Three Kings which was going to be celebrated in a couple of days, on January sixth. Christina and Tracey made sure that Vince included Sebastion and Stefano in his invitation. Naturally they'd be included. They were the sons of his sister Lucia.

The day before the celebration Flora and the kids decorated the huge dining room in the pensione. They scalloped red and green crepe paper from wall to wall, every piece meeting the ceramic chandelier that hung directly over the center of the dining room table. Flora cut out cardboard stars the size of a dinner plate and the kids covered them with shiny foil. Jimmy climbed the ten foot ladder and tacked them to the ceiling, each one dangling by a skinny thread. Their random positioning really made the ceiling look like the sky, especially when the lights were dimmed and the candles on the buffet were lit.The room looked very special.

They also planned on making some *American* specialties. Guido, the sensitive chef of the pensione, didn't seem to happy about that. Not until Vince gave him the rest of the day off. Guido appreciated Vince's kindness because he had three small children of his own and lots of things to do in preparation of the holiday. Besides, Guido was ahead of schedule and had the main course of veal scallopini already prepared for the feast. The side dishes Flora and the girls would have to handle. And, they did.

Working in the big kitchen with the gentle fire burning in the fireplace made Flora feel very much at home. *If only Mama and Bubba...and Cynthia and Irene...if they were here, everything would be perfect.* That's what Flora kept thinking.

The next morning no one had time to notice if the rain had stopped. They were too busy to even care. Jimmy was the first one up at six and started the fire in the fireplace. Emily joined him. She was the official log girl. Brutus was their escort. He followed them everywhere. He was the best dog they ever knew...besides Bubba's HOPPY...and their HUCKLEBERRY.

They felt a little sad for Brutus at first when they realized he had only three legs...but after they saw him in action, they felt silly feeling sorry for such an Olympic canine. Brutus could beat them down two flights of stairs by a mile and he could walk across the room on his front legs with the grace of a prima ballerina! Brutus was their hero. He also saved them from the cooked tripe Vince placed in their dinner plates the night before. Cow stomach didn't appeal to their fast food mentality. Brutus happened to be under the table anticipating their foreign morsels of delight.

Vince was the next one up and congratulated Jimmy on his fire starting technique.

"You make a good fire, Jimmy...when you get to be my age you'll have over fifty years experience... ." Vince sat by the fire with Emily and Jimmy and made them coffee. He also made them *fire* toast.

Vince sliced three thick pieces of bread from the loaf in the refrigerator and then grabbed three long sticks from the pile of kindling. Jimmy slid a twig through each piece of bread and handed one to each of them. Vince taught Jimmy and Emily a trick of the shepherds.

"See, all you really need is a good fire...like you made, Jimmy, and some good bread...a little stick and a little more patience...before you know it you have some good food that sticks to your ribs. But we're more lucky...we have some creamy butter to spread on our toast...and maybe some grape preserves...if I can find them." Vince looked through the pantry which stocked enough staples for an army and found a sealed crock of zinfandel grape jam. They enjoyed his stories and the great breakfast.

Dolly walked in sniffing the air. Jimmy volunteered to make a couple more toast as Vince poured her a cup of *strong* coffee.

"You know what night it is tonight?" Dolly innocently asked Vince. Emily caught Dolly's wink to Vince, which made her look at Jimmy . They both wondered, *what next?*

"Of course I do. That old befana wrecked a couple of the tiles on my roof last year... ." Vince said as he carefully set the story up in his head. He continued.

"Every year, the BEFANA roams the town and causes so much destruction...I'd like to meet her one of these days and make her pay for all the damage she's caused...she's a silly old witch and I wish she'd use the door like everyone else...I keep them open every year on the fifth of January hoping she'll use one of them, but she insists on flying through the air and climbing on everyone's rooftop with her clunky old boots... ." Dolly smiled at Vince but Emily and Jimmy looked more puzzled with each additional word. Vince could see the wonder in their faces, so he asked them a question to pull them into the tale even deeper.

"Would you put up with some old witch landing on your roof every year and breaking up all your expensive tile roofing?"

Jimmy looked at Emily to see if she wanted to go first...she shrugged her shoulders...Jimmy went first.

"It depends...why does she walk around the rooftops...is she really a witch? I'd love a witch to land on my roof anyday...is she really a witch or just some crabby old lady with a hangup for cracking tile...? "

Emily looked to Vince with much anticipation as she waited for Jimmy's question to be answered. Vince was the man to answer them, too. Dolly sipped her coffee and enjoyed the tale told by one of her favorite storyteller's. Vince went on.

"The old befana, or *witch*, is what you would call her, is a crazy old lady who missed one chance in a lifetime to see the Christchild...and in a way I guess you could say she does have a *hangup*. Many years ago, the three wise men came to her on their way to Bethlehem and asked her to join them on their journey to find the BABE...but...she was too busy to go with them...can you imagine, she told them she was *too busy* !"

Emily innocently interrupted. "Why was she too busy?" Vince was taken with Emily's anxious interest.

"Because...she had to sweep her floor...like her floor was the most precious thing to her...can you imagine that? She had to sweep her old floor...that's what kept her from going with the *three kings*." Vince looked seriously sad. Emily and Jimmy felt the sadness of the story. Vince quickly went on...he had to lift their spirits.

"But don't fret, she wised up. . . *now* every year, the

night before the feast of the Three Kings, which we cele-brate tomorrow...she comes back...in search of the Christchild. She leaves bread and sweets for all the good children hoping one day that she might come across the Christchild...that is her dream...she wants to find Him."

"Why do they call her a witch...if she's just an old lady?" Emily asked, truly wondering *why*?

"Well...I think it's because the broom she was sweeping her floor with the night the three kings came calling, became...*magic*! The Angels felt sorry for the old befana, and made her broom able to *fly*. Angels are pretty smart, and they are also very kind...and up until then only witch-es flew on brooms...I think that's why people call her a witch...but she is a *good* witch and she's very old...how far could she get in one night if she had to walk anyway?...I wish they would have given her some soft rubber soled boots."

All of them had much to think about after Vince's tale. Vince loved kids. He had one son, Paolo, who never mar-ried. Vince said he was *too busy making money and building tall buildings in New York*. But, he was coming home soon. That left Vince with a rather small immediate family. His two sisters and brother provided him with seven-nieces and nephews. All of them were grown up now. And, now he had Dolly.

Dolly didn't sweep floors but if the wisemen had approached her in her early days, she would have been rid-ing on her *paintbrushes and memories* that night. Dolly loved Vince's story almost as much as she loved him. That's real-ly why she was there. Everyone knew that, too.

Jimmy and Emily were worried about Vince's tile roof and wondered if the old *befana* was going to visit them that night. The anticipation kept their minds in a dither...and they suddenly missed Flora. She would lend a little more light on the subject. They were ready to go upstairs and get her, then she and the girls walked into the kitchen. They didn't know what to expect from an old *befana*.

Flora and the girls were starving. The smell of the coffee and the toast made their mouths water. While they ate, Dolly and Jimmy and Emily filled the rest of them in on the latest tale of yore. Flora loved it! She reassured Emily that the befana was to be somewhat feared, but more rightfully, welcomed, with great anticipation. Jimmy winked at his mother.

Vince had to shave and get ready for his trip to town. Little Flora made a list of things for Christina and Tracey to pick up at the market. They went with Vince and were to come home with Sebastion and Stefano. Vince had some business in town that day and wouldn't be home till the evening.

Flora and Dolly had lots of last minute things to to tend to. Little Flora stayed back to help them and to wait for Dan's call. She missed him more than she thought she would. They had been each other's best friend for two years. The phone was ultra expensive. But with the mail system being what it was, she knew it might be another week before she'd get a letter from him. And, it could possibly be even longer before he'd get one from her.

Later on that afternoon, Flora wrote to Jack filling him in on all the happenings around the pensione. Although her letter was fat with words, it seemed empty of the little things that truly filled her heart.

Chapter
twelve

"Following Yonder Star..."

Flora walked to mass that morning. It was still dark when she headed up the hill to San Miniato Church. Brutus followed her.

Flora hadn't walked to Church in years; since her Three Mile days. She remembered how wonderful walking in the morning was...how wonderful those mornings were for her. When she walked, she was closer to God for sure, at least spiritually. Now she was in a different neighborhood...a different country, yet she had the comforting sensation that she was exactly where she was suppose to be. Everything seemed familiar...everything welcomed her there. Antiquity fit her soul and Florence was the missing piece of her heart. If home was where the heart was, Flora was home.

The day before had been busy, but nice. Flora and the kids seized the opportunity to make the FEAST OF THE THREE KINGS a part of themselves. They wanted to give back some kind gesture in gratitude for all the pleasures Vince and Dolly had been giving to them. It seemed like they had been there for weeks instead of days. Flora felt very much at home in the pensione kitchen.

Flora was too excited to sleep the night before and decided to wake up early and sneak out to investigate the nearby grounds. She recalled Guido telling Dolly that he and his family were going to attend 6:30 morning mass on Epiphany at San Miniato. Guido's nephew was a priest at the parish and he was going to celebrate the mass.

San Miniato could be seen from Flora's bedroom window. It was a small church and not too far away from the pensione. It was just through the ancient portal at the end of the back road. The night before as she watched the gold winter sun set in the Florentine sky she promised herself to get up the next morning and go to mass. And, she did.

The walk was kind of eerie at first. Flora forgot about being in a foreign country because things had become very familiar and natural.

The sky was clear. The stars were shining but there was a mist that hovered on the street in the distance. It was from the Arno, Flora thought. The country roads in her home town would get that way in early Spring because of the warming temperatures and the thawing lake. She also thought that maybe the stars were shining the same way the night the three wisemen followed the star to Bethlehem. But there wouldn't have been a mist...at least that's what Flora thought.

Cutting through the city, Flora passed another little church. It was almost camouflaged between a market on one side and a shoe store, GIOVANNI'S *le Scarpe Mercato*, on the other.

It wasn't like the grandioso churches Flora and the kids had visited earlier that week. She remembered passing it one day on her way to the *Grande Mercato*. She would have passed it again if she hadn't noticed the light in the window. She peeked inside and heard voices softly singing.

About fifty people were scattered throughout the church. It was more like a cozy chapel in the market district. A small choir sat proudly in the sanctuary.

Flora was only beginning to understand Italian, even though she had taken three semesters during her college days. But, she would have understood the Mass in any language; it was universal...and it was very precious to her.

Communion time came quickly. Thoughts of her Grandparents and family filled her head with memories and stories from the past. So much had changed in her country but that morning...Flora found a piece of long ago and put it in her heart. How could a place stand so still, Flora thought affectionately. Before she knew it, it was time for Holy Communion. Flora walked up to the altar and took the Holy Communion into her mouth. She walked over to the Eucharistic minister and carefully accepted the gold chalice full of the blessed wine.

"Blood of Christ," the Eucharistic minister said in Italian, then he quickly repeated it in English. Somehow, he looked very familiar to Flora.

"Amen", Flora said, taking the chalice into her own hands. Flora looked into the ministers eyes as she drank the Blessed Blood; with her attention more on his eyes, Flora began choking on the blessed wine.

I YI YI...I'm choking, Flora thought with a smile still on her face. A severe panic travelled through the rest of her body. She thought it went down the wrong pipe...but she couldn't catch her breath. It was the kind of choke that happens sometimes with vinegar. Flora didn't want to panic but she felt panic to the limit.

The Eucharistic minister set down the chalice and patted her on the back. Flora began to feel the passage way clearing. She shook her head to motion that she was alright but couldn't hold back the tickling cough.

"I'm...o...kay...," Flora said as if squeezing out those three syllables was an almost impossible endeavor. She walked to the back of the little church and tried to muffle the cough in her scarf. In a few minutes the tickle went away. Then, very quietly Flora slid into the last pew and knelt down, contented to be simply quiet.

The Mass ended and Flora waited for most of the congregation to leave. Many of them smiled with concern at the coughing lady. Flora smiled back politely.

She sat down and closed her eyes while she collected her thoughts. The Church was very quiet. Then her eyes opened and wandered slowly from floor to ceiling. The chipped tiled flooring and the painted walls with old paintings of saints and Jesus made her think again about her journey to Florence. She could hardly believe that she was there. *Betwixt the crumbling and the magnificent,* she thought. Flora took a deep breath hoping to savor the beauty of the early morning candlelight on the painting of Mary above the side alter.

"That happens every now and then," said the tall man who had patted her on the back. Flora opened her eyes quickly in the direction of the deep voice.

"Excuse me?...I'm sorry...," she said, looking up into a ruggedly handsome face. She recognized the man as the Eucharistic minister. Yet, there was something more about him that made Flora feel she had met...or seen him before.

"People choke on the wine every now and then...are you alright now...?"

Flora watched his face as he spoke, not completely hearing his words...there was really something familiar about his face and his expression.

"Yes, thank you...I just feel like a jerk...a *pazzo*," Flora said with embarrassment coloring her cheeks. I really am a crazy person, Flora thought to herself as she looked deeply into the stranger's eyes.

"I'll have to talk to Fr. Tremonte about his choice of wine...," the stranger said as he smiled at Flora. "He is very partial to the dry reds...I'm glad you're feeling better."

"I feel fine, thank you...this is really a nice little church...or chapel...is Mass celebrated here every morning?" Flora wasn't sure why she asked for that information. The stranger bent over toward Flora and answered her question.

"Every morning Mass is celebrated here at 6:30 a.m....

the Franciscan order of brothers run the soup kitchen in back...I volunteer whenever I'm in town...with the holiday I knew the brothers would be celebrating Mass early so I came...I know they'll appreciate an extra hand this morning...plus, there's no better way to start the day than with Mass...and a bowl of Br. Georgio's minestrone." The stranger smiled at Flora. "I'm glad you are okay...I've got to be going now, maybe I'll see you again...CIAO".

He looked at Flora a moment longer; a few seconds that seemed more like an hour to Flora. Then, he walked toward the back of the small building leaving a pleasant trail of cologne; not OLD SPICE, but something nice. She wanted to thank him again...but he was too fast...or she was too slow...she thought his eyes were kind. He spoke perfect English.

Brutus invited himself inside the church and walked up to the pew where Flora was kneeling. She didn't realize she had company until she felt the pooch gently tugging on her coat hem.

"Where were you when I needed you, doggie...?" She scratched Brutus' ears. "I practically coughed the rooftop off this old Church...you should have dragged me out of here a little while ago...no...second thought, I'm glad you didn't... ." Flora patted Brutus on his back and headed for home.

On her way back to the pensione, the gentleman's face came back to her. He was handsome, but something more attracted her to him. She quickly dropped his image when Brutus came running toward her. His limped run which became exaggerated with speed, made her laugh inside.

There was no time for whimsical thoughts or mental pictures of the stranger's face. Flora thought about all the things that had to be done before the guests arrived for the holiday dinner.

Her mind wandered back home...she wondered what her guys were doing...and if Grandma Flora had taken down her tree yet. In between thoughts from home and mental checks on her list of things to do that day, the stranger's face kept coming back to her. Brutus was good company on her walk back to the pensione. He stopped in front of the pensione door. Without that reminder from the loyal canine, Flora would have walked past her Florence home lost in thoughts of the stranger.

Before Flora had both feet in the door, the delicious aroma of something chocolate baking filled the air. Little Flora was already up and had half her recipe of chocolate chips cookies baked. The entire main floor smelled like a bakery. Flora had her coffee and waited for Jimmy and Emily to get up. She wondered what the *befana* had left for them.

Tracey and Christina helped Dolly with the last minute details of decorations. They had a little motivation sparking their artistic abilities. Stefano and Sebastian were coming over early to help them. So, they finished the real work which would make more time for the fun chores. Dolly didn't care why they moved with lightning speed that morning...she was pleased that they were just plain moving.

Jimmy and Emily ran into the kitchen as if the old *befana* was right behind them. Delicious chocolate morsels wrapped in brightly colored foils and sweet breads filled their arms to the brim. Emily talked with Flora about the befana and how she knew that one day God would lead the old woman to the Christ child.

Vince and Dolly watched Jimmy light up the fireplace. Then Vince went into the refrigerator and pulled out a white bakery box tied very neatly with a big red foil ribbon. He walked over to the table and proudly placed it down on the fine lace tablecloth. He begged them all to fill their cups with coffee so they could toast each other on the blessed feast of the Three Kings.

"May we all follow the stars that are inside our souls

and find the love that is there...*buona fortuna!*" Vince clanged his cup with all of theirs. Flora loved his Epiphany salutation.

Vince passed the box to Emily and had her open it. He asked her to serve the little cakes to everyone. The box was filled with all of their favorite dessert...canoli. Flora thought they were almost as good as the one's her Grandma used to make. She thought of her Grandma and how wonderful being Italian was.

The morning was peaceful despite the thought that there would be a house full of people over in just a few hours. Everyone went about their business for the next few hours. The pensione had never been more lived in or loved in. At least, not since those days when Peter, Dolly and Vince were all together.

Little Flora, Tracey and Christina were a big help to Flora that afternoon. They had alot of practice setting things up for big crowds on holidays. Meeting Vince's family was a special treat and the kids appreciated the younger people in his family. Vince's family was quite impressed with Dolly's family, too. His son, Paolo, seemed *more* than impressed with Flora.

Sebastian and Stefano received permission from Flora to take the kids for a ride around Florence and up to Fiesole where they lived. It was a small town but full of many things to see; although that didn't matter too much to the girls...the boys provided plenty of scenery to their eyes.

The boys also called Giacamo, Vince's younger sister's boy, to go along for the ride, too. He would be little Flora's date.. Little Flora didn't appreciate the matchmaking that afternoon but she didn't want to miss going out with the gang. So, she made sure that Giacamo knew she was attached to someone back home. He understood what she told him...but all was fair in love and war.

The holiday was wonderful! Vince's family made Flora and the kids feel very much at home. Zia Antoinette made everyone's day with her fancy pasta. Dolly and Flora made sure that the donna felt the sincerity in their praises. Vince knew how much that meant to his ninety year old Aunt...it had been a good day for everyone.

As quickly as the house filled up, so it emptied of it's special guests. Flora enjoyed the fire in the kitchen fireplace while she finished the dishes. Dolly kept her company and talked about everyone who was there and how they fit in the big family tree. Flora laughed at Dolly's perception of the relatives and fell silent when Dolly's next observation blurted out.

"You are a crazy lady, Dolly...why would you ever say such a thing...?" Flora was careful not to let her voice get too loud. Vince and Paolo had just walked in to sit by the fire. Dolly nodded with a cheshire grin and repeated her words...only this time as if they were some kind of hoped for prediction.

"Paolo has taken to you...and I'm not so sure you'll be able to handle that...I'm not so sure he will be able to handle that."

"*Handle what* ?" Flora asked in a firm whisper and with wide eyes that begged Dolly to stop her evaluation. She quickly looked over her shoulder and continued.

"Dolly...he was nice to me because he felt sorry for me at Mass today...I almost choked to death...I couldn't stop coughing...it echoed in the beams...I was so loud...!" Flora tried to soften Dolly's keen perceptions. Dolly could only smile at Flora's futile explanations.

"Dolly...I couldn't believe it when Vince introduced me to Paolo...when he walked in the dining room I was so embarrassed...Paolo was kind of *shocked* himself...I thought there was something familiar about the Eucharist minister this morning...it really is a small world... ." Flora spoke to Dolly as if meeting Paolo was a big coincidence. Dolly knew it was more than coincidental. So many simple things were written in the stars.

"He's a good dancer...huh, Flora," Dolly said as she grabbed another wet plate from the rack. "I mean for a guy who only felt sorry for a gal with a cough...he danced pretty close...and don't tell me it was *Frank Sinatra's* voice that made you swoon."

"*Swoon*," Flora whispered with a squeak of the ridiculous in her voice, "Dolly...what are you trying to start here...will you keep your voice down...please?" Flora looked at Dolly who seemed to be enjoying their agitated conversation more and more.

"It felt good to have someone hold you...didn't it...don't answer that...I'm just thinking out loud."

"Maybe too loud...," Flora said quietly. She continued washing the dishes, trying not to look in Dolly's direction.

"I don't expect you to answer my questions," Dolly said lowering her voice to an audible whisper, "...I know what I saw... and I'm glad I saw what I did...and you know exactly what I'm getting at." Dolly smiled her slinky grin once more and then put down her towel and walked away from Flora and the sink; proud and with a brand new feather in her hat.

Flora knew exactly what Dolly was getting at and that made her feel like she was transparent and even more than that...vulnerable and predictable. She felt embarrassed.

Sure, it was wonderful dancing with Paolo that afternoon, Flora thought. When the kids brought down their CD player and began playing music from Glen Miller's greatest hits...everyone's foot starting tapping. Vince asked Dolly to dance to MOONLIGHT SERENADE. Paolo followed his father's lead and invited Flora onto the kitchen tiled dance floor. He held her close and tight...like all Italians hold their women. She held him with as much feeling not thinking twice about Jack, only once; he never danced with her like that.

During that dance, and the three that followed, Dolly saw something in Flora she always knew had been inside of her friend. A special desire had been buried deep inside Flora's heart almost to the point of suffocation. There was so much more to Flora than she allowed other people to see...but Dolly saw it while Flora was dancing. Dolly knew she had said enough. Flora had much to think about with Dolly's words. It was time for her to face that long neglected portion of her heart.

The dishes were put away and Flora had no excuse not to join Dolly, Vince and Paolo by the fire. Dolly poured everyone another cup of coffee. Flora sat next to Dolly who was gloating in her new emotional excavation. Flora felt uneasy whenever the conversation came to her; especially when Paolo directed his attention toward her.

Flora knew now that Dolly heard her heart when Paolo walked into the dining room that day; she knew Dolly had seen something wonderful happen to Flora as she danced with Paolo earlier that evening. The stranger's face at Mass that morning became very familiar over dinner and dancing. Dolly knew from that point on, it would be very difficult for Flora and Paolo to forget what each of them had seen and felt on that Feast of the Three Kings.

Vince and Dolly headed up to their room while Flora and Paolo sat by the fire. The large embers were radiant. Vince didn't feel safe leaving a blazing fire alone, so Paolo volunteered to tend the logs. He asked Flora to stay down and keep him company. Flora accepted his invitation and also noticed Dolly's wink as she said good-night.

"My Dad enjoyed the day...it's been a while since we've seen some of the distant relatives...everyone had a great time...the kids will never know how their music made Zia Antoinette's day...she loved to dance when she was young...hearing the old songs again brought back so many memories for all of them...did you hear them talking...the whole day was great... ." Paolo was hyped himself reminiscing about that days events. He poured himself another cup of coffee and asked Flora if she wanted more.

"That sounds good...thank you," Flora said as she wondered what cup of coffee that one was going to be. The vision of her and Paolo dancing from earlier that evening made her anxiously express her next thought.

"You know, Paolo...what are the young kids going to dance to when they are old and gray...what songs and special chords will play tug of war with their hearts...WILD THING?"

Paolo laughed at Flora's last remark and her silly expression. "I think Harry Connick's gonna take care of that...he's really a great entertainer...I saw him when I was in New York last winter." Paolo sipped his coffee. Flora sipped hers.

"I hope more Harry's come out of the woodwork," Flora said agreeing with Paolo, "...nothing can top the old music...it goes right to your heart...did you see the way Dolly looked at Vince when he asked her to dance...the lyrics to AT LAST fit them perfect. Flora sang a line from the song, "*AND YOU ARE MINE...AT LAST.*"

Flora smiled a humble smile at Paolo as if begging him to forgive the squeaky notes that had just come from her mouth. Then, after seeing Paolo's accepting face, she continued.

"And when Vince took Dolly into his arms...did you notice the way he looked at her?"

Sure he noticed the way he looked at her, Flora thought inside her heart. Paolo had the same intensity in his stare while they were dancing. Flora took a deep breath and sighed and then quickly spoke the next thought that had entered her mind.

"The old songs are too beautiful...their words are too, too wonderful...and you know...there will never be another FRANK...he's one of a kind...more than a man...like an angel, a messenger that tells us with his sweet voice that everything is going to be alright...at least in the music world...anyway, I feel so lucky to have lived with his music...ooops...it's the coffee that makes me go on and on like this... ." Between the caffeine and Paolo's sweet attention, Flora began feeling somewhat light-headed. She was in a kind of time warp stupor aggravated by a an overdose of caffeine, Glen Miller and Frank. Thoroughly enjoying herself in Paolo's company, Flora sat down by the fire.

"Here we go...this is nice," Paolo said matter of factly and not taking his eyes off Flora. Flora wanted to say more about the afternoon but she had said enough. Paolo dove into the conversation with something interesting. Flora thought he was very articulate and she could tell in his manner that he felt comfortable sharing his stories. She wondered if he was always that comfortable with strangers.

They talked for hours before they even realized the time. Paolo walked Flora up to her room and wished her a good night. Then he stopped near the stairs. Then, as if remembering something very important, he ran back to Flora.

"I'll be around for a while...actually I'll be staying here at the pensione...just down stairs in fact...so if you need anything, or an extra hand, just let me know...I don't usually ramble on and on...like tonight...but I enjoyed myself very much."

"I was doing a pretty good job of flapping my lips too...," Flora said apologetically, "...but it was fun...I enjoyed your company very much...and...I will let you know if I need any help...thank you, Paolo." Flora didn't know what else to say but she didn't want to say goodnight either. She felt Paolo's apprehension to the finality of their pleasant evening. They looked into each others eyes and for a moment were caught up in that special place in people's hearts that knows no time and needs no words.

"Are you hungry...," Paolo said abruptly, "...all of a sudden I feel like I could eat a horse... ." He invited Flora with his eager expression.

"I could go for something...," Flora said quickly, "...there are alot of leftovers." Flora couldn't believe she said that. She had eaten enough for three days...but she was too excited to sleep, and maybe too wound up to say good-night. She didn't want to say good night.

"I've got just the right thing...," Paolo said excitedly, "...some reheated pasta with pesto...?" Paolo didn't give Flora time to answer but headed for the stairs and motioned to her to follow. And she did, eagerly. She thought if there had been a banister on the stairs Paolo would have slid down on it...and she would have followed close behind.

Paolo was a real chef in the kitchen and he wasn't shy about demonstrating his talent. He sat Flora down at the table and lit two candles. Before Flora's eyes and in a flash he prepared a delicious midnight snack. The candlelight and the pasta and the tiny burning embers in the fireplace made Flora feel very much at home. Paolo made her feel comfortable and safe. She had a difficult time telling herself that she was just having fun. She felt something very wonderful was happening and she knew Paolo felt it, too.

"Now I'm full," Paolo said as he rubbed his stomach, "...actually I could probably eat another pound of the rotini but it's late...and I don't want to have crazy dreams...a little more wine, Flora?" Paolo offered the bottle of Zinfandel to Flora, "I've got to warn you...it's very dry...I don't want you to *choke* again."

"No thanks, Paolo...I'm all set...it was delicious...and I didn't *choke* on the wine this morning...it just went down the wrong pipe...now I know why you looked so familiar...," Flora said with a giggled conviction.

"I guess I do resemble my Dad...that's what people tell me...but Flora, what's the *wrong pipe* ?" Paolo knocked on Flora's head with his knuckles. "Just checking...I thought maybe you were trying to tell me something...like you were made of metal or plastic." Paolo smiled at Flora who smiled back tenderly at his humor. Paolo continued.

"Well...I can't go to bed this stuffed...too much went down the right pipe...God I'm full...how about another log on the fire... ." Paolo walked over to the fire and gestured to Flora pointing at the logs.

"Another log...?" Paolo asked Flora.

"Alright...," Flora said, "...another log sounds great." Flora looked up at Paolo and couldn't stop smiling. "Three logs might be even better," Flora said waiting to see if Paolo picked up on her meaning. "Like a three log snack."

"A three log snack...what's a *three log snack* ?" Paolo asked while poking the wood in the fire. Flora snickered inside at Paolo's question. She liked his perplexed expression.

"You know how the Eskimos have sled dogs," Flora said with *matter of fact* in her voice, "...and when they are on a hunt and the nights are cold and freezing...well, depending on how cold the night is going to be, determines how many of the dogs get to sleep inside the igloo with them...*one* dog if it's just cold...*two* dogs if it's freezing...and *three* dogs if it's totally frigid!" Flora looked at Paolo and paused.

"Yeah...go on." Paolo was anxious to hear the rest of Flora's explanation. His attention and the wine she had been sipping from his glass made Flora feel more giddy...and a bit clever.

"Well Paolo..we didn't have a simple midnight snack...we had a super midnight snack which always calls for three logs on the fire...that allows enough time for a super snack to digest...we wouldn't want to go to bed too soon after we eat, we might have nightmares or bad dreams...capisce?...Do you understand now...what a three dog...I mean a three *log* snack is...," Flora asked as she picked up their plates and rinsed them in the sink. She walked back to the fireplace and sat down with a yawn. Paolo threw another log on the fire.

"Maybe we had a *four* log snack...," Paolo said as he rubbed his stomach, "...actually, it feels like I ate four logs...this fire will start up fast...the embers are really hot." Paolo sat down on the floor near to Flora. They were quiet for a moment digesting the rotini and the nights conversation.

"Spontaneous combustion...," Paolo said with the voice of a quiz show host. His light laugh made Flora look at him. She wasn't sure if she heard his last comment correctly. Paolo responded to her interrogative facial expression.

"*Spontaneous combustion...*," Paolo said again, "...it always amazes me...I can watch a log smoldering and then all of a sudden a burst of flame pops out of nowhere...poof...alot of things combust like that... ." Paolo looked at Flora and paused for a moment.

"Love sometimes...is like that," Flora added with sincerity. Her innocent statement made both of them wonder about what had just been said. "You know...," Flora continued calmly, "...like sometimes how love just pops into the thin air from nowhere...like you said, *poof... .*" Flora tried to make light of her honest observation about love and quickly changed the subject. She tucked the analogy within her minds reach for later scrutiny...for nighttime dreams.

"I think this renovation of the pensione is great for Vince...," Paolo said with a sterile conviction, "...he has to keep busy...he's like me, or rather I'm like him, anyway, we both need to have something going on the fire...I think most people do." The logs were burning strong and Paolo sat silent for a while. Flora felt as if it was her turn to say something but the fire was soothing and the dancing flames were keeping her mind busy. It was peaceful and too comfortable for talk. Her days energy had been long spent and she was simply content watching Paolo look into the fire. She noticed his eyes close and before she knew it, she fell asleep.

Paolo woke up to the grandfather's clock gong on the

half hour. He gently nudged Flora and walked her back up to her room. Flora felt like a kid for falling asleep in front of the fire.

"It seems we've been here before...," Flora said with half a yawn still in her voice, "Excuse my yawn... ." She reached for the doorknob. Paolo didn't take his eyes from Flora's. With eyes that seemed to be begging her to stand outside her door a few moments longer, he finally spoke.

"Thanks for the great day...I can't remember having a better time." Paolo shook Flora's hand and didn't let it go. He looked into her eyes and then kissed her tenderly. When his kiss ended Flora looked at Paolo almost bashfully and then quickly let go of his hand. Something all of a sudden scared her.

"I'm a married woman." Flora cringed inside after she spoke the obvious. Paolo knew Flora was married. For a moment Flora felt like a traitor...not so much to Jack, as to herself and Paolo. She wondered if she had been playing a game by the fire...pretending that it was alright to be so open with her glances, her touches, her heart.

"I'm sorry...it wasn't that you did anything...I just feel a little bit...guilty...for having such a wonderful time...I'm sorry, Paolo."

"No need to apologize, Flora...," Paolo said as he looked directly into Flora's eyes. She could barely stand looking back into his.

Paolo knew he upset Flora and he didn't mean to. He wanted to apologize. "You are married...but you aren't happy...and that isn't any of my business and it isn't an excuse to do whatever I please...but it seemed like you were enjoying yourself...I was having a good time...no one should be miserable in Florence."

"I'm not *miserable*...," Flora said defensively. She paused for a moment to gather her ruffled composure. She couldn't seem to find the words to explain the things she was feeling. But, she continued, hoping to make sense.

"And...there is more to life than being happy...happy in Florence." Her last statement quickly replayed in her mind. At that moment she realized she had lied to Paolo. Flora couldn't imagine anything more wonderful than being completely happy in Florence...or Union Lake...or anywhere else in the world.

"What more is there...tell me Flora...," Paolo said as he waited for Flora to respond. Flora thought about his simple question. Still, the right words weren't there for her. She gave him a quick and guarded reply.

"Like accepting who...and where you are...and making the best of it." Flora thought that sounded good. Paolo walked up to Flora and looked so directly into her eyes that she was afraid to look back into his...but she did. For a long moment neither one could say a thing. Then Paolo looked deeper into her eyes and broke their silence.

"B-u-l-l-s-h-i-t", Paolo said slowly, spelling it out in a low keyed disgust. He came as close to her body as he could without feeling her physically. The resistance between the two created more energy than they could handle at that moment. Paolo continued while Flora kept her eyes glued to his.

"Accepting who you are and making the best of it...is martyrdom.....masochistic...sometimes people go *crazy* trying to make the best of the worst of things...sometimes it's impossible...sometimes it's out of guilt and they accept the pain in their life as some kind of due punishment...but punishment for what...simple mistakes...not having the right answers all the time...?" Paolo seemed to be speaking with much authority on the subject of martyrdom. Flora wondered what happened in his life to make him so eloquently versed on the subject. Paolo pulled himself away from the invisible field of confused passion. Flora could breathe again, at least half breathe again.

"Maybe not punishment for anything," Flora said not sounding as sure of herself, "...but sometimes rolling with the punches...is for the commitment." All of a sudden Flora knew she finally spouted out the words of truth that were bouncing in her heart. She continued.

"You know, *commitment*...the promise two people make to each other." Flora watched for Paolo's reaction. He looked at Flora and shook his head. Flora continued.

"No one said marriage was easy...better or worse, richer poorer...but it seems like whenever things get uncomfortable...or squeamish...we begin wondering if it's all worth it...and we wonder if we should give it all up and move on...that's not what a relationship is all about...and for sure, it isn't what marriage vows are all about...right now I am the biggest hypocrite talking about vows." Flora understood Paolo's steps away from her. She believed what she had just told him, but a part of her...a big part of her...wanted to tell him the hundred other things that were going on inside her mind at that moment, things that had gone through her mind that whole afternoon.

He was a stranger, yet she wanted him to know every single thing about her...she wanted to understand him. Flora wanted to tell him that in their one evening together he looked more into her eyes than Jack had done their entire twenty-two year marriage. Paolo's eyes yanked the next words out of her heart.

"I don't know what Dolly told you about my relationship with my husband...I just want you to know that I'm not just making the best out of something sour...my life is good...Jack is a good man...and it isn't all his fault for the things that are rough in our marriage...," Flora said trying to be fair with Paolo. She continued hoping Paolo would see her situation in life as it really was.

"You only know what Dolly told you...Dolly thinks I'm perfect...or almost perfect...she understands alot of things and naturally takes my side...we're women...and...she's a good friend...and she'll be the first one to admit that Jack is a great guy...," Flora paused, hoping Paolo would break into her discourse. He did.

"No one is blaming anyone here for anything...and no one said you were perfect...or that Jack is some dark villain. Things happen sometimes in a marriage that are no one's fault...they just happen...and it isn't just the things I heard from Dolly...I heard other things tonight...," Paolo paused, took a deep breath and then looked deeply into Flora's eyes. "I didn't mean to cause all this commotion."

"I didn't mean...to blow your kiss out of proportion like this either." Flora looked at Paolo. He deserved more of an explanation. Taking a deep breath, Flora continued.

"Twenty-three years ago, I went after Jack like a missile with a laser lock...I was nineteen and ready for life and love...I convinced myself that it *was* love I felt for Jack...and that I *could* make him love me...I wonder sometimes if I ever really loved Jack...I thought I did...maybe it wasn't love, maybe it was that I wanted to love...and be loved." Flora turned her attention toward the window in the hallway. "We had good weather today, it was nice to see the sun." She sighed a deep sigh.

Paolo brought Flora's eyes back to his by reaching out and touching her cheek with his hand.

"You loved him," Paolo said with much conviction. "Don't ever doubt that you loved him...but love needs nurturing and some of us aren't as good as we preach because we don't truly understand what it's all about sometimes until it's too late." Paolo hesitated a moment, then continued. "Anyway, it sounds like you have love and life all figured out."

"No...," Flora said in a humble tone, "...I only feel that it's more my fault that Jack doesn't love me than his...and that now...I shouldn't be having the time of my life...I came here to help Dolly and... ." Flora paused thinking she was probably saying too much. She couldn't bring herself to say what she was thinking at that moment.

"And what...," Paolo said, almost insisting she go on.

Flora looked at Paolo. He genuinely cared about the things she was feeling. Flora wasn't used to that type of concern. She looked into Paolo's eyes and carefully went on.

"Paolo, I've only been here a few days and already it's difficult thinking about this trip coming to an end...Florence is beautiful...but it's more than your country that has me singing in the morning...so many wonderful people are here...I worry about things... ."

"What kind of things, Flora?" Paolo moved closer to Flora and took her hands.

"Cuckoo things, Paolo, things that might happen, things that might not ever happen." Flora kept her eyes fixed on Paolo's but took a step back away from him. He wouldn't let go of her hands.

"Flora," Paolo said pulling her closer to himself, "...today was wonderful...and tomorrow will be tomorrow, and whatever it brings will be good...life is good... ."

There was a pause in their conversation. Flora felt awkward in her inability to initiate a simple good night. Nothing seemed simple, then everything seemed to make sense. She looked at Paolo and wished he'd take her in his arms once more.

Paolo looked very seriously at Flora. Yet, his serious expression was coated with a sweet boyish charm that said he had something important to say. Flora wished he'd say whatever it was that was going on in his mind...in his heart. She couldn't believe what her heart was telling her. She wouldn't believe it, not yet, anyway.

"You are beautiful Flora...in so many ways...," Paolo said as he held Flora's hands more tightly, "...conversation with Dolly and Vince at suppertime can be very interesting...and to be honest with you, the subject of *Flora and the kids* was getting a bit stale...but now that I met the infamous Americans from Union Lake...I can understand her anticipation of your visit...Dolly's a good judge of character...but I never imagined...or thought I'd...you'd be...I would... ." Paolo fumbled more with his words until the old clock in the hall chimed. It gallantly became the referee between the thoughts in his heart and the words that were rolling clumsily from his mouth.

Flora's face blushed with his awkward compliment. She wanted to respond promptly to his words. The clock stopped chiming.

"Thank you, Paolo...I had a wonderful day." Saying good night was the last thing Flora wanted to do. She looked deeply into Paolo's eyes for a long couple of seconds; they were sincere and beautiful. He smiled at her...with his lips and his eyes.

"I don't want to say good night, Flora." Paolo kissed Flora on her lips, softly. She felt them heavily in her heart; she closed her eyes. It was more of a resuscitation than a kiss; their mouths barely touching, had drawn from the other's soul the love spark time tried fervently to douse.

Paolo let go of Flora's hand. It was more difficult letting go of her eyes. He walked to the stairs, not looking back. Flora watched him till the sound of his cleats on the tile floor diminished. She walked into her room and closed the door.

Flora couldn't sleep. She blamed her insomnia on the pasta, knowing it was really Paolo, his words, and his tender kiss that were keeping her so very wide awake. She sat up in bed and took turns watching Jimmy and Emily sleep. Flora thought about Jack.

Flora noticed her EMERSON paperback on the nightstand, she picked it up and flipped it open. Flora began reading in the middle of the page, carefully and understanding every word as if a beautiful secret of the universe had been shared with her that night.

"IF THE STARS SHOULD APPEAR ONE NIGHT IN A THOUSAND YEARS, HOW WOULD MEN BELIEVE AND ADORE; AND PRESERVE FOR MANY GENERATIONS THE REMEMBRANCE OF THE CITY OF GOD WHICH HAD

BEEN SHOWN! BUT EVERY NIGHT COME OUT THESE
ENVOYS OF BEAUTY, AND LIGHT THE UNIVERSE WITH
THEIR ADMONISHING SMILE."

Flora looked up from the page and closed her eyes
thinking *if the stars should appear one night in a thousand
years, how would men believe and adore*? Tears filled Flora's
eyes. *One night in a thousand years,* Flora thought. God knew
she needed their light...every night. Flora opened her eyes
and went to the paragraph at the bottom of the page.

"THE STARS AWAKEN A CERTAIN REVERENCE,
BECAUSE THOUGH ALWAYS PRESENT, THEY ARE
INACCESSIBLE; BUT ALL NATURAL OBJECTS MAKE A
KINDRED IMPRESSION, WHEN THE MIND IS OPEN TO
THEIR INFLUENCE. "

Flora read Emerson's words again and then went over
to her window to see her friends, the stars. Her mind had
always been *open to their influence*. The sky that night, was
a wishy washy deep gray, full of fast moving clouds. Flora
couldn't find a single star, but she knew the stars were
there. She felt them dancing in her heart. Those thoughts
made her smile.

Flora fell asleep that night thanking God for the wonderful day He had given her. She wondered if Paolo had
been the answer to her morning prayer. Flora wondered if
she had followed the star that fell into her soul, the one
from Gulliver, and if it had brought her to Paolo.

Chapter
thirteen

Orange Tiled Rooftops

Flora worked every day with Dolly, painting and wallpapering and sewing curtains and pillows. The pensione was going through a complete transformation. So was Flora.

Paolo became a kind of permanent fixture in the renovation scheme. He helped out with much of the heavy work and made the decorating very pleasurable. Dolly saw in Paolo and Flora's faces, a little more than what she thought either one of them had originally bargained for. Flora was still married to Jack. Paolo was a confirmed bachelor; that's what he always told Vince, anyway.

Even Vince wondered about the two big kids always laughing and hanging around together. He hoped they knew something he didn't. Like, when two people danced to THEY'RE WRITING SONGS OF LOVE, BUT NOT FOR ME, it didn't necessarily mean that they were in love. But, Vince could see certain sparks when they looked at each other...or when they danced to *Mussetta's Waltz*. He *knew* they were falling in love. Vince knew alot of things about Flora and grew close to her as they shared culinary secrets in the kitchen. *"Who says too many hands in the pot spoil the broth...who likes broth anyway, when you can have chunky beef stew?"*

Vince's philosophy of rolling with the punches and using his knuckles for making *gnocchi* complimented

Flora's view of making the best of things and using half and half in her *canoli* cake instead of heavy whipped cream, *"You can eat twice as many for the same amount of calories...and they taste even better!"* So, Vince kept Flora laughing and Flora kept Vince busy cooking.

"Paolo had to go to Rome for a couple of weeks on business for Vince," Dolly quickly rattled off as she started the morning pot of coffee. "He is such a Godsend to his father." That simple statement was like a bombshell to Flora. She didn't hide her surprised and disappointed reaction to the news.

"Did this just come up," Flora asked, hoping to sound nonchalant. "Paolo didn't mention anything to me last night...not that he has to...but he did tell me he'd be here for dinner tomorrow." Flora looked at Dolly. She hoped Dolly was going to say she was just kidding about Paolo's sudden departure. But, Dolly wasn't kidding. She didn't know if this was an unexpected trip for Paolo. She did hear through Flora's voice a hurt that went a bit deeper than Paolo's missing a dinner engagement. It was time for a woman to woman chat.

"Flora, I don't know if this came up unexpectedly...it's nothing to be upset about... ."

"Dolly, I know...maybe I'm surprised he didn't tell me he was going to leave...two weeks is a long time and we were going to put the moldings up around the fire place."

Flora took for granted that Paolo would always be at the pensione. His sudden departure to Rome for two weeks jarred Flora's recent and pleasant routine. She realized she had been taking alot for granted. Apparently, Paolo was keeping things in perspective. Flora, all of a sudden, felt very silly.

"I'm sorry, I thought, hey, I don't know what I thought...I forgot something upstairs...excuse me for a minute... ." Flora's eyes filled with tears as she walked out of the kitchen. She bumped into Vince on her way to the stairs. She looked up into Vince's eyes and tried to say *good morning*. But, their eyes meeting only made tears overflow from her own.

Vince entered the kitchen with a puzzled look.

"What's the matter with Flora? Bad news from home?" Vince looked as perplexed as Dolly was feeling. Dolly shook her head and then motioned to Vince that she'd be back in a minute. Vince poured himself a cup of coffee. Dolly went after Flora to find out more about the escapades of Robin Hood and maid Marian. Dolly walked carefully into Flora's room.

"Flora, what's the matter? Do you want to talk about it?" Dolly stood behind Flora who was looking out her bedroom window with tears still wet on her face. She stared out from the old window and tried to answer Dolly calmly but before the first word was out of her mouth, she turned around and walked toward the bed. She sat down, took a deep breath and smiled a half smile at Dolly. It was the best she could do.

Flora wanted to tell Dolly a thousand things...so many thoughts were zig-zagging like lightening through her mind. Fr. Bill and the misguided attention she gave him...Matt's affections and her fumbling with such a juvenile situation that past summer...these thoughts made her cringe. Flora remembered how Jack just laughed at her confessions, her cries for he]p. His reactions to the cleansing of her soul disappointed her so much that the rest of the little feeling she had for him died with the late summer roses.

Flora could only imagine what he'd say now if she told him she was *truly* falling in love in Florence. Truly falling, Flora repeated to herself]f. Do I *truly* know what love is? Doubt chilled her heart and all the beautiful things she kept carefully there.

Flora felt sorry for Jack, but feeling sorry for Jack didn't make him love her. Twenty-two years of feeling sorry bought *zip* in the love department. Jack couldn't...he wouldn't even try to understand her heart. Flora was tired of begging for every ounce of affection...Flora wondered if she had been that difficult to love.

She wondered if she expected too much.Was there such an abundance of love in the world that people can toss aside even the smallest particle of it? Flora felt guilty for throwing away the tiny remnants of the love she had for Jack. Those may have been enough to rekindle the fire of their commitment to each other. All of a sudden she felt very lost and unsure of so many simple things. Paolo's trip to Rome triggered a barrage of unresolved questions.

"Dolly I don't know what's wrong...what am I crying about?"

"You've been here three and a half weeks...maybe this is a delayed jet lag...," Dolly said as she gently pressed on Flora's shoulders to make her lie down on the bed. Flora didn't fight it even though she really wanted to talk to Dolly.

"Relax and rest a while...we'll talk later." Dolly covered Flora with an afghan and then brushed Flora's bangs to the side. She smiled and winked at Flora, then started back to the door.

"I feel really dumb right now," Flora said quickly, "...thanks for being here with me, Dolly."

"You know Flora...you are like my daughter...if Peter and I had married...we would have had *dodici* bambini." Dolly opened the door slowly.

"Don't go Dolly...please stay a while...just a little longer... ." Flora sat up on her bed. Dolly walked back and sat down next to her.

"Sure...I'll stay... ." Dolly looked at Flora and smiled at her tenderly.

"Dolly...if I had been content with my life...chances are I'd be home working on a quilt...or I'd be painting the girl's room...why did I have to upset things...my life was alright just the way it was... ." Flora paused for a moment, then continued.

"If Jack were here right now...in front of me...I'd *spit*...listen to me, listen to the anger I have inside of me." Flora threw her arms into the air. "I thought I was over the resentment...and the weirdest thing right now is that a part of me is actually blaming Jack for all of this...I feel so desperate."

"You didn't upset anything by coming here, except your heart...and who doesn't feel desperate at one time or another in their life...especially when things start changing... ." Dolly looked out Flora's window, then back at Flora. She continued.

"Don't you think the leaves on the trees feel desperate in Autumn...I do...first, they change their color, a sure sign of stress I'd say...and then one by one...never knowing when...they begin to fall...some on windy days...some on still days when it seems the journey to the ground below will take forever...then there are those stubborn *oak leaves* that cling till spring...looking pretty foolish in May." Dolly hopped off the bed and sat in the ladderback chair by the nightstand. "Listen to my motor mouth...but you know what I mean, Flora."

"I know Dolly...but those *clingy* leaves in May...they brought so much color to the gray winter days...so many days I'd look outside my bedroom window and the sky would be as white as the blanket of snow beneath it...and the only thing to offset the black and white design of old man winter were the CLINGY OLD RUSTY COLORED OAK LEAVES...so, it's like they are the *brave* ones...our heroes that hang on all winter through wind and snow and rain...to give us joy."

"Like *you* hung on to your marriage...for your family." Flora looked at Dolly responding to her question with her eyes, then her words.

"A little like that, Dolly." Flora paused for a moment. "The kids are growing up...maybe I'm just scared...that one day there will be no one around...and then I'll let go on a blustery day and blow so far away... ." Flora got up from her bed and sat in the rocker with her Grandmother's lace quilt. She rocked slowly in the chair. Then as if the rocking chair had inspired her, Flora went on.

"You know, I shoved my affections in Fr. Bill's face...and what would I have done if he had responded back the same way...I think about it now and...eeeuuuwww...I hated Jack for that...and I hated that part of me that *let* it happen...I probably made Bill's life miserable...like he needed another lovestarved, unhappily married woman crying down his collared neck...and then I have the nerve...the guts to entertain for more than *two* seconds...someone who was half my age." Flora shook her head hoping Dolly would add more fuel to the outrageous fire in her heart. Dolly didn't say a word. She got up from her chair and walked toward the bedroom window. She looked at Flora with eyes that told her to go on.

Flora sat thinking for a while. She played with the string snowflakes on her Grandmother's lace quilt. She continued with humility.

"Dolly...all my fumbled escapades made me open my eyes...Matt's kiss made me feel the hole in my heart...he made me remember how wonderful it is to love...and now, Paolo...meeting him made me find out so many things about myself...being with him makes me feel so special."

"You should be enjoying everything along the way on this journey...and that's the most important thing...not to close your eyes...or your heart...'God does work in mysterious ways'... ." Dolly laughed at her own comment. Flora did, too.

"Yeah, *real* mysterious...I met *you* and then *you* dragged me here...well not, dragged...knowing darn well I'd bump into...you know who... ."

Dolly looked at Flora omnisciently. "You two were bound to meet," Dolly said as she walked back to Flora. "I can't say I didn't think about it before I even asked you to come to Florence, because that was one of the first thoughts in my head after Vince asked me to come...I knew you'd like Paolo alot...and besides, what are women like me for, if we can't see into things and sort of help them along?...but remember *you* did run into him on your own... that blessed event was written in the stars...you met him at Mass...so, you can thank the Man upstairs for that one!"

"I'm not blaming you," Flora said with a chuckle in her voice, "...and I *do* thank God for this whole experience and all the wonderful people I met...but I'm almost positive God didn't have adultery on the agenda for this trip...that's what's really bothering me... ."

"I'm not sure what He had exactly in mind...but I know this...what looks like one thing today...might be something totally different tomorrow...nothing is for sure...except that we have to trust what we feel in our hearts to be true...and those feelings explain themselves in *time*....and time...well, that's the tricky thing...but enough. *BASTA!*" Dolly hugged Flora and then noticed her reflection in the vanity mirror. She leaned closer toward the mirror examining her hair...parting it with her fingers. She saw Flora smiling at her through the mirror. Dolly winked at her as she accepted her smile. Then, she cleared her throat.

"Yup...I need an afternoon with Lady Clairol...these dang roots...they sure grow out fast...seeing my gray hair makes me emotional...see...there is *time* ...right there, that inch and a half of gray is about *three months* of avoiding LADY CLAIROL... ." Dolly shook her hair back into place.

"Dolly. . . I'll put the color in for you...what was your natural color?" Flora stood next to Dolly and looked with her into the vanity mirror.

"*Natural*?...Gosh, it's been so long it's hard to remember...," Dolly nudged Flora with her elbow and a big smile. "Really, Flora...I think I had hair like yours...dark with lots of chestnut highlights...I don't mean to brag, but everyone...even strangers would stop and tell me how beautiful my hair was...Peter loved my hair...yup...it was alot like yours." Dolly turned and looked admiringly at Flora's hair. A huge grin took over Flora's face.

"You mean you had LOREAL number 4...," Flora said smiling at her friends innocent expression of disbelief, "...you really thought this was natural?"

"Of course I did...," Dolly said as she went closer to Flora's head for a better look.

"Uumm...oh yes...*I zee za leetle buggers*...you do have quite a few gray, Flora." Dolly seemed amazed.

"SEE...I'd say I'm about half and half." Flora sat on the edge of the bed and Dolly sat back into the rocker breathing a big sigh.

"One day," Dolly said as if beginning a fairytale, "...I woke up and noticed that all my pretty highlights were gone...it seemed like overnight I was stuck with a mop of blah hair...dark but a *colorless* kind of dark...the worst kind...with strands of gray here and there...*then*, my hair reminded me about the bigger thing that was happening."

"The *bigger* thing...what do you mean, Dolly?"

Dolly took a deep breath before she answered Flora.

"Are you sure we want to get into this?"

"I'm sure...," Flora said eagerly, "...you're not going to leave me hanging in the air with this one."

"Okay...but remember, you asked for it... ." Dolly gently yanked a lock of Flora's hair and took a deep breath, "...here goes." Dolly's face became more serious.

"My *hair* reminded me that I was growing older...but *wiser*. Gray hair is just a sign that there is more to life than the obvious...look what happened to *Moses* after he talked with God...his beard and everything turned gray, at least that's what happened to Charlton Heston in the TEN COMMANDMENTS...but back to the subject, the chestnut highlights, the shimmering auburn and golds...they went away...all that wonderful sheen went deep *into my soul*...where it turned into a quiet, soft wisdom...a special wisdom that only comes with age...okay, maybe it wasn't all that *quiet*...or *soft*." Dolly winked at Flora who was wearing a silly grin.

"Dolly, your hair must have been *full* of highlights," Flora said not meaning to sound sarcastic. "I mean...you have so much wisdom...I mean you know so much about everything... ." Dolly laughed at Flora who was trying to make her compliment sound *complimentary.*

"All kidding aside," Dolly said with a very serious expression and gently rocking in her chair. "Just because the chestnut leaves our hair doesn't mean it's gone forever...it stays inside of us with all the other beauty that sort of *disappears* with time...the older we get, the wiser we get, most of us anyway...so much is planted in our soul everyday...if we only have the courage to see more than the fading reflection in the mirror...there are so many things to discover, there are so many secrets life wants to share with us, things we just can't comprehend when we're young." Dolly stopped rocking in her chair and looked at Flora with anxious eyes.

"That's beautiful, Dolly...when did you figure all this out?" Dolly thought for a minute as she looked into Flora's eyes that were begging her for a great answer.

"About thirty years ago...," Dolly said pausing for a moment in mid sentence. Then, as if suddenly receiving the rest of her thought from Providence, she continued with great confidence...and a cocky grin.

"Yup...about thirty years and *three hundred thousand* gray hairs ago...I was walking to my Art class one day when a flock of geese flew over my head. I looked up at them flying in tight formation and then I realized I wasn't afraid to look up at them anymore...I wasn't worried about getting pooped on, I really used to worry about that... ." Dolly looked at Flora who was trying to hold in her laugh. "Trust me, Flora...when a goose poops it isn't pretty...from that day on something inside of me knew that if I got pooped on by a goose or any other bird...it would be a *bless - ing,* it would be good luck...not a shitty mess!"

"GOOD LUCK?" Flora asked as she laughed whole-heartedly, "...I'd *rather* find a penny and pick it up...you know, not so *messy.*" Flora smiled at Dolly. Dolly took Flora's hand and squeezed it.

"I know you know what I'm talking about,Flora, how often does a person get pooped on by a bird?...seriously, when you're young and it happens, you could faint at just the thought of it...but that day as I looked up into the sky full of geese, I felt privileged to be on the ground beneath them...that night when I brushed my hair I didn't see chest-nut highlights in the mirror...but something was shining in my soul, the *geese* in the beautiful Autumn sky...from that day on I began to see alot of things differently...I realized that lots of things that seemed terrible when I was young...really weren't that bad...like growing older...or being alone."

"Little things are making more sense to me everyday." Flora squeezed Dolly's hand back with as much affection.

"Things change...leaves...hair color...that's the story of life, girl...but *nothing is ever lost*...you just have to know where to look for it... ." Dolly looked at Flora with sinceri-ty.

"Thank you, Dolly... ." Flora hugged her wise old friend...she hugged her hard. "Dolly...I don't know where I would be right now if it wasn't for you...and Vince...you are making me look at myself...and making me understand that alot of the things I'm feeling are just part of the whole big thing." Flora looked gratefully into Dolly's face. "You would have made a wonderful mother, Dolly...really." Flora hugged Dolly again and thought of her own mother back home.

Flora thought of her Grandma Bolone and her Grandmother LaCroix. She thought about Emily and little

Flora and their role in the world as women. A woman learns from her mother and her grandmother...her sisters, teachers. How much she has to learn on her own...in the bedroom...in the kitchen. Then, on the porch or waiting for a bus or walking through dried leaves, the secrets of the universe unfold, one by one...sometimes with geese flying overhead in perfect formation. She thought maybe that was why coffee klatches started...one woman needing to share a special gift of knowledge like Dolly had shared with her. So many times they're lost. That thought made Flora hug Dolly harder. Dolly hugged her back.

"Don't be afraid to love...," Dolly said breaking her embrace and placing her hands on Flora's shoulders, "...just don't be afraid to love."

Dolly walked to the bedroom door, "Flora...no more words...we have lots of work to do...so perk up...GOSH...I forgot about Vince...I told him to wait for me...thank heaven we didn't get on the subject of wrinkles ...or *double chins* or *sagging*...you know... ." Dolly winked at Flora then headed back to the kitchen to see Vince.

Vince knew the delicate condition of a heart that loved and for whatever reason wasn't loved back. He almost wrote Dolly out of his script until the pensione came back to him. He picked up the phone one day and just called Dolly. From out of nowhere he found himself dialing a long distance number, that's how he explained it all to Dolly.

Dolly entered the kitchen and Vince asked her if she wanted a cup of coffee.

"Make it a double...we have to talk." Dolly sat down and related the whole morning episode to Vince. He understood Flora's response and knew this would only be the beginning of her coming to terms with her problem. How she went without the love she deserved for so long was the biggest mystery to him. Flora neglected herself long enough and the natural desire to be loved was too big now to hide. Flora could no longer pretend that the void wasn't there.

Flora had the love of her children, but that was different...and maybe for a while Flora had convinced herself that loving them and their loving her back, would be enough. But, things were changing and the absence of Jack's affection became more keenly noticed. When Flora began looking at the scenery she realized the world was full of love. She wanted more.

Down deep in Vince's heart he knew Paolo needed Flora as much as she needed and wanted him. What a huge emotional volcano could erupt if things weren't handled with a special trust and faith. If anyone could handle that type of situation, Vince knew Paolo could. Vince had total confidence in Paolo concerning that delicate matter of the heart. Afterall, he was his son.

Vince took a deep breath and stretched in his chair. He nodded up and down in a deep thinking kind of way and said, "Che sera, sera". Dolly knew what he meant. She sighed her own deep breath of wonder.

"You are such a romantic." Dolly looked into Vince's smiling eyes. "How I stayed away all these years I'll never figure out, but I'm so happy we are together now". Dolly reached across the table and squeezed Vince's strong hand. He squeezed Dolly's back.

"Don't ever let me go Dolly...you know...we're alot like the trees...like the little ones that are overshadowed by the big, we somehow manage to twist and turn and find our sunshine...it's in our nature to love...and to be loved in return...Flora only wanted to be the cream in Jack's coffee...that's all."

"Too bad he stopped drinking coffee after they were married...you know what I mean, Vince... ." Dolly smiled at Vince. Vince stretched across the table and kissed Dolly's cheek while Dolly poured the cream in his coffee.

"Wowwy zowwy...two love birds here...," Christina said as she and Tracey entered the kitchen. They immediately started talking about the *guys* and how much fun everyone was having. Dolly was glad to see their contented souls, and asked how little Flora was doing with Dan.

"Little Flora and Dan are going to be married one day...," Christina said more than half serious. "That is if Giacamo doesn't upset the old apple cart. He is so dang nice and if Dan doesn't get here soon...maybe little Flora's defenses will break down and whoa, whoa, whoa...Giacamo rides again! He's a persistent kind of guy...and if the *Italiano* postal service continues it's pace of delivering mail from back home... who knows what will happen?"

Christina and Tracey jabbered on and little Flora joined them. Not long after that, Emily and Jimmy came bouncing in the room with Brutus. The sun was shining and they had big plans that morning, too. Sebastian and Stefano...and Giacamo, were going to take them to an afternoon opera. The opera didn't excite Jimmy, but he wouldn't miss going anywhere with the new three *Italian musketeers*. That day was a holiday for everyone!

Flora heard the commotion and came back down to the kitchen. Dolly was happy to see her smiling again.

"Ready for Lady Clairol?" Flora asked Dolly.

"Ready...!"

The afternoon came and the pensione was quiet. Dolly's hair turned out very chestnut, just the way she liked it. Dolly and Vince went visiting friends and the kids went to the opera. Flora wrote some letters to send home till the telephone rang.

"Flora?"

It was Paolo.

"Flora, are you there"? Flora couldn't speak. She didn't know what to say or how to react to the flood of emotions she was feeling inside herself.

"Hello...Flora...are you there?"

"Paolo...I'm here," Flora said as she gained her composure.

"Hang on...I've got to deposit more coins... ." Flora hung on and heard the clang of the *gettone* through the receiver, each one plunking heavily into her heart. She was so happy to hear Paolo's voice.

"Flora, I've been trying to call you for hours...but it was busy...Vince called me last night and wanted me to take this Rome trip for him...he and Dolly have some visiting to do...he needs the break anyway...I know we had a lot of plans, and I'm sorry if I've disappointed you...but I'll be home soon, and if I put my nose to the grind I'll be able to cut this trip short by a week... Flora are you there?"

Flora was so happy she didn't know what to say, his voice sounded so good to her.

"I'm here, Paolo...and don't worry about me...there are alot of things I can do this week and...you just be careful and hurry back." For a moment Flora was tempted to say more...Paolo interrupted.

"I thought of you on the train...and the moldings for around the fireplace...we have to talk when I get home...don't do too much while I'm gone...ciao, Flora...I miss you...tell everyone I miss them."

Flora held the phone to her heart. She was falling in love with Paolo. She would accept whatever came to her in that relationship. Without love, Flora thought, a person only existed.

Flora threw on her heavy sweater and boots and walked to the market on a cloud. The kids would be home soon and the young guys ate like an army. Flora tried not to think about Paolo...but the more she tried, the more he came into her mind. She missed him terribly. As, she dropped the mail off, she wondered why she couldn't make herself miss Jack...even a little. She felt ashamed for her lack of feelings for him and that quieted her hearts joyful song for Paolo.

Flora stopped thinking and enjoyed the sky. It was

vivid blue and clear like an ektochrome picture postcard. How much she enjoyed being exactly where she was...exactly where she needed to be. As she headed back to the pensione her eyes caught the rooftop of San Miniato and that made her think of God...her family and her commitment to both of them. Paolo was not a mistake. He made her feel that everything was good. She didn't want to let him go.

The orange tiled rooftops against the clear blue sky of Florence made her heart warm. Cloths drying in the breeze and the smell of early springtime made her think of time and how precious every moment is to people who love. Tears filled her eyes and the warmth of their overflow onto her cheeks made her smile with gratitude that she was able to feel such happiness.

Chapter
fourteen

Guilt

"Dolly, the room is beautiful...bravissimo!" Vince congratulated Dolly and Flora on their decoration of the dining
room. He was more than happy with the results and kind
of surprised how all the colors and ideas went together.
Dolly laughed with delight at the expression on his face
and hugged him. She pinched his cheek affectionately and
then said dramatically, "Oh ye of little faith."

Flora was actually surprised at the outcome of the project, too. She never let Dolly sense her doubts at certain
phases of the renovation...like when she painted the window wall *ultramarine* blue. She always trusted Dolly's
senior judgement and the dining room was, afterall, an
example of her artistic expression. Something clicked and
made the whole room come together. It really was a work
of art... and love.

That night was the pre-lent celebration dinner at San
Miniato; a mardi gras bash, only instead of the day before
Ash Wednesday, it was celebrated the week-end before.
The people of Florence took this time of year very serious-
ly. Time to celebrate and get out all their *wild* flirtations, in
a respectable way, before the penitential season of Lent.

The girls were excited for the celebration that evening.
Sebastian and Stefano were going to go, but Giacamo
bowed out when he heard little Flora wasn't going. She

wanted to wait at home for Dan's phone call and baby-sit for Emily and Jimmy. Christina called her a *party pooper* in one breath and then in the next made her know that she would have stayed home, too, if she had a guy like Dan calling her. Tracey seconded that declaration, Emily *thirded* it; Jimmy thought they were all crazy.

"Let's catch a few afternoon winks," Vince said in between two yawns, "...we'll be up late tonight and I don't want to fall asleep in the middle dinner...we've been pretty busy this week and it caught up with me." Vince headed for the stairway. He bid all of them *adieu*. Dolly followed Vince. Flora sat at the table and admired the dining room a little while longer.

After Flora finished the afternoon dishes she went upstairs to lay down. When she passed the kids room, their chattering and giggles were too tempting to pass by.

The girls were doing their nails and Tracey was setting Emily's hair. Jimmy was writing to Jack.

"Mama," Little Flora said sweetly, "...come on in...I was just going to ask you if I could borrow your gauze skirt tomorrow." Little Flora looked sheepishly at her mother. "I'm going to the museum on a private tour...and I want to look...*sophisticated*."

"I'll have to look for it," Flora said hoping to accommodate little Flora's request, "...but I haven't seen it the whole trip, maybe it's tucked underneath something...I'll look for it when I go to my room... ."

"I know where it's at", little Flora said as she pulled the closet door open. She dangled the skirt in front of her waist. "Sorry, Mom, I thought you hung it here".

"Sure, " Christina said as she walked by little Flora and pulled on her ponytail. Then Tracey and Emily grabbed Flora's arms and led her to the bed then directed her to sit down.

"Let's talk, Aunt Flora." And so they did. Everyone blurted out stories about their tutors, about Sebastiano and Stefano...about Giacamo's persistence with little Flora, Jimmy's spy adventures...it was good to hear about so many of the things that were going on in and around the pensione. Flora was very happy to hear they all were having as good a time in Florence as she was.

Emily put the ROBIN HOOD compact disc in the player. That music made them all quiet for a while and Flora could see their thoughts turning toward home. Flora suggested calling home. Jimmy dialed as quickly Flora tossed that idea in the air.

"If it's almost three o'clock in the afternoon here...it's almost nine o'clock in the morning at home. Daddy should be up. . . huh Mom?" Jimmy looked to Flora for her answer when all of a sudden he connected with someone on the other line.

"Dad? It's Jimmy...how's it going...Come sta?" Jimmy smiled so proudly and listened attentively as Jack spoke to him.

"Ask Dad if he picked up his tickets yet...has he gotten our mail...did he get the watercolor I sent to him?" Little Flora spurted out questions faster than Jimmy cared to hear them

"BE QUIET...I can't even hear what Dad is saying...you can talk to Dad later." Jimmy was growing very impatient with little Flora's intentional rudeness. Flora covered little Flora's mouth with her hand and Jimmy thanked her for that effective muzzle .

One by one all the kids talked to Jack...then he asked for Flora and they talked for a while...mainly to get the logistics of Jack's upcoming trip straight...he was excited.

Their words with Jack put everyone in a good mood. It was like they were energized with a boost of magic that left them all contented. They were saving the major tours of Italy for when Jack arrived. Jack had promised to take them on a trip to Rome and Pompei...and alot of other *neat* excursions.

Flora left them jabbering a mile a minute. All during her bath she felt guilty for having *fantasies* about her and Paolo. Especially after talking with Jack. Especially after seeing the anticipation in the kids eyes after they heard his voice. Flora felt a terrible guilt for leaving him out of her mind as easily as she had those past few days. He didn't love her, but she couldn't let go. She blamed herself for Jack's incompetence.

When Paolo was around her, or when she'd hear his voice on the phone, love was real. But, when he was away...when the days passed without hearing a word from him...it was as if he never existed and that all her recollections of him and their good times together had been just a dream.

Reality was, that she was married to Jack. A good marriage or not, that's the way things were. She didn't have the courage to really look at her life seriously, it hurt too much. Her heart ached for someone who could just love her for who she was and would accept her *as is*.

Though their acquaintance was a relatively new one, Dolly came to know Flora very well, maybe even more than Flora's own sisters. Flora's sisters had a suspicion of her discontentment, but knew also that Flora was strong and that she would never, jeopardize her family's happiness, no matter how wretched things became for her. Flora was their big sister, their mentor. Dolly knew Flora's strength and her commitment to her family, but she also knew the sacred niche in Flora's heart that had been neglected.

Flora accepted the designated *crown* of leadership many years ago, and would never think of relinquishing it for her own personal gain, for her own pleasure, that's what she told Dolly, anyway.

The past few years had been exceptionally difficult for Flora. Moving in with her parents, with Jack's approval, proved to be a huge mistake. Jack swore many times curs-

ing the day he made that *terrible* decision. He never let too
many days go by without reminding Flora of that horrid
mistake either.

Flora's own mother felt the tension in their marriage
and the resentment Jack held since their living together.

Jack made the lottery his prayer and winning it his only
hope for a normal life again. If he won ten million dollars
Flora didn't think that would *cure* Jack's ailment. She knew
it wasn't the prescription for her.

But, Dolly saw beyond the pain that bound Flora to a
vow that was empty. Flora grew up believing everything
gets better if you try hard enough to make it that way. She
was as stubborn in that belief as she was persevering. So, it
was up to her to change things...even if she had to wade
half her life in water Jack was making impossible to tread.
Jack's gloom had almost eradicated all sense of joy from her
heart. Then, Dolly dived in to save her drowning spirit
from the merciless force of Jack's negative current. Dolly
knew this trip was a must, a desperate attempt at rescuing
a helpless soul. Flora had to find the strength to reach out
for help and not feel traitorous for taking such a valiant
stretch toward finding happiness.

"*Mom*...the telephone...it's Paolo." Flora ran to the
phone.

"Buona sera, Paolo...how are you?"

"Flora, I won't be coming back to Florence tonight...it
seems there was more to this contract than I thought...and
no one knows where the Cardinal is."

Flora's spirit fell, but understood Paolo's predicament.
It took a good amount of faking to sound as if she hadn't
been disappointed in his not returning in time for the celebration.

"I want you to go to San Miniato tonight with Vince and
Dolly...you'll have a great time...I'll probably be back sometime on Sunday...I'll call before I leave."

Flora told Paolo she would go that night, but knew she

wouldn't. She thought it would be nice just being home with little Flora and Em and Jimmy. That morning Jimmy had mentioned how hungry he was for a good old *American hamburger.*

Dolly could have persuaded Flora to go with them but she thought Flora might like some time for herself and for her own family. Dolly made a mental note to talk with Flora in the morning, she wanted to know what was going on.

Flora heard the doorbell ring.

"Giacamo...what are you doing here," little Flora asked as she opened the heavy carved door of the pensione parlor. She almost sounded rude in her greeting to Giacamo.

"I had to drop my Aunt off at Church for the celebration ...and since she only wanted to stay for the dinner...I thought that maybe you wouldn't mind if I waited here for a few hours." Giacamo felt embarrassed with his unexpected visit. "I'll go into town...if you have something more important to do."

Little Flora didn't mean to embarrass Giacamo with her abrupt greeting.

"No, you aren't interrupting anything, but I do have a couple of things I want to do tonight...but I'm sure Jimmy will love your company...come in." Little Flora walked Giacamo into the kitchen.

"*Buona sera,* Mrs. Filippi."

"*Buona sera,* Giacamo...come in and sit down. Flora finished wiping the crumbs from the table. "Here, sit down and I'll get you guys some snacks to munch on."

"Thanks Mrs. Filippi." Giacamo sat down and Jimmy sat across from him opening the gameboard and getting anxious to begin. They played the game and Emily watched patiently, knowing she was going to play the *champ.*

Flora made hamburgers and Giacamo couldn't seem to get his fill of them. Jimmy laughed at how fast the *guest* ate...and how much he could eat. Little Flora noticed how easy he was to talk to...and his eyes...how penetrating they pierced through hers.

Just before they were finished with supper, Dan called. Little Flora talked. Giacamo pretended to be distracted with the dishes and the clearing of the table. Little Flora didn't care though...it was good that he was there to see that there really was a *Dan*. Emily brought down the compact disc player and played her favorite song, EVERYTHING I DO. Giacamo said he hadn't heard anything that beautiful since *Puccini*. Emily thought he was talking about some kind of noodle.

"Not *fettucini*, Emily...*Puccini*...the great Italian composer. I'll take you to see LA BOHEME one afternoon. It opens at la Scala soon." Giacamo looked toward little Flora and quickly invited her to come along, too.

"What about ME?" Jimmy jokingly pouted.

"You too, especially you Jimmy...you'll love it." Giacamo winked at Emily.

"Then you have to watch ROBIN HOOD one afternoon with us," Emily said anxiously, "...you'll like it, Giacamo." Emily smiled at the new checker champ of Florence.

Little Flora hung the phone up and politely accepted Giacamo's invitation to the opera. Giacamo knew then that she had been half eavesdropping while she was talking to Dan. That was good, Giacamo thought. *Very good.*

"LA BOHEME is my favorite Opera...," little Flora said to Giacamo with demure excitement. "Ever since I heard the music in the movie MOONSTRUCK, I've become an Opera fan...even though I've never really gone to an Opera."

"Well," Giacamo said, "...you are formally invited to one next week and you will fall in love with it...I guarantee it." Giacamo smiled at little Flora and was taken in by her natural charm...until Emily broke the spell.

"Just don't forget me you guys...I like Opera, too."

"I could never forget about you, Emily." Giacamo gave Emily a big hug.

"I have an idea," Emily said rushing out from the kitchen. "I'll be right back."

"I bet she's going to get her MOONSTRUCK video...and she'll ask if anyone wants to watch it with her...I think Emily's seen that movie twenty times!" Jimmy acted like he was imitating a psychic.

"I think that's exactly where she went," little Flora chuckled in agreement.

"HERE IT IS," Emily said completely out of breath, "...here's the MOONSTRUCK tape...anybody wanna watch it with me...please?"

Little Flora volunteered her company and Giacamo followed quickly with his resounding *yes*.

"I guess I will, too," Jimmy said with far less enthusiasm, "...what else is there to do *alone*?"

Flora finished up in the kitchen and excused herself from the last half of the movie. She could see everyone was having a good time around the television. Flora noticed the special smile little Flora couldn't wipe from her face. She warned Jimmy not to tease and then headed up the stairway feeling pleasantly exhausted. Little Flora's face came back to her. The familiar love smile convinced Flora that her daughter would fall in love with more than a dead Italian composer. And, Giacamo would end up being remembered as more than just the *checker champ* of Florence.

Chapter
fifteen

A Daring Decision

Flora was surprised that everyone was sleeping in after the big bash. Flora fell asleep fast and hard the night before and didn't even hear the girls come in or the usual noises from Dolly and Vince after they'd had a good time. The bright sun woke Flora up. It rose outside her window and was the first thing she saw each day, even if it was hidden by the clouds. She looked into the sky and thanked God for such beauty and the opportunity to be in Florence...and for the row of parasol pine trees that lined the via San Miniato.

Flora went downstairs to start the coffee brewing and maybe get some pancake batter ready for the kids. She saw some fresh bacon in the refrigerator the day before and thought a big breakfast after a late night would hit the spot for everyone.

Flora loved the kitchen in the pensione. She wrote home about it in full detail and sent pictures from Emily's polaroid camera. She was still waiting for Irene's response to her letter...which was due anyday.

Flora's phone call to Irene about the *trials and tribula - tions* of teenage-hood in Florence made all the folks back home anxious to hear more about the big adventure. Irene felt like hopping on the next plane so she could join in the fun...frolic...and...a more *rigid* supervision of the girls. Flora was known to be *softee* when it came to giving in to the girls and their whims. She always denied that accusation and defended her decisions with conviction. She always expected the best from the kids and usually they never let her down.

Rose called twice and talked to all of the kids. She was confident that they were keeping a level head. Christina had to concentrate more on history and geometry during her stay in Florence. History, Sebastiano was taking care of in his special tours off the *beaten path*, and Stefano was good with equations and figures...he definitely held her attention when he tutored geometry.

Giacamo and little Flora pointed Christina in the right direction of studies with their reminders on the disadvantages of *summer school*...especially if they really did plan on returning to Florence in July. Flora let them dream. If that was what they really wanted, they would have to work very hard for it...and if they were resourceful enough to save and plan for such a big venture, they would deserve the privilege of coming back.

The batter was mixed and the bacon was fried. Flora wrapped the bacon in foil and placed the bundle on the back grille to keep warm. She stuck the batter in the refrigerator. The coffee brewed, relinquishing it's tempting and hearty aroma...still no one got up.

Flora started a small fire in the fireplace and sat by herself thinking of what a great opportunity the trip had been for all of them.

The sun was strong and the temps were warming up the earth quickly. Spring was a little way off on the calendar, but she could feel the sun getting stronger. The days were definitely longer.

Flora was anxious to start on the parlor the week ahead. Dolly more or less gave Flora that room to decorate on her own. Flora wanted to make it feel like springtime. The huge ocean which separated her homes was becoming smaller; she understood there was not that much difference in places. All people were bound to the main purpose of existence, love. Lilacs smelled as sweet in Florence as they did in Union Lake...the wisteria were just as beautiful.

Ideas galore passed through her head, along with visions of one day *decorating* on a regular basis.

Then someone knocked on the back door. The knob started turning and Flora wondered who it could be at such an early time in the morning.

"Flora...it's me...," Paolo said as he poked his head in the door. He came into the kitchen.

Flora couldn't believe Paolo was standing in the kitchen. "I didn't think you'd be back till tomorrow evening...even Monday...," Flora said as she looked into his eyes. She saw that wonderful radiance that attracted her to him in the beginning. Flora felt herself trembling inside but tried to stay calm.

"After I hung up with you, Cardinal Alberto called me in his office, looked at the plans, listened to my story, and bang!...he liked it alot! I was shocked at how smooth it went...not that I didn't have faith in the project...God it's good to be back here...and what smells so good? Paolo looked around the kitchen. "Where is everybody?"

Paolo always talked fast when he was excited about something...but Flora had never really saw him that hyped...she knew he accomplished what he set out to do, and she was very happy for him. His excitement over-flowed into her spirit. Paolo grabbed a piece of bacon.

"Sit down and I'll get you some...," Flora tried to finish her sentence, but Paolo did for her.

"First let me show *you* something... ." Paolo grabbed a sweater off the hook near the door and wrapped it over Flora's shoulders. "Hope it's yours." He took her hand and they walked outside and up the road toward San Miniato.

The morning was mild and there was just enough fog to make everything look mysterious. Flora felt like she was walking through a cloud, like Paolo was taking her into his dream. Paolo held her hand tightly and didn't stop talking until he reached the point where he needed to be. Paolo took a deep breath, scanned the countryside with eagerness and awe, then looked at Flora .

"This is it...this is where dreams will come true for a bunch of little kids that otherwise might have gone through life without a fair chance...without knowing someone cared." Flora watched his face as he talked about his dream.

"God, I love it here," Paolo said with sincerity. He was coming back to earth. Paolo apologized for being so impetuous and for literally dragging Flora out of the kitchen. But Flora understood his exuberance and she felt fortunate to be sharing such a grand moment with him.

"Paolo, I'm so happy for you...this is such a great thing that you are doing... ."

"It's something I've wanted to do for a long time...and my business is in kind of a slump...so I'm sort of *seizing* the moment...thanks for letting me share this with you...it means alot to me to have you here, Flora...at the pensione and right here on this very piece of ground...that's what I wanted to tell you Flora. "

Paolo noticed Flora shaking from the cold. He took off his jacket and put it on Flora. "Here, I'm warm...I know this morning air can go right through you...I can smell Spring in the air."

"Thanks, Paolo...I'm not really cold...I think I'm just shaking from all the wonder of this place...and I can smell the Spring coming, too." Flora looked into Paolo's eyes. "Maybe it is a little chilly." Flora knew she was shaking from the pure pleasure of being with Paolo.

They walked back to the pensione at a much more leisurely pace; a contented quiet held their attention. Paolo's big dream was coming true. Flora kept silent till they reached the pensione. Only then did Paolo let go of her hand. He sat down by the fire while Flora fixed a good breakfast for both of them.

Flora brought a tray of pancakes over to Paolo. He took the tray from her and then made her sit down next to him.

"I am so hungry...this is great, Flora...," Paolo said as he put a forkful of pancakes into Flora's mouth...then one into his own. With her mouth full Flora thanked him.

"Thanks, Paolo...there's more syrup if you need it." Flora looked up at Paolo who was eating heartily. "I'm glad you're home... ."

"It's good to be here, Flora...real good."

Paolo thought of the change Flora had brought to the pensione. She put life back into it with her decorating but even more with her gaiety and her smile. He felt himself growing very fond of the visitor. He didn't want to think of her as just a temporary guest, either.

Paolo talked about his trip to Rome and his upcoming journey to Perugia, where he had to meet with the Franciscan monks and discuss the details of the orphanage. Flora brought into the conversation Jack's arrival date and some plans he had made for the whole family when he arrives. When the reality of the two of them not really being two isolated people set in...a cool silence filled the room.

They had been dreaming the past few weeks. Paolo seemed to have finally found someone whose spirit immediately entered his. Flora gave herself to him; no words spoken. She needed a friend. She wanted someone to want her, to look forward to her, to need her. Paolo, for whatever reasons made his attractions known in a subtle yet very real way that took Flora's heart by surprise. Neither Paolo or Flora thought too far into the future. That would have shocked them into a world they had already spent too much time.

"Come with me to Perugia tomorrow," Paolo said with excitement, "I want you to meet Brother Georgio, he's in charge of all the technical arrangements of the building of the orphanage...you will like him." Paolo looked deep into Flora's eyes and blinded her better judgement. She said *yes* to his sudden invitation.

Dolly walked into the kitchen and brought a huge chunk of reality in with her. Flora needed that reminder.

One by one, the late sleepers walked into the kitchen. Flora fixed everyone their breakfast. She thought, as she flipped the pancakes, that maybe she flipped her own lid. How could she have said *yes* to Paolo's invitation? Was she totally crazy...or had she finally come to her senses?

When Vince and Dolly sat down to breakfast, Paolo repeated the details of his visit with Cardinal Alberto to them. Vince was so pleased that tears immediately began running down his cheek. Dolly gently dried them with her handkerchief as if she planned on keeping them forever in her possession. Dolly noticed Paolo's sweet attention toward Flora. Little Flora noticed it, too.

Little Flora volunteered to stay and help with the morning dishes. She wanted to talk with Flora. Dolly gave the rest of the crew the nod to go ahead with their chores and Vince and Paolo went into the formal dining room to talk more about the pensione and the orphanage. Little Flora was alone with her Mom.

"Mom, did you notice how Paolo looks at *you* all the time...I can't blame him...you look extra beautiful lately...have you bought some secret Italian lotion that you're not telling me about?" Flora laughed at little Flora's comment and reached over sideways to kiss her arm. Little Flora kissed Flora's cheek and went on with her conversation.

"Really, Mama...I think he has an adult type...you know...like a *crush* on you... ."

"No, no...not a crush...he just appreciates the company here at the pensione...he likes being with all of us." Flora tried to sound confident in her tone. Flora didn't want to lie but at this point she wasn't sure of what the truth was.

"No, really, Mom, he looks at you *different*...it's nothing to be ashamed of Mama...you can't help it if he's falling head over heals for you...I think he has great taste."

Flora kept washing the dishes and hoped little Flora would drop the subject of Paolo. Flora felt deceitful in her response to little Flora's perceptions...but it wasn't time to get into it. Little Flora changed the subject.

"Dad's due in next week...I hope he can stay till we go home."

Flora didn't want to talk about Jack's coming either. She had to inform little Flora about her trip tomorrow with Paolo. How could she delicately drop that bomb on her? Little Flora would for sure know that something *more* was up than just a casual acquaintance. And that her *observation* wasn't as farfetched as Flora had made it seem. But, Flora had to tell her.

"Tomorrow I'm going to drive up to Perugia with Paolo... he wants me to meet some of his friends who are going to be in charge of things at the orphanage when it's completed." Flora stopped drying the dishes and looked at her daughter. Little Flora wasn't sure how her mother really felt about going.

"Do you really want to go, Mom?"

Flora looked dearly at her daughter.

"In a way I do...I sort of promised him I'd take the day off...what do you think...?"

"I think it will be good...if he does have any serious feelings for you...then would be the time for you to find out...but *if* he does...what will you do?"

"I don't think I have to worry about that...but he's so open and I've enjoyed working with him...he's helped so much with the renovation and Vince appreciates his company...everything will be okay...and I'm a little bit excited to see the town of Perugia, it's suppose to be beautiful this time of year...and it's where they make those luscious *BACI* chocolates...you know, the one with the hazelnut in the middle...and the tiny love note in the wrapper."

"The ones that have the little *hazelnut* in the middle...I *love* them." Little Flora hugged her mother. "I'll take care of Jimmy and Emily only if you promise to fill me in on every detail of the trip...and bring home a *pound* of the BACI'S...promise?" Flora promised.

Little Flora looked at the clock, then dropped her towel and ran out of the kitchen yelling back to Flora that Giacamo was going to pick her up in twenty minutes to visit the *Villa I Tatti*.

Little Flora always dreamt of going to Harvard...so Giacamo knew she would love to see the Villa. He told her about it's history and how it ended up being bequeathed to Harvard University in 1959 when Bernard Berenson died.

Dolly ran into little Flora on her way to the kitchen and wished she had all that wonderful energy of youth. Dolly confronted Flora about Paolo as she was wiping off the table.

"So what's up Flora?"

"You're the second one to ask me that this morning...little Flora asked me if I noticed Paolo looking at me in *admi - ration*.

"Admiration? I think that's a polite way of putting it...what did you tell her?"

"What do you mean, Dolly?" Flora knew exactly what Dolly meant.

"Flora, I know that you have grown fond of Paolo...," Dolly accented her firm belief by taking hold of Flora's hands, "come on...tell me what's going on... ."

Flora hesitated. But, once she began...she felt relieved to get so much out in the open.

"Dolly, you know I care about him so much...but I'm not sure if I completely trust my feelings.""

"Well...why not...Flora the *woman*, the *lover of life...moth - er of five* and *angel* to five-hundred more?" Dolly waited for Flora's answer.

"Dolly, you make me sound so good...and wise...but the truth is, I *don't* know what I think about all of this."

"But, *you do know.* You have one of the most loving and purest hearts I know...but, you've been conditioned over the years to block out what you really feel...because it's been tossed back to you so many times. You've got to trust yourself again...even if it means getting hurt again...sometimes that's the only way you'll ever find out... ." Dolly didn't want to hurt Flora but she could see in Flora's face that her words had gone straight through to her heart.

"I'm scared, Dolly. What if certain things...do happen? Is my happiness worth all the pain a decision like that would cause everyone...my time for love and romance is over...I should have outgrown these needs... ."

"*Poppycock!*" Dolly said admonishingly. "You don't believe that for one minute...you never outgrow your need to love...love is for all ages, love is for all times... it's about truth and living what a person believes in. If other people are hurt because they can't accept that reality...it's their problem...not yours. *You* have to live with yourself and the decisions you make. *You* have to be happy with your life if you ever hope to make any sense of living...*whew*...why do I get myself all riled up like this...you're going... ."

"Well...that settles it Dolly, I'm going to Perugia tomorrow with Paolo...I think being with him away from the pensione will make me see things in a different light."

"Flora...see things the way they *are*...open your eyes and your heart an *see.* Don't worry about the gang. I'll keep things in control."

"Thanks Dolly... ." Flora felt better after Dolly's encouraging words. *Perugia or bust,* she thought. Flora gave Dolly a big hug.

"What are you two hugging about," Vince said as he entered the kitchen, "...not that you need a reason to hug each other...but it's been a slow day and *I'd* like to hear some good news...or *something.*"

Flora poured Vince a cup of coffee and then politely excused herself from the hotseat Dolly had her perched on. Dolly's words kept Flora going the whole day. Now the trip to Perugia was something she *had* to do. Flora's night prayer was vague. Her eyes wandered to the clouds hanging heavy in the night sky of Florence. Things had to be brighter in the morning. Flora hoped for that.

Chapter
sixteen

Votive Candles

"Your Mama got off on an early start," Vince said chirpily. "She's going to have a good time...the weather is bellissimo and this time of year in Perugia is as mystical as the season of Lent!" Vince filled the kids in on Flora's agenda as he whipped this and tossed that.

Vince loved making breakfast and Jimmy and Emily were the first ones up. They looked forward to Vince's cooking...breakfast, lunch *or* dinner and all those neat snacks in between. He was an unconventional breakfast maker, which meant you never knew what you were going to get until it was placed in front of your face. It always tasted good, no matter what it was.

"Dolly, have a seat right next to the signorina Emily...you are in for a *real* treat...," Vince said as he winked at Dolly and then at Emily...Jimmy was busy eating and relishing every bite.

"Vince...you can make anything taste great...you must *use* a SECRRRET INGRRREDIENT,"

Dolly said rolling her R's and waiting for Emily to fill in the missing word.

"You mean...GARRRLIC...?" Emily said, mimicking Dolly's rolling R.

"You're too smart, Emily...," Dolly said as she hugged Emily affectionately. Dolly's eyes roamed over to the kitchen window. "It looks like Flora and Paolo will have good weather."

"Not a cloud in the sky, Dolly." Vince smiled at Dolly who kept the window her view for a few moments longer.

"What are you looking for in that beautiful sky, Dolly...," Vince asked as he tapped his spatula on her shoulder.

"Nothing...nothing, Vince, it's just that it's so clear but...," Dolly said, sounding unsure of herself. She paused for a moment and smiled at Vince's crooked smile. "But, I feel rain coming...and what's that silly grin all about?"

"Nothing...just eat your omelet and enjoy it while it's hot... and enjoy the sky while it's blue...we'll worry about the rain when it gets here." Vince filled Dolly's plate with her favorite omelet, green pepper, mushroom and pimento.

"You know, it's the darn pimento and your wine mustard sauce that makes this taste *out of this world*...you are full of sweet surprises, Vinny."

"I know, I know...I'm full of sweet surprises, morning, noon and *night*... ." Vince touched Dolly's hand with his fork and her heart with a sly smile.

"Yup...I really like your *night* surprises," Dolly said with added enticement in her voice. She cleared her throat. "But it's morning, so *manga*, you *dolce diablo*." Dolly poked Vince's hand a bit harder with her fork. She smiled at her good friend.

Christina and Tracey and little Flora had big plans of their own that morning. Little Flora decided, at the last minute, to go to Fiesole with the gang. Giacamo's family lived there and they were going to celebrate his older brothers ordination into the priesthood. It would be a celebration worth participating in, and Stefano and Sebastiano had to be there. The girls were excited about being a part of such a wonderful family gathering...especially Tracey and Christina...they were going to meet Sebastiano and Stefano's parents. Little Flora was more or less just *going along for the ride.* At least that's what she told the girls.

Giacamo was very interested in little Flora but she kept up her guard even after the great time she had with him the night before. Little Flora knew Giacamo was a great guy; she even felt at times that she would like to get to know him better. But, she knew if she got to know him any better, she'd probably fall head over heels for him...and she couldn't do that to Dan.

The night before had been wonderful for little Flora. She enjoyed Giacamo's company very much. Giacamo was perfect...she kept hoping something about him would repulse her...instead, he was becoming more and more attractive. Giacamo was becoming a part of all their hearts. He was a good sport with PICTIONARY which won over the hearts of Jimmy and Emily. Little Flora understood their attraction one-hundred percent.

"Stefano will be here for us in about an hour," Tracey said as she doublechecked her watch with the clock on the mantle. "I've got to wash my hair real quick and figure out what I'm going to wear...wasn't last night a blast?" Tracey nudged Christina who was finishing up the last few breakfast dishes.

"Hey, I've got to get ready, too...so help me and dry these dishes...and then wipe off the grill, ok?" Christina was usually fast and efficient but had a difficult time concentrating on what she was doing that morning. Sebastiano threw her for a loop the night before with his sudden declaration of his intentions.

"CHRISTINA...," Tracey said loudly with a bit of *impa - tience* in her voice, "...we'll never be ready in time if you keep washing *clean* dishes...what's the matter with you this morning...HELLO...HELLO IN THERE...EARTH TO CHRISTINA." Tracey hoped Christina would snap out of her early morning fog.

"Tracey...EARTH TO TRACEY," Christina said sarcastically, "...God, Tracey, I'm so sick of that expression...*I really hate it."* Christina wiped out the sink, and headed out of the kitchen and up the stairs toward her room.

Tracey followed.

"What's up...? Little Flora asked as she put on some clean cotton socks.

"What's going on Christina," Tracey asked impatiently. Christina hesitated...then quickly closed their bedroom door.

"Gee...you're acting a little strange, Christina," little Flora said half teasingly, "...I mean more strange than usual...come on tell us what's bothering you."

"Okay...but you have to *promise* not to tell anyone today...Sebastiono wants to tell his parents first...so promise me you won't say a word." Christina waited for little Flora and Tracey to promise.

"Okay...okay...we promise...," little Flora said taking Tracey's hand and then directing her total attention to Christina.

"Well...I guess there is only one way to say it...I'm...I mean...Sebastiano asked me to marry him...so I guess... that means... we're *engaged*...!"

Little Flora and Tracey screamed their typical screech whenever news was *good* or *strange*....or both. Christina's news was definitely both.

"YOU LIE...YOU'RE KIDDING...," Tracey said expecting Christina to tell her that she was only joking around. Christina didn't say a word. She stared at Christina turning more pale with each breath she took.

"YOU'RE NOT KIDDING...you're not kidding...OH MY GOD...!" Little Flora ran up to Christina and hugged her.

"I don't know what to do...you know how much I like him...how I like him...I...I *love* him...but NO WAY did I ever think he was going that *ga-ga* over me...NO WAY did I ever imagine him asking *me* to marry him...are we in Italy or what?"

They laughed and made up a hundred different scenarios. Then, after the laughter came the sudden realization of the seriousness of that matter. Despite Christina's flip and carefree attitude toward Sebastiano, Tracey and little Flora knew there was *something* big going on between them. Sebastiano loved Christina and as many times as Christina privately dreamed of becoming engaged...the reality of it was making her feel very uncomfortable and very much afraid. She was *only* eighteen.

Little Flora couldn't believe the news either. She was happy for Christina, if Christina was going to be happy. She wondered then about Tracey who looked to be deep in thought. If Sebastiano was crazy about Christina...Stefano wasn't far behind his brother. He was absolutely crazy over Tracey and made no effort to conceal his attraction or his affections.

Tracey must have been thinking along the same line, all of a sudden she felt a huge knot in her stomach. She wasn't sure if it was Vince's breakfast *conglomeration* or the thought of meeting Stefano's parents...the day all of a sudden seemed like a page from the twilight zone.

Little Flora wondered about the moon last night and definitely blamed her *amorous* feelings on that old man in the sky. She realized he must have zapped all of them last night...*real* hard.

Vince answered the doorbell and yelled up the stairs for the girls. Sebastiano was waiting outside the pensione in the car. Stefano wrestled around with Jimmy as he waited for Tracey, who was stuck upstairs pondering the twenty-four hour flu. But, she couldn't do that to Stefano or Christina...it was time to face the music.

Little Flora found herself excited to see Giacamo...she wondered if he knew what the scoop was on Sebastiano and Christina? The day would prove to be very interesting...confusing...but for sure, fun. No matter what the ending...they were off.

Paolo and Flora took care of business in Perugia. The ride there was beautiful...but, very quiet. Paolo seemed distracted. Flora wished she had stayed back at the pensione. Paolo wasn't as talkative as he usually was and he seemed to be almost in a kind of blue mood. That wasn't like him and Flora felt uncomfortable for the first time in his company. Flora felt like he was shutting her out? It was too much like being with Jack. She hoped it was just a case of the project jitters for Paolo. She didn't want to be the blame for his change in disposition.

"I love this country," Paolo blurted out. Talking more to the road than Flora he continued.

"I can't imagine living anywhere else in the world...you must feel like that about your country, too...," Paolo didn't give Flora enough time to respond but repeated his same words, "...I can't imagine anyone leaving the place of their birth...and their family...for *anything*."

Flora took Paolo's sudden remark personally. It rang very cold in her ears.

"I don't know what you mean...I can *imagine* alot of things...Paolo...but I can't read minds...what exactly are you trying to say?" Flora was hurt. Jack always made her read his mind and she was tired of that old game. She thought about keeping her mouth shut...but she didn't.

"Paolo, I can imagine the world not even existing if it were filled with selfish, stubborn, scaredy-cat people like those who *can't* imagine anything," Flora said quickly. "Sometimes people have to leave everything they love and cherish for economic or political or private reasons." Flora wanted to defend her own motives.

"You know Paolo, I came to Florence because Dolly invited me...but I'm not going to pretend that decorating the pensione was the main attraction...I want to visit my Grandparents hometown and see the land they talked about so much...maybe to even mingle with the people whose grandparents rubbed elbows with my mine...I

thought maybe coming here would bring them back...at
least for a while...and in a way, it has. They left this beautiful country to find a better life... ."

"And, you left your country to find something, Flora?"

Flora looked at Paolo and realized she did come to
Florence to *find* alot of things.

"I guess I did."

"To find a better life?...," Paolo asked, "...maybe to fall in
love?"

"Paolo...I don't know what to say." Flora was interiorly
flabbergasted. Flora felt very uneasy.

Paolo looked toward Flora. Their eyes met. Flora quickly turned her head in the opposite direction. She stilled her
thoughts. Nothing seemed to be making any sense to her.
She wondered why he was asking her such crazy questions? Flora looked out of her window and recognized the
countryside. She knew where she was, even if she didn't
quite recognize the fella sitting next to her. Flora kept her
vision straight ahead and wondered if Paolo was going to
ask her anything else.

Paolo felt the absurdity of the conversation. He wanted
to start over again.

"I didn't mean to upset you...I don't even know how
this stupid conversation started... ."

"Conversation? I thought I was being quizzed...maybe
things are moving too quickly for us, Paolo...you have the
right to think and ask questions...I did leave my home and
country and half my family...what kind of woman am
I...what kind of woman is sitting next to you right now...tell
me Paolo...I'd like you to answer these questions for me."
Flora was hurt and she felt foolish taking Paolo's questioning so seriously. She was four thousand miles from
home and with a man, practically a strange man. Flora was
tired and in a dismal mood. As dismal a mood as the sky
had turned. She wished she had kept her mouth
closed...and her heart a little more open.

They drove for a while longer and weren't too far from the pensione. Paolo wanted to stop and stretch his legs. The damp weather had made them knot up with cramps. Flora stepped out of the car. She felt rejuvenated as the tiny raindrops touched her face. The drops of water made her cry, not a sad cry, a relief cry...a kind of sad relief cry.

Without a thought or hesitation Flora began walking down the road. She thought about all the walking she and her children used to do in the old neighborhood...to the market, to piano lessons, to school and Church. The song they used to sing when the weather was bad or when the jaunt had been extra long, came back to her. "PUT ONE FOOT IN FRONT OF THE OTHER...SOON YOU'LL BE KNOCKING AT THE DOOR." And, for a moment, she wished she was in her old neighborhood and walking home...heading for her home and it's beautiful green frontdoor.

Paolo got back into the car and drove slowly down the hill till he met up with Flora.

"Come on in...we'll be home soon...please get in Flora...?" Paolo motioned to Flora to get back inside...but, she ignored him. His words didn't tempt her to get inside the dry car...but his face did.

He followed Flora and tried to convince her that it was a long way home and that she would catch pneumonia. But, Flora knew approximately where she was...and the rain was soft and sweet and it was the most real thing she had felt all day.

"Just go, Paolo...I want to walk...really." Flora didn't look at Paolo while he begged her to get back into his car. She stared straight ahead and walked with determination down the hill. Paolo took her words seriously and drove away feeling very unsettled.

It was sort of a mixed up day, going completely in the opposite direction of her dreams. Flora was stubborn and stuck to her decision about walking the rest of the way home. It was all downhill from there anyway. The misty droplets of rain woke her up and helped her set things back in perspective. She wondered if Paolo could *imagine* any woman ever being that pigheaded and stubborn.

In the old country of her dear grandparents, Flora found new horizons...in the landscape...and in her soul. She couldn't believe the magnificent landscape of Tuscany. It made her cry. But, the crying made her feel good. Flora saw the tiny church of San Miniato not too far away. She wanted to stop inside the church to say a prayer. She was glad she left Paolo and walked the rest of the way home but also knew in her heart, that she had behaved like a child.

Her shoes squeaked with wetness as she walked to the altar. She knelt down and looked up to the crucifix that was hanging above the fancy altar.

"Dear God...," Flora said in her heart., "...I'm such a jerk sometimes...I wish I could say that in Italian." Flora felt ashamed in front of the crucifix, but comforted, too. Her mind wandered and many thoughts of the day popped in and out. Flora wanted to stop her racing thoughts. She began reciting the GLORIA.

"You alone are love...You alone are the Holy One, Jesus Christ... ." She made that familiar recitation her prayer.

Flora let her mind travel back home to St. Mary's Chapel where she made many visits. Whenever she felt the need to be extra close to God, Flora would visit there. Then her mind drifted back to that Holy Saturday when she stopped in at Our Lady of Good Counsel Church and prayed that Jack would be the one to love her. She was so insistent in that prayer. She had felt enough love for both of them, but, she eventually found out that loving enough for two people could never be a substitute for loving someone and then being loved back.

Flora sat still for a while with no thoughts except that her feet were wet and cold...she was wet and cold. She continued her prayer.

"I'm so mixed up about so many things, dear God...I'm glad You have a sense of humor...I feel like the past few years have been tests from You...and You know I've never done well on tests...I mean You always know what I need...and my whole life You have taken care of me...but lately...I guess I'm just tired...I'm tired and I feel like I'm going in circles...I'm going in some big crazy circle searching for love...searching for love...that makes me think of Sandy back home and a few summers ago when we were up north together and had to go into town. We pulled up to the town bar and pretended to go inside...she started singing, *"searching for love in all the wrong places"*, we laughed so hard we cried.

"Even here, I've managed to jumble things up by thinking Paolo had some special interest in me...help me to be who I am and help me to be content with my life each day and to see the love that is always there."

Flora sat for almost an hour and didn't want to leave. She thought about the day and the beautiful car ride through Umbria...what a mystical province...she thought of St. Francis as they passed by Assisi and Fr. Bill and his stories of that small town, especially his visit to the church in San Damiano where St. Francis received the stigmata in front of that altar's crucifix. She remembered how excited he was to share everything about his trip to Italy. Flora remembered how she *thought* she was in love with him.

Brother Georgio had that same enthusiasm as he shared his ideas for the new orphanage. His face looked saintly and Paolo's face beamed with joy as the plans unfurled. Paolo had worked for years on this project and finally the day had come to get things started. He had so much on his mind and at times he seemed a million miles away from Flora. She thought she should have stayed back at the pensione. For a few moments she wished she was back home...maybe that's where she was suppose to be.

It was quiet and warm and the light from the votive

candles burning on the side alter inspired more reflection. She enjoyed their flickering flames and was mesmerized with the soft glow that poured from each red candle holder. Every flame represented a special intention for someone in that town. She prayed for all of them. She prayed for her Grama and Grandpa.

Flora closed her eyes and thought of the Florence sky where she was positive she heard the stars talk of love.

Flora was getting ready to leave when she heard the old wooden Church door squeak. She saw a shadow of a figure walking up the aisle.

"Flora...is that you...?"

Flora tried to makeout the silhouette in the back of the church. It looked like Dolly.

"Flora...," the familiar voice said bouncing off the hallowed walls. Flora smiled inside herself at her worried friend's call.

"Dolly...what are you doing here?"

"What am *I* doing here?...*I'm* getting a woman to come to her senses." Dolly huffed as she met up with Flora half way down the aisle.

"I'm sorry Dolly if I worried you...I was just starting for home...Paolo must have told you about our car ride through Umbria...I'm sorry I worried you."

"*Worried me*?...*everyone* is worried," Dolly said as she took a deep breath. She continued, trying to be more calm.

"That road is *curvy*...and *swervy*...and *dangerous*, especially in the rain...you and Paolo talk about the kids, you two behaved like...like...oooooo....who should I worry about more...not to mention the kids...what do you think they're thinking right now...and Paolo...talk about not making any sense...I knew, even though the sky was perfectly clear this morning, that something was brewing in the distance... ." Dolly locked her arm in Flora's. "Let's get the heck home."

Dolly and Flora walked backed to the pensione. Dolly

asked about the trip to Perugia. Flora didn't want to frazzle Dolly anymore than she already was. She wanted to explain the little things that had bothered her that afternoon but knew it would take too much time. If Dolly wasn't back soon...the whole pensione would have gone out looking for both of them. Flora thought another time would be better. So, Flora kept her excuses simple.

"Dolly, you know how impetuous I am sometimes, well, this afternoon Paolo seemed to be hinting around at something...and I just didn't like the sound of it...so I decided to walk the last couple of miles home...that's all...no big thing." Flora hoped Dolly would accept her explanation. She didn't.

"THAT'S ALL...NO BIG THING!" Dolly said while shaking her head in a negative direction. "The world could be falling apart...*no big thing*...let's go." Dolly smiled at Flora. Flora smiled back, grateful to Dolly for everything.

"Thanks Dolly...I'm ready...," Flora said eagerly, "...and tired...and hungry...any good leftovers when we get home...I just want to sit by the fire and have a hot bowl of soup."

"Me too...and while we are enjoying the fire and drying our drenched bones...I'll fill you in on some *really* good news."

Dolly couldn't wait to be sitting by the fire before telling Flora the news. She wanted to lift Flora's dampened spirit. The news about Christina and Sebastiano...and the *possible* news about Tracey and Stefano...made Flora ecstatic. She couldn't wait to hear more from the girls.

The sky was clearing on the horizon and just enough light from the set sun escaped to warm her heart. With the persimmon glow reflecting in her eyes and sinking deeply into her soul, she thought of Paolo.

"This isn't SPRINGTIME IN THE ROCKIES...but it is a really rocky road...," Dolly said while huffing and puffing, "...*like life*." Dolly hung on tightly to Flora's arm for support.

"You know, Flora, talk about *men*...they can build sky-scrapers that reach to the moon...and *orphanages*...but they can't see in front of their own faces sometimes...oh well...ain't love grand?"

Flora thought of her mother with Dolly's last remark. She realized how much she missed her. Taking big steps over muddy puddled water, Flora wondered if she'd ever tell her mother about Paolo. Maybe there would be nothing to ever tell.

Chapter
seventeen

Souls Turned Inside Out

The next few days were full of excitement for Christina and Tracey. Flora thought it would be a good idea to wait and call home with their *news* until Jack arrived. Sebastiano and Stefano would ask Jack for his permission to marry them, since he was the Godfather of the girls. Jack was in for a big surprise and the girls were becoming more and more apprehensive as the estimated time of arrival drew nearer.

The girls met Sebastian's and Stefano's entire family at the ordination celebration and they were well accepted. Not even Lucia, the mother of the future grooms knew about the boys serious intentions toward the girls. She thought they were just being good friends to the visiting American family. Much was hanging on the shirttail of Uncle Jack and his reaction to the boys...and his acceptance of their marriage proposals.

The girls had nightmares about the impending phone call home and announcing that grand news breaker to their parents. Tom and Danny sent their little daughters off to study in a different country. They knew alot of fun and excitement was in store...but not a *marriage proposal*. Irene was still struggling with Tracey going out on dates. Rose had finally painted Christina's bedroom.

Dolly had the best advice for the girls. "Worry is worse than trouble because the worst never happens." And, "live, love and be merry...for tomorrow there is enough time for tears." For now, they would live on the brighter and the drier side...they were having such a good time in Florence. No one was going to spoil this precious time in their lives, not as long as Flora was there.

The parlor was on hold for a few days, till the wallpaper came in. Everything that could be completed, was. The next day Jack would be there; lots of things were cooking on Guido's stove.

Activities around the pensione were getting a bit more hectic. Flora had to talk to Paolo before Jack arrived. The past week they had been easily avoiding each other. With all the unexpecteds that popped up...and Paolo very busy with his own projects, Paolo and Flora managed to keep their cooled distance, at least physically. In the mornings when he'd leave for San Miniato, or at night when he'd try to be inconspicuous in the kitchen fixing a snack, Flora found it very difficult to turn her head in a different direction. That busy morning, seeing Paolo's luggage parked by the front door, made Flora's heart drop to her knees. She had to find him.

Flora ran into Vince who was on the ladder in the hallway. He was shining the old brass fixture hanging from the ceiling. Vince was always busy but never too busy to lend an ear to the forlorn or a hand to someone in trouble. Flora asked him if he had seen Paolo. He dropped the cleaning rag from between his lips and told her Paolo was in his room the last time he saw him. Flora ran up the stairs and caught him as he was closing his briefcase on the bed.

Paolo looked up when he heard Flora enter the room. There was a definite tension in the air. Flora fought her inclination to let the whole thing go, to just say good bye...and leave it at that. Afterall, Paolo was just going to walk out without a word being said. But something kept her there.

Paolo asked her to sit down and then he closed the bedroom door. Seeing Paolo's briefcase on his bed made Flora feel like things had already been decided. He was leaving and maybe for good. Flora had resolved many things in her heart but all the resolutions then, had seemed unrealistic.

Flora judged many things in her life rigidly, especially her marriage. In her bed that morning she had sad thoughts about dying. On her deathbed she envisioned the kids standing by her side. She looked into all of their faces and felt the love they had for her and knew they felt the love she had for them. In her early morning daydream she couldn't see Jack's eyes, he wouldn't look at her. When he finally did, she saw something in his eyes...the capacity to love was there...the look that told her he was sensitive...but for whatever reason...allergic to her. She felt angry at herself for not being the person Jack could love. She kept asking him why...he could only shrug his shoulders in her dream. She cried at that sad nightmare and felt it was like a ghost from Christmas past...and possibly, the future. She pushed that thought from her mind.

Paolo had been more than just a happy episode in Flora's life. She stopped trying to justify her attraction to him and finally, just allowed it to be.

"A lot of things are going on...this is one busy place," Paolo said as he pulled up the window chair and sat at arms distance from Flora. He reached out and took her hand. He held her hand and the tension between them left. He looked into her eyes and apologized for his behavior from the Sunday before. Flora apologized and suggested they forget about the whole thing.

"No...I can't forget about it...I hurt you...I don't know what happened that day," Paolo said sincerely, "...I didn't mean to upset you, yet in a way I wanted you to do just what you did. It's like I needed a reaction...a reason to let you go...I wanted to make it easier for both of us...I wasn't thinking...or maybe I was thinking too much." Paolo sounded more than apologetic. He let go of Flora's hand, got up from his chair and walked toward the window. He looked outside at the familiar view and put his hands in his pockets. Paolo continued.

"I thought about our Sunday together and I know we both said some things that were nonsensical...but they made me think." Paolo looked carefully at Flora. He continued.

"I'm not leaving Florence...but to make things more *comfortable* for you, with Jack coming in tomorrow, I decided to move in with Fr. Cellini at the rectory...he'll appreciate the company and I'll be on hand if the surveying people need me. The digging starts next week...and I should be there on call anyway." Paolo insisted it would be easier for all of them if he moved out.

Flora got up from the bed and walked toward Paolo. She stood next to him; he, with his hands still in his pockets and she with hers aching to touch his face. The silence yanked at Flora's heart. She couldn't just stand there anymore ignoring the real feelings that were ready to explode inside her. So, Flora hugged Paolo, carefully at first.

She didn't worry about his responding to her affection. She knew what she felt and had to trust those feelings...she had to trust her heart...even if it meant being broken again. With every second that passed, her embrace grew stronger.

Things had changed since their trip to Perugia and they couldn't seem to talk comfortably about anything. Flora thought that it was going to take more than words to rectify the huge rift between them. Flora felt like a fumbling awkward teenager again, until she felt him respond in a body language that needed no explanation. He held her tightly and asked her not to let him go.

Paolo looked into Flora's eyes repeating with his gaze the words he had just spoken. Flora gently pressed her lips on his but the desires pent up inside both of them were more than they could handle. Paolo wanted her completely and Flora thought of nothing else than being wrapped in his arms.

Then, a knock on the door.

"Paolo...you've got a phone call...it sounds urgent," Vince yelled through the closed door.

Paolo kissed Flora again and then walked to the door not taking his eyes from Flora's. He answered Vince while still looking into her eyes. " I'll be there in a second, Dad."

Paolo kissed Flora again then sat her down on the bed and told her not to move. Paolo slipped out of the room calmly. He followed Vince down the stairs into the kitchen. Vince knew Flora was in Paolo's room but didn't let on to Paolo. Vince didn't want to meddle. He hoped things were better between them.

Paolo took the receiver from Dolly.

"Pronto...," Paolo said, he listened for a few moments. His voice sounded impatient as he continued the conversation.

"It really *does* matter...I'll catch the next train to Rome...meet me at the station...no, I'm glad you called me, it's just that your timing is way off...talk to you later...ciao."

Paolo was upset but something needed his attention immediately in Rome if the orphanage was going to get started the next week. He went back to his room and asked Flora to drive him to the train station. She said, yes.

It was only a fifteen minute walk to the train station but the ride gave them time to be together. Paolo wanted to be with Flora.

Flora didn't want to believe the upset in their plans. Jack was coming in the next day and so many things were *jumbled*. So many things in her heart were unresolved. She wondered if they were ever going to have a chance to sort things out. First, the misunderstanding and then the confrontation up in Paolo's room. Flora felt like she was saying good-bye to her best friend...forever. Her tears were ready to overflow and her heart was pounding in her ears.

"Flora, everything will be alright. Maybe this trip wasn't badly timed...," Paolo wanted to make Flora feel better. He continued.

"You know Flora...everyone would have been wondering where we were all day...and you know where we would have been...in my room, you know, getting things...*together*." Paolo smiled a silly grin at Flora. She smiled a silly grin back. Paolo continued.

"I don't want to get on that train in just a few minutes either...but something good will come from all of this...believe me Flora."

Paolo ached inside his own heart for both of them; he believed, though, that everything had a good purpose. The *good* that was going to come out of that situation wasn't very clear...but one day they would both understand. He believed that with all of his heart...he wanted Flora to believe that.

"I'm sorry Paolo...," Flora said as she slowly got out of the car. Paolo grabbed his bag and jumped out of the car. He rushed toward Flora and hugged her hard. He cupped her face in his hands and kissed her.

"I'll be back soon. I'll call you tonight no matter how late this meeting runs." Paolo didn't want to let her go. He saw her begging him to stay with her eyes. The train was leaving, he kissed her one more time and then ran to the train. Flora walked back to the car. She couldn't look back.

When Flora returned to the pensione, she immediately began to prepare supper. Everyone was hungry and keeping her hands busy sort of kept her mind off Paolo. She made Grandma Filippi's cheese *cassetelle* and served them with chicken soup. Vince had never eaten anything like them before and was anxious to try the dumplings. His people made *tortellini* with veal and spinach.

Vince made the pasta dough for her. Flora wished she had her ravioli cutter...but she had lots of time and even more hands to help her. Emily was a pro at making the braid in the dough to seal the ravioli closed; Grandma Fran taught her how to make the braid that past summer. Jimmy was pretty good at braiding the pasta dough, too. At least they stayed sealed.

Little Flora noticed the unusual quietness in her mother as she was making the *casatelle*.

"Is everything okay Mama?"

"I'm fine Flora...I'm just a little preoccupied with the big week coming up."

"Are you sure that's all there is...," little Flora said as she touched her mother's cheek with her hand. "Your face is so soft...it must be this Italian air that brings the blush back to our cheeks... ."

"You think it's the air...Vince says it's the *garlic*." Flora teased little Flora.

"The air...the garlic...and the *people*.." Little Flora picked up a paring knife. "What can I do to help?"

"I think it's a combination of all three...," Flora said still smiling at her daughter. "You want to help...first, go wash your hands and then get the salad ready to mix...the tomatoes are in the refrigerator and there are a couple cucumbers under the lettuce."

"You know Mom...you never did tell me about your trip with Paolo to Perugia...just because we were all too *busy* to listen doesn't mean I forgot about your promise." Little Flora was persistent.

"Well...I can't say this is the most perfect time...," Flora said as she pointed in the direction of Jimmy and Emily, "...or place, not to mention some little ears getting *bigger,* I promise we'll talk tonight. I *promise*."

Little Flora agreed, she forgot about Jimmy and Emily's *big ears*. "No rain, or sleet, or tide will keep me from our rendezvous...*where* did you say the tomatoes are?"

Dinner was delicious. Vince ate like the casatelle were made in heaven. Flora was so proud. Everything turned out great...even the salad was special. Flora thought that maybe they were all extra hungry.

Jimmy and Emily stayed to help Flora clean the kitchen. They took their time and made the best of that dreaded chore while Flora fixed a batch of tapioca pudding. She especially thanked Jimmy for volunteering to take little Flora's place in the kitchen that night. Giacamo unexpectedly showed up with two tickets to the opera. Jimmy liked Giacamo and couldn't see two tickets going to waste...or a brand new soccer ball being returned to the store. Jimmy traded his sister for the ball and the supper dishes. It seemed fair. Jimmy liked the way Giacamo operated.

It was time for bed. Jimmy and Emily put the PICTIONARY gameboard away and kissed Flora good night. She stayed down by the fire and put her feet up on the hearth.

Dolly and Vince walked into the kitchen and smelled the pudding. "Is there any desert left for us?" Vince asked while rubbing his stomach.

"There's plenty left...," Flora said as she took off her apron. "Your bowls are on the stove...it should be just the right temperature...hope you like it."

"We'll love it, Flora," Vince said anxiously. "Come sit down with us and have your coffee."

The threesome sat down together. They all passed yawns for a couple of rounds, then started laughing.

"You'll have to make those cassatelle one night when Paolo is here...he'd love them...they taste like my sisters tortellini recipe...even better." Vince flattered Flora with his compliments. The mention of Paolo made her feel a bit uneasy.

"Too bad he had to go back to Rome," Vince said as he tried to sneak a wink at Dolly. "The orphanage is like his baby...I haven't seen him this excited about anything in a long time." Vince was trying to get at something. Dolly thought she'd help him *get* to where he was going.

"He hasn't been this excited about anything, well, not

since Flora came to Florence, right Vince?"

Flora's face beamed embarrassment. "You two are like kids...the girls have been rubbing off on you." Flora said, trying to be funny, but almost gagging on her tapioca pudding.

"We'd say, you and Paolo are acting like kids...what's up anyway?" Vince asked as he leaned forward in his chair.

"Nothing like being *subtle*, Vince." Dolly couldn't believe his way of easing into things.

Vince cleared his throat and directed his next statement to Dolly.

"*Subtle*? Dolly...life is subtle...love is subtle, sometimes anyway...look how many twists and turns it threw into our lives but it doesn't mean that those days we weren't together were empty of love...I lived each day of my life always ending it with a deep breath and thanking God for the love he brought to me that day, the love in whatever shape or form...the important thing I always try to remember is that love is always in our hearts to give...and it's always being given to us...we have to keep our hearts open to it and accept everything in our lives as gifts of love...," Vince reached over to Dolly and kissed her forehead, then he directed his attention and next words to Flora.

"And you, little lady...today you filled our bellies with your love and tenderness...thank you for that treat."

Flora blushed from Vince's words and even more from his kind expression and the wisdom of his simple words. Flora understood what he said and was grateful to have such wonderful friends in her life. The phone rang. Vince got up and answered it.

"Pronto...," Vince said with gusto. His face lit up as he listened carefully to the caller.

"It's Paolo!" Vince excitedly said to Flora. "Yeah, *she's* here sitting by the fire with Dolly and myself...sure...you take care and we'll see you soon...okay...I've got it...CIAO". Vince handed the phone to Flora with a cheek-to-cheek smile.

Flora took the phone and tried not to seem as nervous as she was feeling.

"Hello, Paolo...how is everything?" Flora could barely contain her excitement. Dolly and Vince excused themselves to give her some privacy.

"Your father is so good...he knows something is going on... ."

"He should...I told him how I felt about you the first time I saw you... ." Paolo spoke with charming ease.

"When will you be coming home?" Flora asked excitedly.

"Flora...I'm home."

"Honest?" Flora couldn't believe Paolo was home so soon.

"Honest...as soon as I hopped off the train, Cardinal Alberto's aide was waiting for me. He had the papers for me to sign in his briefcase. We sat down in the station and did it right there, it took about forty minutes. While I was clearing up the discrepancies...Fr. Natale bought my return ticket...so here I am...Flora...meet me by the side door and we'll go for a walk...I have to see you."

"I'll be ready." Flora's heart was in her throat. She hoped everything that could be straightened out would be by the next day. Finally, they might have some time to really talk out their feelings.

Flora sat down at the kitchen table. Then, she couldn't wait another minute and decided to start up the hill to San Miniato.

The temperature was unseasonably warm and made Flora feel the springtime that had crept into the night air. Flora met Paolo on her way up the hill. They met almost exactly where the orphanage was going to be. The sky was clear and there were at least a million stars in the sky. The moon was a tiny fingernail. Paolo brought a thick wool blanket that gave away it's age through it's musty odor.

Flora thought perhaps it's younger days saw many picnics in the surrounding hill country. They sat down and stared up at the sky hoping maybe to find some of the answers to life in the almost Spring night. Then, Paolo noticed a falling star.

"There...right there...nope, it's gone...," Paolo said as he pointed in the right direction. "Falling stars fall fast." He took Flora's hand and made a circle in the air and told her to concentrate on that one specific section of the sky...he told her that the next one to see a falling star would get one *wish*.

They stared at the sky for a good while. Flora wanted to break the star watch...but Paolo was taking it very seriously.

"Did you ever see PINNOCHIO...?" Paolo asked Flora not taking his eyes off the sky.

"I did, Paolo...I loved that story...especially Jimminy Cricket," Flora replied keeping the sky her view.

Paolo spoke seriously, "I remember one rainy afternoon,Vince and I watched that cartoon three times...we actually stayed for *three* shows! We went to bed that night singing *'when you wish upon a star'*...that seems like yesterday." Paolo kept looking into the sky.

"Did you wish for something that night," Flora asked while turning her head to Paolo's direction...as she brought her heart into the conversation.

"I probably did...I can't remember exactly what it was...but I probably wished for something." Paolo smiled at Flora and asked her if she had wished for something.

Flora hesitated a moment. Paolo's question opened up a secret drawer of put-away and forgotten treasures. With excitement, she answered his question.

"It's funny...I remember how Jimminy's song touched me...I loved that little cricket...I probably wished for a cricket like him...or...for a *nose* like Pinnochio's." Flora laughed at her last remark realizing that as funny as it sounded...she probably did ask for the growing nose.

"I know I pictured myself as Pinnochio," Paolo said assuredly, "...and Vince as Geppetto...I probably wished to see my mother...I would have given anything to have known her." Paolo looked into Flora's eyes once again and smiled. Then his attention went back into the dark night sky.

Flora felt sad for Paolo as she thought of him growing up without his mother. But, she felt his strength and knew he had handled his sorrow with courage...and he made the best of his life despite the terrific void. For a long while, no words were spoken.

Flora looked into the night sky...through her heart. She had questions and wonderments that came back to her with Paolo's verbal reflections. She imagined the sky as a never ending space...full of wonder and love...a great divide separating her earth from other lands...miles and miles and light-years away...yet they were so much like her land and full of all the good things that make life worth living...she knew that in her heart.

Flora thought about time and distance. They were loosing their significance...they were becoming false boundaries to her. Flora thought how her world had changed since she came to Florence. Visiting the museums and walking through ancient countrysides made her realize that time was a deceiving kind of measure...time was loosing it's power...it's status as one of the major guide's in a person's life. Flora felt time had become an overrated measure for the inexperienced and lonely heart; an hourglass for those who had nothing better to do than keep track of days spent. Only those who hadn't found love needed to measure things...to keep their minds busy and off their broken hearts that could only be half living.

Flora felt so many things changing inside of her mind and her heart. The days that had passed from the age of the great Roman empire...the crusades and St. Francis...the

Renaissance...Puccini...were just seconds in the grand scheme of things...yet, each and every heart that had lived and loved, uniquely marked the universe forever. Architecture and statues and paintings and music and roads and ruins reminded her that time had passed...and people, too. Flora thought how many artifacts of man managed to survive...only to remind her of how much more the heart and soul of man survives; they are in the distant stars...yelling out in their brightness that *love* is all that really matters!

Flora turned to Paolo. She watched him watch the sky. And, as if some invisible curtain had been lifted from the universal stage, Flora saw things at that moment the way they were meant to be seen; with her mind so full of the heavens wisdom and her heart so full of it's trust.

"How about," Paolo said abruptly as he looked at his watch, "...in ten more minutes, if nothing happens in the sky, we'll both get a wish?"

Paolo's voice startled Flora...it brought her back to Florence and simple things. Flora smiled as she went over his words in her mind...*if nothing happens in the sky*. If he only knew what was happening...what had happened already. She looked at Paolo and made him her wish...he was the sun and the moon and the stars...he was love. She would take a chance on loving once again.

Flora looked into the sky. She felt love's kindred spirits dazzling her emotions. She thanked God for that awareness of His greatest gift...the gift of love.

"Times up...," Paolo said as he tapped Flora's shoulder. He kept his hand on her shoulder. She raised her shoulder bringing his strong hand closer to her lips. She kissed it tenderly. Flora didn't turn around to look at his face but she felt his smile in her heart. She was lost in that smile.

"Paolo...you go first...since you saw the only falling star tonight." Flora spoke with a kind invitation in her voice.

"What!...wait a minute...I'm the guy who saw the falling

star...so I should at least get to choose who goes first...fair?" Paolo rolled over onto his stomach and scooted as close to Flora's face as he could. Flora could smell his pleasant aftershave. She wanted to kiss his eyes that always seemed to be saying say so much of the things he was feeling.

"Three wishes would be a heck of a lot easier," Flora said honestly. "*One* wish...let me think a while." Flora felt like she was on the spot...she wasn't sure what she wanted to say first. She wondered how a person could fit so many things into one wish?

"Take all the time you need...I know what I'm going to wish for... ." Paolo hung his head down as if keeping it up would give Flora a peek into his thoughts. He waited patiently for Flora.

"Then why don't you go first?" Flora bonged Paolo on his head with her fist *softly*, yet hard enough to make him feel her giddiness.

"It wouldn't be fair...besides...I kind of like watching you think." Paolo rubbed his head...faking his pain. "God...you have a pretty tough fist!"

"I'm thinking...I'm thinking...I know what I want to say but the words...I want them to come out right." Flora was stalling for fun. Her wish had been inside her heart a long time, but her courage to say it needed prompting.

"I guess you can't rush a woman... ." Paolo said teasingly.

"OKAY...I'm thinking...let's see... ." Flora tried to muster up more courage. She didn't realize it would be that difficult for her to say the simple things that were in her heart.

"Take your time but remember," Paolo said admonishingly, "...if the sun comes up before you make your wish...it might not come true." He looked at Flora with an anxious expression. Flora laughed at Paolo's serious face.

"*Really,* Paolo...who makes up all these rules?" Flora looked at Paolo with a big grin. Paolo turned onto his back again and propped his head up with his hands for a pillow.

He looked at Flora with an even bigger grin. "Okay...I'm ready."

"I wish...," Flora paused for a moment. She couldn't finish saying what she really wanted to say. She thought for a second more. "That you...will...always be happy." Flora couldn't believe she turned chicken...she lost the courage to tell him her real wish. Paolo understood her words. He heard the truth through them.

"Gratzie...thank you for that generous wish Flora, but falling star wishes have to be something you want...for *yourself*."

"I *do* want that for me...," Flora said seriously. "You happy...would make me happy...even if I'm not a part of that happiness." Flora wondered how really stupid her last remark must have sounded. Paolo felt her hesitation but he wanted to make her say what she was feeling...he needed to hear the truth. He wanted Flora to hear the truth. Flora didn't know what to say next.

"I couldn't be happy without you...," Paolo said seriously, "...it's my turn...my wish Flora, is a little bit selfish...but it is my wish." Paolo stood up and asked for the stars attention. He reached for Flora's hand and made his wish known. Paolo's cocky grin and political voice left him. The expression on his face turned humble and real. His voice became sincere, low...soft and full of feeling.

"I wished for you, Flora." Paolo helped Flora to her feet and held her in his arms, gently at first. As their emotions grew so did the intensity of his embrace. Flora felt his total being in his caress. She felt his inner spirit, so kind and strong. She hugged him back.

"I need you, Flora...I want you to know how I feel, how I've been feeling ever since that morning when you choked on the blessed wine. That night, after we talked till almost morning, I wanted to hold you...just like this...and I wanted to tell you that I loved you... ."Paolo broke his hold on Flora and looked into her eyes as he continued.

"I'm not going to pressure you or do anything that would make you feel unsure of yourself. I want you to be sure...I want you to be happy...I can wait...me and the stars will always be here for you." Paolo kissed her cheek and wrapped her again in his arms.

Flora didn't know what to say...or worse...where to begin. She hoped that he would never let her go...that, the moment they were sharing, could last forever.

"I love you, Paolo." Flora couldn't believe she finally said those words out loud...it was good to hear them.

She didn't want to think of Jack during that tender moment...but he was there, back in her mind. She loved Paolo and, Jack would have to understand. I did love Jack, Flora thought to herself as she let go of Paolo.

"Paolo...I'm really cold...could we head back to the pensione?"

"Here...let me cover you with this blanket.." Paolo carefully wrapped the old wool blanket around her. They headed down the hill for home.

The night air had grown much colder but not as cold as the gust of guilt that passed through Flora's heart. She couldn't stop shivering. The sky lost its stars and it was very late.

Paolo walked Flora to the pensione but when they reached the front door, neither one of them could say good night. Flora leaned up against the brick pillar on the front stoop of the pensione. Flora smiled at Paolo but couldn't stop her teeth from chattering. Paolo pressed up against her gently, yet firm. He bowed his head and placed his forehead on hers. Flora felt his breathing. It was calm and comforting. He wrapped his arms around her. Flora stopped shivering. They danced standing still to the love waltz that was playing in their hearts.

"This is good...," Paolo said looking into Flora's eyes. He kissed her as if to seal a private promise that he made to himself. Flora felt his unspoken words and silently gave herself to him.

"Your eyes remind me of the stars," Paolo said very tenderly. Flora looked into his eyes and found herself in a silly mood brought on by the night...the stars...and love. Paolo saw that impish look on her face and asked her what she was thinking.

"What are you thinking right now with that crazy grin on your face...I thought I was being very romantic."

"You were, Paolo...it's me...a crazy line just went through my head with your compliment... ."

"Well...are you going to share that *crazy* line?"Paolo squeezed Flora a little tighter.

"JUST SO MY TEETH DON'T COME OUT," Flora said rather quickly.

"TEETH...what do you mean...?" Paolo said looking baffled at Flora, yet knowing something funny must have provoked her last comment.

"Yes...*teeth*...it's a line from an old joke...I don't know what provoked me...it just popped out!"

"Well...how does the joke go...," Paolo asked sincerely. Flora knew Paolo was probably just being polite. She wished she would have kept the whole thing to herself, but she had to continue.

"First you say, YOUR TEETH ARE LIKE STARS...and just when the person believes it's a compliment, the joker quickly adds...THEY COME OUT AT NIGHT!...see," Flora said with an apologetic tone, "I told you it wasn't funny." Flora started to laugh from embarrassment.

Paolo looked puzzled at Flora.

"No," Flora said as she shook her head back and forth, "...it *really* wasn't funny...and I want to apologize for blurting it out...when you're twelve anything makes you laugh...especially if it's about your math teacher who wears dentures...and then when you're forty-two, all kinds of things come back to haunt you from out of nowhere...like that corny old joke...or a husband who's going to be here tomorrow... ."

"Flora, tonight is for us...things are going to change but let's not analyze all that right now." Paolo took Flora closer to himself and kissed her tenderly.

"Flora, your eyes are like the stars."

"Thank you," Flora said sincerely, "...you are a gentleman...and a poet, Paolo." Flora was taken with Paolo's openness. She took his hand and placed it on her heart.

"This is all so good, Paolo...I feel like nothing this wonderful could be happening, it seems I can't accept the beautiful things that come my way...I don't deserve so much." Flora turned away from Paolo for a moment.

"Flora...," Paolo said bringing Flora's eyes back to his, "...most of us have a hard time accepting the good things...maybe we think too much...let's enjoy what we have right now." He hugged her hard. There were things in his heart that were surfacing, too. He thought about telling Flora about Francesca. Then, he set that thought aside for another time.

"Okay," Flora said in light spirit, "...I owe you some poetry...only my words are from someone else's heart."

"That's okay with me...," Paolo said, relieved that now he had an excuse not to divulge the secrets of his past. "Just so they're not from some Edgar Allen Poe collection. Although, KNOCKING-KNOCKING AT MY CHAMBER DOOR has a certain charm." Flora smiled at Paolo's humor. She politely cleared her throat and began.

"WHAT MATTER TO ME IF THEIR STAR IS A WORLD? MINE HAS OPENED IT'S SOUL TO ME; THEREFORE I LOVE IT. Robert Browning wrote that for Elizabeth Barret...I think I understand what he was trying to say in his poem...maybe because I'm here in the land he loved so much." Flora felt silly in her recitation.

Paolo took Flora's other hand and gently pressed an imaginary circle around his heart. "I open my soul to you...," Paolo said very seriously. "Mr. Browning probably had a night like this under the stars holding Elizabeth...maybe he was standing right where we are...what do you think, Flora?" Flora thought for a moment before she answered Paolo's question.

"I think you might be right," Flora said taking Paolo's hand and holding it tenderly. She continued with her thoughts on the night sky.

"Paolo...I think we're all under the same sky...you and me...Robert Browning and Elizabeth Barret...BOGIE and BACALL...," Flora said with a small chuckle in her voice. Her face was full of romantic conviction. Paolo listened carefully and with a smile as Flora continued.

"Really, when you think about it Paolo, what is the sky, what is that space that has no end?" Flora looked at Paolo who was encouraging her with his eyes to go on. She did.

"I think *we* are that space...each one of us sees himself...his soul." She surprised herself with her sharing that intimate observation with Paolo; but, she knew he would undcrstand. Flora continued.

"Like, when we look into the sky...we are really looking into our own souls that have been turned inside out from love...and only after we love, do we see things the way they were meant to be seen...the sun and the moon...the beautiful colors of sunrise and sunset...the clouds and the stars...they become more than just decoration...we see life, past, present, and future." Flora looked deeply into Paolo's eyes. He kissed her forehead.

"Flora...if the sky is our soul turned inside out...what are the stars...?" Paolo was completely enjoying their conversation.

"The stars," Flora said confidently, "...they're all the lucky souls that lived and loved...and their brightness is what they left behind for us...can you imagine a sky without them...what would we do without them? They dot the grand reflection of our soul...they give us a glimpse of the eternal...hope...they make us see that nothing that ever lives and loves ever dies." Flora paused. She looked into the sky and then quickly turned to Paolo somewhat embarrassed. "I-yi-yi, listen to me...but you did start it." She excused herself for philosophizing so rampantly. Paolo took her into his arms.

"You don't have to excuse yourself...I'm enjoying it too much...one day we'll be up there Flora...inspiring young lovers...see, you've got me doing it...but you do it better, tell me more...I'm serious...I'd like to hear more about the things up there." Paolo looked up into the sky. He tried to coax Flora by squeezing her a bit more tightly into his arms. Flora could only smile back at Paolo. His eyes prompted her to go on. She felt embarrassed for a moment and then tried to explain herself.

"Sometimes a person can say too much...sometimes I say too much...," Flora chuckled at her last statement, "...you know what I mean."

Flora smiled at Paolo hoping he'd say something that would turn their thoughts to another subject.

"You could never say too much." Paolo tightened his embrace even more and kissed Flora softly.

They accompanied the night until it faded into a quiet gray dawn. The new morning light made them say good-night. Paolo waited for Flora to go up to her room. She opened her window and waved to him as he began to walk back to San Miniato. She wanted to yell out to him, "*Wait for me...I love you, Paolo!*"

Flora went to bed still feeling Paolo's hand on her heart, still hearing the stars in the sky.

Chapter
eighteen

"When the father comes..."

"...Maybe distance does help a person see things more clearly. The other night Paolo made me realize how foolish I have been about so many things. I want to love. The stars in the sky told me so. Paolo heard them, too." Love, Flora.

"Fr. Cellini, Paolo said raspily. He cleared his throat and continued.

"I'd like to talk with you if you're not busy." Paolo couldn't sleep and he saw light under Fr. Cellini's bedroom door.

"Paolo...is that you?"

"Yes, Father Cellini...it's Paolo, may I come in for a minute?"

"Come in...come in...the door is open." Fr. Cellini greeted Paolo with open arms and a big hug. "It's going to be like old times with you here, Paolo...I am so proud of your commitment here."

Paolo served as a Deacon to Fr. Cellini at San Miniato for two years. That seemed like such a long time ago. It was there that Paolo began his dream of an orphanage. It was there that he made promises in his broken heart.

"I'm happy to be here...and excited as heck for the orphanage to get started." Paolo hugged Fr. Cellini again.

"Paolo, what can I do for you...you can't sleep...something heavy on your mind?" Fr. Cellini knew Paolo intimately, and knew by the look on Paolo's face, that something was bothering him.

It seemed to Paolo that Fr. Cellini never slept. He was always dressed in his cassock and his eyeglasses were a fixed feature on his face. Although in the afternoon, if he wasn't with someone in his office or working in his garden Paolo could always find him catnapping in the rectory parlor, eyeglasses dangling from one ear. Paolo looked at the old man and realized what a blessing he had been for him in his life. Without Fr. Cellini, Paolo would have given up on life completely.

"Something heavy...but something good, I hope," Paolo said trusting Fr. Cellini to listen with an open heart.He confided completely to Fr. Cellini. He spoke of his attraction to Flora, and how in the beginning he never thought it would turn into anything serious...or that wonderful. Flora made him feel love again. He didn't feel it was wrong...something that good could never have been wrong. He had to trust his heart, but that was something Paolo had difficulty doing.

Paolo had lived alone long enough. His promise to himself to be self sufficient turned into a constricting chain that was squeezing all the love out of his being. He was slowly becoming a person he didn't even recognize until Flora made him see flashes of the person he used to be. She made him feel things he tried for many years to ignore.

He left nothing out in his verbal catharsis. He even shocked himself with his openness. He had been so sure of things earlier that night, but with the morning and Jack entering the picture, he had to clear his conscience, he had to empty his heart. Paolo wanted to convince himself that what he felt was good...true. Fr. Cellini would understand him. Paolo counted on that.

"I'm not asking you to bless what I'm doing, or to tell me that I'm making a big mistake...I just want you know what's going on in my life. I need to know that you know...I want you to pray for me and Flora and our situation."

"I'll pray for you...you are always in my prayers...and who am I to tell you that you are making some huge mistake? There is only one mistake a person can make in the name of love,Paolo, and that's not allowing yourself to love because you are *afraid*. Paolo, I understand what you are feeling...I wish I could give you God's blessing, too...but I can't...God will bless you if your heart is pure. I can give you my best wishes...and I will pray for you and Flora. I will always be here for you...you know that Paolo."

"Thank you, Fr. Cellini...I'm just a little, heck...I'm alot scared. I don't want to hurt Flora... ." Paolo fidgeted with papers on Fr. Cellini's desk.

"She's *good* for you...," Fr. Cellini said with a question in his voice. He wanted to hear more of the things that Paolo was feeling in his heart.

"Father...she's *very* good for me." Paolo said while nodding his head in pleasant recognition of Fr. Cellini's expression.

Fr. Cellini shook his head knowing nothing he could say was going to change Paolo's mind. He cleared his throat and went on,in a very serious tone.

"When the husband comes to Florence, you know the picture will change for all of you...he will turn everything upside down...it's...how you say in the romantic heart...bittersweet? You understand what I'm saying...?" Fr. Cellini wanted to make Paolo understand the seriousness of his attraction to Flora if he was to take it a step further.

"I understand, Father...," Paolo said respectfully. He looked into Fr. Cellini's eyes hoping not to see some of the things he didn't want to understand. Fr. Cellini felt his visual plea and could only bow his head down. Fr. Cellini waited a few moments before he started talking again.

"You know I can't tell you what to do...but, you are a smart man, Paolo, and you know what deep waters you are jumping into... ." Fr. Cellini looked into Paolo's eyes and continued.

"The facts of the situation are...soon the husband will be reunited with his wife and family...things will change...not Flora's feelings toward you or yours toward Flora...but the husband and wife together...and being again with his children...this makes a woman realize her duty and commitment...she will give up her own happiness for her children's happiness...what the two of you are sharing right now is wonderful...but a time will come when this woman will realize the things she is keeping buried in her heart...this I know is true."

Paolo understood what Fr. Cellini was saying...he thought the same things himself...he knew Flora would die for her children. But, the kids seemed to understand their mothers relationship with their father and Jack's absence made it easy for Flora to pretend for a while that Jack didn't really exist. The thousands of miles between them made it easy for her to be *brave* and daring with her future plans. That distance would have been a bridge in her relationship with Jack if he had truly loved Flora...but it seemed to be more of a mote, protecting her from a relationship that had been slowly pulling her spirit under.

Paolo left Fr. Cellini's room discontented. He was sure of Flora and all the things he loved her for...but would Flora be as sure of him when Jack entered the scene again? Flora's heart was vulnerable. Paolo wondered if his had been simply a simpatico heart that just happened to be in the right place at the right time. He had to believe in Flora and he wanted to believe in himself.

The next few days were busy for Flora and Paolo. Jack was keeping his family busy sight-seeing and the surveyors were keeping Paolo on his toes with snags in the orphanage plans. Paolo was grateful, in a way, for all the extra running around he had to do. It had given him the extra will-power to stay away from the *crowded* pensione.

How much he wanted to see Flora. Maybe Fr. Cellini was right, Paolo thought. Jack, back into the picture, could change things alot.

Flora felt overwhelmed when Jack knocked on the pensione door. His arrival made the kids crazy with excitement. He was like the forgotten Dad and Uncle who decided to come home again. Vince and Dolly were impressed with the profound influence he had on his children and Tracey and Christina. Sebastiano and Stefano appreciated his understanding about their proposals, too. He seemed to have brought everything together. Flora felt his importance in the family...she began to doubt the blatant resolutions she had made only days before about their marriage. She realized now it wasn't entirely up to her to dissolve the DEATH DO US PART vows. Everything that was so black and white in her plans only hours before, had melted into a dangerous shade of gray.

"She isn't here this morning, Paolo," Dolly said with more than a twinge of impatience in her voice. "No one is here... everyone went to Napoli...I know it isn't any of my business...but where in the heck have you been...you know, you *could* drop by." Dolly was the only one home so she invited Paolo to come for coffee. Paolo accepted Dolly's invitation and he looked forward to talking with her that afternoon.

Dolly was happy to see Paolo that morning. She was very curious to hear how all of his plans were coming along. She wondered if he had been as miserable as Flora. She wondered if he could hide it as well as Flora had been doing.

Jack and the kids were keeping spare time at a minimum the past week, Flora always went along; always without her heart. Flora was hoping the wallpaper would have come in that morning but it didn't. She wanted an excuse to stay home and work on the parlor, and maybe get a chance to see Paolo. Flora thought it was ironic that the paper she picked out was from a company based in Michigan. It looked so Italian but they had to send to the United States for it.

"Paolo...it's been a long time," Dolly said as she opened the door for Paolo to come into the kitchen, "..you look *great*...maybe a little thin...anyway, how is everything going with the orphanage?" Before Dolly could ask another question Paolo grabbed her and twirled her around the kitchen. They laughed at each other's dizzy expressions.

"We're not as young as we used to be," Dolly said as she sat down into a kitchen chair, "...but that did feel *invig - orating*...who am I trying to kid...my head is *spinning out of orbit... .*"

Paolo kissed Dolly on her cheek and then walked over to the fireplace and sat down.

"It's been a while...," Paolo said as he looked around at the kitchen.

"*Too* long, Paolo...," Dolly said softly. She got up from her chair and started kneading her egg bread dough while trying to update Paolo with the latest happenings around the pensione.

Paolo could barely keep his attention on Dolly's conversation...or rather soliloquy. His mind kept drifting back to the afternoon when he accidentally met up with Flora on the Ponte Vecchio. It was the day after the big Epiphany get together. The day after *their* long night by the fire. Flora wanted to get out and soak up some of the good Italian sun that had been evading her since her arrival to the sunny land. She looked beautiful to Paolo even though Flora told him that he had caught her at a bad time.

He remembered how they talked until the sun made them feel the time that had too quickly passed. They walked home slowly. Paolo took a few wrong turns to extend their walk. Paolo felt Flora's overwhelming need to share some things that too rarely are shared with another person; things people feel more comfortable sharing with strangers. He felt close to her. Paolo wanted to tell her about Francesca, but hesitated. He thought there would be a better time for that. Flora told him that afternoon, how she never would have thought, in a *million, zillion years,* that she'd be in Italy...that winter. She never dreamed of being in Italy in the winter ever! Flora told Paolo that she had imagined herself in Venice in the summer, and even walking around St. Mark's square in the springtime. Paolo loved her imagination and her simple way of looking at things. He wished he could get all the little things she said and all the simple things they enjoyed, out of his head. Dolly cleared her throat and snapped Paolo out of his trance.

Paolo apologized to Dolly for being rude and inattentive. Dolly understood and she wished she could make things easier for Paolo.

Paolo sat back in his chair, then he looked at his watch.

"I was hoping to see Flora...but she's been very busy with Jack and the kids... could you give her a message for me...?"

"Sure, Paolo...but you have to know that she'd love to see you or at least hear from you...," Dolly looked up from kneading the dough, "Maybe you could try and make it over for dinner...Flora and the girls made lasagna for supper and Vince is going to put together his famous salad...and you'll get to taste some delicious bread." Dolly lifted the bread dough in veneration. Paolo laughed.

"It all sounds so tempting, but I'm leaving Florence tonight...for a couple of weeks. A million set backs have to be taken care of and...I may as well get going on them...and I don't think my coming to dinner would be the wisest thing."

"You're going away for two weeks?...then you'd be crazy if you didn't come for dinner tonight." Dolly was flabbergasted at his announcement. She interrupted Paolo as if to make sure she heard wrong. She heard him correctly.

"The rig we're using for the digging broke down and I decided to replace it instead of repairing it...the nearest dealer is in Naples...if the orphanage was going to be completed some time this century, I'd better run this errand myself."

Dolly went over to the calendar on the refrigerator, "...the twenty-first of February...and....when are you coming back?" Dolly flipped the calendar page over to March and told Paolo that Flora would be heading back home on the eighth of the month.

Paolo wasn't positive about the duration of his stay in Naples, but, if he had anything to do with it...he'd be home on the sixth or seventh of March. He wasn't sure of anything; the rig in Naples, the bricks from a builder he knew in Pompei, not to mention the legal paper work he had to deliver to the Cardinal in Rome. He was sure of one thing: he wanted to see Flora before she left for the States.

"I'm going to make a few calls and try to postpone this afternoon's trip, till at least tomorrow morning...your bread is worth even catching the five a.m. train. I'll let you know if I'll be able to make it for supper...either way I'll try to see you before I leave."

"Make sure you do...really, Paolo...try."

Dolly knew her bread wasn't the only reason Paolo wanted to be there for dinner that night. He wanted to see Flora. He wanted to look into her eyes and see if everything he was thinking and feeling were the same things she was thinking...the same things she was feeling. He would know so much by just looking in her eyes. They were the *mirror of a man's soul*".

"What did you want me to say to Flora...?"

Paolo thought for a second.

"Dolly...nevermind...wait...just tell her that I hope she is doing okay...whatever that means...Dolly no...just tell her I'll see her before she leaves...you know what I mean." As the words left his mouth he somehow knew they were only sounds of a wishing heart...sounds Dolly could translate into what he was really trying to say.

"I know what you mean...and Paolo...you *have* to tell her about Francesca."

"Where did that come from," Paolo asked Dolly with surprise. He walked up to Dolly and nervously began scattering the flour on the bread table.

"I know...and I've been meaning to...but there hasn't been a lot of time for confessions." Paolo sprinkled more flour onto the kneading surface. Dolly tapped his hand.

"*BASTA*...enough, Paolo...now quit playing with my flour...seriously...you have to tell Flora before she takes off for the States...it will be terrible if you two can't get together one more time before she goes back home...she may never come back...I don't know about you men sometimes." Dolly hung her shoulders low and took a deep breath as she kneaded the bread dough half-heartedly.

Paolo heard the exasperation from Dolly's hope. He hugged Dolly wrapping her back completely in his big arms. He kissed her tenderly on her raspberry blushed cheek. Dolly held on tight to the promise in Paolo's kiss but didn't allow the tears it stirred to overflow. She responded tough to his sensitive peck, hoping to stop her tears...hoping to make him think of Flora and all the things that should be resolved.

"Be careful Paolo...you'll get flour all over you!"Dolly raised her shoulders and shook her head as if trying to chase away a pesky fly.

"I'm not afraid of a little bit of flour...," Paolo said as he dipped his hand in the flour sack. He rubbed some on his face...and then walked toward the door. Paolo turned around so Dolly could see his floured expression.

"No, you aren't afraid of a little flour...*other things* scare you lately...," Dolly said as she shook her head back and forth in concern. "But what do *I* know...get out of here...and get your work done so we can see you tonight?"

"I will...and say a prayer for me, I know the bread is going to be delicious." Paolo walked away quietly.

Paolo reminded Dolly so much of Vince and Peter when they were young. As she rinsed off her sticky hands, Dolly saw Paolo from the kitchen window walking up the hill. He made her realize that time plays tricks with people in love. The flour on Paolo's face didn't hide the concern Dolly saw in his eyes. Dolly knew the expression Paolo was wearing in his lonesome heart.

Chapter
nineteen

That February Night

The wallpaper came in from Michigan and Flora was finally able to finish the parlor in the pensione Belloni. Flora and her family would be leaving in three days. Sebastian was going to fly back with them to the States to meet his future in-laws, Tom and Rose. He had to make his intentions known and prove that he would be a loving and supportive husband. Christina was in seventh heaven.

Tracey thought she wouldn't be able to wait until December when Stefano would come to visit her. They were in love, but no matter what anyone could say over the phone, it wouldn't satisfy Dan's parental instincts. Jack convinced Tracey that her father was doing what he felt was the best for her...and that out of respect for him and her mother, she should at least go home and talk things out face to face. Tracey loved her parents and agreed that going home would be the best thing. For the time being.

Jack was very diplomatic and saved alot of hurt feelings. He helped the girls out of some tough predicaments and made them grow up a little, he hoped. It was difficult not falling in love in Italy, Jack knew what they were experiencing. It's basically a simple thing...yet, so many people are perplexed by it and eventually let it go. Jack knew about letting things go.

Jack not only kept the kids going in a hundred directions, always with a museum at the end of every one, he also designed the parlor menu for the upcoming tourist season and helped little Flora mix the paint for her *moon* mural.

Little Flora's mural captured the full moon in the Florentine sky. Their first night there, the full moon beamed in through their window and gave little Flora the idea for the mural. She wanted to leave the final touch for her next trip. That made her believe she would have to come back one day to finish it. It would be like her *coin* in the Fountain of Treve.

Everyone loved the results of the whole pensione renovation, especially Vince. He couldn't say enough about the outcome of their labor of love.

Guido couldn't wait to get his kitchen back. Dan was calling everyday for little Flora; she was anxious to get back to him; Giacamo had been making her feel things she couldn't explain. Dolly was getting teary eyed at the end of every meal and Jimmy and Emily wanted to stay at least another month. Flora dreamt of that herself every night. But, their nights were running out. Every hour left of their trip had been spoken for. Flora worked on the parlor hoping Paolo would drop in to say hello...or good-bye. That was her daydream those last few hours in Florence.

"The paper was worth the wait...it's absolutely beautiful Flora...," Dolly said as she peeked in the parlor to check out Flora's progress.

"Thanks Dolly...it really does look nice...nothing like finishing things at the last minute." Flora just about completed the room. She had all the windows open and the smell of springtime made the delicate sprigs of lavender lilacs in the new paper come alive.

"It really is beautiful... ." Flora stepped back to admire the walls.

"Why don't you take a break and have some lunch with me...," Dolly said to Flora, "...we'll sit on the veranda and *soak* up some sun."

The sun sounded good to Flora, so did having lunch with Dolly. It was almost noon.

Italy was sunny...mostly sunny in every season. Dolly admitted that the past winter in Florence wasn't all that it was suppose to be. Flora washed the wheatpaste off her hands and met Dolly out on the veranda.

"It seems so quiet..., I bet it's really different during the summer," Flora said as she walked toward Dolly who was setting up their lunch on the table.

"Maybe you'll just have to come back and see for yourself," Dolly said seriously.

"I'd fold out a cot...and sleep right up here," Flora said wanting to make Dolly laugh, "...talk about a room with a view...!" Dolly smiled at Flora.

"If you *did* come back", Dolly said hopefully, "...I mean *when* you come back...you can set up your easel and paint anywhere...here on the veranda or up the road at San Miniato...you could probably sell them to the tourists...it's so beautiful here!...you wouldn't have any trouble finding inspiration in the summertime...it's hot and full of people." Dolly placed the fruitbowl on her head and struck a serious pose.

Flora had to admit, the proposition sounded extremely tempting; it was something she had proposed to herself many times the past days.

Dolly and Flora talked about their meeting last Fall at the community college, the holidays in Union Lake, and the *unexpected* phone call that whisked them all there in the first place. It was all so good to remember. Dolly and Flora talked about everything and everyone...almost everyone.

Flora began feeling sentimental. She had become very attached to Vince and Dolly...and all the pleasant commotion around the pensione. She didn't know how she was going to leave. It all of a sudden hit her like a frigid cold December wind. But, it was March. She didn't want to think of leaving Florence when the most beautiful season was only beginning.

"Dolly...a big part of me wants to stay here forever." Flora looked to Dolly and read her expression. She continued as Dolly rolled silverware up in napkins.

"I've gotten so attached to this place...being here these couple of months makes me feel like I'm leaving home...," Flora looked over to the direction of Santa Maria del Fiore, "...and what about the beautiful bells...they make me think of the really important things in life." Flora walked over to the balcony railing stretching her arms out to catch the warmth of the sun. The bells from the Duomo were ringing the *mezzagiorno Angelus*. Flora continued after the bells.

"This...this beautiful place is like my home...I'm excited about seeing young Jack and Joe and my parents...and I can't wait to tell them about everything...but what happens after that? What will I do two days later when the suitcases are emptied and all the clean laundry is put back inside drawers...and the souvenirs are given away?" Flora left the sky and turned to Dolly. "One rainy evening I'll climb up into the attic to put away the luggage...I'll look out the window and it will hit me and this trip will seem like a dream...I'm not ready for it to be over."

"It was more than a dream, Flora...and...you know what they say, *'it ain't over till the fat lady sings'*...and you don't hear me singing now, do you honey...?" Dolly had her pleased as punch expression on her face. It made Flora smile.

"No...you aren't singing...and it's been so wonderful here...and not just because of Paolo...but because of him and everything he made me see...and feel...the things we made each other see and feel." Flora took a deep breath and sighed.

"Flora...everything will be alright."

Dolly knew there was nothing left in Flora's relationship with Jack. He was a great guy, but Dolly wasn't blind.

Jack had as much affection for Flora as he had for his artistic talents. All the paperwork was in order; he had a marriage license and a fine arts degree, but that was it. Dolly imagined he held Flora as much as his paintbrush...and both suffered from the lack of use. It wasn't like Jack was a jerk. He was intelligent, witty, fun and a great father, and he was loaded with talent. His one big fault was that he didn't love Flora. No one could make anyone love another person if it wasn't there.

"Dolly...you know me...and I know you are honest with me and now...I have to be honest with you."

"What is it Flora?"

Flora placed her elbows on the table and folded her hands as if she was going to pray. She rested her head on her hands and began to speak looking deeply into Dolly's wondering eyes. Dolly listened intently.

"Last night...I couldn't sleep...I got up and sat in the rocker and just thought and thought about the past few months...my mind kept going back to Paolo...and then back to Jack...and then way back to my first years of marriage...maybe I wanted to find some good excuse to blame myself for every single thing that went wrong with my relationship with Jack...but I can't blame myself for everything...I did love him...I made a commitment to love him forever...but being here in Florence and meeting Paolo, made me think about alot of things...I used to think that if Jack and I stuck it out long enough love would have to come from such a valiant effort...but love takes two people...and a promise...I broke that promise." Flora paused for a moment.

"Excuse me, Flora , for breaking in, but I know that a part of you wants to believe that things could work out with Jack...and wouldn't that be wonderful...but you're kidding yourself...*it ain't gonna happen*...not in a million years...and do you know why?...because, *Jack doesn't love you*." Dolly paused for a moment and looked at Flora. She continued more diplomatically.

"Flora...Jack has too many personal problems that need to be resolved before he can ever truly love anyone...in a way, by making things bearable...you made them *unre -solveable*...you never faced the problems with an attitude of resolve...that was your only mistake."

"*My only mistake*...I looked out my window last night and I thought about Paolo and his work at the orphanage and our wonderful time together...and maybe that's all it was suppose to be...a wonderful time for both of us."

Dolly took Flora's cold hand.

"You deserved that time...Paolo deserved it...," Dolly said firmly. Then as if struck by some grand illumination Dolly continued.

"Maybe your time together was for the courage it's going to take to make you do what you should have a done a while ago." Dolly's eyes grew as big as saucers making Flora smile at her friend's sincere expression.

"Flora...take one day at a time...I feel the same way you do...like maybe this whole trip was a dream...because it was so good. Flora, we've been so close the past weeks and your being here has made such a difference in my life...in Vince's life...the kids have made this place come alive...even Brutus is going to feel the emptiness when you go back, he loves Jimmy and Emily." Dolly carefully petted Brutus' head and then went on.

"When you came here, not just the pensione needed renovation...all of our lives were in some need of repair...and none of us realized how much, until we were all together...but now it's time to get back to our little niches and go on from there." Dolly nodded and continued.

"I'm glad the tourist season will be starting soon," Dolly said excitedly, "...that will keep Vince and I busy...and you have a big family to take care of...and lots of painting to do...I saw the sketches on your dresser of San Miniato...they are beautiful...keep it up, when you get home and whenever you finish something, send it to me...I'll hang them in the parlor...and if anyone inquires about your work...I'll give them a price." Dolly noticed the spark in Flora's eyes come back. Dolly winked at Flora and motioned for her to sit down at the table. "Besides...you'll be back before you know it...because this wasn't just a dream...and there are people here who will never forget you."

"Dolly...," Flora said sincerely, "...what do I want...this trip was heaven and I'm grateful...afterall, I didn't come here to fall in love, that was the bonus on this trip...and I turned out to be a pretty good decorator, too." Flora smiled at her friend and reached across the table to squeeze Dolly's hand. "I do love painting...that will be my driving force...I'll paint...and whatever money I make...I'll set aside for my return...and I will be back."

"You will come back...now let's eat...," Dolly said trying to change the subject, "...the prosciuto is delicious."

Flora felt relieved getting her frustrations out in the open. Since Jack came the kids had been going in a hundred different directions. She had felt like the fifth wheel on most of their excursions. She kept up her jovial facade for everyone else, though her heart wasn't really in it. No matter where they went she ended up thinking of Paolo. She felt like a hypocrite walking through the Sistine chapel. When she stared up at the miraculous wonder of the *Story of Creation*, she felt God was staring back at her heart. He knew she dissolved her marriage vows with Jack a long time ago. She hoped He would understand.

They ate their lunch and enjoyed the mild breeze. The sun warmed their bones. Dolly poured two glasses of Aunt Lucia's homemade muscatel wine. She stood up and raised her glass to Flora.

"*Saluti primavera e sempre Firenze...*," Dolly said in perfect Italian.

"Let me see if my Italiano has improved...," Flora held

her glass up and clanged Dolly's, "...*greetings to Spring and always Florence*...not bad huh, Dolly." They both laughed.

Dolly didn't want to bring the mood down but time was running out. There were some things Flora had to know. And, against the wishes of Vince, Dolly decided to butt her nose into Flora's life anyway. Dolly didn't want to upset any applecarts, but she had to get one rolling. She couldn't sit back and let something as wonderful as love slip away from two of the nicest people she knew.

Flora wasn't a saint. She had enough rough spots to keep her humble and Dolly knew that. Paolo asked for alot of his own loneliness in life, too. But, neither deserved a life without love, especially after finally finding it. Dolly was well aware of their shortcomings but knew their hearts were as good as gold. For many of the same reasons Flora and Paolo accepted life as it had been given to them and managed to survive. They fought for everything in the world, except for the one thing they both were starving for. Each of them had written love out of their scripts. During the past couple of months, Dolly tried to make them see their folly.

"Did you and Paolo ever discuss the reasons why he felt so close to the orphanage project."

"It was something he always wanted to do...he loves children...," Flora said pertly. Dolly didn't let Flora finish her answer.

"Did Paolo ever mention that he was a priest? Did he tell you about Francesca...about Roberto? Dolly rattled off those questions faster than Flora's mind could digest them. Flora couldn't say a thing. She looked at Dolly and waited for her to go on.

"Flora...bear with me, I should probably keep my mouth shut and leave well enough alone...but well enough isn't good enough...I'm not trying to cause any trouble or make you upset...but it seems like you are letting too much go for granted...lady, you're leaving in three days! Maybe

I'm old fashioned because I think it takes two to tango...but...maybe that's done solo these days, too... ." Flora still couldn't say anything. Dolly wished she could have taken her words back. Instead, she went on.

"Flora, maybe I shouldn't have opened my big mouth. These are very personal matters and it should be Paolo who tells you...and he's wanted to explain all these things...he does plan on telling you, but who knows when...what the heck is he waiting for...he knows you are leaving soon...Flora, sometimes I could scream at the *snail-icity* of men!" Dolly continued more calmly.

"You and Paolo have something very special and I don't want you to go home and forget about him...promise me that Flora." Dolly took Flora's hand and squeezed it hard.

"I promise...wonderful things happened here...I won't forget...how could I forget." Flora squeezed Dolly's hand and then kissed it. Dolly sighed a deep sigh.

"Flora...things happen in a person's life that make them turn a complete *about face*...and I'm glad they happen...like you meeting Paolo...it made you look at your life and examine your relationship with Jack...which made you realize that it was *your* relationship...and through the years, despite the pain you carried in your heart...you still managed to love...you loved your family...you loved life...and your love, Flora...it never seems to run out...that is your strength." Dolly didn't want to say anything more...but she did. She promised Flora that Paolo would be back...soon, and that he'd get in touch with her before she left Florence. Dolly understood the rough road of life. She prayed that no hearts would be broken and that Flora would come to understand the way Paolo loved her.

Flora had other thoughts and prayers going on in her head. She hoped with all her heart and soul that Paolo wasn't doubting her, or the special night they shared under the stars. He told her he would always be there; he and the stars in the sky. It was that simple and good. She held onto those words with all her might. No matter how things would turn out, Flora would treasure that February night forever.

Later in the afternoon, Flora hung the last three strips of wallpaper and felt the early evening dampness that suddenly blew in with the breeze. The parlor smelled like their night on the wool blanket, under the stars at San Miniato. She closed the window and thought of Paolo.

Chapter twenty

Back Home

"HERE THEY ARE!" Little Tommy yelled out. It was the third time that evening he made everyone hop and look out the window, for nothing.

"Cry wolf again, and I'll personally throw you outside and set you on top of your Grandpa's flagpole...then you will be able to spot them coming for sure." Dan was half teasing...but Tommy could see in his eyes that the *here they are* joke wore thin, at least for Dan.

Dan missed little Flora so much and the past few weeks were almost too much to bare. Everyone knew how Dan felt about little Flora and they all loved him. Dan was a pretty tough guy who had a sensitive heart. Liking him, came very easy.

"Hey Dan...are you sure little Flora is coming back...we *heard* she was *staying*...a dude named *Giacogogo* or was it *Giacanono*...or wait...it was *Giacamo*...yeah, that's it, GIA-CAMO wanted her to stay and go to school there. His father is a professor in the Art department at the University." Donny could have said more, he could have gone on for hours. But, Dan had enough goofing around with the little guys.

"OKAY...*Donnoroony*....or is it *Donnatelli*...or wait... now I know...it's *DONNA*...and *your* ass is grass." Dan put Donny over his shoulders while Matthew came to the aid of his cousin who was about to get walloped. They were heading outside when Matthew saw Jack's van pull up the drive.

"Dan, wait! Grandma, Bubba, they're home...," Matthew shouted excitedly. "Danny-boy, your little Flora is backy...wacky... ." Everyone ran to the door. Dan plopped Donny off his back and ran outside to meet the van. He couldn't wait to see little Flora.

Grandma Flora's surprise *welcome back* party was a success. The flight was long and everyone was starved for some good wholesome food. Grandma Flora satisfied all their taste buds and appetites. Irene and Danny, Tom and Rose, and Sandy and Larry were all there to hear about the trip. Cynthia and Larry even drove in from the farm anxious to hear about the trip and to see the future *in-law*. Everyone knew the party wouldn't be complete without Aunt Cynthia's famous apple pie or her delicious cherry-nut sheet cake. Everyone was impressed with Sebastiano and he felt at home being with all of them...as long as Christina was standing close by. Aunt Irene liked his eyes. Aunt Cynthia thought he looked like TOM CRUISE.

"Mrs. Filippi, would it be alright if little Flora and I left for a while?" Dan barely finished his request when Flora handed him his jacket and motioned to little Flora who was sitting by the fireplace to *Vamoose!*

Flora was so proud of little Flora who handled herself with such demure the day before. Giacamo had asked her to stay and study at the University. She was so tempted, but realized that Giacamo would take her acceptance of the invitation to mean that she would be staying for him...when little Flora really knew she'd be staying to pursue her studies. She thought.

It wasn't that little Flora didn't care for Giacamo, he was very handsome and she loved the same things he did. If she hadn't had strong feelings for him it would have been very easy to stay and phase him out of her plans. But, she couldn't write him off; she was afraid that he would come to mean too much to her. And, Dan was waiting for her to come back home.

"I kept trying to picture your face in my mind," little Flora said as she looked into Dan's eyes, "...it scared me when I couldn't, I dreamt about you alot...I'd see your face and then sometimes it would leave me...and no matter how hard I'd try...your face wouldn't come back...then right in the middle of dishes...or looking up at the tower of Pisa, you'd be there again...and I'd feel so close to you."

Little Flora hugged Dan. They walked out to his car then decided to walk for a while. It was a mild night and the lake just thawed. There was a quarter moon that night.

"It looks the same in Florence...I mean...almost," little Flora said as she turned around landing clumsily in Dan's arms. "It does looks the same." Flora said convincingly. She took another glance at the moon hoping to convince herself that it was true. Hoping to swish Giacamo out of her mind.

"Whoa, this feels good...you and the moon," Dan said trying to be as romantic as he could be. He let go of little Flora...almost as if suddenly remembering he wasn't suppose to be enjoying himself. He walked toward a tree stump near the shore and sat down.

"What's the matter?" Little Flora walked down to him and stood behind him massaging his shoulders. She felt his strength...she remembered his strong hold when he'd hug her goodnight...that she could never forget. She rubbed his back long and with her hands she tried to make all her love penetrate through to his heart. She loved him very much. But it was *different* now. She knew how much he needed her those past few weeks and she wanted to ease all his fears and erase every single doubt he had about their relationship. But she had doubts now, too. He stilled her hands on his shoulders. He talked to her while looking into the night lake.

"I didn't think you'd come back...at least not with

everyone else." Flora wanted to walk around to him but he wouldn't let go of her hands that were resting on his shoulders. He went on.

"When we'd talk on the phone and after you would say *good-bye*...I'd die inside...do you know how many times I wanted to drop everything and come to you?...little Flora, I could never go through this again...I knew I loved you before you left...I know I love you now...but I know you had things to work out...I didn't plan on a GIACAMO dude coming into the picture...that freaked me out!"

"I'm sorry...but it wasn't easy for me either. Christina and Tracey fell in love and all the *gush* they gooed all over...Giacamo was actually my saving grace...he made me think of you. That probably sounds weird...but he did. At first, it was comforting when he'd stay with me at the pensione. We walked alot...and always brought Jimmy and Emily with us, they were your undercover little chaperones...it's funny now that I'm thinking back on it...really Dan, no matter where we went Jimmy and Emily were there."

"Thank God for Emily and Jimmy...remind me to hug them again when we get back to the house." Dan laughed thinking about Jimmy and Emily being his *body guards*. He scooched little Flora on his lap.

"They have the same moon in Florence," Dan asked as he looked into little Flora's eyes. "If it was shining like it is right now...and Jimmy and Emily weren't with you...who knows what might have happened." Dan wrapped little Flora in his arms and kissed her. *Who knows what might have happened,* little Flora thought.

"I'm happy to be back, Dan...," little Flora said, realizing there was a big part of her that was missing Giacamo. But it wasn't the *same* moon, little Flora thought as Dan held her tightly. She was content in his arms yet wondered about Giacamo and how she would have felt in his embrace if she had given him the chance to hold her the night they went to the Opera. She shoved that thought out of her mind. She was with Dan now and Florence was a million miles away. It was difficult keeping Giacamo all those miles away...but she had to try.

Jack opened up the sofa bed for him and Flora. Their room near the attic was like a studio apartment...big but not big enough to waste good space on a conventional bed. Jack was happy to be back in his niche and he was excited to go over all the memorabilia in the morning. The trip was great and he accomplished everything on his agenda of *must* things to do. It had been a long trip home and he needed a good night's rest.

Jack stacked envelopes of pictures from the trip on his lap and carefully looked over each one. "It went too fast...huh, Flora?"

"It did...I hope we'll get back there one day." Flora took off her socks and looked out from her bedroom window. The familiar view brought her mind back to where she was. Florence was wonderful, it was like a dream now, but the dream was over. She was home, and her life was good. If only Paolo had called her before she left. Flora wanted to put him out of her mind. But, she was keeping him too real in her heart.

Flora looked in the mirror as she brushed her hair...she combed her bangs back and wondered if she should let them grow out.

"Do you think I should let my bangs grow out and kind of curl them back?" Flora asked Jack as she struck a demure pose for him.

Jack glanced up from his reading and looked to the top of Flora's head for one second. "I think I'd keep them the way you always wore them...they kind of hide your frown lines...and little wrinkles... ." Jack went back to his book. Flora took a deep breath and then another quick look into the mirror. Jack was right...they did hide her little forehead wrinkles...but she did look sophisticated with her widow's peak showing.

"Are you sure...," Flora said to Jack really looking for a milder assessment and something more in favor of her new inclination.

"I think you look better with bangs...," Jack said to Flora, not looking up from his reading. "And, since when do you care about my opinion...hey, just do what you want Flora, it's your hair."

It is my hair, Flora thought. If only he would have looked in her eyes...her face...he wouldn't have answered her so hastily. It wasn't just about her bangs.

The phone rang and Flora ruffled her hair not caring what fell for bangs and what stayed back. It was late and everyone was sleeping. Flora heard the phone and wished she could have just let it ring, but the caller was insistent. She walked into the boys room and answered it.

"Hello...Hello... ." Flora was ready to hang up...then a familiar voice began to babble on the other end.

"Flora...is that you...it's Dolly."

"It's me...Dolly...it's great to hear your voice...it's been a whole day and a half." Flora tried to keep her voice down.

"Flora...it's great to hear your voice," Dolly said very chirpily, "...you made it home okay I presume." Dolly didn't need an excuse to call, but she didn't want to seem like a pest either. She knew Flora left Florence unsettled and she wanted to hear how things were going back home.

"Dolly...I'm alright," Flora said taking a deep breath, "...I'm just trying to decide if I should let my bangs grow out." Flora didn't want to even mention Paolo's name, so she rattled on to Dolly about the day's happenings.

"We missed the storm in New York and no one lost any luggage...and Mama had everyone here waiting for us...it was nice...Sebastiano seems to be right at home...Rose fell head over heels for him...Tommy likes him, too...my sister Cynthia thinks he looks like *Tom Cruise.*" Flora filled Dolly in on everything from the train ride to Rome to the expressway ride home from the airport. She told Dolly she hadn't realized how much she missed young Jack and Joe...they seemed so much older. She went on and on hoping to evade the main thing on her mind.

"Dolly, you better hang up...your bill is going to be outrageous...I'll call you in a couple of days."

"Flora, not yet, and don't worry about the bill...I've got to talk to you about something...and I want you to be honest with your answer or just don't say anything."

"I'll be honest in a nice long letter...Dolly this phone call is going to be expensive...I promise to write as soon as we hang up."

"DON'T YOU DARE HANG UP...just listen...Paolo's back at San Miniato...he wants to stay there while the orphanage is going up...he accomplished alot in Naples and thinks things are going to move a bit quicker now...finally. Anyway, we talked all last night about you and the kids and your stay here at the pensione...he couldn't believe how beautiful the parlor turned out...look I'm getting off the subject...he wanted me to tell you how sorry he was and then told me not to...that he would write to you himself...but he seemed so...I don't really know the word that would perfectly describe his mood last night, except that he wasn't PAOLO...he wasn't himself...he was very tired...but more than tired... ."

"Maybe he *was* tired...he's a busy man and has a full life with his work and the orphanage...maybe I read too much into his just being himself? I have to forget about him, Dolly. I have a marriage that needs all the attention I can give it and more...I had the time of my life with you and Vince and the girls and Jimmy will never forget our winter rendezvous in Florence." Flora wanted to go on but Dolly interjected abruptly.

"Go ahead and convince yourself of everything your saying. You probably started your self-brainwashing on the train to Rome! Tell me I'm wrong."

Flora couldn't tell Dolly she was mistaken; Flora promised herself not to take her thoughts of Paolo into Union Lake. He belonged in Florence with her memories and the other half of her heart.

"Flora, don't pretend that what you felt for Paolo or what Paolo felt for you wasn't real...it might be the most real thing you've felt in years. Florence was wonderful for you and you made Paolo feel alive again...I don't know why things were left so up in the air...I just don't know...but please don't forget or pretend it was all a dream...it was very real and beautiful." Dolly realized she had said enough to Flora. "It's getting late...I'll write to you tomorrow...ciao, Flora...and let them grow for a while...you'll look beautiful either way." Dolly hung up before Flora had a chance to say *buona sera*.

Time would help Flora straighten things out. Everything Dolly said was true...except maybe the part about her hair. Dolly was a romantic. Flora was a dreamer. But, Flora was home now and it was time to *wake up*. Why did Dolly have to call...why did she have to mention Paolo?

Flora couldn't sleep. She tossed and turned in bed for half the night. Finally, at four-thirty she got up from bed and called Dolly in Florence. Flora let the phone ring ten or eleven times, till someone picked up the receiver.

"Pronto!...Pronto...Hello... ." Flora recognized Vince's voice.

"Vince?...it's Flora...I woke up hungry and thought I'd call and ask what you have in the fridge...anything for early morning blues... ."

"Flora...," Vince said with his strong voice, "...we have... let me see...pasta and chicken for the hunger pains...and a...what's that piece of paper sticking out of the butter dish?...OH...an airline ticket to Rome...kind of greasy though...but very good for the blues... ."

"I'll take it greasy, even dipped in anchovy gravy with whip cream and a cherry on top... ." Flora chuckled at her last comment.

"Flora, since you people left, all we do is sleep and nap...when are you going to come back?" Vince's voice was sincere. It seemed as if he were in the next room. Flora wanted to talk more with him and look into his kind wise eyes. Vince heard through Flora's silence. He tried to cheer her up.

"So, Flora...get back here and wake us up...not to mention you took the good weather back with you...it turned cold and it's raining hard...so come and bring the sunshine back to Florence...ooops...I've got anxious eyes on me...Dolly wants to talk with you...ciao, Flora...we miss you...take care and we'll see each other soon...bye Flora."

"Ciao, Vince, we'll be back soon...tell Brutus we miss him...," Flora said with a lump in her throat.

"Flora...," Dolly said excitedly, "You're darn tootin' you'll be back...is anything the matter...you should be sleeping...it's about four-thirty over there?"

"No...no, nothing's the matter...I just kept thinking about the things you said and I kind of said some things that really weren't true...I don't want you worrying over there... ."

"Flora...hang on a moment... ." Dolly handed the phone over to Paolo who was having breakfast with her and Vince.

Paolo took a deep breath, "Flora...it's me... ." His voice melted every bone in Flora's body. Flora's eyes welled immediately with tears.

"Paolo... ." Flora's heart ached, she couldn't say another word. Paolo wanted to say so many things.

"Flora...I'm sorry I didn't get to see you before you left...but I honestly thought that us not getting together would be the best way to handle things...at least for the time being."

Flora still couldn't speak. Paolo hesitated for a moment before he continued.

"Flora... ." Paolo hung on to the phone hoping Flora would respond.

Flora bit her lip as her tears rolled steadily down her cheeks. With their release, came the words her heart had been holding for a long time.

"Paolo...you're what was best for me...all I wanted was you...to hold me in your arms and tell me that everything was going to be alright...I just needed you to be there...you stayed away...maybe you were afraid that I wouldn't have been able to say good-bye...but for you I could have done anything...we did so much to spare each other pain, we shouldn't have thought so much...you know what I mean."

"Flora...*nothing* should have come between us...not time...or miles...I thought I had to give you another chance with Jack...I had no right to call that shot, I realized that when I saw you board the plane yesterday... ." Paolo paused. Flora couldn't believe that Paolo was at the airport in Rome.

"Paolo, *you were there*...in *Rome*?"

"I was there...I should have said good-bye to you...I'm sorry... ."

Flora hesitated before saying something she really didn't believe herself. She felt so far away from Paolo.

"We'll get over our winter in Florence, Paolo...we'll manage...people always do...but, Paolo...I'll always treasure the time we had together, every minute of it...forever." Paolo heard through Flora's tough words.

"Flora, you don't have to be brave for both of us...don't be brave and sensible for me...Flora...I shouldn't have stayed away...I made things worse...so don't you try and be the sensible one now...it won't work."

"Paolo...I've got to go...," Flora said as she looked out into the snowy March night, "...I love you, Paolo...*buona notte.*" Flora's throat tightened. She wanted to say something heroic...something she could really understand. But she wasn't feeling heroic and nothing was making sense.

"What happened to all our plans," Paolo asked seriously, "...to all the things we talked about? We can't let things
end like this...Flora...I made a mistake...we have to
talk...say something...please... ."

Flora hung up the phone hearing Paolo's words fade
slowly...hearing muffled words and sounds her tired heart
couldn't understand.

Chapter
twenty-one

A Stolen Pinch of Cinnamon

The season of Spring passed quickly. The days grew longer. Flora's wish to hear from Paolo began to wane. She felt her heart letting go and it hurt more than anyone could ever know; she wouldn't expose that timid part of her heart to anyone, except to her good friend, Fr Bill.

Flora confided many things in him. She trusted him completely. In the beginning it was the miles apart that helped make it easier to be so honest with her problems. But as their friendship grew, Flora understood what a blessing he was to have in her life. Maybe the distance made that possible. Maybe she was beginning to really understand what her heart had been telling her all along.

It was easy for Flora to talk to Bill. He never judged her. He enjoyed her letters as much as she looked forward to hearing from him. He understood the rocky road her marriage was on. Bill knew the vulnerable side behind Flora's basically happy-go-lucky disposition. He understood what brought her to that point and tried to make her see the right way out of it. He convinced her that she had to look within for the answers...be patient and most of all trust God. And, she did.

Bill thought the trip to Florence was great for Flora and her family. She finally was able to develop her talents as an artist. Flora could take her newfangled role as designer very serious; Florence proved that to her. She was flattered by all the responsibility Dolly placed on her. Bill never met Dolly but loved her for what she did for Flora.

When Flora was in Florence she called Bill from the pensione and talked about everything. He sensed in her excitement and exuberance that Flora had found what was missing in her life. When *Paolo's* name entered their conversation, Bill had no doubt that Flora's empty heart had been filled. Flora found the love her life was missing; the love that was always meant to be there. He worried too, about her saying good-bye to that love, he wasn't sure if she would be able to handle that. Too much had been left unresolved. Bill felt that would wear on his best friend's heart. And, it did.

Jack grew more and more distant from Flora. He would never admit to it, though. He always blamed everything that went wrong on Flora or her family or the kids; never himself. He was slowly dying out of love and he didn't care. Flora tried to convince herself that things would get better.

Flora's kids were her life. She thought that they would be her saving grace. They were growing up but somehow she was standing still. It was the time in her life when she and Jack were suppose to start doing more things together. Their relationship was suppose to be taken out of *neutral* and put back in *drive*. But, there was no where to go.

The kids were just about finished with school when Jack suggested that they spend the summer up North. Young Jack and Joe were working on the island that summer. It was only seventy-five miles east of the cottage so their days off could be spent with the summer gang. Even little Flora loved the suggestion...she had graduated the week before and was ready to move on. Jimmy and Emily loved the north so much they wanted to *live up there*, that's what they were always telling Flora anyway.

"Why did you have to say that in front of everyone,"

Flora asked Jack. Jack didn't acknowledge her question. Flora continued airing her views.

"It was like you knew they'd be all for the idea...and who am I to fizz out the great plan?" Flora was upset with Jack's sudden outburst, then she realized that it was probably the best suggestion he ever came up with. She would have time to work on her paintings and maybe even start the portfolio she needed. And, the kids wouldn't have a better time anywhere.

That night before Flora went to bed, she climbed into the attic to put some boxes filled with winter things away. She turned the dangling bulb Jack had rigged up for light in the dark loft. Flora made a couple of trips, up and down, stacking scarves and mittens and heavy wool sweaters next to the Christmas decorations. Then, Flora walked over to her empty luggage and sat down on Jimmy's big suitcase to rest for a few minutes. The airline tags caught her eye. ALITALIA, how sweet it sounded to her as she repeated it once again in her head. It was raining a soft drizzle. The sound of it on the rooftop made her think of Florence.

Flora pulled an old letter from Dolly out of her sweater pocket and began to read it...again.

"Dear Flora, It's been raining here all month...actually it's been raining since you left. Work on the orphanage has been slow...Paolo has been working between the raindrops...oh well...the flowers will be beautiful in May! How about you? Have you decided to come back for the summer?

"I don't know what to think anymore. Some days it's all so clear to me. On others it's confusing. I see Paolo almost every night for dinner. I know he loves you but I won't dare bring up your name. Vince did a couple of times and Paolo just got up and left...he walked out not even finishing his supper.

"And, your letters. It's like you never were here...you don't mention anything that's in your heart...what are you afraid of...what is everyone afraid of?

"So, I've learned to screen my thoughts and not to bring up anything from last winter. Vince is the only one who feels the same way I do. Br. Georgio seems to have taken a convenient vow of silence lately, too. I hope Paolo can at least talk with him.

"I'm working on a water color of the Ponte Vecchio. I sold three more of your pastels and put that money in your account here. It's building up...then you will have no excuse to not to come!

"Oh well, 'you can lead a horse to water'...whatever you decide to do this summer...be happy! I know everything will work out in the end.   Ciao...and love, Dolly"

Flora smiled at her friends letter and philosophy. She knew there were big decisions to be made and hoped the summer would help her see things clearly.

That past spring, as soon a she returned from her trip to Florence, Flora thought of spending the summer at the cottage. But, she didn't want to leave Jack. When he made it clear that he wouldn't mind everyone leaving, Flora really had no excuse not to go. If there had been the slightest gleam in Jack's eyes when Flora was around him, she would have stayed in Union Lake and been content. Jack's empty eyes, his blank stares guaranteed the adventure that was in her soul. On the first of July she and the kids headed for their cottage on the great Lake Michigan in the north woods.

The whole three hundred and eighty-five mile trip up to the cottage seemed strange. Flora was driving. Jack wasn't telling her not look at him...the kids were being completely civil. It wasn't the typical scenario.

Flora was used to little bickerings about breath blown in the wrong direction and pop spilling purposely on someone's pillow. The kids were definitely growing up. Especially little Flora who finally accepted the *little* in her name. She was eighteen and a half and on to the University. People could call her anything they wanted to now. She was more than Flora's oldest daughter...she was Flora's best friend.

Mary and Bruno Dacys were already up at their cottage which was right next door to Bubba's. Bruno mowed the lawn for Flora while she put together some pizza dough. It was a kind of chilly night, so the kids started the wood-stove and decided to eat inside. Emily ran next door to invite all the Dacys over for supper. It was a good night. The pizza was excellent and the *Chianti* made it *molto delizioso!*

Flora went to bed grateful that things turned out the way they had...she was anxious to see young Jack and Joe on the weekend. The sound of the gentle waves unwound Flora's mind, taking her peacefully to sleep.

The next morning came with a clear blue sky. Everyone slept in till Jimmy woke them up at a lazy nine-thirty in the morning.

"I know we are on vacation," Jimmy said softly to Emily, "...but you gotta see the lake...it's like a sheet of glass and the sun is so warm...let's have our cereal down by the beach...then we'll walk to the dunes." Jimmy fixed the huge breakfast tray including the cereal, fruit, bowls and spoons. Emily carried down the gallon of milk. Flora loved to see them excited and didn't want to see their effort go unnoticed. She sprinkled water on little Flora's face and made her scream...which woke up Tracey, Christina and Sebastiano. That strategy of waking up sluggish teens always worked.

They all walked over the dune and onto the beach, some with eyes only half opened. Emily took each break-fast order and Jimmy served them. You could hear a fish break water on their beach that morning.

Sebastiano was impressed with their little hide away on the lake. He felt like he was looking at the Mediterranean Sea. He kept drinking from the lake and couldn't believe it was *good* water. Christina laughed at how many simple things impressed and sometimes even shocked Sebastiano. He won all their hearts.

"Flora...there's a phone call." Mary yelled that message down to the beach. As Flora walked back up to Mary's cottage she felt embarrassed. The phone call had probably woken Mary up...she hoped Mary didn't mind.

"Hello." Flora tried to talk softly. She was alone in the kitchen.

"Hi Flora! It's Irene! You are going to think I'm crazy but yesterday after you left Mama's, Dolly called and told us about Stefano coming to stay at the cottage for a few weeks...then before that bit of news digested...guess who knocked at the door while Mama was still talking to Dolly on the phone...you'll never guess, so I'm going to tell you, STEFANO! *Stefano from Florence!*"

"*Stefano?*" Flora asked in disbelief. Flora giggled at the whole scene Irene was trying perfectly to describe.

"Can you believe it? Flora, did you have any *inkling* he was coming to Union Lake?"

"Irene, if I had any *inkling* whatsoever, would I be up here...no, I'd be down there making some good Italian food...and changing sheets...and...going crazy...so, where is he now?"

"Okay, Flora, listen...when we told him that Tracey was up north with everyone else...he wanted directions on how to get there...and before I could say anything, like what was I suppose to say...Daddy started writing down directions and telling them how easy it would be to find the place! In the meantime me and Mama were flipping! I don't want him up there with Tracey, you know, the two of them *alone*...who knows what will happen...he is so dang good-looking...Danny will probably head up there tonight after I give him the news about the *unexpected visitor*, I won't even mention how handsome he is."

Flora tried to calm Irene down. She was very protective of Tracey and knew the possible *forest fire* of passion that was heading in their direction. They all knew how the *north* affected young hearts in love...even old hearts in love! Flora managed to put things in perspective for Irene and then asked for more details.

"Well, when did he leave...?" Flora asked calmly. Irene tried to answer just as cool.

"He and his cousin, or maybe Stefano was with a friend, anyway, they left about twenty minutes before I called you...Mama thought of calling...we didn't want you to be shocked out of your gord the way we were...can you imagine, they just pulled up into our driveway, I mean, no phone call to announce their arrival...they could have called from the airport... ." Irene's *cool* frazzled.

"Flora...I'm sorry for being so upset...but, you know how I worry about Tracey."

"You don't have to worry about Tracey...but Irene...*time*...what *time* did they leave?"

Irene paused for a moment, gathering her composure.

"Flora...they left around ten o'clock...they had just eaten breakfast and were going to drive straight through...Daddy thinks they'll be there at about four-thirty, five o'clock, if they don't get lost or break down anywhere, which they shouldn't, he rented a *Lincoln* at the airport...Flora, *please* keep an eye on Tracey...talk to her as soon as you hang up...and have her call me tonight...make sure! I'll stick to my schedule as planned and come up on the nineteenth with the boys...but Tracey has to call me *every* night...promise me you'll make her call?"

Flora promised. She understood Irene's apprehensions about Stefano joining the gang up North. But there was nothing anyone could do about it now. Stefano was a great guy...and this trip might give him the chance to get to know Irene and Danny. Flora walked down to the beach to give the kids the *good* news.

"SWEAR TO GOD...*swear to God*, Aunt Flora...is he really coming...if you are teasing me it's a bad joke." Tracey couldn't believe what she heard, eventually it settled and it was like the kids were little and someone just yelled from the top of the dunes that *Santa Claus was coming to Gulliver!*

Sebastiano's eyes filled with tears...he had missed his brother. Now things would be perfect for him.

"Oh, I almost forgot, Stefano's coming with his cousin...Irene forgot his name...but I would imagine that Giacamo made the trip with him, what do you think Sebastiano?"

Sebastian agreed. "He's off from school this summer and always loved coming to America...his mother must be feeling much better...now we have double reason to celebrate...it will be like a reunion...I must go to town and pick up some things...who wants to go with me?" Sebastiano was in his glory. "My brother and my cousin are coming to this beautiful place... ." He picked up Christina and carried her over the dune. He whispered in Christina's ear. "I knew he wouldn't be able to stay away from his *cara mia*... ."

Christina and Jimmy went with Sebastiano while Emily picked up the breakfast dishes. Tracey and little Flora straightened up the sleeping bags and then sparkled up the bathroom.

"Do you really think Giacamo is coming with Stefano," Tracey asked little Flora who was shining the mirror over the bathroom sink.

"I don't know, it would be nice, though...but I can't imagine him coming here...he has so much work to do since his father is busy taking care of his mom...I don't know...plus...I can't imagine him leaving home when his mother is so ill...we'll know in a while." Little Flora was acting very nonchalant about the whole situation at hand, at least on the outside.

"I guess we'll just have to wait...," Tracey said as she smiled at little Flora, "We'll wait... ."

Flora started some coffee cake dough...the kids loved her cinnamon coffee cake with the vanilla icing. Flora knew the appetites of young people. Kids could eat all day...especially up North.

The temperatures climbed and there was a nice breeze coming in from the Lake. It reached 92 degrees, but it felt very comfortable. Little Flora set the deck up with chairs and opened the big canvas umbrella over the table. Everyone was too excited to eat. So they talked...and talked...and talked.

Flora drilled Irene's command into Tracey's head without being too tyrannical. Tracey pleasantly accepted the message from her mother and told Flora she called every night anyway. But, things would be different now with Stefano in the picture. His being there would make things a *little bit different*, in a very pleasant kind of way.

"OH MY GOD...I think that's them!" Christina yelled as she was rinsing out a few glasses in the kitchen sink.

"If you're kidding, I'll pull out all your split ends," Tracey said impatiently. She wasn't in the mood to play *THEY'RE HERE*, all evening.

"NO, *honest*...it's them." Jimmy verified the announcement and everyone ran to the car to greet them, except Flora. She wanted the young kids to be alone a few minutes. She hurried and rolled out the coffee cake dough on the kitchen table. Flora imagined how the girls were feeling right then...and she thought of Sebastiano and how good it must be feeling for him to have his brother back again.

The back door opened. Stefano walked up to Flora and kissed both her cheeks. He hugged her like she was his long lost Aunt. Flora thought he was very kind to make her feel so special.

Everyone was standing in the kitchen hugging and talking and then Paolo walked inside.

"Mama...*Paolo* came with Stefano," little Flora tried to soften the blow of her announcement by talking slowly and clearly, like a kindergarten teacher. "Isn't this a...nice... *surprise*?"

Little Flora saw the shock in her mother's face and was embarrassed for her...and Paolo. It wasn't like Flora to become so unnerved at *anyone's* arrival, ever! She welcomed and entertained anyone and everyone who entered her home. After a couple of deep breaths and a quick swallow to clear her tight throat, Flora's shock melted into a polite, yet chilled welcome.

Flora tried to keep her eyes from meeting Paolo's.

"Come on in and sit down...I have to get this dough going if we're going to have some cake with our camp coffee tonight." Flora motioned to everyone to sit down but the kids wanted to go right out to the beach. Her *stomach* felt like it had already run there...without her.

Sebastiano excused himself and Stefano. He couldn't wait to show his brother the *great Lake* that you could drink! Stefano grabbed Tracey by the arm while Flora told all the kids to go and have a good time. Little Flora whispered to her mom that she'd be back up in a little while to help out with supper. That left Flora and Paolo alone in the kitchen, at least for a while.

Flora wondered about all the flour on her face. She felt it on her cheeks like she felt Paolo's eyes that were watching her. She quickly rubbed her hand across her face and dusted some of the flour away. Flora couldn't brush Paolo's burning stare away that easily. She could barely look at him. Flora was afraid she would see what she tried to talk herself into not ever seeing again. The shock of his presence made her laugh at her futile resolution. At that moment in the kitchen, it seemed as if they had never really left Florence...and that her feelings for Paolo were even more real than she remembered.

"The drive up here was beautiful, Michigan is huge...the map your father made was really easy to follow." Paolo tried to break the silly silence that was wearing on both of them.

Flora's funny face made it almost impossible for Paolo

not to laugh out loud. He hoped Flora would say some-thing, but she was stubborn...and she didn't.

"*Stefano* couldn't wait to get up here...I can't blame him...," Paolo said as he snitched a pinch of cinnamon sugar while looking sideways at Flora. Flora caught his sneaky fingers and his side glance. That made her finally smile a *genuine* smile.

"I can't blame him either...I always thought that when two people were in love...not even distance or the great wall of China itself could get in their way...Stefano is young but he's a darn smart guy for his age." Flora stopped at that and Paolo knew exactly what she meant. She offered him another taste of cinnamon. Paolo took Flora up on her kindness and thanked her with a quick kiss on the cheek.

Paolo had alot to talk over with Flora. He realized what a shock it must have been for her to see him at the cottage. He decided to go down to the beach to give her some time alone. Paolo walked toward the door. Before he opened it, he turned around.

"Save me a few minutes tonight...I've got to talk to you...and *don't burn the buns.*" Flora looked up from the table and smiled at him. She knew in her heart that she would save him all the time he needed.

Flora could barely function after the door closed behind Paolo. She couldn't believe how such a grand obstacle like *resentment* could dissolve so quickly. With just a stolen pinch of cinnamon sugar and a twinkle from Paolo's eye, Flora found her heart smiling again.

Chapter
twenty-two

More Falling Stars

"You guys bring the good weather with you every year...honest, before yesterday, we had *seven* gray days in a row...you can ask Mary...seven completely overcast days, and that's unusual up here...one more gray day and I was going to head back down to Chicago." Bruno poked Mary as he finished his evening summary on the weather conditions of the Upper Peninsula.

Flora was fortunate to have Bruno and Mary as neighbors. Back in Chicago they were school teachers. In the summer they relinquished their city home and teaching responsibilities to become small town dwellers...beach bums... *boat potatoes*. Summer was a time to be hassle free and full of whatever moved them. Their son, Matt, would always have a special place in Flora's heart; he made her watch for things in the sky.

Supper on the grill always turned out great. Anything grilled, even potatoes ,tasted extra good in the North country.

The sun set that evening through the pines behind the bar-b-que pit. Flora watched Paolo enjoy the family around the fire. Mary noticed her expression and knew there was more to this guy *Paolo* than his being a cousin to Stefano.

"Flora...wait up, I'll help with dessert." Mary followed Flora up to the house with some dirty dishes.

"Thanks for carrying the dishes up, Mary...I think the coffee pot is ready to go...let's see, if you want to get the cream out of the refrig...I'll frost the cake." Flora went into the kitchen drawer to get a spatula.

"Those hamburgers tasted great tonight," Mary said as she opened the refrigerator door, "...I think I ate three...actually two and a half...I couldn't ignore Flopsey's begging eyes...do you want me to fill a pitcher of milk for the kids?"

"That's a good idea...maybe we'll bring out the fruit bowl, too...I'm so glad it warmed up today, the kids are having a great time."

"Flora, if you don't mind me asking...where on earth did *Stefano* come from...he looks like the guy on the cover of GQ...Tracey really seems to *like* him."

"I think it's more than *likes*, Mary...I think she's in love with him...don't say anything to Matt or Eric...hey, they probably already know, news travels fast up here... ."

"It must be the *whispering pines* that divulge all our secrets...," Mary said under her breath but loud enough for Flora to hear.

"Yup...I think it is the pine trees... ." Flora smiled at her friend's wise face. As Flora took the frosting knife out of the bowl, she looked sheepishly at Mary.

"The other day one told me that Tracey and Stefano are sort of...*engaged*."

"*Sort of* engaged...when did this happen?" Mary asked in complete shock.

"While we were in Florence...back in February." Flora looked up at Mary who seemed to be in shock for a couple of seconds.

"Who could blame him?" Mary shook her head in bewilderment. "But...*marriage*...it seems like *everyone* fell in love in Florence...Matt was telling me about little Flora and a cousin of the S and S boys."

"Oh...you mean Giacamo," Flora said with a question

in her voice. Mary nodded.

"Oh Giacamo...he was a good friend to little Flora, but you know, she's still going with Dan... ."

*"All is fair in love and war...*does he have *money?"* Mary ran her finger across the rim of the frosting bowl and licked it. She carefully went on with more questions...hoping to get honest and direct answers.

"Have Tracey and Stefano set a marriage date...will it be in Florence...I hope I'm not being nosy or out of line asking so many personal questions...but I feel like I'm part of the family...like an Aunt."

"Mary...you could never ask too many questions...but you might end up eating all the icing...you're not being nosy either...the girls love you and consider you part of the family...like a big sister...they tell you everything up here...so if you hear anything I should know, please fill me in...got it?" Flora and Mary laughed.

Everything Flora said was true. Mary was very dear to all them.

"Now that I know how much I'm part of the family...what about *Paolo?* Who the heck is he?...don't take me wrong...he seems like a nice guy...he's pretty good looking...was he born in Italy...he has no accent...in fact, I'd never guess that he wasn't born and raised right here...how does he fit in this whole Italian plot to marry off all the Bolone girls...? Why is the dude here? Please don't tell me he's waiting for Emily?" Mary grabbed Flora's hand and continued.

"Remember our pact, Emily will be *Eric's* bride...one day." Mary laughed...but not too hard.

"Mary, we'll talk about that tomorrow on the beach...I think everyone must be wondering where the dessert is...and the kids wanted to have their own bonfire down on the beach." Flora was grateful Emily came up with the message from Bruno to *get the lead out.*

"Okay, Emily...you carry the fruitbowl...and Mary, you

take the coffee pot down and I'll get the tray...here we go!"

Flora knew that Mary could have gone on and on and Flora would have enjoyed filling her in on the details of *who was who from where and why*...but she wanted to make sure Paolo was okay.

When Flora placed the tray of goodies on the picnic table she caught Paolo looking at her. He gave her a quick wink and went on listening to Bruno's tales from *high school hell*. Everyone got a kick from Bruno's stories. It was a good night.

One by one the kids excused themselves and headed down to the beach. Even Jimmy and Emily, who normally were so content sitting with the big people, *flew the coop*. That left Mary and Bruno and Paolo and Flora by the fire alone. It was awkward at first. It took a few minutes to get used to the silence.

"So, Paolo," Mary asked with gusto, "...how do you like the United States...or rather, Michigan?"

"I love the United States...I lived in New York for a while and then only visited the eastern States...I was never this far north or west...it's very beautiful."

Bruno asked where Paolo lived in New York and if he knew this person and that place. Bruno held the floor with the story of his coming to America from Lithuania and seeing the Statue of Liberty for the first time. Bruno's voice and his mannerisms made Paolo feel right at home.

Flora was learning about Paolo, too, that night. It was a relaxed atmosphere considering no one but Flora knew what to make of the stranger, although Mary had a pretty good idea. Bruno made sure no one's wine glass emptied...and that no one's mind went unentertained.

Mary kept any lull in conversation short...she had a hundred and one questions. So did Flora.

"What are you doing now, Paolo, back in Florence?" Mary asked the question but Flora was anxious herself to hear what he had to say.

"I'm in construction...and I do a little bit of this and that... ." Before Paolo could elaborate, Mary anxiously interrupted him.

"What are some of the *this* and *thats...if you don't mind me asking...*?" Mary threw another log on the fire. Flora smiled hard at Mary for being the character she was.

"*Mary*...the poor guy might just want to relax...," Bruno said admonishingly. He was the diplomat in the family.

"No, no, no," Paolo said sincerely, "...that's okay...I don't mind." Paolo looked at Flora and then went on.

"Right now I'm building an orphanage, I've had this big idea in my head for years, and finally last winter everything jelled and started taking shape. It's really off to a great start...in fact, the exterior is completed and the kitchen and bathroom facilities were practically finished before I left." Flora couldn't believe the building was that close to completion. It made her feel the great lapse of time between March and July. She listened to Paolo's every word, imagining every detail.

"The painting and the simple decorating will be done at a much slower pace...as long as the game room and library are set by the end of September...that's when Fr. Cellini will transfer the boys from St. Gregorio's to San Miniato."

Flora was glad to hear about the progress on the orphanage. She wanted to ask him about Br. Georgio, then Bruno asked another question.

"You sound like a busy guy, Paolo...what made you become interested in a big project like this in the first place?"

Mary suddenly blurted out, "You look more like the type to be building VIC TANNIES all over the place."

Flora watched Paolo's expression wanting to see if he took Mary's words the right way. She wasn't sure if he understood Mary's humor...or the way she *stream of con - scioused* her compliments. Paolo understood the compliment. His eyes were smiling.

Paolo didn't want to go into his reasons for the orphanage right then. He hadn't even shared that with Flora yet. But, Bruno's sincerity and Mary's personality made Paolo feel like that was the right time to go into it. He began his story looking at Bruno, then Mary. When he came to the part about Roberto, he fixed all of his attention on Flora.

"And when the little boy was given to his distant relatives...I knew there had to be a better way."

Flora knew *Roberto* was Francesca's son. Francesca *was* in love with Paolo, but he was more in love with his vocation. He loved her in his own way, but couldn't give up the priesthood for her.

One night, Francesca left Paolo in a panic. She sped away down the hill and slid off the road into a tree. She was killed and Roberto was snatched out of Paolo's life, only to be neglected and abused. Paolo left the priesthood when the Bishop wouldn't allow him to adopt Roberto. Flora felt numb inside after hearing so many private insights about the man she thought she knew so well. Paolo went on.

"Roberto lived with me till he was thirteen. Brother Georgio helped me out when I had to go out of town on business. I was working all the time, so when Roberto's best friend was being sent to a private high school in New York...I thought the best thing for Roberto, would be to go along. He loved the idea and that's when I made New York my part time home for a few years."

"How old is he now?" Flora asked, completely caught up in his story.

"He'll be twenty-one in September...in fact he'll be coming to the University in Florence for his graduate work about a week before his birthday."

There was silence. It was getting late and Bruno had to get up early for walleyed-pike fishing the next day. Bruno nudged Mary and that was her cue to head up for bed. They had a nice evening...and it was time to call it a day.

Paolo moved over by Flora and they sat for a while not

saying anything. Neither one of them wanted to say a single word. Flora heard so much that night and understood alot more about Paolo's past life. Paolo was hoping he didn't say too much. So much more had to be said.

The fire was warm and the glow from the large embers was comforting. Flora knew Paolo's life didn't start on the day they met. She loved him for what he was to her that wonderful stay last winter. She hoped he loved her for what she was to him.

"Catch a falling star...?" Flora thought they had enough heavy duty questioning. The stars were magnificent and brought Flora back to that special night when she knew she loved him.

Paolo looked up at the sky and breathed a heavy sigh. He was tired, but more in love. He put his arms around Flora and looked into her eyes, then kissed her.

"I couldn't help myself...I wanted to do that for a long time, Flora."

"I've wanted to kiss you for a long time," Flora said sincerely. She turned away from Paolo and looked into the fire hoping that would bring her halfway back to earth.

"Paolo, we're really not this nosy...I hope you didn't mind the hundred questions."

"No...I think it's flattering to have people ask about your life...especially friends of a good friend...Mary and Bruno seem like good people...I'm glad they're your neighbors."

"You made me feel at home in Florence...we did become good friends, didn't we?" Flora's composure went to pieces with her last comment. Tears came into her eyes, she tried to hide them.

Paolo leaned over toward Flora, slowly he bent his head down and kissed her tenderly.

"I'm sorry, Flora...I know I hurt you...if I could take it all back...I would...it was wrong for me to leave you the way I did... ." Flora looked forgivingly into Paolo's eyes. She didn't let Paolo finish.

"I'm sorry...for everything...I should have been more reasonable...but, I've come to the conclusion that some-things just can't be figured...like the time we spent togeth-er, it was good for both of us...then, we all had to get back to things the way they were...I understand that now." Flora stood up and walked by the fire.

There were many things to talk over, but now would-n't be the time for big discussions. The stars were shining and love was so full in their hearts. Flora and Paolo were feeling the past months loneliness and they needed to feel each other again.

Paolo took Flora in his arms and held her tightly. He kissed her with his entire being. Flora kissed him back ten-derly, then passionately...giving herself completely to him.

"Let's go for a walk on the beach," Flora said, not real-ly wanting to end their embrace but feeling as if things were moving too quickly. She felt his passion which made her forget about everything else on the entire earth. Flora took Paolo's hand and led him toward the cottage. She looked at the cottage and decided to forget the walk on the beach. Inside they could be alone.

"What happened to the walk on the beach...?" Paolo said innocently as they climbed the wooden porch steps. Flora opened the door.

"It's pretty nice in here...and...we could be alone for a while," Flora said teasingly. "Seriously, I think we could both use a cup of hot tea."

"Tea sounds good... ." Paolo swooped Flora into his arms and carried her inside.

When the cottage door closed it was as if Paolo and Flora had been snapped out of a dream. He set her down gently in the kitchen. Maybe it was all the reminders of ear-lier days for Flora, and for Paolo, the awareness that he wasn't in the kitchen at the pensione. He was on Jack's premises. As much as they both wanted to begin their future together, that wouldn't be the time or place. Flora knew that. Paolo felt it, too.

"I rented a cottage at the Inn up the road before Stefano and I came here this afternoon. In fact, Stefano has to come back with me...I know that will make your sister feel better...I know it will make my Aunt feel better...and it's the way it's suppose to be."

Paolo hugged Flora. She was glad he had made proper arrangements. They sat on the loveseat and talked about the orphanage. Flora was happy to hear how much it progressed. Flora could visualize the building and could picture a tiny nightlight softly glowing from every window.

What they didn't talk about made them understand that life was a winding road and their journey had once again taken another wonderful turn. The clock chimed midnight.

"I know they're going to kill me when I drag Stefano away from the fire...but it's late...we'll have tea tomorrow." Paolo brought Flora closer to himself. He felt good holding her. Flora could have stayed in his arms forever.

"These past few months were crazy...I can't even begin to tell you how much I missed you, Flora." Paolo took a deep breath and then got up from the loveseat. He took Flora's hand and helped her up. He walked slowly to the kitchen door. They stood facing each other, neither one wanting to say goodnight. Flora finally spoke.

"I'm so glad you came...," Flora said softly. With one foot out the door Paolo turned to Flora.

"I still can't believe I'm finally here...pinch me."

Flora squeezed his hand and then kissed him on his rough cheek. His twenty-four hour whiskers felt good to Flora. Paolo kissed her on her forehead.

"I'll see you tomorrow...," Flora said in a whisper. She watched Paolo walk till the darkness made him disappear. As if in a trance, she went to bed.

While lying awake and with the sound of the waves

from over the dunes, Flora thanked God for the wonderful surprise that had come to her that day. Flora had strong feelings for the man from Florence. She knew she loved him very much; this man who stole her heart in a few seconds of time. Flora was anxious for morning to come.

Chapter
twenty-three

Tears In The Sand

Flora heard something on the deck. She was curious about the noise but not curious enough to even think of opening her eyes.

She wasn't sleeping very sound. When the noise stopped, it replayed in her mind. That replaying echo finally woke her up and made her wonder if she had imagined it in the first place. She rolled over and tried to fall back to sleep. Then, Flora heard the noise again. Something or someone was definitely out there.

Flora slowly got out from her bed and walked over to the doorwall. She carefully pulled the heavy floral drapes back and stood behind them. She looked around thinking a raccoon would suddenly pop into the picture and solve the mystery of the noise.

Then, Flora saw Paolo struggling to climb over the rough cedar deck railing. Their eyes met. Paolo motioned for Flora to come outside. She was relieved that it wasn't some strange wild animal. Seeing Paolo trying to squeeze between the rail made her smile. She wondered why Paolo would be there at such an early hour. It was 6:00 a.m. But for Paolo it would be like 12:00 noon. Maybe, he couldn't sleep.

"What are you doing here?" Flora said as she quickly combed her fingers through her wild morning hair. How good it was to see him, she thought.

Paolo jumped off the deck and reached for Flora to jump. She jumped and fell...not into his strong arms, but into the sand. She giggled softly while brushing the excess sand from her flannel nightgown. Paolo smiled hard at the falling lady and then politely shushed her with his finger. He took Flora's hand and together they walked to the beach.

It was a beautiful time of morning. The sky was purple with a hint of deep rose in the East where the sun would be coming up soon. The lake had stilled, becoming so smooth it looked more like a mirror than a majestic fresh water sea. Flora loved the early mornings in the North. The sky...and the lake always said so much to her.

"To think we sleep through all this beauty...the Chinese have the right idea." Flora was talking in a whisper yet straining her voice so Paolo could hear her. Sound carried far on mornings when the lake was still.

Paolo snuck in a quick kiss.

"That's one more reason why I love you," Paolo said looking very carefully into Flora's eyes. "Which way do you want to go?"

Flora nodded east with a tilt of her head. "The sky is too wonderful to put behind us, Paolo."

Paolo smiled at Flora and they walked for a while very contented in each other's company. Finally, Flora thought it was time to ask a few questions.

"What's the matter Paolo...couldn't you sleep?" Flora was hoping to hear something flattering but Paolo's expression looked too pensive for that kind of frivolity.

"I slept for a while...but I have too many things on my mind," Paolo said squeezing Flora's hand tightly. They walked for quite a distance longer keeping silent...like the great lake that morning. Flora squeezed Paolo's hand tightly back.

"I called Vince last night when I got back to my room,"

Paolo said as he stopped in his tracks. He put his hands on Flora's shoulders and continued. He looked deeply into her eyes.

"I wanted to hear how things were going and to let him know Stefano and I arrived in one piece, Stefano's mother is the most protective mother I ever met...so my father was worried for her. When Dolly said he couldn't come to the phone I knew something was up. She said he was feeling sick all day and that if he wasn't feeling any better by tomorrow, she was going to take him to the doctor. He had to be really feeling awful...for him not to come to the phone...and heaven knows he would only think of going to the doctor if he was near death...if that...so I thought about him all night. Then about five thirty, the phone rang...it was Dolly. She didn't want to upset me but I could tell from her tone that something was up...then she told me that she brought my Dad to the hospital...I've got to go back."

"When will you leave?" Flora was as upset with the news about Vince as Paolo was. She touched Paolo's cheek with her hand and told him not to worry

"I'm trying not to...anyway, I called the airline...and the first flight available is at three forty-five this afternoon. I'll leave here about nine o'clock.

That will give me plenty of time to drop off the car and pick up my ticket...I'm scared Flora...if anything happens to him before I get there...I...don't even want to think about it... ." Paolo took steps away from Flora.

"Nothing is going to happen...your Dad is strong...and... ." Flora couldn't finish her sentence. She saw strong men die before. Vince became real in her mind and she remembered how good he was to her and the kids. He couldn't die...he was too young...Paolo needed him. She thought of Bubba and how empty life would be without him. They both realized how unpredictable life was and how in a moment everything could change.

There was a huge log on the beach. Paolo sat Flora

down on it. Paolo sat next to her and folded his hands while looking down at the sand beneath his feet. He stared at the sand as if needing to count every grain.

"Do you want me to go with you?" Flora asked. She wasn't sure about anything, but she felt that it was her place to be there for Paolo...and Dolly. Paolo didn't answer her right away. Flora thought her invitation seemed, all of a sudden, very dumb.

"No...you've got your hands full up here...you stay and take care of the kids...it might just be something he ate." Paolo was trying to be optimistic but his doubts quivered through his tone.

Flora hoped Paolo's words would be true. But, deep in her heart she believed there was more to Paolo's sudden need to be there than just a case of indigestion in Vince; he wouldn't be flying home because his father had a stomach ache. Paolo loved his father dearly and sensed something more serious was going on.

"Let's go back and I'll make you some coffee...I can wrap up something for the trip back to the airport, it's a long drive when you're alone?"

"Thanks Flora...but I couldn't eat now or drink any-thing...just be here with me till I have to leave."

Paolo's hands were like ice and there was a look in his eyes Flora had never seen before. He was scared. She put her arms around him and felt his inner chill. She began rub-bing the sides of his arms to make his blood circulate...to make his goosebumps go away. He rested his head in his hands. He wouldn't look up, but Flora knew his eyes had filled with tears. She saw them drop to the sand.

"Paolo...come here and rest...put your head on my lap." Flora made the log her back support and sat in the sand. She took off her chenille robe and made a pillow for Paolo by placing it on her lap.

"Don't let me fall asleep," Paolo said as he stretched out on the beach. He nestled his head on Flora's robe pillow.

"Let's talk about us...," Paolo said as he looked up at Flora. He coaxed her with his eyes. She thought it was a good idea to keep their focus off Vince...for a while anyway.

"You and me...we are *so* boring...you said you didn't want me to let you fall asleep...if I talk about us, we'll both be sleeping here in five minutes." Flora wanted to make Paolo laugh...or at least smile.

"Hey, *I'm* not boring...well, maybe a little?" Paolo picked up a handful of sand and slowly sprinkled it into Flora's hair.

"Now a boring guy would never think of doing that...would he, Flora?"

"No...I've got to admit, *only* a real nut would dare tamper with a woman's hairdo...especially this woman's...you know it takes me *hours* to perfect the look I want." They both laughed.

Paolo looked like himself again. He sat up and tried to shake out the mess he made in Flora's hair. Flora didn't care about the sand...she'd have eaten it if it would have made Paolo feel better.

"I'm not sure if I'm discovering something here...your hair...it...it looks terrific!" Paolo tried to keep the joke going. It was good to see him laugh. He stood up and began tossing stones in the lake.

"Flora...I wish I had my wish back...you know...the one I made in front of you and the stars at San Miniato?...I wished for you...now I'd wish that I would have met you twenty-three years ago, and that we...," Paolo couldn't finish his sentence...it all seemed so childish to him now. Flora knew his thoughts...she had the same. But she, like Paolo knew that no one could go back...the best anyone could do, was to go forward...happy. That's what Flora was trying to do. Paolo continued.

"Time is kind of weird, isn't it...it moves too fast...then, it seems like it moves too slow...when something like this happens...it makes you feel the reality of it all...we're so cocky...what makes us think that we call all the shots." Paolo kicked around the sand. He went over to Flora and helped her up from the sand. They started walking again. He held her hand.

"Flora...I want you in my life...this whole trip was suppose to be about us...and...now...I can't keep things in perspective...I just don't like the perspective I'm feeling...it isn't fair of me to put you on this...stupid roller coaster ride."

The sun was just about to dawn. The sky was vivid scarlet, and it's colors were reflected on the quiet lake...it looked like a dream. It affected Flora deeply. Paolo was making her think about the future...Vince was making her think about time, the sky made her think of God. All three made her realize that everything has it's time. But, love...love is always in season and it's always there to give.

Flora gave her love to Paolo knowing one day she'd probably have to say good-bye, maybe for good. But she put that thought way back in her mind.

In the beginning it was easy for Flora to tell herself that she was enjoying a special time that she deserved. But, as she grew more and more fond of Paolo and when she sensed he was feeling the same way, it became difficult for her to pretend that they were just being good company for each other and that it wasn't going to last forever. In her heart she knew her love for him was going to last forever.

"Paolo...I want to be with you...now and for whatever moments God gives us...even if they're few and far between."

They walked for a few steps in silence. Flora continued.

"I won't think about anything else but today...and you being here right now...we waste too much time thinking about tomorrow." Flora felt the extra pressure that was on them at that moment. She wanted to keep an atmosphere they both could handle, no matter what was going to be tossed into their lives that day.

Paolo was listening so Flora went on with the thoughts

that were on her mind.

"I feel like a hypocrite sometimes, Paolo...I loved Jack...he gave me five wonderful kids and I love them so much. He took alot of guff...gave up alot of the things he could have had if he had married someone else...someone he truly loved. He didn't really love me...and he wouldn't let me love him...and the worse part of this whole thing is that maybe *I never really loved him enough*...you know, unconditionally...at first I did...it was easy...but after a while I could feel things changing...I always thought my love would be enough for both of us... ." Flora felt herself going in circles, and she was confused. The sky was making her feel things that maybe were too real to ignore, but too painful to see right then. The sky was changing, so was her world. And...Paolo was leaving, again.

Paolo listened to Flora and heard exactly what she was saying. Her words made him think of his own guilt and how painful it was getting through it.

"I understand what you are saying...love isn't easy...and forget putting it into words...all I know right now is that I love you... ." Paolo was very serious.

"Flora, before I came yesterday...I thought of you and me...being together. I couldn't get that thought out of my mind. I wasn't sure of how that was going to come about...but I knew that it would. I loved Francesca but not with my entire body and soul...and that's what it has to be...love is completely selfless. I was young and gallant and too much into myself, I thought I'd change the world...I thought I could mold Francesca into a kind of image that would make her more worthy of my special love...I thought with time, she would come to understand my relationship with God...and my commitment to him...I thought I'd be able to handle anything that came up...I didn't count on Francesca loving me the way she did. I couldn't even understand that kind of beautiful love...I was a blind fool when it came to understanding the way

Francesca loved me. Her love was pure and complete...the greatest kind of love there is...love to me then, was regimental and very rigid and I had to understand it...it had to make sense completely...I was very firm in my beliefs... ." Paolo took a deep breath and continued.

"I wanted Francesca to get her life straight for her little boy, Roberto...he's why we met in the firstplace...do you mind me talking about this?" Paolo looked into Flora's eyes.

"I'd like to hear more...if you feel comfortable talking about it... ."Flora smiled at Paolo. Paolo smiled back and continued.

"It was brought to Fr. Cellini's attention that young Roberto was being left alone while his mother worked at night. Francesca was a maid for a wealthy family in Fiesole. When she worked late and the babysitter had to leave early, Roberto would be left all alone in his bed. One night a neighbor found Roberto wandering the countryside... *alone*. I went to talk to Francesca about her situation and she was very honest. She told me she was doing the best she could in her predicament, she had no family to help her out. I went and spoke to the Galino family and they made arrangements for her and Roberto on the nights she had to work late. Francesca felt she owed me her life...I didn't understand her affections.

"The night she was killed...a part of me died...and I blamed myself for her death...it was my fault...I watched her walk out of my room upset with the world...disheartened with me...*rejected* by me...I had some deep soul searching to do." Paolo paused for a moment and then continued.

"It killed me to see Roberto leaving in the arms of a complete stranger. I was ordained a year later and on that day I promised Francesca in my prayers that I would never loose sight of Roberto.

"So...I'd go visit him once or twice a month...I wasn't a

very welcomed guest and after a while I realized his new family didn't really even want *Roberto*...I couldn't leave him in such an unloving atmosphere...on one of my visits he cried to go back with me and the family just threw up their arms and packed up his bag and practically threw us out with a *good riddens*.

"When I was denied permission to adopt Roberto...I had to make a decision...that's when I left the priesthood and became Roberto's father."

Paolo and Flora had walked a couple of miles along the shore. Flora sat on the beach to rest. Paolo sat behind her very close and wrapped her in his arms. They looked into the great Lake.

"Flora, I believe in God...and I know everything that happens is for a purpose...I prayed every night that you'd be safe and that one day we'd be together...maybe I'm being selfish...wanting so much...so much that isn't mine...God knows how much I thought about you all these months...and how I dreamed of us being together...like right now...with you in my arms." Paolo broke his hold on Flora and stood up and walked around to the front of her, then knelt down and took her hands. He looked deep into her eyes and continued.

"You are so close to your family...would it be fair of me to take you away from all this and the people out love...I want Emily and Jimmy to be happy...and Jack...I just want you to be sure. I talked with Fr. Cellini before I came...he knows how much I love you...but he made some things clear...and cautioned me about my plans...I don't ever want to hurt you...I guess a part of me has never grown up...I want everyone in this situation to be happy... ." Paolo hoped Flora understood what he was saying.

"Paolo...there is so much to think about...somedays nothing makes sense, then there are the days like now. It hurts me to think of leaving so many of the people I love behind...but I'll never stop loving them...I'll never forget them...they will never forget me...but, without you...if I had to completely let go of you...my heart would break."

Flora didn't care if she sounded corny...she had to make Paolo understand her feelings. Flora paused. She waited to see if Paolo had anything to say. He looked away from her eyes and at the sky. The sun made his eyes well up with tears. Flora continued, holding Paolo's hands even tighter.

"We all want what's right and good, I worry about making the right decisions, how a bad one would affect everyone else around me...for a long time I convinced myself that I could be happy without Jack's love...so many other people loved me...but I cheated myself...I deceived myself. I wanted to be the rock...but I wore down...the past few years wore on my heart...I ran out of the strength it took to keep up such a strenuous position...I gave up...then, like a miracle...Dolly entered my life...her invitation to Florence turned everything upside down and made everything right side up...I met you, Paolo." Flora was upset but she had to get all the jumble that bounced around her mind out in the open. She let go of Paolo's hands and went on.

"Paolo...some days I feel like I betrayed love itself...I'm an *adulteress* Paolo...I feel guilty for having to admit to myself that I was wrong about alot of things, so wrong, that it makes loving you seem like a miracle...like something from heaven...shoving my true feelings under the carpet wasn't going to change how I felt about you...I didn't want to let go of something that precious because I was afraid or scared of making another mistake...instead, I decided to trust my heart again...and if I got hurt, oh well...I'd just have to take the pain...the love was there...I couldn't let it go."

"It was meant for both of us," Paolo quickly interjected, "...don't you think God knows what we all want from life...what we need....can't He bless us with special surprises? And I don't believe that stuff about not always getting what we want...God knew I needed you...I want you with me." Paolo paused for a moment to calm his peaked composure. He continued more mellow.

"Flora...have we grown up that much that we can't recognize a miracle when we see it? Our meeting in Florence was plotted by the angels!...why does there have to be a logical explanation for everything all the time...Flora...you aren't an adulteress because you were never really married to Jack...if anything, you were a *prostitute* those years...you sold yourself out for everything but love."

Paolo saw the surprised look on Flora's face. He tried to explain himself more clearly.

"Flora, you know I didn't mean it like that...I, of all people, have no right to call you anything...I was the blind pompous fool...the emotionally retarded idiot who preached love, yet didn't see it looking in my face...at least you tried...I was like Jack, a fool who couldn't see beyond the big nose on my face...then you came along and made me open my heart and really love...I never loved a person the way I love you...it scared me at first, Flora...it scares me now...but I feel your confidence and trust...Flora, I don't know what's going to happen right now...but I do know that I want you in my life, I want to be a part of your life." Paolo took Flora's hand and they headed back to the cottage.

Flora felt Paolo's strength in the firm grip he had on her hand. It was good to have him by her side. The walk ended too soon for them. Flora wished they had taken two steps back for every step forward. She thought somehow, that would have taken them back to where they started.

Paolo felt sick inside knowing he had to leave Flora but his watch told him it was time to go. They walked up the steep driveway not saying a word. As they approached his car Paolo stopped and hugged Flora. Flora didn't want to cry...but she couldn't keep back her tears.

"I'm sorry Paolo...I'll pray that everything turns out well for Vince...be careful."

Paolo wiped the tears from Flora's cheeks.

"Flora...I love you." Paolo wanted to say more but he was too aware of the time and his mind kept drifting back home to Vince. For a second he felt Vince had already left him, that he was already an orphan. As much as Paolo tried to shake that horrible feeling, it lingered deep in his gut.

Paolo headed down the road. He caught the rear view mirrored reflection of Flora waving good-bye. He wanted to throw the car in reverse and back up. Vince would understand his delay. Instead, Paolo drove off confused and upset.

Seeing Flora in the mirror made Paolo think of the day when he met up with her on the Ponte Vecchio. They talked about so many things that day. He remembered how they couldn't stop talking...they didn't want that afternoon to end. Paolo didn't want their morning to end.

Flora walked back down the driveway. She noticed how green the leaves on the birch trees were. Almost fluorescent in the morning light. The only things left of Paolo's short visit were his tire prints in the driveway, the dust his car kicked back in the air, and the hole he left in Flora's heart.

Flora went back to the cottage and started getting breakfast ready. She kept thinking of what she'd tell the kids when they got up. As Flora filled the tea kettle with water, she saw Mary walking over the lawn to the porch. Flora walked over to the door and let Mary in.

"Gosh, it's quiet in here...the older the kids get the later they sleep in the morning...one of the *perks* of having teenagers." Flora smiled at Mary's quick anecdote, then went over to the stove and started the tea water brewing.

"Flora, I saw Paolo's car in the drive when Bruno left for fishing this morning. I thought he went to the Inn with Stefano last night." Mary wasn't being nosy, she was just concerned. Flora thought it was time to fill her in on a few things about Paolo. Mary would understand, and Flora needed someone to talk to.

"Mary...," Flora hesitated, then went on, "...he did go with Stefano...but he couldn't sleep so he came over earlier to walk on the beach." Flora wanted to tell Mary about her relationship with the man from Florence, so she continued.

"Mary, Paolo is a good, good friend to me...even more than a friend...we met in Florence...we sort of hung around together...he showed me so many neat things and POOF!"

"Poof?" Mary asked mimicking Flora's descriptive word. Flora paused for a moment then continued.

"You know...*poof* as in *it happened quick*...from out of nowhere... ." Flora was actually blushing. Mary sat motionless...and speechless. Flora carefully continued.

"I don't know what else to say, Mary...my whole world is literally upside down right now...Paolo had to fly back to Florence...he got a phone call early this morning and found out his father was in the hospital. Vince is like my dad...he's strong...God I hope everything is good." Flora poured the steaming tea into their cups.

"Mary, want a piece of toast...or a chocolate chip cookie?" Flora invited Mary to take a cookie from the green glass jar.

"No, no...this tea is fine," Mary said as she looked at the glass jar full of cookies. "I won't be able to eat just one...it is tempting...but... ." Mary quickly returned her attention to Flora. "Flora...are you going to be alright?"

"I'll be fine," Flora said, hoping to make Mary believe her words more than she believed them. "I'm just...you know, a little wound up from Paolo's visit...he and his father are so close... ."

"Hey, don't worry...*look on the bright side!*" Mary's voice sounded gruff. But, Flora knew Mary was very compassionate.

"You say to look on the bright side...it's not so easy, is it, Mary?" Flora didn't wait for Mary to respond. She went on.

"Like our lives are flashed before us a page at a time, like on WHEEL OF FORTUNE...only instead of a letter missing...words are missing...and we're always trying to figure out the story. Like, today's page would have dealt with *unex - pected* things...like *Paolo's coming here, Stefano's coming here, and the news about Vince*...we don't have to worry about the next page...we only have to understand today... ." Flora paused.

"What's the matter Flora?...why did you stop...and why are you looking at me like that?

"Like what?"

"I don't know..., " Mary said as she stirred her tea. "Your nose was starting to get all squinched...and your eyes were intense...I was just getting into your spiel."

"Mary, I'm sorry...it's just that your face made me realize how I was going *on* and *on*...and I didn't want to bore you."

"Bore me?...not yet," Mary said as she smiled a wicked grin, "...but you know I'll let you know when you do...Flora...are you sure you never taught PHILOSOPHY 101?"

"You should have told me to shut up when I gave you the chance... ." Flora chuckled as she poured more tea into Mary's cup. "I get like this sometimes...you know...a little rambly... ."

"Na...you never *ramble*...you simply *filibuster*... ."

"FILIBUSTER?" Flora laughed at Mary's descriptiveness, "...wow...I haven't heard that word since high school."

"And that's been a *real* long time." Mary sat back in her chair with a big smile on her face. "God...I'm good."

"You are," Flora said thoroughly enjoying her friends mellowness. Mary quickly sat up, with a more serious expression. Mary continued.

"I think alot of it...is our age...I think the older we get the more we doubt what our hearts are telling us...and that's sad...instead of becoming more wise and believing in ourselves...we begin to *doubt* things...big things...you'd think Oprah, Donohue, Geraldo, even Dr. Ruth would devote an afternoon to BELIEVING IN THE POWER OF ONE'S HEART...I suppose no one would watch, not *gruesome* enough I guess...how did I get on this subject?" Mary didn't really want an answer to that question. She went on.

"Sometimes we're *blinded* by the ways of the world...I'm glad you weren't...Flora, I'm happy for you...I'm glad you fell in love in Florence...we're suppose to live and love, every single day...what did Robin Williams tell his class...oh yeah...CARPET DEMI...no wait, that's what he told Bruce Willis...anyway, you know what I mean."

"You mean CARPE DIEM," Flora asked with a chuckle.

"Yeah...that's it...anyway, that's what we are suppose to do." Mary's words made sense to Flora. Flora knew Mary was right...and she was grateful for her kind words of encouragement. They stirred their teacups in unison. Mary continued her thoughts on the matter while she gazed into her swirling tea.

"You don't want to worry the kids...especially Sebastiano and Stefano...Vince is their...*uncle*?" Mary said as she snapped out of her tea-swirling stupor.

"Vince is their *favorite* Uncle, that's another big thing...we'll just have to wait for Paolo's call." Flora said feeling half drained.

"You gave him my number I hope...I'll try to stick close to the house today, just in case." Mary was very considerate.

"Mary, thanks...you might not have to worry about today though...he'll probably be calling sometime early tomorrow morning...I figure around six o'clock. He won't get to Rome until way after midnight...then, if he connects right away with the train...that's another hour and a half to Florence...well, anyway it won't be until tomorrow before we hear from him...and today if you don't mind me using your phone again...I'll call and order a phone for the cottage...we've put it off long enough...it's time to hook one up...you and Bruno have been very kind and accommodating... ." Flora squeezed Mary's hand to make sure she understood her sincere appreciation.

"Hey...no trouble...we got to hear all the news as it happened...and every time I had to deliver a message I always got to sample dinner simmering on the stove." Mary squeezed Flora's hand back.

"A trip to Florence," Mary continued in her robust way, "...and this gosh darn commotion! Was it worth it?" Mary threw her arms in the air and grabbed a cookie on the way down. She continued as she bit into the chocolate chip cookie.

"God...these *are* good...Flora...I'm only kidding of course about the commotion...but think about it...two nieces just about ready to bite the dust without even considering *my* two guys, who have been in your own backyard...but isn't that the way it goes...*the grass is always green - er...* ."

"Mary...you are my saving grace today...before you came over I felt like the world was falling apart...now it feels like maybe it won't...thanks."

"I'm here for you Flora if you need me." Flora knew Mary would always be there for her, she was like a sister. Mary didn't want to keep things so serious. She quickly went back to typical *Mary* conversation.

"Yesterday I bought a bunch...I mean a *huge* bunch of really ripe bananas...remember how many we went through last summer in the muffins and cake...I gained twelve pounds last summer all because of you Bolone's...talking about *big banana's*...what about Jack...will he be coming up this year...?" Mary winked at Flora. Flora laughed at Mary's analogy.

"The *big banana* would never miss his summer time up here with the kids and *you* and *Bruno* and the Dacy dudes...Jack will be up around the same time as Irene and her boys."

"Don't mind this next question...and you don't have to

answer it...but is this *separation* thing legal?...I mean have you and Jack taken legal steps toward a divorce? Gosh...how can I ask this more gently? It must be rough on him, too...tell me to shut-up, Flora."

"*BE QUIET MARY,*" Flora said teasingly, at least half teasingly. "Jack is handling it well...I think my family is taking it worse...it's a sad thing, Mary, for everyone...I've disappointed more than a few people... ." Flora looked at Mary trying to hide the tears that instantly welled in her eyes. Mary quickly changed the subject.

"Okay...okay...we'll talk about the kids...um, how is Irene handling Tracey's romance...and Rose with Christina's foreign fling...I still can't believe it...two of the prettiest girls in *Michigan* marrying some foreign *Italians*...you know Flora, I smacked Matt on the head last night for letting Tracey get away...how did he know some Italian hunk was going to rob the cradle...how old is he anyway?" Mary poured more tea into their cups.

Flora smiled at Mary.

"Stefano is twenty-three...a wonderful age to get married." Flora cut the conversation short when Sebastiano walked into the kitchen.

"*Good morning,* Flora...*good morning,* Mary," Sebastiano said as he walked toward the kitchen cupboard for a coffee mug. "I didn't want to sleep in this late...but we were up until about *three o'clock*...we were going to come up at midnight when Stefano left with Paolo...but the night was beautiful and the fire was *too* romantic...how could we let all that go to the wind." Sebastiano smiled at the two smirking women.

"You're not in *love* or anything, are you Sebby," Mary asked with a huge grin on her face.

"No...he's not in love... ." Flora smiled at Sebastiano as she filled his mug with fresh hot coffee.

"Well, maybe just a little bit...," Sebastiano said as he took a sip of coffee.

Chapter
twenty-four

Good News

That sunny day, full of gloomy faces, dragged. Sebastiano and Christina walked the beach all day and well into the evening. Sebastiano and Stefano were anxious to hear from Paolo. They were as patient as any two young Italian men in their situation could be. They had to weather it out like everyone else. But, everyone else didn't have a sick Godfather in the hospital. Zio Vicenzo was very dear to them.

Flora wrote to Fr. Bill that afternoon. She confessed her love for Paolo in the letter and hoped he would understand. After the letter, Flora thought she'd better unpack her suitcase. But, a strange feeling passed through her when she tossed the old bag on the bed. Maybe it was the *ALITALIA* tag that triggered her uneasiness. Flora quickly stashed it back in the closet. She didn't want to tempt fate.

Later on that evening, Flora excused herself from kids bonfire; the stars reminded her too much of Paolo.

Emily and Jimmy asked to stay down on the beach and enjoy the fire with the gang. Flora gave her permission with one condition; when little Flora said it was *time for bed...they had to listen.* They agreed.

The next morning came with no interruptions during the night. Flora felt that was a good sign; *no* news meaning *good* news. Then as she heated the griddle for pancakes,

Mary's son, Eric, knocked on the door.

"There's a phone call for you," Eric said conscientiously. Flora couldn't read Eric's face, but her heart dropped. She wondered if she should wake up Sebastiano...she decided to let him sleep. Flora turned off the griddle and followed Eric.

As Flora walked across the dewy lawn to Mary's cottage she thought of Paolo and his tears in the sand. Flopsey barked at her when she went inside to the kitchen.

Mary handed Flora the phone and then politely went back to plucking the shriveled petunias off her well groomed plants. "I'll be on the deck... ." Mary winked at Flora and walked out onto the deck.

"Hello, Paolo, how is everything?" Just hearing his voice made Flora feel better.

"Flora...Vince is doing fine...believe it or not...it was a case of *indigestion...severe* indigestion accentuated by stress...can you believe it?"

Flora was relieved, she sat down by the kitchen table, feeling her body begin to relax.

"Paolo...I'm so glad...I still can't believe it...thank God it was something that simple."

"I thank God everytime I think about it, Flora... how are you holding up?"

"I'm okay...I can't wait to tell the kids...how are you doing?"

"I'm completely wacked...I slept on and off the whole flight...when I missed the train I decided to take a taxi to the hospital, I was a nervous wreck...I should have called first because when I got there...they told me Vince had been discharged...I didn't believe it at first...it was too good to be true. All those nasty premonitions for nothing...God, I was relieved." Paolo unwound on the phone. Flora was content just to hear his voice.

"Flora, I wish I were back with you...hope I didn't cause too much havoc... ."

"Believe it or not, we were just saying how much commotion *your* coming here caused...," Flora said kiddingly. She heard him laugh. That made her smile.

"Really, Paolo...I'm glad you made it back safe and sound and that Vince is doing fine...tell him we all love him very much...and that we'll see him soon."

"I hope so...Flora...I've got to go to the pharmacy and pick up a few things for Vince...I'll call you later on...there are a few things I have to tell you...keep in touch...and you be careful...thanks for your prayers, Flora...and tell the *big* kids...to *behave*."

"They will...and *you* be careful, too...Ciao... ." Flora heard the click of his receiver. Vince was doing fine. *Thank you, God,* Flora thought affectionately, *thank you, so much.* Now, time, would smooth out the wrinkles of yesterday.

Mary walked back into the kitchen and Flora gave her the good news about Vince. She saw the kids coming and wanted to give them the news.

Sebastiano and Christina led the caravan of concerned faces. When Flora announced the glad tidings, they all *whoopdeedooed.* Flora was happy to see the gloom lift from their spirits...everyone's appetite came back, too.

"Could we have blueberry pancakes this morning, Mama...we have tons of syrup...and alot of Aunt Cynthia's blueberries from the farm in the freezer...*let's celebrate!*" Emily looked at Flora with her big brown eyes. Flora couldn't say no to that face and *blueberry pancakes* sounded pretty good to her, too.

Flora quadrupled the pancake recipe. Not one drop of batter was left after they had all eaten breakfast. The table was joyous and Sebastiano and Stefano were back to their frolicking ways. Little Flora helped with the dishes and Tracey and Stefano went along with Sebastiano and Christina for a walk on the beach. It was good seeing all of them smile again.

Before Flora knew it, was time to get thinking about her

supper menu. She found some ground round in the refrigerator, left from their bar-b-que on Monday and a fifteen pound bag of Michigan potatoes in the pantry that were growing some serious *eyes*. So, she put together a spaghetti sauce and boiled the potatoes for her *gnocchi dumplings*.

Usually, Flora would have called the kids in to help her form the potato dumplings...but that afternoon, she decided to make them by herself. She figured that the kids needed to be together and carefree. And she needed to be alone, at least for a while. At least until little Flora walked in and asked if she could help.

"Thanks...I'd love it...but could you please go and stir the sauce...if it's sticking, lower the burner...and taste it...tell me if it needs a little more oregano... ."

Little Flora stirred the sauce, then filled the big spoon and tasted it.

"Ummmm," little Flora said as she sat down at the kitchen table where Flora was mixing riced potatoes with flour, "...it tastes great, mom...as *usual*...have you ever made a *bad* sauce?" Little Flora finished licking the big metal spoon and then tossed it in the soapy dish water with a perfect aim. Flora laughed at her daughter's question.

"*Bad* sauce?...a *few*...," Flora said matter-of-factly. She paused for a moment and looked sheepishly at her daughter.

"No...," Flora said now with a more humble tone, "...actually it was *more* than a few."

"Get out of here... really?"

"Really...I've made more than a couple of *nasty* batches...one I called *rosemary's baby*, I read one half *cup* of rosemary, instead of one half *tablespoon*, only the devil could say that sauce was good and keep a straight face....then there was the sauce I made with diced tomatoes because I didn't have tomato paste in the cupboard...after three hours of simmering it was still watery, so I decided to thicken it with a little *flour...you* thought it was *pretty* because it was so *pink!*..you kids were little when I was becoming the chef I am today...too young to remember the really *shitty* meals... ." Flora and little Flora laughed.

"Anywho...," little Flora said after a deep sigh, "...I'm glad Vince is doing okay...will Paolo be coming back?" Little Flora hoped he would. She liked Paolo and knew he was good for her mother. Flora answered little Flora's question while she started the big pot of water on the stove for boiling the gnocchi.

"I don't know...I hope he relaxes a while before he does anything...he's going to keep in touch." Flora looked up at the clock. It was two twenty-two.

"Don't let me loose track of the time, Dolly will be calling at three...you come with me and we'll both talk to Dolly.

"Paolo had a long trip...I don't know how he did it," little Flora said as she grabbed a chunk of dough to taste.

"I know...remember how long it took us to get back into the swing of things when we got back in March?"

"I'll never forget that trip, Mama...I'm so happy we had the chance to go...I wouldn't mind studying there...it's beautiful and life seems so much more...you know...like, *easy.*"

"I miss being there, too."

"I love Union Lake...and this place is heaven, but there was something very special about Florence." Little Flora took a deep breath and continued.

"The pensione, my room, everything was so great...you know I think about the mural...and I miss it...I miss my painting on the wall...there was something about it that just seemed so *divine*...like while I was painting it...something *in* me was moving the brush...I know I'll go back and finish it." Little Flora was a sentimental artist.

"Mama, I know I shouldn't bring this up right now...but it seems we barely have time to talk anymore." Little Flora kept plugging away at the mound of dough while she talked.

"I love Dad...but I see things now that I'm older...I understand a little more of what a relationship involves." Little Flora was trying to make some point. Flora kept still even though she knew what her daughter was going to say. Little Flora went on.

"I see how you seem to *radiate* when Paolo is near you...I think it's beautiful...," little Flora watched her mother's face as she went on, "...how could you have gone so many years without that kind of love in your life...I know you were busy with us kids...but how could you have survived not having that special attention...that special love a woman needs to have from a man...from her husband?"

Flora sat down and was still for a moment. She smiled at little Flora and wondered what to say. Little Flora wanted an honest answer from her mother's heart. Flora wanted to be honest.

"I love your Dad...Jack is a good man. Maybe I was never the right woman for him. Maybe I never really loved him the way he needed to be loved. The years go by, I thought one day things would change...that I could change, in the meantime...things happen, like you grow older and wiser...and some things that seemed so unbearable kind of become...okay... ."

"How could you live like that or why would you want to go on living like that when you know that there is something more out there, someone out there who loves you so much?" Little Flora blurted out, defending Flora yet reprimanding her.

"There are things people do just to keep peace...so many people get hurt when... ." Flora didn't know exactly how to say what she had to say. Little Flora thought she knew what her mother wanted to say. She finished Flora's statement.

"When someone goes after their own happiness... ." Little Flora waited to see if she was correct in her presumption.

"Yeah, a little...but it's more than that little Flora...I was happy...you and young Jack and Joe and Jimmy and Emily...look how much I have...I wouldn't go back and change a thing in my life...see, it isn't about one thing...it's about everything...sometimes if we dwell too much on one thing...we loose everything...oh, look at the tray of *gnoc - chi*...they look like golf balls... ." Flora started laughing at her mounds of dough that were suppose to be the size of marbles.

Little Flora glanced up at the clock. It was two fifty seven. She yelled out the time again as they dashed over to Mary's for Dolly's phone call at three o'clock. They knocked on her door and ran in.

"Mary...it's us." Flora went into the kitchen and sat next to the phone. Mary left a note on the table telling them she went to town and that they should make themselves at home.

"I bet Dolly calls at exactly three o'clock... ." Little Flora said as she placed a dollar on the counter, "...three, two, one". As little Flora imitated the ring on the phone and pretended to answer it, the real phone rang. It surprised her and she laughed as she picked up the receiver.

"Dolly...I just won a dollar...you called exactly at three o'clock!...I miss you, too...okay...I'll get my Mother...see you soon I hope...CIAO." Little Flora handed the phone to Flora and sat down to listen.

"Hi, Dolly... ." Flora listened to Dolly as little Flora tried to read her face, hoping to figure out what was being said.

Flora nodded and repeated, "Yeah...yeah...", as Dolly went on and on. Little Flora could only imagine what was being said. She knew through Flora's tone and facial expressions that it was *good* news anyway.

"Okay...okay...I'll do that...yup...tonight...okay, hear from you soon, and thanks for everything, Dolly, CIAO." Flora hung up the receiver and smiled at little Flora.

"Gosh...nice conversation," little Flora said as she

yawned. "What did Dolly say...?" Little Flora was anxious to hear the news.

As they walked back home Flora went over Dolly's conversation verbatim. And, little Flora repeated it, almost word for word. Little Flora went over the *news* items once again...counting them on her fingers.

"At least you know now for sure that ONE, Vince is okay...TWO, the orphanage is beautiful...THREE, Vince is on a pre-ulcer diet...FOUR, Sebastiano and Stefano's mother misses them and she's on high blood pressure medication since the *girls disrupted Florence*...FIVE, Dolly had a hundred compliments on the pensione and wants us to come back...SIX, she burned the custard for the canoli and Guido almost quit, then Dolly said she was sorry and that she would never interfere in the kitchen again...and SEVEN, everyone misses us...even *Brutus*...I love that dog...and EIGHT, she knows Paolo *loves* you. What if he comes back and asks you to go to Florence again...?" Little Flora was in love with love and everything seemed much more simple than what it actually was. Flora forgot how easy it was to follow her heart because of the many obstacles that had been tossed in it's path. But Paolo filled her heart with hope, and with his love the strength to hurdle any rock that got in way. She only had to trust him and believe in his love. Flora opened up to little Flora.

"Paolo might want me to go to Florence... ."

"*Will you go*...would you go?" Little Flora wanted an honest answer.

"I'd really have to think about it." Flora looked at little Flora's face while '*I'll have to think about it,*' replayed in her mind.

"Mama, there should be *nothing* to think about...you can't tell me you never thought about something like this...even in Florence there was a time when I thought you'd stay...I was thinking about it myself...you and me and Jimmy and Emily."

"I did think about it...but it's never that simple...thinking, and doing what you're thinking, is two different things... ."

"Act on the one that will bring love back into your life...Mama, whatever you decide on doing, I will stand by you." Little Flora hugged her mother.

"Thanks Flora." Flora hugged little Flora. It was good to hear those words from her daughter.

Little Flora appreciated Flora's openness. She would have alot to think about, too.

Flora went inside the cottage with little Flora and finished preparing supper. They all ate that evening with a hearty appetite. The girls shooed Flora out of the kitchen when it came time to do dishes. They told her to take a long walk on the beach.

Flora headed east so the sunset would be in front of her on her way back. She played tag with the waves. The sky made her think of Paolo. She said a prayer of thanksgiving for Vince's good health. With the sun caressing her back she prayed that everything would work out for the best.

Flora heard someone calling her. She turned around and scanned the beach. Matt came running toward her.

"Thanks for waiting up, Flora...do you mind if I walk with you?"

Flora didn't mind at all. She was grateful for the opportunity to talk with Matt. She really hadn't talked with him since Thanksgiving.

"Matt...I'd love the company."

They walked for a while down the beach quietly. It was a beautiful evening and the waves were picking up momentum. Their rhythm was like a third party keeping Flora and Matt entertained.

"Flora..., I just want to tell you that I'm happy for you." Matt ran in front of Flora and walked backwards so he could see her face as he talked with her. He went on.

"I love Uncle Jack...he's the beach dude of all

dudes...but...I think I know you too, and I know you are doing what you have to do...you needed to be loved and he was there...kind of like the mountain that has to be climbed."

"Matt...thanks for sharing that with me... ." Flora chuckled inside at Matt's mountain analogy, but she felt in that awkward comparison his sincerity and she was extremely grateful to him for that.

"Remind me when you're a young old man and I'm an *ancient* old woman...to tell you a little story...about falling stars."

"Why wait...I've got the time...and I'm due for a good story."

"First, let's turn around...look how neat the sky is!" Flora turned in the direction she was looking.

"It is," Matt said as he twirled around, "...okay let's hear it storylady... ."

"Well...it's kind of long," Flora said with a chuckle in her voice, "...and I'm not so sure it would sound that good right now."

"I'll like it no matter what...come on Flora."

"Nope," Flora said firmly, "...it's one of those tales that has to be heard with an *aged* ear...and a mellow heart...I'm not even sure if I'd be able to do it justice right now...there are parts of it that might not make sense if I'm not careful with the words I choose ...the whole story might be lost forever...just know that we have a good story one day to enjoy...I promise."

Matt looked at Flora with an anxious face, an almost begging face which tempted her to divulge every crazy thought she ever had. She wanted to explain to him all the wonders of the world. He deserved that. Flora knew though, that wonders can't be explained...at least not perfectly with words. Flora looked into her young friend's eyes. Matt reached out for Flora's hand, then shook it.

"I'll hold you to it...count on that, Flora." He squeezed

her hand hard and then let it go gently. Then he smiled a very wonderful smile at Flora.

Matt's smile tempted Flora to make herself believe he already had that *aged* ear, but., the excitement in his eyes gave away his impetuous heart; it was far from mellow. Flora locked away her story about a starry sky and two hearts that had been anxious for love. She smiled back with a wish...a prayer. She believed Matt would one day find the love that satisfies every imagining. Then, Paolo's face whisked into her mind when the tangerine sun caught her eyes.

"Flora...remember Josh's brother...the one that was going out with his professor...he ditched her." Matt's eyes looked to Flora for her reaction to his bit of gossip.

"I knew he would...," Flora said with a proud smile.

"And do you know why, Flora...?" Matt asked sounding legitimately concerned.

"Maybe their *age difference* had something to do with it...," Flora said sincerely.

"I don't think so...or maybe it did...anyway...the bottom line is that he's going out with her *older* sister now."

Flora and Matt laughed till their jaws ached. They knew that love was something very precious and that most of the time it was a pretty tough thing to figure out. One year made Flora appreciate the many years she had on her summer friend.

Chapter
twenty-five

Gray Wool And Memories

"A miracle! We did it, you did it Paolo, all the running around and the ten thousand back and forths to every-where picking up this and that, you are our hero...without your being here through it all...we could never be starting operations next week. In a few hours...imagine...only hours, Paolo, that building will have a soul." Brother Georgio bubbled. He stepped out of the car to admire the view of the orphanage.

Georgio and Paolo were on their way back to San Miniato from the pensione where Dolly had made them dinner. They had to go over a check list of leftover supplies with Fr. Cellini, so they excused themselves early.

The sun was setting and the color of the sky made them stop and view their project in a magnificent light. It was finally completed and the boys would be transferred to San Miniato that weekend.

Paolo was the driving force and the *gopher* for the orphanage project. Since June, his relationship with Flora and the uncertainty it left in his heart, had propelled his energies. He felt guilty for accepting Georgio's praise. He also knew he could have never done it without the support of Brother Georgio and Fr. Cellini...and the memory of Francesca.

"Georgio, it is wonderful, but you deserve the credit...you were my inspiration...you kept me going...you crack a mean whip... ." Paolo hugged Brother Georgio. They continued to admire the orphanage.

"A real mean wet vermicelli noodle would be more like it... ." Br. Georgio wanted to see Paolo smile.

Brother Georgio noticed Paolo's disposition had changed ever since Flora's name was mentioned in their dinner conversation. Paolo seemed far away in thought. the whole evening. Br. Georgio knew where to go looking for him.

"Dolly and Vince mentioned Flora and the kids are living alone now at her parents home in the northern peninsula of Michigan."

"Yea, she decided to stay up a while longer...," Paolo said, seeming distracted.

"A while longer?" Br. Georgio asked innocently.

"Georgio, what do you *really* want to know." Paolo looked at his good friend. "You always beat around the bush...just ask me what you want to know...and maybe I'll *tell* you what you want to know."

Paolo and Georgio had known each other for a long time. They met at a retreat fifteen years before and became more than best friends. Paolo considered Georgio to be his brother.

Georgio knew Francesca and was there for Paolo the night she was killed. Roberto was only five years old then, and it was Georgio and Paolo who cared for him till his next of kin was notified. The *next of kin* didn't work out at all. When Paolo gained custody of Roberto two years later it was Georgio who was there when Paolo went away on business. Paolo used to call Georgio Roberto's guardian Angel.

"Paolo, I won't beat around the bush...," Br. Georgio said smiling, "...now you've got me cracking whips *and* beating bushes...what I really want to know is, *when is Flora coming back here*...is that in the near picture...I could use her artistic expertise with the interior design of the chapel...and the secret to her chewy chocolate chip cookies...so, what's going on?" Georgio knew something was bothering his good friend.

"I'm not sure...I mean I want her to come back...someday she will be back...but I want to make sure she really wants that...does that make any sense?"

"Yes...and no...how will you know when she is ready...have you asked her lately?"

"No...I'm waiting for her to say something...or do something."

"*Do something*? Moving to the summer cottage was her way of telling everyone that she was going to make some changes in her life. It was her way of telling you that things in Union Lake couldn't go on the way they were...*capis - ci?*...do you understand what I'm getting at...you gave her reason to change all the things in her life that made no sense...you gave her the courage. Now it's your turn Paolo, if you plan on staying in the game, that is. If you love her...tell her...it's that simple."

"Okay...I'll leave in the morning...," Paolo said facetiously. "Is that soon enough for you...?" Paolo walked back to the car and jumped up to sit on it. Georgio stood next to Paolo.

"What would be wrong with that? If I were you...I'd have been on the plane yesterday...last week...c'mon...do something really wild...the orphanage is almost perfect...you deserve the time off anyway... ." Brother Georgio took a deep breath and went on.

"You think I'm *fooling around*...but I'm telling you right now, I haven't been more serious about anything in years. I tried to keep an eye on you and your life and Roberto and things have gone pretty good, so far. After Francesca was killed, you blamed yourself...and you were wrong, but acting perfectly natural. You seemed to work your way through the guilt and even forgive yourself. You buried yourself in your father's business and Roberto's life. You *thought* everything was perfect! Then Flora came to town. She became the friend you never thought you needed...you fell in love not even realizing you wanted to...then you got scared...what are you *afraid* of Paolo? Do you still feel bound to the priesthood...or Francesca...are you still punishing yourself for something that was never your fault?"

"I'm not afraid...maybe too much happened these past few months...and Roberto is moving back here, the orphanage is still on my mind...Vince needs my attention... ." Paolo looked straight into the sunset ignoring Georgio who was shaking his head.

"Paolo, your looking in the wrong direction right now...look inside your heart...forget everyone else for just one minute...you try to be everyone's savior...when are you going to save yourself?" Paolo knew Georgio was right, but he was embarrassed to have so much thrown in his face all at once. He had been kidding himself about his true feelings and Georgio made him realize it wasn't funny.

"I don't need this shit Georgio... ." Paolo jumped off his car and headed back around for the driver's seat.

"No one needs this garbage," Br. Georgio said defensively, "...I'm sorry if I overstepped my bounds, but I'm your friend and I want you to wake up...you've got a woman who loves you...and you love her...Paolo, just think about it?" Georgio hopped off the car and spoke to Paolo through the passenger's opened window.

"Paolo...you are like my brother, I want what's best for you." Georgio fell silent. Paolo put his head down on the steering wheel for a minute then got out of the car and walked back to Georgio.

"Georgio, I'm sorry." Paolo was very apologetic. Georgio hugged Paolo with his big arms and apologized to Paolo for his harsh assessment of things.

"I'm just a romantic fool, I didn't mean to sermonize but... ." Br. Georgio smiled at Paolo and suddenly stopped talking. Paolo understood his cliffhanger. They both turned around and leaned on Paolo's car. They talked looking into the sky.

"Georgio, remember last March when I came to Perugia to have you sign some final papers? Georgio nodded his head in affirmation.

"And Flora came with me... ."

Georgio continued nodding.

"That's when I knew...I loved her." Paolo looked at Georgio to see his reaction. Georgio wanted to hear more. He encouraged more words from Paolo by keeping silent. Paolo continued.

"That night on our way home I freaked out inside. I loved her...I knew I loved her...but instead of telling her that I did...I began saying things I knew would push her away...I wanted her to wonder about the things she was feeling, I wanted her to blow up at me and tell me to go to hell...I felt I deserved that. I almost needed her to bash me...for Francesca. I actually thought that would be poetic justice...I made Flora the executioner by proxy...and I didn't realize till after I thought about it, how insane I was for thinking such a thing. Flora thought I snapped...she even got out of the car and walked the last two miles home." Paolo paused, and waited to hear if Brother Georgio wanted to comment. Georgio just listened. Paolo continued.

"I wanted to go and talk to Flora that night...I knew I hurt her. I got as far as her bedroom door. I waited a while before I knocked...I heard her talking to Emily and Jimmy about the hills in Umbria...I went back to my room.

"The next morning while I was packing Flora walked into my room. She looked beautiful. I was packing up to move into the rectory with Fr. Cellini...I thought it would make things more *comfortable* for everyone when Jack arrived...but when I saw her I knew I couldn't leave...walk out of her life...we were just getting to know each other...and already, I loved her. I held her in my arms that afternoon and I told myself not to let her go...and then I did. I didn't want to say good-bye to her. I didn't want to upset her life again.

"Then I went to Rome and I thought about her the whole trip...I tried to tell myself I didn't love her...I barely knew her...I didn't need to love someone that way...but she was there, in my mind...in my heart. Even after the night we talked for hours under the stars...right here...I let go of love and tried to talk myself into something that would make more sense for everyone...like maybe her life with Jack could work, if I stayed out of it. So, I stayed away...patting myself on the back for being so gallant...a real Lancelot. I watched her board the plane back to the States. I thought I'd get over her...I prayed to get over her...I wanted everything to get back to normal. It didn't. How could it?

"The trip to Northern Michigan with Stefano was suppose to be a kind of *second chance*. Then Dolly's call about Vince made that impossible...I went a little crazy...I thought Vince was dying...because I went after Flora...that God was going to take something from me...because I was taking something from Him.

"After Francesca...I vowed never to love anyone again...but I never really knew what this kind of love was all about...then Flora came to me." Paolo paused for a moment. He looked at his watch and walked back around the car. He looked at Georgio who was still staring into the sunset sky. Paolo walked back to Georgio and looked into his eyes.

"Georgio, you are too wise and I am a fool. I'm thousands of miles away from the woman who means everything to me...but I'm *afraid* to take the next step...I haven't been able to relax...I've got to keep busy just to keep my mind off of her...last week I went to Rome three times and then I volunteered to go to Naples to pick up one last shipment of wallboard. You know, I call her every other day...the days I don't call, I have to steer away from the phone...I don't want to be tempted. When we talk, I don't want to hang up...I try to bring things up that will make her think of our good times here in Florence hoping she says...*Paolo come get me.*"

"To ease your conscience," Georgio said, not taking his eyes off Paolo's. "You want her to take the next step for you... ."

Paolo looked at Georgio as if he'd become suddenly enlightened. Georgio continued.

"I haven't told you anything you haven't already told yourself a hundred times."

Paolo looked away from Georgio.

"I've been a fool, Georgio...I'm ashamed of myself for not trusting more in God than myself. For not trusting my friends...I know what I have to do." Georgio smiled at his wise friend's decision.

"She's waiting for you, Paolo. Tell her how you feel...no, words aren't enough...don't tell her...*go get her!* Paolo, *she loves you!* If you would have asked her to stay last March...she would have. You didn't even call her to say good-bye, do you know how that *hurt* her?" Georgio didn't wait for Paolo to respond. He went on.

"The night before Flora went back to Michigan, I drove down to the pensione to say my good-byes. Dolly prepared a fantastic supper and we spent the whole evening in the kitchen. Flora couldn't bring herself to leave the kitchen. She was waiting for your call. She did the dishes...and then the dessert dishes...then we had coffee. Flora asked me to sit with her by the fire after everyone else excused themselves to do last minute packing. Sebastiano invited me to go with the young kids for a walk to Vivoli's for gelato. I made up some excuse and stayed back...I wanted to talk with Flora.

"We sat by the fire with our coffee. At first we talked about everything in general...then there was big silence...she looked into the fire and then into my eyes...as if begging me to see what she was really feeling. All I knew for sure was that she ached inside...she was leaving the next morning...and she didn't want to.

"I wanted to console her in some way but I didn't know how, except to tell her that I would be there for her and listen. She wanted to talk. She spoke of love...life, the whole scheme of things. But, after a while she opened up and told me things that had been tying her stomach in knots for a long time. She didn't have to tell me everything she did...but she couldn't help it.

"Flora loves her family...she loved Jack, but she needed to be loved. Meeting Dolly was a blessing in her life that took her by surprise...but she felt it was all meant to be.

"She came to Florence in a whirlwind...she was caught up in Dolly's exuberance. She was simply happy to be here with all of us. She never planned on falling in love...then she saw you at Mass...she saw something wonderful in your eyes. Flora told me how scared she was at first of her immediate attraction to you...when she saw you at Mass and then when she met you at the dinner table on Epiphany, she knew you were going to be someone very special in her life. You took her heart. She didn't realize how empty her life had been without you.

"She loves you, Paolo...I'm wrong about alot of things...like the amount of wallboard we needed for the chapel...or the amount of pasta we needed to cook for twenty hungry teenage boys...but not when it concerns love." Br. Georgio knew Paolo was having a rough time inside his heart. Falling in love with Flora made him have to jump back into an inner war that he wasn't ready to fight. But, he was a fighter and Georgio knew if Paolo would just pick up his sword, he could win.

"Let's go...," Paolo said impatiently. "We've got a meeting with Fr. Cellini. He wants to go over some of the curriculum...and Georgio...*gratzie*." Paolo heard enough. He wanted to get back to the orphanage. Paolo and Brother George finished their short drive back to San Miniato in silence.

They met for a while with Fr. Cellini then took inventory on the excess supplies. It had been a long day for all of them. The hectic day and the special wine Fr. Cellini poured for them had taken their toll on Paolo. He was exhausted and excused himself from the meeting and went to his room feeling depleted.

Paolo showered hoping to soothe and relax his body and his mind. He went to bed only to stare up at the rough stucco ceiling, he couldn't fall asleep. He cracked open his window to hear the night's noise, thinking that would bring his tired mind to sleep. He loved hearing the crickets. Paolo needed to hear something besides his own thoughts. His eyes canvassed the room like it was the first time he had slept there.

That night he was more conscious of the plainness of his room. His bed, a nightstand and a dresser with five drawers were the only pieces of furniture. A three way lighted floorlamp and a copy of DaVinci's LAST SUPPER, hanging over the nightstand, were the only decorative accents.

Paolo looked at the gray wool bedspread draped across the bottom of his bed. It made him remember the night he and Flora had spent under the sky...wishing on stars. That night everything seemed possible, everything seemed good. He loved Flora. Paolo wondered why he was still alone at San Miniato. He could have moved back to the pensione but there were too many memories of Flora there.

He thought back to earlier that evening when he was having dinner with Dolly and Vince. Everything reminded him of Flora. The kitchen curtains, the wine decanter she bought for Vince that looked like a bunch of grapes and her Grama's lace coverlet on the rocker by the fireplace. She told Dolly that coverlet would make her come back one day. That was her most treasured possession, besides her pendant necklace.

Lying in bed made Paolo feel very much alone. Brother Georgio's words kept coming back to him...*go get her if you love her.* His mind travelled back to the shores of Lake Michigan and to Flora. He loved her. He wished things could be that simple.

Brother Georgio made Paolo think about alot of things. He wanted to think that the past had been long forgotten. Brother Georgio's words made Paolo realize that there were still ghosts in his conscience. Paolo was unaware of their invisible presence in his life until he fell in love with Flora. Then the guilt of his unsettled past woke up with all the other emotions he unconsciously buried deep in his soul.

Paolo never thought he'd have to look that deep into his heart again, but he had been wrong. He knew that every encounter and every relationship affects who we are and what we become. Paolo learned that lesson the hard way. It was up to him now to make the next move. He wanted to begin by listening to his heart and not to be afraid of really hearing it's song. He had to have love in his life again. He wanted his life to include Flora.

Paolo reached down to the bottom of the bed and pulled the wool blanket up over his body. How he wished Flora was there with him. Paolo fell asleep thinking of Flora.

The next morning came quickly.

"*Paolo...wake up!* They've started the meeting without us." Brother Georgio shook Paolo from a deep sound sleep.

"Give me five minutes...," Paolo said as he jumped from his bed. With his eyes only half opened, he began dressing in yesterday's clothes. Brother Georgio handed him a clean shirt from the closet and suggested with his eyebrows that he wear the fresh pressed shirt. Paolo nodded his head and accepted the judgement of his friend. Before he had the back tails tucked in they were off to Fr. Cellini's office.

"I feel like shit this morning Georgio...I couldn't fall asleep last night and when I finally did...I had to wake up to your ugly face...," Paolo said teasingly and in between a couple of yawns.

"Talk about *ugly* faces...you can take off your mask now...or maybe just get rid of the whiskers by this afternoon. Oh, remind me to buy you a comb and brush for Christmas."

"I look that bad?"

"Almost," Br. Georgio said with a sly smile. "Fr. Cellini is waiting for us." The two good friends started laughing.

Their jovial mood took leave when they entered Fr. Cellini's room and saw his worried expression. Paolo walked up to the old man and began massaging his narrow shoulders.

"What's up...?" Paolo asked, feeling the age of his friend. Fr. Cellini turned his head slightly toward Paolo, acknowledging his question.

"I cancelled our curriculum meeting." Fr. Cellini closed his eyes, hung his head down low. Paolo could feel the tension in his friend neck.

"That's great, Fr. Cellini...you should be *clicking* your heels instead of mopping the floor with your face." Georgio tried to lift Fr. Cellini's spirit.

"You two quit clowning around," Fr. Cellini said impatiently, "...don't you ever take anything serious...sit down...both of you...in front of me...I have something serious to talk over." Fr. Cellini sat up as straight as he could and shook his shoulders. Paolo understood his body language and walked around to the front of Fr. Cellini's desk. Georgio dragged another chair from behind the door. They sat down and were ready to be serious.

"Okay...we're listening," Paolo said sounding like an obedient schoolboy.

"We're listening." Br. Georgio added to accent their

readiness.

"Remember my brother Alfredo," Fr. Cellini asked, now with a more civil tone. "He called me last night from Belgrade...he's very worried about the children in his village. There have been skirmishes and villagers have been seriously, very seriously hurt...he needs our help."

"What does he want us to do?" Paolo asked anxiously. Alfredo was a major influence in Paolo's decision to build the orphanage in San Miniato. Alfredo was not a priest or a missionary but he, like his brother, Fr. Cellini, devoted his life to helping the poor and less fortunate. He was one of those men that made things happen even when things seemed impossible. With the old Yugoslavia in turmoil, the impossible was an everyday affair.

"Tell us, Father...what can we do?" Brother Georgio's expression matched Paolo's.

"He needs supplies and manpower...with all the fighting and revolts and the absurd dallying from outside resources, Alfredo is desperately seeking aid...his people are dying." Fr. Cellini spoke with much remorse in his voice; his mannerisms spoke of disgust in the system...disgust in a world that stood by bartering ways and means, weighing motives and actions while brothers lost their dignity...their lives.

"I can't send both of you now ," Fr. Cellini said directing his attention toward Georgio, "...but Alfredo would appreciate a quick response...Georgio, I need you here at the orphanage... ." Then, Fr. Cellini looked into Paolo's eyes. Before Fr. Cellini could get out another word Paolo volunteered his services.

"I guess that leaves me...I'll go Fr. Cellini."

"I knew you would help, Paolo." Fr. Cellini accepted the heroic offer quickly...before any words could be taken back...before any sane man would have the time to reconsider.

"I'll do all I can from this end...," Br. Georgio said as he hugged Paolo.

"Well," Fr. Cellini said, "...let's get started...thank you Paolo. I thank you for Alfredo, too." Fr. Cellini realized there would be more there to deal with than anyone expected. Even optimistic Paolo had his doubts and reservations.

"Hey...don't thank me yet...first let me get there...you know how I am with directions," Paolo said trying to brighten Fr. Cellini's eyes. All of them knew going into Yugoslavia was not going to be easy, especially with all the civil uprisings. Despite the risk in his upcoming venture, Paolo seemed anxious to get it over with. Fr. Cellini chased the two big guys out of his office with well wishes and a prayer.

"Now get going...we'll talk more later... ." Fr. Cellini hugged Paolo hard. Paolo felt the courage in his old friend's embrace. Paolo couldn't look to long into Fr. Cellini's eyes. Father Cellini saw some of the things Paolo didn't want him to see.

"I know, Paolo," Father Cellini said sympathetically. "I'm not asking a small favor...I wish I were young again so I could go with you...I know you will do your best...and you will be in my prayers constantly." Paolo hugged Fr. Cellini one more time, then he quickly left the room. Georgio followed.

"Wish I were going with you...this is sort of bad timing huh, Paolo?...I don't want to add more grief to this matter...but you know you are going to miss the CALCIO STORICO."

"I know, Georgio...hey...do me a favor...let Leonardo know about the change and he'll get a replacement...maybe that young guy who looks like Fabio...the one who tackles like Dick Butkiss...you know who I'm talking about."

"I'll go tomorrow...the young kid will take this as a *mir - acle* from heaven...the green team really has a winning chance this year...we'll be thinking of you anyway."

"That should be enough to give you guys the edge against the blues...*my* face in your minds cheering you on...give Gabriel a *good jab* from me...anywhere it will hurt...and make sure you tell him it's from his buddy Paolo."

Paolo was used to wrenches being thrown his plans but this had to be the worst wrench ever. Going to meet with Alfredo was going to be a bigger challenge than Paolo cared to let on. But, now it was something he had to do.

"You were going to see Flora... ." Georgio put his arm up around Paolo's shoulders as they walked.

"Yeah." Paolo sighed a deep sigh.

"You know, Paolo, not that your volunteering to go see Alfredo wasn't admirable...I know how much he means to you...but it wedged it's way into your plans with Flora... ." Georgio paused for a moment while looking at Paolo. Georgio continued.

"We're too much alike...I know about the battles we fight in our own hearts..don't turn your head and ignore what has to be accomplished on the homefront first...I'm gonna miss you." Georgio stopped their walking and stepped in front of Paolo like a brick wall. He grabbed Paolo's face and kissed Paolo's cheeks firmly. Paolo smiled at his big friend who had the heart of a little kid.

"Things will work out Paolo...*just get your ass in there and get the heck out*...don't pull any *St. Paolo's*...hear me?" Georgio wrapped both of his strong hands around Paolo's neck, as if to choke some sense into him. He looked sincerely into Paolo's eyes and warned him again.

"If you dilly-dally...if you hang around being everybody's hero...I'll personally come and beat your butt...so read my lips, DO WHAT YOU HAVE TO DO AND THEN GET OUT!"

Paolo laughed, half from the expression on Georgio's face and half because he knew Georgio was being dead serious.

"You know I will...don't worry Georgio, everything will be alright." Paolo hugged Georgio very hard. He wished his friend was going with him to Bosnia. Somberly, Paolo walked into his room to pack.

Paolo thought of Flora and how much he needed to talk with her. Things weren't settled on the homefront. Honorable intentions weren't going to win the war there either. His thoughts back to the shores of Lake Michigan were tender. He remembered the sky crowded with stars. They would be his strength..he needed their optimism. He really needed Flora.

T. Stellini

Chapter
twenty-six

Straining Ahead

"Carissimo piccola Flora,

"Hope you are enjoying the north country of your state. Cousin Paolo could not say enough about your grandparents cottage on the great Lake Michigan or about all the relatives and friends who gathered there for the summer. He wished he could have stayed longer but Zio Vincenzo gave all of us a scare. The only good part about that whole fiasco was how Zio Vincenzo ended up in the room next to my mother in the hospital and they both came home on the same day. Vince was relieved to find out his discomfort had been only gas and my mother was happy to have her big brother at her side. Now everyone is home and happy.

"My mother is doing well but her recovery will take much time. She talks to me about you. My mother likes you very much. Who wouldn't?

"Dolly and Vince bring baskets of food and wine up the hill to the orphanage for the workers everyday. The orphanage is almost complete. From the outside, it looks like it's been lived in for years. Dolly has planters of geraniums all over the grounds. The inside carpentry will take a while longer but it is livable. The boys will enjoy it very much.

"I have enjoyed working alongside my father and Paolo my father and Paolo. They teach me something new everyday and not everything they teach me is about hammers and wood. With

280

the heat so unbearable in the afternoons, we take long, long
lunches in the shade and wait for the scorching sun to settle in
the sky before we finish our agenda for the day. That gives us
time to talk and dream.

Paolo said he missed the bells when he was in the north and
hearing them now makes his heart sad. Paolo loves your mother very much. He has never come out and said this to anyone
but we all can see it in his face when he talks about Flora. And,
when he mentioned the bells in Florence, I knew it was the
thought of your mother and how she loved the bells that makes
his heart ache.

"I imagine I look the same way to him and my father when
I talk about you. They look at each other with the grin of omni-
scient wisdom. I don't mind their poking fun at me, in fact, I
enjoy it, I look very forward to it! I know there is nothing they
can say that I haven't already told myself a hundred times.
And, you know I am a patient person but don't be surprised if
I don't come and knock at your door one day, when you least
expect it, piccola Flora, I will be there. I'd have been there
already if I wasn't needed so badly here for my work and the
care of my mother. I know you know that. Maybe it is a blessing in disguise that I'm situated here so tightly. I know you
need the time to think.

"Today was very hot. We worked until the sun set (9:15)
because the sky was full of rain clouds for tomorrow. When I
arrived home this evening, a letter from you was on my desk.
Your letter made me so happy. It refreshed me more than any
swim or shower could have done.

"Thank you for sharing how difficult it was for you to leave
last spring. Spring did not come into my heart after you left,
you took it with you. I could not smell the air or watch the flowers bloom. To know that you had those same feelings gives me
hope that one day you will understand what happened to us last
winter.

"I look forward to hearing from you. Enjoy the wonderful
season of harvest.

"*Con mille abbracci e baci, Giacamo   P.S. Tell Emily I watched MOONSTRUCK tonight with my mother. And even though my mother speaks very little English, she enjoyed the movie more than she has enjoyed any movie, ever. She told me, after I kissed her goodnight, that it isn't Cosmo's moon anymore. "It's Giacamo's moon!" That made me think of your mural and the "bella luna" you captured on that wall. Was it our moon you painted, piccola Flora?*"

Flora made a special trip into town when she noticed the wood pile had almost diminished. She had to find out where to call and order the firewood. That was something Jack would have done very well, but this season, Flora was on her own.

Flora knew the best place to find anything was at the grocery store. DICK'S IGA's bulletin board was jammed with *want ads* and *for sale* notes. With her own list, she ventured into town in search of wood and the best price. She found both and felt as if she accomplished a great deal in such a short time. The money she saved on the wood, she spent on special groceries. That night she wanted to make something delicious for supper.

Little Flora stayed home and worked on her painting of the pine trees that stood tall on the lot next door. The sky was partly cloudy that morning and the deep gray billowing clouds in the west made a beautiful backdrop for the evergreens. Little Flora thought the pines looked like soldiers guarding their cottage. She was really *getting good* as Flora would say. Each day brought a new discovery about art, and herself. It was slowly becoming the biggest part of her life. And, Flora saw something very special in little Flora's work. Flora was proud of her daughter.

"Little Flora?" Flora yelled into the house as she plopped the groceries down on the floor. Flora walked into the living room and looked out from the doorwall window to see if little Flora was still painting. She watched her paint for a few minutes and then stepped out onto the deck. Flora walked over to the painting and was surprised to see how much the painting had changed since she last viewed it.

"It's beautiful...I love the colors...and the pines are look- ing so *real*." Flora complimented her daughter as she tucked little Flora's hair inside the neck of her turtle-necked sweater.

"Thanks mom...I've been wanting to do that for a while but I didn't want to get paint all over my sweater...do you really like it...," little Flora asked excitedly.

"LIKE it?...I love it!" Flora responded with sincere delight.

"There's still so much I have to do on it yet...but I kind of like where it's going...the sky today made the whole mood of the painting change...it's funny how a little more green...or a little more blue can change the whole mood of the sky." Little Flora squinted her eyes at her painting and then dabbed her paintbrush in cobalt blue and continued.

"You can sure tell Autumn is here, Mama...look at the clouds...there so thick and heavy...and the sky is more cobalt blue in the Fall. In the summer and winter, ultrama- rine is the predominating color...don't you think so...?" Little Flora was enjoying her carefree days in the North. Flora agreed with her perception on the seasonal skies and appreciated her verbal treatise on the effects the seasons have on sky color. Flora wanted to see if her own percep- tions concerning her daughter were as keen.

"Are you okay...was there *good news* in Giacamo's let- ter," Flora as she came around to the front of little Flora.

Little Flora answered her mom as she continued dab- bling with her paints. "It's always good news from Giacamo...happy news...I never met a guy who could write six or seven pages and not repeat himself...he makes every- thing sound so good...he says the winds were kind this summer and that the winter in Florence should be especially mild...he's working for his Uncle full time before the rainy season begins in October...and he wants to complete his last semester at the university in January...in the meantime he's saving his money just in case something *big* happens in his life, the extra cash will come in handy...he also wanted me to know that my mural is still unfinished...and that he's anxious for the day when he can look at it completed...oh...and Dolly sends her love... ." Little Flora put her paintbrush down and looked at Flora whose eyes tempted little Flora to say more.

"Why are you looking at me that way," Little Flora asked with a big smile. She smiled harder and shook her head knowing if she didn't share what was inside her that moment she would burst.

"Even though I never said anything to anyone about Giacamo...," little Flora said with a bit of embarrassment in her voice, "I know you know I care about him...you know I care alot...but...I want to take my time."

Flora didn't say anything to her daughter. Her smile told little Flora that she was pleased. Little Flora continued feeling more comfortable expressing her thoughts.

"I have so many questions in my mind...I think taking this whole thing slowly is the right thing for me...and I thank God there is an *ocean* between me and Giacamo...although after his letters I always feel like I could swim across if I had to...but that's beside the point...you know what I mean...I guess I just need more time...for everything."

Flora looked at her daughter, then looked at little Flora's painting. She picked up the paintbrush and touched little Flora's nose delicately, putting a small blue dot on the tip of her shiny nose.

"Time makes everything a masterpiece," Flora said with a big smile. She hugged little Flora and walked back inside the cottage.

Flora was happy the kids were enjoying the North.

They had decided together about staying up till spring but Flora knew how quickly kids could change their minds...how quickly things could change.

The phone rang and Flora ran inside to answer it.

"Hello?" Flora said.

"Hi...Flora!" It was Paolo. Flora was surprised at his early call.

"Paolo...you're calling so early...is anything the matter...?"

"No, no...everything is fine...I woke up early and did alot of running around today...it seems like I've gone thousands of miles...I'm ready for a nap...what have you been up to?"

Flora picked up the groceries and started placing things in their proper place as she talked with Paolo.

"Not too much...I went into town this morning and ordered some firewood...we're just about out...I know it's early but I don't want to be caught out of our heat supply when the snow starts coming... ."

"*Snow*...it's only *September!*," Paolo said in amazement, "...sounds like you plan on staying up there for a while." Paolo was hoping Flora was only teasing him.

"Well, I just want to be prepared...but I am growing pretty fond of this place... ." Flora wanted to hear Paolo's reaction.

"Nothing wrong with that." Paolo was positive Flora was playing a little game.

"I imagine *Christmas* will be beautiful up here and next Spring...to see everything green again." Flora didn't believe her words for one minute. She wanted Paolo to tell her she wasn't going to be there for Christmas...at least, not without him.

Paolo became impatient with talk of things that might not be. The reality of his present situation left him in limbo once again; between what was and what he thought would be. He kept the conversation loose...and then changed the subject.

"I've been putting together some book shelves in the recreation room for the boys...Fr. Cellini politely dropped a hint when he stacked some leftover plankwood over my desk along with a note mentioning there were also a half dozen crates filled with books for the boys in his office that still had *no place* to go...so I put up a few shelves and had enough wood for a makeshift entertainment center."

"Wow...you have been busy...I'd like to see it...what does it look like?" Flora asked, concerned but more grateful for the new direction in their conversation.

"A little like the one Vince rigged up in his room for Dolly when she bought her new television...," Paolo said realizing Flora was being more polite than interested. He continued trying to make what he had to say informative.

"Only the boys didn't have a television...or a stereo...but, Fr. Cellini took care of that...last Sunday he dropped a nice hint during his homily that the orphanage was near completion but some things were still needed...like a used television or an older stereo set...the next day two cardboard boxes were delivered to the rectory...someone donated a brand *new* television and a *compact disc player*...that really made our day...and it really made the entertainment center look pretty dang good... ."

Flora was happy that things were going well at the orphanage. Paolo's voice and his enthusiasm filled her lonely heart.

"That's great Paolo...everything sounds like it's going smooth at the orphanage," Flora said, with true excitement.

"Flora...I'm overwhelmed with the support everyone has given us...the next day I walked into the rec room and a brand new ping-pong table was set up! Brother Georgio and I broke it in...he beat me bad...even two out of three...I suggested best out of seven but Georgio only laughed... ."
Flora laughed at the picture Paolo created for her imagination. She knew how competitive Paolo and Georgio were

in any sport. Flora wanted to hear more about the orphanage.

"Are the boys in the orphanage yet?"

"Most of the little guys are here and we are waiting for the others who are due in this weekend...and Flora...your pillows came the other day...they are great...even the ninja turtles...I put one on little Giuseppe's bed...he's only three and a half and reminds me of your Joe...his eyes are black and his hair is so dark and bushy...he walks all over the place with it...I can't wait for you to see him...oh, and the other two pillows with the PISTONS logo, we're going to raffle off after first report card marking...for now they are on one of the new bookshelves...thanks again Flora... ."

"I'll send you a few more...little Flora is working on one now that has the University of Michigan colors...Brother Georgio will like that one...how is he doing, Paolo?"

"Were your ears burning the other day...he was talking about you and reminiscing about your visit with him the night before you left Florence...he likes you alot...and your chocolate chip cookies...he wanted to know when you were going to come back."

Flora wondered the same thing.

"What did you tell him...?" Flora asked anxiously hoping to hear something positive.

"I sort of told him that I was waiting for you to call the shots on that one." Paolo waited for Flora to respond. Flora took her time before responding to Paolo's last statement even though the words were on her lips before he finished.

"What did he say about that?"

"Something like...*you already called the shots*...and that you wanted to come back."

"He's a pretty smart guy...Georgio's pretty smart... ." Flora felt the tears in her eyes well and her throat tighten. She couldn't say anything more.

"He is a wise man...," Paolo said feeling the tears in Flora's voice. "He wanted me to go get you and bring you back here the same night we talked about it...he told me you would be *ready*." Paolo knew Flora was missing him just as much as he was missing her.

For a *long* moment, it was silent.

"I would be ready, Paolo...if you knocked at my front door right now...I'd be ready in fifteen minutes." Immediately Flora's words spoke to Paolo's heart. She heard them echo in her own. Flora wondered if she had said too much...should she have said more? Paolo heard the truth that Flora kept deeply in her heart.

"*Fifteen minutes*...that reminds me, I've got to get going...I'm late for an important engagement...I've postponed this meeting for quite some time and I feel guilty about it. I'll get back with you. Ciao. I miss you". Paolo hung up the phone. Flora couldn't believe how abrupt Paolo had ended their phone call. He seemed almost rude or maybe it was just her present disposition that made Flora feel his good-bye had been calloused. Flora tried not to think about it.

Flora looked out from the living room window and noticed the waves had grown bigger. The sky looked stormy but there was a crack in the cumulus blanket of clouds that allowed the sun to sneak through. That tiny opening made the escaped ray of light immediately bounce into Flora's heart. She was grateful for that burst of radiance...it inspired her. Flora turned on the CD player and played the music from WHEN HARRY MET SALLY. Flora started her supper as she sang IT HAD TO BE YOU.

Jimmy and Emily came home from school starving and excited. They loved the bus ride even though they were the only two kids riding it the last seven miles of their trip home. They sat in the back and Jimmy made Emily giggle the half hour Journey.

"Hang up your book bags and I'll look at all your papers after supper... ." Flora gave Emily a kiss and handed her a cupful of sliced pears.

Flora gave Jimmy a head lock and rubbed her fist knuckles in his hair. Flora stuffed a pear slice in his mouth and then pointed to the overflowing garbage bag. He shimmied it out of the old rubber pail and then plunked it on the porch with the promise to take it to the dump after supper with little Flora. Emily kept munching on the pears. She was always starved after school.

"Thanks, Mom...I'm *so* hungry...I don't have any homework...but I do have a lot of notes for you...my teacher is really nice. Yesterday I thought she was a little *mean* but today she smiled at me." Emily meticulously began sorting out a stash of papers from her bookbag.

"If you were in my class, I'd smile at you all the time...my little *poopoodoo!*" Flora tickled Emily and grabbed one of her pear slices.

"Emily, when you're finished with the pear, you can set the table and Jimmy can stick the bag of garbage in little Flora's trunk...then we'll take it to the dump tomorrow."

"*Yeah you big stinky poopoodoo...you can set the table,*"...Jimmy said echoing Flora's request to Emily.

Flora seasoned the chicken and placed it in the oven. She set the timer and peeled the potatoes. Jimmy snatched a piece raw potato. They all heard thunder in the distance.

"Mama...it's starting to rain...I'll bring in all our paints...Jimmy, you want to help me...?" Little Flora peeked her head in the from the doorwall and yelled in. Jimmy helped her bring everything inside.

"Now will you help me with my homework tonight...I saved your artwork from washing out into the sea...?" Jimmy tried to bargain with little Flora.

"Okay, Jimmy, I'll help you...but I won't DO it for you.

"That's all I'm asking for...a little help from my *big* sister." Jimmy was getting to be a big joker and a kind of picky thorn to his sisters.

The chicken was a little dry but the potatoes were great.

After the dishes were done Emily set up the PICTIONARY game hoping someone would want to join her. They all played for a while. Just as Flora was going to announce bedtime for Em, little Flora stood up and looked out the window. She saw a car coming down the driveway. It was dark outside and no one recognized the car.

"Are you expecting anyone?" Little Flora asked as she took a closer look out the window.

"It might be the wood delivery...but I thought he mentioned tomorrow would be the soonest...maybe he changed his mind." Flora got up to look out the window.

"Nope...it's a car...and someone's getting out." Little Flora announced to the rest of the anxious audience. Flora went over to the light switch in the basement hallway and flicked on the floodlights; that light made everything look like it was midday.

"Mama, I think it's a guy and he's walking toward our house...wait...I can't believe it...*it's Paolo!*" Little Flora ran to the door and Jimmy and Emily were directly behind her. They opened the door and ran outside to greet him.

Flora could not believe her ears and then couldn't believe her eyes. He was there...Paolo was really there...how could he be? He was just talking to her a few hours ago.

Flora darted into the bathroom to primp her hair...she felt faint. She forgot about her hair and her pale face and ran out to greet Paolo. She felt uncontrollably giddy thinking that he had actually come back.

Flora walked into the kitchen where Paolo looked like a Christmas tree. Jimmy's head was in a strangle hold under one arm, little Flora was under his other, and Emily was the Angel, sitting around his neck topping the tree. Flora walked up to him and put her arms around Paolo's waist. She squeezed him affectionately. Flora and Paolo looked at each other, lost for a moment in each other's eyes. Tears rolled down Flora's cheeks, and she didn't stop smiling. Little Flora grabbed Emily off Paolo's neck and Jimmy slid out from the limp strangle hold. Flora placed her hand on her hip and smiled at Paolo.

"*I was wondering*...Paolo," Flora said still smiling from ear to ear, "...either you're a wizard or you have *secret* wings none of us know about...how in the heck did you get here so fast?"

Paolo looked at Flora with wide eyes and shaking his head in contemplation.

"Tell us Paolo..., " Emily said pleadingly.

"OKAY...it was simple...I *never* said I was calling from *Florence*...I called from the airport in Detroit...pretty slick, huh...?," Paolo said as he directed his attention first to Emily and then to Jimmy.

"I like the way you do things, Paolo... ." Jimmy quickly said in a congratulatory tone.

"Pretty slick...I should have guessed that," Flora said as she hugged Paolo again.

"Anyone for some fresh coffee?" Little Flora stepped in to bring Paolo and Flora back to earth.

"We'll all have a cup... ." Flora smiled at Paolo and then went to help little Flora get their coffee ready.

"I'm so glad he's here...Little Flora said teasing her mom and quickly moving away to avoid the *pinch of agony*. She smiled at Flora and walked back to the table with a large tray of warm rolls.

"Gratzie tanto...piccola Flora...by the way...I have a message from a fella in Florence...he said to make sure a certain *little flower* gets his message...what was it he told me to say...oh yeah...'*tell my little flower...I love her*'...Giacamo is a poet at heart...even when his hands are full of wet cement...you should have seen how silly he looked when he gave me that message...all the crew was teasing him...but he didn't care...he repeated it *three* times and made me promise not to forget to give you this letter...I made him promise to finish the tile work in the boys shower... ."

"A *letter*...you have a letter," little Flora said excitedly. "Where is the letter?"

Paolo purposely fumbled around his jacket pockets pulling the linings out. "That's why he made me promise...*see*, I almost forgot to give it to you." Paolo reached into his back pant pocket and pulled out an envelope. "Here it is...not very neat...but at least I delivered it. Paolo handed it to little Flora.

"Thanks Paolo... ." Little Flora said as she folded the envelope in half and tucked it inside her sweater pocket. "I'll read it later...it will be nice reading something that's isn't *four* or *five* weeks old...although most of what Giacamo tells me has no expiration date." Little Flora smiled at Paolo and thanked him again.

"You're welcome...and that reminds me...I have a couple other little things inside my pocket that do have expiration dates." Paolo reached into his jacket pocket and handed Jimmy and Emily some mini bags of nuts from his flight...and a small bottle of wine.

"Just for looks big Jimmy...not to drink." Paolo said watching Flora's expression take on a look of wonder. Jimmy's face lit up like it was New Year's Eve. Jimmy promised Paolo that he wouldn't open the bottle until he was twenty-one...and then he'd probably have to use it on a salad. Everyone laughed.

Flora poured Paolo a cup of coffee and placed the cake plate full of cinnamon buns directly in front of him. Paolo loved them. After a little while full of questions and good conversation, little Flora took charge of bedtime. She corralled the crew for bed and avoided walking past her Mom who still owed her the *pinch*.

"Thanks honey...I'll forget about the pinch, too."

"Little Flora just wants to read her mushy letter from Giacamo," Emily said as she walked away grumpily. "But I don't care...I guess I really am tired anyway."

"Sure," said Jimmy teasingly, "You just want to read your new BABYSITTERS CLUB book...talk about mushy stuff."

"We'd rather not right now *James*...so head for the bed or I'll make *you* read *my* mushy letter...," Little Flora said with giddiness in her voice.

"I'd puke if I read that letter... ." Jimmy kissed Flora goodnight and hopped over his chair almost flying his way down the hall to bed. Paolo smiled at little Flora and winked at her as she left the kitchen. He smiled at Flora. She smiled back at him, tenderly.

Flora and Paolo took a few minutes to absorb the shock of being together again, alone. Flora stared across the table at Paolo. He looked at her while he shook his head with a big grin.

His eyes were beautiful to Flora. His eyelashes looked like worn down paintbrushes...short and thick, carefully outlining the mirrors to his soul. Flora broke the silence.

"You're a pretty funny fella...," Flora blurted out to Paolo as she cleared the table. She kept busy, hoping her composure wouldn't go as wild as her thoughts had been running.

"I'm a *funny* fella? I really felt like ALBERTO TOMBA the way the kids greeted me." Paolo chuckled inside as he recalled his warm reception. When the table was cleared he grabbed Flora by her elbow and took the towel from her hands.

"Get your sweater...let's go outside." Paolo led Flora away from the sink. Paolo put his jacket on and walked out to the porch. Flora quickly grabbed her sweater off the hook and met Paolo outside.

Flora walked out to the middle of the lawn, "You know, it rained like crazy this afternoon and then it cleared up so nice...look at the stars...," she said as she looked straight up into the night. "Come on Paolo."

"God...they're beautiful and so many...wait a minute,"

Paolo said as he ran back to the porch. He carried down two outdoor chairs and placed them on the lawn. "It's so black out here...really you can barely see in front of your face...where's the old moon tonight? Let's sit down for a while and talk." Paolo placed a chair under Flora and made her sit down. It was a beautiful night. For a while no words were spoken. Then, Paolo took Flora's hand.

"Flora...it's good to be here...I hope I surprised you! Last night I couldn't sleep...I kept thinking about things...I realized what a fool I've been for waiting...waiting so long to come see you...I thought you needed more time, when actually it was just me who needed more time." Paolo let go of Flora's hand and reached over to put his arm around Flora. His chair tipped and knocked them both over. Paolo held on to Flora during the slow motion fall and didn't let go. He braced the fall with his shoulders. They laughed like they were silly kids and stayed in their awkward position on the damp September grass for a while longer.

"Flora, this *falling down thing* isn't so bad ...things kind of look good from way down here...are you alright?" Paolo looked into her eyes and then kissed her tenderly. Neither of them wanted to end their antics on the lawn. Paolo became very serious as he spoke.

"I came here because I...I want you to know that I need you in my life...this long distance stuff doesn't work."

Flora watched his face. She didn't need to hear his words, his tender embrace and his eyes had said everything she wanted to hear. Flora managed one arm loose and touched his lips with her fingers. She waited till he smiled and then removed her hand and kissed him slowly and passionately making that intimate touching of their lips speak more than any words could ever say.

Even though the ground was wet and the air had chilled, Flora and Paolo were content. They were acting foolishly and didn't want to break the spell. So many times before unexpected things made them come back to reality...or what they thought was reality. They realized the world, unlike lovers, did things differently. They were lovers of life and love and had to decide their own course. They had to follow their hearts; each one warming the others. That would be their reality.

Flora wanted to say so many things to Paolo. Everyday she'd think of something she wanted to share with him. Her journal was fat with writing and articles and poems. She memorized a Bible verse that morning and was going to send it to Paolo the next day.

"Paolo, I came across something neat this morning while I dusted the coffee table. I picked up the Bible and started going through some of the treasures I stuffed in between the pages for safe keeping. An old Easter card from Jimmy fell out and when I went to put it back this verse popped out at me...do you want to hear it?" Flora sat up on the grass ready for Paolo's reply.

"Sure...go ahead." Paolo smiled at Flora. He was thinking of the important things he had to tell her.

Flora looked into Paolo's eyes. "Forgetting what is behind and straining toward what is ahead, I press on toward the goal to win the prize for which God has called me heavenward in Christ Jesus." Flora tried to absorb the words again in her own heart. She had difficulty justifying her motives for leaving Jack...for wanting to start a new life. She knew Paolo had his own doubts. She hoped their love would be strong enough to overcome every obstacle. It had to be.

Paolo didn't say anything after Flora spoke her words. He stood up and walked to the porch steps. Flora followed him.

"I think these are a little safer." Paolo invited Flora to sit down on the wooden porch steps. He sat next to her.

"At least they are a little drier." Flora didn't know what else to say. All of a sudden they were both feeling the cold and the wet and the discomfort of the night.

Flora knew the decision to leave Jack went against everything she ever believed in and the very strict teachings of her Catholic Church. She knew, after Florence, that her life would never be the same. She could not go back to Jack and continue to live her life as if nothing had changed. Flora had decided to live her life with love as it's core...not as it's reward. She needed to love and be loved all the time not just when things went okay or when Jack was in the mood to be civil. She needed more than that. But, she felt very selfish with her reasoning. And she knew, love was always kind.

Flora was vulnerable. When she met Paolo, she tried not to make the same mistake with her emotions as she had with Fr. Bill. She was a wiser woman in Florence...but more afraid of the simple truth; love is all there is. Paolo had been drawn to her as much as she was taken by him.

Paolo, ever since Francesca's death, chose the philosophy of the world. He stopped believing in himself and tried to ignore the strong faith he had in God. He denied his own heart and reasoned with his guilty conscience. Flora contented herself with keeping busy and not looking to hard in the direction of her real feelings, blocking them out and convincing herself that she had outgrown such needs. Both accepted the world as it had made them...never protesting it's cold fallacies, until they met each other.

The whole evening seemed like a dream to Flora. Paolo had surprised her. She remembered the day he scooted her out of the kitchen in the pensione wanting to take her to the Opera. He didn't know the Opera had been canceled that day. They laughed all the way back home. The sun was warm and Flora loved the way it felt on her shoulders, Spring was in the air. Paolo had stayed for supper that night and helped Flora make pizza...American style; piled high with everything from the refrigerator. They stayed up that chilly night till three in the morning sitting by the fireplace and sipping on Vince's homemade Zinfandel wine.

They toasted Vince and Dolly and Bubba and Flora and the fireplace and the wine, the grapes, the sun that made them so sweet and the moon that brought them together...the stars, Florence and love.

Then, the moon coming up over the pines caught both their attention.

"Flora...there's the moon...wait here a minute...I have something in the car for us."

Paolo walked over to the car and opened the back door. He reached across the seat and grabbed something that looked like a jacket. He walked back to the porch and flung open a blanket on the lawn. Flora caught a whiff of a familiar musty odor. He made her sit down and he sat next to her and stared up into the sky. Flora pulled up a corner of the wool blanket and brought it up to her nose. She smelled it and started laughing. It was the musty blanket from their evening at San Miniato. Flora stood up and confronted Paolo who was still playing *Mr. Innocent* with his eyes in the sky.

"You mean you brought *this* all the way from San Miniato...?" Flora took a deep sniff into the blanket.

"Yeah...and now I kind of feel sorry for the poor guy who sat next to me on the plane...I kept this on my lap because it kept falling off the shelf...whew...it does sort of smell...oh well."

"Paolo...I knew you would come, I would have waited forever...or at least till the firewood ran out." Flora pushed him flat on the blanket and knelt beside him. She wrapped her arms around his neck.

Paolo kissed Flora knowing that he wouldn't have wasted another minute of his life living without the woman who came to Florence, answering his prayer. But, the next announcement he had to share with Flora made him wonder if he hadn't bit off more than he could chew. Promising Fr. Cellini his services just hours before, suddenly made Paolo feel regret. Being with Flora made him realize going to see her in person might have been a bad decision. He loved Flora. Before, the miles had taken the edge off their passion. The safe distance between them painted a distorted picture of the way things really were. The way things were, was more than he planned on dealing with. Seeing her and feeling her made him realize that leaving again was going to be the most difficult thing he'd ever have to do.

Paolo didn't want to be under the stars that shouted everything good. He felt guilty hearing such good news from the heavens. Atrocities prevailed half a world away...under the same sky. As their glimmerings caught his eyes, so they filled his eyes with tears. Things became jumbled in his heart.

"Flora...let's go back inside...I'll start a fire and we can talk."

How much Paolo wanted to forget about the words that were pounding in his head. There were words that were going to change many things.

"It is getting chilly...I have something nice to warm us up...," Flora said, agreeing with his suggestion. "You've got to be tired...let's go." Flora took his hand and walked back to the cottage.

"I'll be there in a minute," Flora said as she turned the burner on under the tea kettle. Paolo went into the living room and started a fire in the fireplace.

"The fire will be great, Paolo." Flora tried to make some light conversation. "Here...try this...and then we'll have some hot tea... ." Flora handed Paolo a glass of wine.

"Gratzie, Flora...," Paolo said charmingly. He sipped the wine. "Zinfandel...whoa...that'll knock the chill out of an elephant." Paolo rubbed his stomach.

Flora laughed at Paolo's expression."My sister-in-law's father makes it every year. She brought a bottle up when they visited last summer and told me it was from a good batch...I guess it is...," Flora said as she winced her eyes from the potency of the drink.

"It's gotta be more of a brandy...but I like it...whew... ."

"I'll have to tell Debby that her Dad's wine was a hit," Flora said as she sat down on the couch by the fireplace.

"Well...it's sure hitting me," Paolo said as he moved to the couch with Flora. Flora sipped her wine, wondering what was to come.

"Flora...it is good to be here... ."

"It is good... ." Flora clinked the tip of her glass to Paolo's. Before her toast left her lips, Paolo interrupted.

"To us...right now...to...being together... ." Paolo clinked his glass to Flora's. Flora smiled at his words.

"To us, Paolo... ."

Paolo took Flora's hand. He held it tightly.

"Flora...I have to tell you something important."

"I'm listening... ." Flora couldn't imagine what he had to tell her. By his expression she knew it had to be serious. She listened. Paolo began his announcement carefully.

"Fr. Cellini called me into his office yesterday and asked me to do him a favor...he asked me to help his brother who runs an orphanage in Bosnia... ." Paolo hesitated a moment, then asked Flora if she remembered him talking about Alfredo.

"I'm not sure...is he the missionary brother?"

"No...his missionary brother is in Asia...Alfredo's just a super man who threw up his arms one day and headed for Yugoslavia to help a friend for a few weeks...that was ten years ago...now he runs an orphanage...he was an inspiration to me ever since I was a kid...Alfredo used to have dinner with my family and he'd tell the best stories...he was always moving from one end of the world to another...helping anyone who needed help...no matter what it was...he would help to change things...make them better."

"Where is his orphanage now...?" Flora began putting the pieces together.

"That's the tricky part...it's just outside of Bosnia."

As Paolo went on, the disappointment in Flora's heart grew more intense. She knew he was going to leave her again.

"Flora...don't look so worried...Georgio made me promise to get the job done and to get the hell out of there...so don't worry about me spending too much time delivering the relief...it's not that big a deal...really." Paolo realized he had said enough.

"I don't know what to say, Paolo... ." Flora didn't want to believe her ears, but a part of her deeply understood Paolo's concern.

"Say what you feel...that's why I came here...I couldn't have told you this on the phone...I had to tell you in person." Paolo looked into her eyes with a look that said so many things. Flora was still for a moment. Then, she looked away from Paolo's face and into the fire.

"Why...why was it so important to see me...you came all this way to tell me that you're going away for who knows how long...on some kind of quasi-*kamikaze* mission...and you want me to say what I feel about all this...in twenty seconds?"

"NO...how about thirty seconds," Paolo asked facetiously hoping to make Flora smile. His comic relief didn't make her smile.

"Flora...I'm not trying to be funny...and I'm not goofing around...I know that you know I care deeply...it isn't fair dropping all this on you...but I had no choice...no...I did have a choice but I had to make sure you understood the reasons why I made the decision I did...I want you to understand." Flora hesitated for a while, then finally spoke.

"I do understand...that's part of the reason I love you...but seeing you now is so good...I can't imagine you going away again... ."

Paolo stood up from the couch. He poked around at the fire. Then he spoke.

"This whole trip might have been a bad idea...the thought of never seeing you again distorted my judgement...I don't want to think of the worst, but if I had gone away without seeing you...I can't predict the future...and I didn't want to risk loosing you...all I knew a few hours ago, was that I had to see you...maybe I should have called or written this whole farce in a letter." Paolo sat down next to Flora feeling strangely discouraged.

"Flora...I did what I thought was best for you and me...maybe it was selfish...but if you feel the same way I do right now...this trip couldn't have been a mistake...I remembered the morning you called Dolly and when she gave me the phone you told me that you only wanted me to hold you and tell you that everything was going to be okay...I want to hold you tonight and make sure you know that everything is going to be alright."

"I'm glad you came," Flora said as she looked into Paolo's eyes, "I'm very glad you came." Paolo followed his heart to hers. Flora reached over to the coffee-table and picked up a magazine. She placed it on Paolo's lap.

"I just read an article in the TIME magazine about the conditions in Bosnia and Croatia", Flora said as Paolo began leafing through the pages. Flora went on.

"The Serbs and Muslims and Croats...it's absolutely like hell there right now...so many innocent people dying and the children are starving and being abused and...believe it or not...when I read this last week I thought of you...especially after I read the article on the two children who were murdered on a bus...not victims of war...victims of everyday life."

Flora turned on the lamp closest to Paolo. He skimmed through the article and then carefully placed it back on the table. Like it held no secrets. He looked carefully at Flora.

"Flora...it is that bad...even worse," Paolo said looking directly into Flora's eyes. "Alfredo had some grim tales of his own first hand account...it's like, even while Fr. Cellini was telling me about the situation in Bosnia...I felt guilty...it made me feel sick...no one realizes the situation over there...and it isn't going to just go away...when he asked for help...how could I have refused him?"

"You couldn't have," Flora said understanding his decision to help Alfredo. She went on very carefully.

"I'm sorry Paolo...I think if you had refused him...I'd have been more disappointed...it's just that seeing you made me flip...when you held me in your arms I thought we were finally going to get on with things...with our life together....hey...don't mind all this...I'm a romantic fool...I'll be alright...you will be alright." Flora poured wine into their half emptied glasses as her eyes filled with tears. For a moment she lost her sense of timing. She wondered about love and how, even in the face of a desperate situation, it kept two hearts hopeful.

Paolo's sneeze snapped Flora out of her philosophical wander. He was there now, his sneeze and his commitment to something he believed in. Love overflowed from their hearts like the wine glass on the coffee table that had been filled dangerously full to the brim.

"You know, after I saw you Flora...and held you in my arms...I wanted to forget about the promise I made to Fr. Cellini...do you know how tempting that is for me right now?"

Flora didn't say anything right away but allowed Paolo's words to go through her mind once more. She sat up straight and finally answered his question and his begging expression.

"I know how tempting it is...and...I'm glad you aren't going to change anything...I understand what you have to do...I wish it were done and over though...I mean...I'm glad you told me about it...but...I'm *scared* Paolo...I'm petrified in fact."

"Flora...I'm scared...," Paolo said taking a strong hold of Flora's hands. He continued.

"Last night...I prayed that everything would be resolved with Alfredo...that he wouldn't need me...that you would come back to Florence...and that we could get on with our lives...I was sincere in my prayer...and as much as I tried not to listen to that tiny voice in my soul...I couldn't block it out hard enough...then I laughed inside...about my juvenile petitions...finally I gave in to the situation...the next prayer was about you, and how I had to tell you in person about my decision...Flora...you...in my mind, made everything else fall back into perspective...I knew I had to see you if anything was going to make sense...I'm glad I came." Paolo hugged Flora with most of his strength; the portion he held back safeguarded his promise to Alfredo. It would have been easy then to call the whole thing quits...but that whole thing now was a part of Paolo...it lived and breathed inside of him.

"Flora," Paolo said still holding her hands, "...everything will be fine, no matter how things go tomorrow, or the next day, or the next month...something inside of me knows that we are going to be okay, and that's what's giving me the strength to do what I have to do." Paolo looked into Flora's eyes a look that made her believe that everything would be fine. His words enforced the things that were inside of her own heart. Flora was completely taken with Paolo's intimate sharing. She listened to every word as he continued.

"You know, it isn't just our lives that have changed...it seems the world is begging for our help so it can change...love and truth will always prevail...you know Flora...no matter where I went in the world...especially when I lived in New York...I never felt settled...there was the feeling that no one..no one, especially me, was content...a city of people thinking they were somewhere...but going where?I was nowhere. In Florence with Vince and Georgio and Dolly...everyone, even the orphans seem to be exactly where they should be...where everyone should be at this point in time...do you get what I'm saying?"Paolo caught his seriousness. Noticing Flora's tight smile, he asked why she was grinning.

"I understand... ." Flora looked up into Paolo's face...scanning his features one by one as if she was making a copy in her mind of the face she loved. She touched his lips; she told him that no more words needed to be said. Like a sculptor, she slid her thumbs down the bridge of his nose telling him to keep it out of trouble. Finally, she outlined his deep dark eyes with gentle kisses. "I love you Paolo." Flora whispered her commitment to him .

It was difficult...it was almost impossible for them to think of parting again. They spoke of things that bound their hearts and souls. They agreed that the world was sometimes cruel. Many misdirected and unsuspecting souls, capable of so much love and compassion walked around with blinders on their hearts; wearing masks society will accept. Paolo didn't believe in masks or anything else that would hide the truth. He was too full of love and it's clear vision.

Paolo's vision was keen and he heard the sound of hope in Alfredo's plea. That commitment drew Paolo to Flora like fire to oxygen; he needed her encouragement, he needed her love to survive.

Paolo realized that he was never self sufficient...that no one is complete on their own. Their night was full of love, and like all good things, moved too quickly with time's apathetic rhythm. People made things happen...their love made things happen...that's what Paolo believed. That's what Flora always believed.

"It's getting late... ." Paolo said as he looked at the old German clock on the fireplace mantle. "We're gonna be okay." He kissed Flora tenderly and carefully. Thoughts of his upcoming journey made him cautious. He kissed Flora's tears. He made his move abruptly from the couch.

Paolo stared out the doorwall while pulling his heavy

sweater down over his head. The brilliant stars that joined their hearts celebration, had melted in the pale morning sky. The still lake reflected the empty, colorless heavens. He didn't want to say good-bye.

Flora saw too much in Paolo's stare. She knew she would have to make the best of the next moments...she wanted him to go away with her courage and love tucked inside his gallant heart. He gave her courage that night as he shared his deepest thoughts.

"Paolo...take this...," Flora said as she removed her treasured keepsake from around her neck. "I'm sure you'll find good use for it sometime." Flora handed her pendant to Paolo.

"It's your gold pendant...your good luck charm," Paolo said as he smiled at Flora. She turned away and started folding the Afghan, pretending to be brave.

"I don't need anything for luck," Flora said with determined courage, "...you are my charm...I want you to have this just in case... ." Flora didn't want to finish her thought out loud. She didn't want Paolo to know that she was afraid for him.

Maybe her fancy filigree gold necklace would make him think of her and their night in the north...maybe it would remind him of her love in a land where so many things will shout despair. She believed her pendant could be whatever he needed it to be.

"Just in case what?" Paolo said knowing exactly why Flora gave him her special token. He sat down, heavily into the couch. Paolo pulled Flora down with him.

"Just in case you forget...I...hey...I don't know...just in case...you need a cup of coffee and you haven't got a dime." Flora smiled at her quick thinking and her silly comment. They looked at each other's costumed expression. Flora felt wonderful sitting so close to him.

"I'm not going to the RITZ." Paolo said as he went along with Flora. He clenched the necklace tightly in his fist.

"This would buy one big cup of special brew," Paolo teasingly said as he held Flora closer to his body, "...I love you so much." Paolo pressed Flora's head on his chest and prayed silently that God would keep them safe and that his return would be soon. Flora returned his sentiments with a quiet aspiration of her own. She would keep him tenderly in her heart, forever.

Paolo stretched out on the couch. Flora started to get up to give him more room to get comfortable.

"No...don't get up...there's plenty of room...come here." Paolo scooted on his side which made just enough space for Flora to fit. Flora scooted as close as she could to Paolo, facing him. She could feel him breathe. As Flora concentrated on his breathing, as she looked deeply into his kind dark eyes, she wondered how she ever lived without him...how she was going to have to say good-bye.

"Will you hold me tight, Paolo...," Flora said as a chill swept through her body. Paolo pressed his fingers against her cool, smooth cheeks. He held her tight hoping to warm her body and her soul. Flora's loose robe slipped off her shoulders. Paolo brought it back.

"No wonder you felt chilly...you're not exactly dressed underneath your robe."

"Not *exactly*," Flora said, trying to mimic Paolo's sincere expression. "I'll go get a t-shirt...hang on a minute." Flora watched Paolo's face as she tried to slowly maneuver her way up from the couch. Paolo saw her game, then drew Flora closer to himself.

"Nope...you're not going anywhere...we'll be chilly together... ."

"If that's the way you want it...but, I've got an idea...," Flora said as she awkwardly slipped her chenille robe completely off, "...cover us up with this...and we'll both stay warm." Paolo took the robe from Flora and diligently tried to cover them without disrupting both of their comfortable positions on the couch. Flora giggled at his tenacity.

"Go ahead and laugh at me," Paolo said with a laugh of his own. "It's more difficult than it looks...remember, I'm doing this with one hand."

"Whose fault is that...just ask me to move and I will, then you'll have two arms to struggle with," Flora said trying to tease Paolo even more.

"This could be an *olympic* event...I'm almost out of breath...now we'll be warm."

"This feels good and warm...I'd give you a gold medal for your persistence." Flora kissed Paolo's hand.

"I am a good cover-upper...," Paolo said, pleased with himself and their folly. "I'm pretty good at a few other things, Flora...so...if there is anything else I can do for you my lady...please, ask." Paolo looked at Flora with an expression eager to please.

"Paolo...," Flora softly whispered, "...do you think we could stay like this...till the sun breaks through the clouds...or the kids get up for pancakes?" She brought her lips to his and kissed him tenderly.

When their kiss ended, Paolo looked into Flora's eyes. They invited him again to be her lover. His eyes told her that he'd do more than wait for the clouds to dissipate. With fire inside his heart and with the gentle strength he harbored in his soul, he loved her passionately and with no reservation.

Chapter
twenty-seven

Time Heals

Heavy clouds hung low in the December afternoon sky;
more full of cold than snow.

Everyone had packed their bags for the big trip home
the night before. Flora sat on the cold cement porch steps
waiting for the school bus to drop off Emily and Jimmy.

She skimmed through her journal which had become a
friend to her the past few months. Her ordinary and extraordinary thoughts had been written down daily...faithfully.
Reading the recent past echoes from her heart that cold
afternoon made her more anxious for her trip home...but
also very thankful for the precious time she had up in her
northern retreat. She knew those days had emptied her
heart of the nagging clutter that had neatly piled up over
the years. Bit by bit, the autumn days and their profound
example, made Flora let go of the person she thought she
had become. She began to see herself as she really was, not
just the person she thought she was suppose to be. As the
trees changed their color and as the autumn clouds
resounded their seasonal song, Flora moved along with
them; trying to learn from their simple and natural obedi-
ence. Her fingers, stiff and clumsy from the cold, fumbled
through the pages until her entry from October 20 caught
her special attention. She read:

Dear Paolo,

With every word, I pray, that as the ink absorbs into this paper, so might these words be received into your heart.

I miss you...alot...and I wish you were here or I was there...everything up here reminds me of you. Our time together seems like a long ago dream.

We're having snow today...an early snow I've heard from all the radio people...it is so soft and beautiful. The leaves are still clinging to their branches which make the snow in this mid-morning light seem pastel...like the snow on early springtime buds. The flakes are large and fall softly down to our dear mother earth. I close my eyes now and can feel their gentle touch. I should go outside right now and let them bury me with their heavenly message.

I couldn't resist the temptation...I ran outside and stretched out on the lawn...I closed my eyes and pretended the snowflakes were kisses from you...I know you are fine and healthy...I have to keep thinking that everything will be good.

The accumulation of the magic snow is melting from my hair now and dripping on this note to you...can you feel them, Paolo? The whole world is crying for you and me...we have to be strong.

Then, a letter from Dolly written a few weeks before fell from Flora's journal. She opened it and read it.

"Dear Flora,

"It doesn't get any easier, does it? Of course you know I'm talking about life and not the art of squeezing into my girdle!

"Vince and I sat up last night wondering and thinking, thinking and wondering...about the past, the present and the future. The older you get the less sleep you need...that's what I heard, anyway. Or, maybe it was Lucia's visit that wound us up. The zinfandel wine was the best yet...maybe we had too much new wine!

"The past we can smile at. It comes and goes through our

minds so often it's become a familiar friend. The present is new and somewhat mysterious...but has a way of fitting into things if we just let it be. Now the future is the bugger, especially if we begin spending too much of "today" worrying about it.

"Lucia asked one hundred questions about Paolo and what he was doing in Bosnia. She told us many stories about things she had heard...where the heck does she get her information...I'd love to book her on UNSOLVED MYSTERIES! We love her but it does take a few days to unwind from her visits. She is going crazy making plans for the big weddings next Fall. She also heard that Giacamo's mother isn't doing well after her surgery. You probably know this already.

"Giacamo still very much taken with little Flora. He tells me that he knows she will be back one day and then she will fall in love with him. I think she has already. It seems little Flora is alot like *her* mother.

"Flora...I hope you are doing fine. Your last letter was down in the dumps. Don't worry about things you have no control over. Do what you can do and go from there.

"I think that you and the kids going home for the holidays is a good idea. Going home and being together with your big family will help put somethings to rest. Enjoy the turkey for me. Vince and I are going to celebrate, too.

"Flora, no new news from Paolo. I think we are going to have to take the bits and pieces as they come. In between time we will pray that he is safe; I know he is in God's care.

"Don't eat too much turkey!...Could I go for a piece of pumpkin pie with whipped cream! "

Love, Dolly"

"P.S. Tell Emily and Jimmy we found Brutus a playmate. A little puppy followed Vince home from the market-place...we all fell in love with her...we call her BEFANA...she'll grow into it!"

Flora folded Dolly's letter and put it back in her journal. She wiped the tears that snuck into her eyes as she heard Little Flora slam the door behind her. Little Flora could barely contain her excitement about the holidays...and going home. Flora tucked the journal in her travel bag.

"It was nice up here Mama...but I'm really looking forward to seeing everyone...I'm so dang excited." Little Flora threw another suitcase in the trunk.

Flora was excited for the kids. She knew they had been gallant for her, above and beyond the call of duty. She knew too, that their Fall adventure made them grow up as much as it had forced her to evolve. It was time to go home for all of them.

"Me, too, little Flora...in fact, if we didn't have to chop down the trees...we could meet the kids up the road...and we'd be off from there." Flora stood up and rubbed her fanny hoping to warm it up.

"Gosh...it's freezing...*hurry up bus!*" Flora jumped up and down like a kid...and little Flora did the same...together they started walking up the driveway screaming with delight oozing...pouring out of every bone in their bodies. They laughed at each others anticipation.

"You know Mom...I used to worry so much about the word *little* in my name...it used to bother me alot...but now...now I don't ever want that endearing adjective to be dropped...especially by my family...it will always remind me to keep a part of my heart open and trusting, like a child...I love this jumping up and down...but I'm getting a headache."

Little Flora hugged her Mom. Flora hugged her back,

hard.

"Okay my *little* Flora...wait here and I'll get the saw and we'll be ready for the kids."

No sooner had Flora run down to the car to pick up the saw, the school bus came into view.

"Bye Mrs. Glynn...see you next year." Emily giggled at her salutation to the bus driver. Jimmy just shook his head as he waved good-bye to Mrs. Glynn.

"Have a Merry Christmas...too," Jimmy said hurriedly. He was too wound up to even tease Emily about her *ancient* departing line to the bus driver. He ran down to get the saw from Flora.

They all walked across the road and chopped the two trees they had picked out a few weeks before. One tree for the inside of Grama's house and one tree for just outside the living room bay window.

"Are you sure these trees are big enough?" Emily asked in a truly concerned voice.

"Yeah, Emily...they'll be big enough...look...this one is way taller than me...and this one is double my size...we'll probably have to chop a little off when we get home...*home*...that sounds sweet." Jimmy handled the tree job very well. He took charge of tying the knots on the roof carrier. He made sure he tied them in triple knots.

"When I take them off...I'll just cut the rope with my knife...if they aren't too frozen...we're all set...let's go!"

"Anyone have to use the bathroom?, Flora asked, taking a last minute check on the house, "...we'll stop for lunch in Gaylord...okay...lead the way...!" Flora slammed the door and locked it. She straightened the Christmas wreath that swung off center. She thought it looked so much like Christmas there. Little Flora was thinking the same thought.

"Maybe we'll celebrate next Christmas here." Little Flora smiled at her mother as she verbalized her mental note.

"I'd love that...wouldn't that be neat Jimmy if everyone came up here...?" Emily didn't wait for a response.

Jimmy went directly into Emily's face and exaggerated his response, "IT WOULD BE E-M-I-L-Y-...but let's not talk about NEXT year...let's enjoy THIS Christmas...FOR-WARD...HO...!"

The Mackinac bridge was closed for an hour. The fifty-five miles after that were slick with frozen snow. Gaylord was a welcomed stop on their schedule. Lunch turned into supper and a little shopping. The weather cleared and the rest of the trip was smooth sailing. Emily and Jimmy fell asleep. Taking advantage of the quiet time, little Flora talked to Flora about her plans for the new year.

"I've been thinking lately...and I don't want you to take this the wrong way...because I loved it up north these past few months...I'll cherish the time we had together forever...but...I've got to get on with my life...I'm not sure what that means yet, except that I know I have to find out about some of the things I've been wondering about...you know."

Flora looked at her daughter and smiled. She knew little Flora had been ready for quite some time *to get on with her life.*

"I understand...in fact the past few weeks I've felt guilty about dragging you kids with me...but in August...I had no options...and I knew we would make the best of it...and we did."

"We did Mama." Little Flora smiled back at her mother's face.

"Tell me more about your plans." Flora was anxious to hear about little Flora's ideas for her future.

"I know you might be going to Florence soon," little Flora said in a confessing type tone, "...and I've given that alot of thought...I'd love to study in Florence...but things are so up in the air with you...and I need something definite...so, I'm going to apply at the University in Florence and go on from there."

Flora looked at little Flora and smiled. She looked back at the road hoping little Flora would tell her more. She did.

"And...I think...I love Giacamo," little Flora said with an expression that even surprised herself. She continued with much confidence.

"Mama, I think I've loved him from the first time I saw him...but I wouldn't let my mind believe it...I didn't want to hurt Dan...but I hurt Dan more by dragging him through months of wishy-washy decision making...he wasn't ready to accept it anymore than I was...and I after I broke things off completely with him...I felt guilty for loving Giacamo...a guy I only knew for weeks and hadn't seen for months...but this time up here and writing to him and reading his thoughts and feelings...I know I have to give this a chance...so after Christmas I'm going back to Florence...Dolly said I can live at the pensione with her and Vince...and I am concerned about Giacamo's mother...I'd like to visit with her again...so, what do you think?"

Flora wished she had things as balanced in her mind. Her little girl had grown up.

"I know you are doing the right thing...how could you not follow your heart to Giacamo...?"

"I know...and it scares me to think I almost talked myself out of it...I almost convinced myself that things would have been wonderful with Dan because he is such a great person...but...I didn't really love him...he deserved better than that...I deserved better...I knew that the moment I met Giacamo, can you believe I actually fell in love with him the moment I saw him?"

"I can believe that...and...well...all I can say right now...is...that the best thing that can ever happen between two people has happened to you and Giacamo...treasure it and keep it good...I'm so happy for you."

Little Flora poured her mom a cup of hot coffee from the thermos. They toasted Christmas...going home...the family...life...and...Grama's raspberry tarts.

"AND...one more toast...to Dad...and that one day he will be as happy...he deserves that, too."

"Yes...he does deserve to be happy...," Flora said with soft conviction.

Little Flora heard a tinge of remorse in her mother's calm words. The next question came unexpectedly from little Flora.

"Mom...let's see if I can phrase this correctly...what one thing...no...what was the biggest reason for Dad and you ending your marriage...I mean...I don't want to sound dumb...or nosy...but...I know you love Dad...and in his own way I know he loves you...and you guys love us kids so much...and our family was fun...good...we had so many good times...and it freaks me out to think that the whole time...or part of the time, something was missing in your life...I don't know exactly what I want to say...but...I just want to know why you fell in love with Paolo?.. when did you stop loving Dad...if you hadn't met Paolo...would you still be with Dad...?" Little Flora touched her mother's hand gently and waited for her mom's response.

Flora didn't say anything for a good mile. She wanted to answer Little Flora with the simplicity and honesty her daughter was looking for. But, there were no simple answers to her loaded question.

"Still be with Dad? Probably...and we would be okay...I don't want to belittle my years of marriage to Dad by saying too much or by not saying enough...love can't be reasoned...or explained. I think Paolo and I just happened to meet at a time when not falling in love with each other would have been the greater misfortune...we were both given a second chance to love and be loved...and even knowing that it was wrong to be unfaithful to Dad...I let myself fall hard and fast, but not *from* love...into love...love made me let go of a relationship that was empty...only love could have ever given me the courage to let go...Paolo did that for me...he was there for a purpose...he was there for me to love...I hope that one day we'll have a chance to be together again...now, I'm happy for you...and it's the holidays and we are going home...and you are in love."

Little Flora understood her mother's words...and her watery eyes. She smiled at her mother, not saying a word.

"And...that settles it...," Flora said after clearing her throat, "...if you aren't going to go back up...we'll all stay back home for the winter...Jimmy's been hinting around about staying down home and Emily's teacher confided in me last week that Emily mentioned not coming back for the winter...I think we all need to be back home with everybody...although...I will miss *the quiet days*," Flora said with tongue in cheek.

Little Flora looked at her mom with a big grin .

"*Miss the quiet days*...NAAAAAA...we've had enough for a while."

Flora laughed with agreement.

"Look at that little farm house, Mama...it looks like a Christmas card...," Emily said in a half yawn while pointing out her window. It did look like a Christmas card, Flora thought.

The last hour home was the best. They passed so many little towns with decorations and countryside. The thrill of the holiday was making them giddy. Smoke from distant chimneys and evergreens decked out with twinkling lights made them grow more anxious for Union Lake. Flora had dreamt of pulling into the driveway and then surprising everyone with their carols on the porch. She had dreams of Paolo, too, that kept a part of her seriously sober. Thoughts of him on his dangerous mission made her sick with uncertainty. Dolly's letters had been her only communications from him. She'd have given up that Christmas to be with him...with him anywhere, if that had been possible.

The holiday came. It was Christmas Eve.

"It's really like we never even stayed up there...I mean,

now that I'm home...it seems like I never was gone...," little Flora said trying to answer everyone's questions at once. The young kids swarmed around the *Northerners* for information on the trials and tribulations of the past months.

"Are you guys going back up...?" Little Larry asked Emily politely.

"I don't think so...little Flora wants to go to school here and Jimmy misses all of you guys...alot."

"No I don't...that's not it...you are so stupid sometimes Emily."

"OH...so you didn't miss us huh, JIMMSY POO...well we missed you...you big jerk." Donny knew what Jimmy meant but had to tease him. Jimmy took the bait...hook, line and sinker.

"No...you know I missed you guys...but we're not going back because little Flora wants to start school...that's all she did was paint and write Giacamo mushy letters...and *smoke* on the deck!"

"And I suppose you didn't write to *Hillary*." Little Flora had to get back at her brother's wise crack...even if it was Christmas Eve.

Jimmy turned to his cousins in defense and swore up and down trying to set his record straight about Hillary.

"I swear I never wrote to Hillary or any other girl on the face of this earth...swear to God."

"Jimmy, since it's Christmas...I'll just drop the whole thing...like, JOY TO THE WORLD...but we know the truth...and quit swearing." Little Flora winked at her brother teasingly as she walked like a proud peacock by him to answer the knock at the front door. She turned around and reminded Jimmy about *Alice* from Gulliver and how his cousins might want to hear about THAT.

"WHOA...JIMMSIES...the ALICEMEISTER...we gotta hear about that cookie." Danny and Donny were anxious to hear more. Little Flora promised to talk to them later as she reached for the doorknob. When she opened the door she was very surprised.

"Come in, please come in...MERRY CHRISTMAS...what a surprise...I'll get my mom." Everyone's attention went to the vestibule. It was Fr. Bill.

"I knew you'd all be together tonight celebrating...so I invited myself over...hope you don't mind."

No one minded. Bubba was used to unexpected guests on Christmas Eve...that was part of the specialness of the evening. Long lost relatives often stopped in to see Bubba and relish the extravagant way the night was spent enjoying old times, great food, and treasured friends. The greetings subsided and after a taste of everyone's special treat, Fr. Bill asked Flora if he could talk with her a few minutes alone.

Flora put the leash on KIRK and then walked outside. That was about as alone as she could be with the entire house full of merrymakers. She wondered what Fr. Bill had to say.

KIRK pulled on his leash and practically dragged Flora to his hook on the tree; the dog was well trained to his spot for eliminations. Fr. Bill laughed at Flora's composure...she wanted to strangle the pooch for making her trip on the patch of old ice. Fr. Bill helped her up.

"Thanks for the lift," Flora said with a twinge of embarrassment in her voice. "The dang dog is a BRAT!...not really, he's got a pretty cute disposition...but he's young and full of piss and vinegar." Flora wrinkled her nose and then smiled. Fr. Bill tapped her nose with his finger.

"We were all full of it when we were young." Bill smiled at Flora.

"So...how have you been Bill?"

Bill handed the dog a piece of Christmas cookie.

"I'm okay."

"You look fine...maybe just a little tired," Flora said sensing that everything wasn't as good as Bill wanted her to believe. "The holidays do that sometimes...we get so wrapped up...excuse the pun...but really...it's so good to see you."

"Flora...it's nice to see you," Bill took Flora's hand, "...you are a good friend to me...you're the only one I know from the old neighborhood that still writes."

"I enjoy it, Bill." Flora squeezed Bill's hand.

"I wanted to see you before I went in for surgery at St. John's on the twenty-seventh...for a *quadruple* bypass...they say the procedure is an everyday thing now, like going in for a hernia operation...anyway...I volunteered to say midnite mass for Fr. Ron tonight so I better get going."

"Wait a minute, Bill, a quadruple bypass? When did all of this come up?" Flora held his hand even tighter.

"My doctor's been hounding me about it for a few months now...so...I may as well get it over with...don't worry about me...I'm gonna be fine...but I've got to go Flora."

"I'll keep you in my prayers Bill...everything will be fine." Flora was at a loss for words. Bill's face had aged and he looked too thin for his healthy frame. The wind had picked up and it was getting late. Flora walked Bill to his car. She wondered where all the written words had gone that used to pour out from her heart.

"If you get a chance...drop me a line...I'd like to hear more about your art career...I always liked your artwork you know...and I want to hear more about your friend from Florence."

Flora wasn't surprised at his request. Bill was a lover of life...a lover of his God. She was magnetized once by that love confusing it with something she wanted it to be. How that something seemed so foolish to her now.

"I will Bill...you know me and letter writing...and don't worry about writing back...I know you care about all of us...I know writing isn't something you enjoy...I do enough for both of us anyway."

Fr. Bill smiled at Flora.

"I'm happy for you, Flora." Flora reached through his open window and kissed him on the cheek. Flora wished him a Merry Christmas.

"I wouldn't mind a visit after the big *gig* Flora.

"Call me...and I'll be there...*ADESTE FIDELES!*

Flora watched as he pulled away from the curb. She thought about the timing of things and the old saying of Ben Franklin on the plaque in the laundry room, *Time is a herb that heals all wounds.*

"Aunt Flora...everyone's wondering where you are...come on in, Grama's cutting her special cake." Little Larry came outside to get Flora. He knew how much she loved that raspberry whipped cream torte. Flora walked back to the tree to unleash KIRK. She walked inside holding little Larry's hand. "Thanks *Lorenzo DiMedici* for coming to get me."

"Where's Fr. Bill... ," Jimmy asked, "...does he want to play some poker?"

"He left...he'll just make it back in time for Mass...maybe we'll see him later on next week."

Flora helped Grama pass out the special holiday dessert. The night was typically wonderfilled. Fr. Bill's visit made it even extra wonderful. It proved to Flora that she had grown up even more than she thought. She looked at Bill and saw why he was her friend. Seeing him made her realize that time did heal many wounds.

After Flora and Grama had straightened up the party house and nestled the younger kids in their beds, Flora sat by the fire and examined the Christmas tree with great peacefulness in her heart. The ornaments collected over the years made Flora nostalgic. Almost a quarter century adorned that tree. Angels and stars, muppets , clothespin people the kids made in Mrs. Verlinde's art class, Hallmark special edition ornaments that celebrated birthdays and special days, all told their stories again to her that night.

In the soft radiance that hallowed each colored light on

the tree, Flora saw the good things in her life; her family and friends...the traditions that gathered all of them together. She fell asleep with those visions that were sweeter than sugarplums. The past, present and future filled her mind with memories, smiles and dreams.

Chapter
twenty-eight

Scars And Stars

Flora wondered what Bill had to talk with her about. His surgery had been a success and he was heading back to the windy city the next morning, that she already knew.

The snowstorm, from a couple days before, was neatly piled up into banks along the highway. Flora was grateful for the clear roads and the day off from her full schedule. There were things she hoped to confess to Bill...if the opportunity arose.

"He's fine...and...he's in room...three twenty-three, bed two," said the nurse at the front desk. "Take the elevator two floors up and make a right when you get out of it. " Flora followed the directions from the helpful nurse and hopped on the elevator. When it stopped, she stepped out and turned right.

Flora walked down the hall counting down the room numbers. One floor above...which seemed a world apart from her then, was the room her five children were born. Flora peeked inside room three twenty-three. A strange face greeted her glance.

"Nope...I'm three twenty three, bed one...I'm the *sassy* guy in this room...Bill's over there getting his staples out."

Flora laughed politely at the character in three twenty three, bed one. He motioned for her to go behind the drawn curtain.

"Knock-knock," Flora said, waiting for the *who's there?*

"Flora...is that you...come on in...Doc's pulling out the last *zip* in my zipper...OUCH!"

"Bill...hold still...or you might need a few more stitches...you're all set...I'll be back tomorrow to discharge you and...have a nice visit." Bill's doctor smiled a plastered smile at Flora, then walked out of the room.

"I'm glad that's over...you know...his bedside manner would make *Marcus Welby* cringe...but *Ben Casey* would be proud of him...really...he's a great guy...look how neat he stapled me up." Bill opened his unbuttoned shirt. Flora's arms went weak, but she pretended the raw scar didn't offend her.

"He is pretty neat," Flora said as her eyes quickly fled Bill's chest, "...his mother must have been a seamstress...and his dad had to have been a tailor." She watched Bill button his shirt back up. "Bill...you look great...you're cheeks are rosy again." Flora thought Bill looked one-hundred percent better than he did on Christmas Eve.

"Rosy cheeks?...thanks Flora," Bill said looking in his tabletop mirror, "...you're looking kind of peaked now...let's go to the sitting room...I need a cigarette."

As they walked down the hall, Flora watched Bill light up his cigarette. She shook her head and wondered for a half second about saying something admonishing...she decided not to. Bill had probably heard it all before, anyway. He deserved that cigarette. Flora thought it was good to see him smile his boyish grin. She thought it was funny how much pleasure a little paper and tobacco could bring to a grown man.

"Thanks for coming, Flora."

"Thanks for asking me...and here's a little gift."

Bill opened the tissue package while holding his just lit cigarette tightly between his lips.

"Flora...I love it'...it's the cottage...the lake." Bill looked

up to Flora. "You did this?" Bill held the painting at arms
length and smiled.

"You act so surprised," Flora said as she crunched the
tissue and ribbon and squished it into her tiny purse. "I'm
glad you like it...your the one who always told me to *do
something* with my talent."

"Flora...this is beautiful...I'll hang it in my room when I
go home...and one day when you are famous...I'll charge
admission to anyone who wants to see it...and... ." Bill
looked at Flora and couldn't seem to end his sentence.

"And," Flora interjected as if trying to save the game,
"...and then you'll send *all that cash* to the missions." Flora
smiled knowing that would be exactly what Bill would do.

Bill set the painting down and sat deep into the lounge
chair. He sighed a deep sigh and smiled again at Flora.

"Talking about the missions," Bill said in a very conser-
vative tone, "...Fr. Buddygig, a friend of mine, wrote to me,
he's a missionary in Malta, his home is in Yugoslavia
though. In November, he went home to visit his parents in
Sarjevo...he was worried about them with all the trouble
there...I thought you might want to read the letter he sent
to me. He's still there." Bill pulled he letter out of his shirt
pocket and handed it to Flora. She read it anxiously while
Bill pulled on his styrofoam slippers that were curling off
his heels.

"It gets pretty much into things," Bill said after taking a
deep sigh, "...what do you think...does it jive with the
things you've been hearing?" Bill looked to Flora who was
still engrossed in the letter. Flora looked up to Bill.

"I don't hear that much but it doesn't sound very good
over there...does it Bill?...you know, I can't stand listening
to the evening news anymore, but I do." Flora handed the
letter back to Bill. He saw the worry in her face and the concern in her eyes.

"Things are going to turn around...there are problems
in Eastern Europe that have never been settled...they've

been fighting for centuries. But, you know we have a responsibility to help in whatever way we can...as a nation...and as individuals. Listen to me...I feel like I'm in one of my history classes...but Flora, if and when I get through to my friend...I'll ask about Paolo...everyone knows everyone over there." Bill touched Flora's hand.

"I'd appreciate that so much...I know Paolo's alright...Christmas, a message came through to his father...Vince called me right away to fill me in on the news...the little news there was."

"How long does Paolo plan on staying there?"

Flora shrugged her shoulders. "I wish I knew... ."

"You know, Flora...people like Paolo make the impossible things in this life easier to bare...he gives people hope...and not just the people in Yugoslavia...but people like me and you...knowing there are people who will dedicate their lives to helping others...for me, that's like a shot in the arm."

"Me too, I wish I were there to help... ."

"You're exactly where you should be in your *condi-tion*...Flora...does Paolo know about the baby?"

Flora looked surprised at Bill's question and his expression. She smiled at his blushing cheeks.

"Baby? A baby?" Flora looked at Bill with complete surprise. "I didn't think I'd show with this heavy sweater... ."

"Flora...remember...I saw you through *three* of your pregnancies...so...does he know?"

"No...I think it's best he doesn't know...I haven't even told Dolly...she'd be a nervous wreck for all of us...and Paolo has enough to worry about. Everything is fine...I had an ultrasound exam last week and everything is fine with my little son." Flora's face beamed with pride. "Do you know how good it feels to share this with someone? Bill I'm so glad you noticed."

"Flora...you glow...but you're no *spring chicken* so take this pregnancy easy, try not to worry about anything...that's the best thing you could do for the little tike...and I think you're doing the right thing by waiting to tell Paolo...he has enough to worry about...Paolo will be home soon... ."

Bill lit up another cigarette which made Flora sit back in her chair and sigh. Bill thought her sigh was for him and his second cigarette; he looked at her sheepishly.

"I know what's going through your head...I shouldn't be smoking...and you're right...and I probably shouldn't be smoking in front of you in your condition... ."

"Don't worry about me..., if you have to smoke, I don't mind...I'll just hold my breath... ." Flora took a deep breath and held it, then exhaled slowly. "See...I don't mind." Bill laughed at Flora's face.

"Thanks Flora...I'm grateful you understand enough not to say anything about this nasty habit...believe me...I've heard it from everyone." Bill took a long drag from his cigarette and savored it.

"You're a big boy...you know what you're doing...and if you wanted to quit...you would have already...we all have our bad habits...and I've been thinking about taking up smoking myself, of course after the baby...what do those cigarettes have...maybe there is something in them...like vitamin C...?" Flora said imitating honest wonder. She shook her head at Bill, smiling a big smart-alec grin.

"Don't you dare start this shitty habit...I wish I *could* quit...but I like it too much...getting back to you...you DON'T have any bad habits," Bill said, looking at Flora with a pleasant seriousness .

"Sure...I wish...," Flora said as she shook her head, "...I have a million bad habits...ask Jack."

"Come on Flora...you know what I mean."

"Yeah... ." Flora got up from her chair and looked outside from the third floor window onto the traffic below. She walked back to her chair and sat on the edge of the cushion. She saw Bill was thoroughly enjoying his cigarette, so she continued to make conversation.

"I've made some big mistakes Bill...you of all people know that...but I've tried to learn from them...just when my life seemed to be settled...just when I felt really content with everything...BAM...I meet Paolo...at Mass yet...choking on the blessed wine...I fell in love with him...and now I'm waiting...and in between all that waiting, I'm trying to be productive, excuse the pun...and happy, eventhough the biggest part of my life is far off on a mission of mercy." Flora ended her confession when Bill crunched out his cigarette butt in the ashtray.

"These things are hard to come by in here," Bill said with a crooked grin when he noticed Flora watching him put out what was left of his cigarette butt. Bill brought his total attention over to Flora.

"Flora, you needed someone to love you and someone you could give your love to without having it shoved back in your face...your heart wasn't going to rest until it found that love.. you contented yourself for a long time, and maybe everything was the best it could be, but that morning in Florence your heart knew things could be better...things were only beginning...you can't stop your heart from reaching out to love...no one can do that...and Paolo was there, with just as aching a heart as yours...talk about something you can't fight...why do you think you choked on the wine?" Bill chuckled with his humor. Flora did, too.

"For courage," Flora said quickly, "That's what Dolly told me a couple days before I had to leave Florence...she said I met Paolo for the courage it was going to take for me to face my life as it was and then to do the things I was going to have to do from that point on...the past few months have been real eye-openers for me...it wasn't easy for me to admit that things weren't as peachy as I made them seem...hey...I didn't come here to talk about me...you wanted to tell me something...what is it Bill?"

"Dolly sounds like a smart gal...anyway...I did want to see you...because I needed a visit from a good friend who wouldn't mind my smoking...and, I wanted to apologize for intruding on your holiday, Christmas Eve. I should have called before...but then, I might not have had the courage to come."

"No apology necessary...Bill...you will never need an invitation to come by...our home is open to you...you're part of the family...remember that."

"That's kind of you Flora, but...if you won't let me apologize...at least let me explain reasons for crashing your party... ."

"Go ahead, Bill... ."

"It wasn't just a holiday stop...I was scared...and I had to see you."

"I'm glad I could be there for you... ." Flora reached over and squeezed Bill's hand.

"It wasn't so much the surgery that frightened me, as it was the feeling of being so alone...and of all the people in my life...I thought of you...you always made me smile." Bill leaned heavily back into his chair. He continued as Flora listened.

"I needed to see someone who could smile at me...just because...I'm *me*...do you understand what I'm trying to say." Bill saw Flora's understanding of his words and continued.

"All those letters you wrote...I took them out of my closet and read a few of them one night...they always made me feel good...and despite the pain you were wrestling with...you always ended on an upbeat note...or some wonderful perception of life...or something neat you noticed that day...you were a blessing in my life...I knew time would sort out all your problems...you got over me and the world still spinned didn't it...so...on the twenty-fourth of December, I followed a star...to your house...and not that I didn't have faith in DR. GAYBLADE, but people *do* die during surgery...and what if the *big guy* was ready to take me...I wanted you to know all this...I'm not the best letter writer and I know mine are few and far between...but I can always count on you...thanks Flora for everything...especially for being my friend." Bill sat deeper into his chair.

Flora understood exactly what he was saying. Paolo came into her mind with Bill's words. She wondered how many times Paolo had wished for the opportunity to talk with Francesca about his feelings. How many times Flora had wished Jack had spoke to her about things. Life made no deals with time. Love was the only conqueror of time and it's steady motion. Love was sharing...and love was always kind.

"Bill...all the writing I did and the justifying in my own mind for writing to you...in the beginning I believed you *needed* me...I wanted to believe that...I needed someone to need me then...and you were the poor cus who got the 'object of my affections' shoved down your throat...how did you stand it...I'm sorry...all I can say now is that I'm glad you appreciated the letters...and that we stayed friends...I hoped for that all along." Flora was flustered but it felt invigorating to get that horrible confession out of her heart. She had carried it long and deeply. Bill sat forward on his chair and rested his elbows on his knees. Flora continued.

"After I realized...that I wasn't going to find what was missing from my heart in Jack...I turned to other people...well you know all about that...," Flora touched Bill's hand and continued.

"I felt so vulnerable last Fall...going back to school was good for me...I met Dolly who loved my work and then like my fairy Godmother, she whisked me and the kids to Florence...you know the rest...Bill, life is for love...and living only makes sense if you love...so I didn't fight it anymore...I fell in love with Paolo...and there were days when I tried to talk myself out of it...but the stars wouldn't let me... ."

"The *stars* wouldn't let you? I hope I don't sound stu-pid...but this fascinates me... ." Bill touched Flora's hand and asked her about the stars that talked.

"Bill, remember the stars up north?...well, that's how they look in Florence...only bigger for some reason...I remembered the stars up north the summer before my trip to Florence...and how for a long time after they affected me...then, I saw them again one night with Paolo...affecting me the same way...they were practically shouting at me...*YOU FOOL...IT'S LOVE THAT REALLY MAT-TERS...AND HERE IT IS IN FRONT OF YOU...TAKE ANOTHER CHANCE*...and not just that...it seemed like everything there was making sense...," Flora paused and looked at Bill. Her expression was bouncing off his face. Bill motioned for her to go on with his anxious brow. Flora continued.

"Well...maybe they didn't shout all that...but, Bill...whatever it was they said...I heard it...they were try-ing to open my eyes...open my heart...love is all that ever truly matters...give it away and enjoy the giving...like the stars...they're there for us and never ask for anything in return...how much I love them now!...even on nights when the clouds hide them...I love them even more...because they are there...like love...for all of us, for all time." Flora stopped and then as if forgetting something important with only twenty seconds to squeeze it in...she added another personal thought.

"My heart is content...I guess that's what matters...that's what makes a heart content...to love someone...because the love is there...it was always there to give...and Paolo accepted it... ." Flora looked at Bill and hoped she wasn't sounding crazed. Deep in her heart, she knew he under-stood what she saying.

"Flora...everything worked out and I'm really happy for you...you and Paolo are two lucky people." Bill said as he picked up her watercolor painting. "WELL...what are you working on now...Flora?"

Flora felt the shift from the subject of love...she went along with it.

"I'm working on a study of the night sky... ."

"What makes me wonder why you'd ever pick a subject like that?" Bill said with a big smile.

"The kids reacted the same way...they know I've gone a little cuckoo over the stars...they tease me about going from the American flag on everything...to stars hanging everywhere...I just laugh because their accusations are true...this year the stars have hit me hard...in my reading, my painting, decorating,...I even made Emily a STAR quilt...I got my inspiration a song from HOOK...about the star the angel sends *'when you're alone'*."

"Flora...I saw the movie twice with my nieces and nephews...my sister's kids bought me the soundtrack for Christmas...how the heck did you make a quilt out of a song?" Bill and Flora laughed...then Flora explained her design...then they laughed some more. They talked about the stars and love and staple stitches and scars. Bill agreed with Flora's observation that *scars might really be fallen stars* that leave their mark reminding us that life was spent...love was spent.

The lounge grew dim in the late afternoon light. Flora noticed all the time that had whizzed by. She pulled herself up from her chair.

"Bill...this was nice...," Flora said as she politely yawned. Her bones cracked as she stretched her shoulders back. Bill stretched a bit and winced from the pain.

"I wish I could stretch like that, Flora...a simple little stretch to get the kinks out."

"Hey...hold still...!" Flora said emphatically. "I'll massage your back for five minutes...that will get some of the kinks out...*just don't stretch*." Flora cringed at the thought of having blood and guts all over the floor.

"Don't worry Flora, I'm not going to *pop open*." Bill laughed at Flora's face as she walked behind him. She rubbed his shoulders. She felt good about being able to cater to her friend.

"Let's not take any chances, Bill, you went through enough."

"Aaaahhh...*this feels great Flora*...," Bill said as he seemed to relax with Flora's massage. He kept still for a couple of minutes then as if suddenly remembering an important thought, he continued.

"Keep following your heart, Flora...and take care of the little bambino...Paolo's a lucky guy." Bill hung his head down, totally trying to relax his neck. "Have any names picked out?"

"I want Paolo to name him...the baby is due in mid May." Flora noticed the time and then patted Bill's back signaling the end of the massage. Bill took Flora's hand and kissed it.

"Keep in touch Flora... ."

"You know I will... ." Flora hugged her friend hard. A hundred thoughts seemed to pass through her mind with that embrace. How much she had grown up in her middle-age. Maybe every gray hair represents a hard time gone through. Dolly would like that theory very much. Flora let go of Bill. She looked into his face and noticed there were tears filling his soft grey eyes. Bill quickly took Flora's arm and led her slowly to the elevator.

"Flora...trust in all the things you know...trust in all of the things we can't explain."

"I do, Bill...," Flora said firmly. And then, as if following a secret plan, Flora backed into the opened elevator. She looked at Bill as she pressed G floor and then thanked him again, not concentrating on her farewell but on his face. Bill stood worn but brave and watched the doors slowly close not saying another word, only smiling and wiping the maverick tear that dared to spill onto his rough cheek.

As Flora rode down on the elevator, Bill's solemn face came back to her. She was keenly aware of some of the pain he suffered in his life. His heroic smile never hid that from Flora. He made great sacrifices in his life for the things he believed in. They all had made sacrifices. Then, Jack and his words from two weeks before echoed in her mind, stunning her as much in their replay as they had the first time she heard them. Tears filled her eyes. Maybe they were the tears she should have cried the night Jack told her that *he never really loved her.* Flora couldn't cry that night. In a queer kind of way, his words seemed more honest than anything he had ever shared with her. He took his stuffed army duffel bag...kissed her on the forehead and said good-bye.

The elevator stopped on the ground floor. The door opened. She hesitated for a moment as if she wasn't sure of her next step. But, it was time to step out...out of the elevator...out of some things that were over. It was time to move on.

The drive home was quiet except for the hills and the trees...and the glorious sunset. The moon was a tiny sliver...a waxing moon, Flora thought. Her heart was filled with the pink of the sky's horizon. She said a prayer for Bill. She prayed for Jack, the kids, Bubba and Grama Flora, Grandpa Pete and Grama Fran. She remembered Dolly and Vince and her friends in Florence, little Flora, Giacamo, and his sick mother. As Flora turned into her driveway...and with the dark bare branches of the oaks against the just night sky...she prayed for Paolo and his new little son growing strong inside of her.

Chapter
twenty-nine

April Showers, May Flowers

"*Dear Mama,*

April is beautiful here. Springtime is spectacular. I finally finished the mural in my room. You are going to love it! All this inspiration made it go so easy!

Dolly and I have been getting ready for all of you to come. We have lots of sauce made in the freezer and lots of other things that will save time in the kitchen when you arrive with the whole clan. I can't tell you how excited I am to see you...all of you again.

The wedding plans are going pretty good. We're keeping things simple and traditional. Br. Georgio is letting us use the gymnasium at the orphanage for the reception. Giacamo has already drawn up plans for decorations. He recruited plenty of artists for help with them. Actually, Br. Georgio is letting his art students use their Saturday's for extra credit if they help out. Plus, they love hanging out with Giacamo...he is their hero. Mine, too.

Mama, he is so good. He tries not to show how much he misses his mother, but he does, very much. I'm glad I came right here after Christmas and had the opportunity to be with her before she died. She shared so many little things with me about her life, Italy and Giacamo. We'd watch movies together and some nights we'd just listen to opera music, mainly Puccini. Giacamo was her baby and yet he was the man in the family especially during the last couple of months. He'd make her smile whenever he walked into the room, he'd feed her and wash her, he'd carry her to bed and sit with her till she fell asleep. He would talk about me and how many kids we're going to have. *Dodici bambini, Mama!* (Mama Mia!)

It's hard to believe I'm going to have another little brother soon. Hope you're taking it easy! We are all quite anxious here, but are very careful when talking about it. Especially, Dolly. She says the women here have an uncanny way of finding out things they shouldn't, and we wouldn't want Paolo to hear &'bout it from anyone except you.

Grama Fran wrote to me the other day. She didn't come out and say it in so many words...but she hinted big enough that she and Grandpa wouldn't be coming to the wedding. She really wants to come but I know she will do what Grandpa wants her to do. I feel sad that there are such bad feelings still between Grandpa and you. I know you've tried to explain things to him...but for me, could you try again to get him to come? Have Dad talk with him. I wrote to Grundpa Pete yesterday. Maybe he will mellow. I never knew he was that stubborn! Giacamo is saying his prayers for them.

No word from Paolo for three weeks. Vince is worried but not to worried. He told me that one day Paolo and Roberto will just show up at the door. I hope so. I think that's why he's always got something cooking in the pot on the stove. Vince is wonderful for Dolly. They love each other so much.

Well, I'm going to go. Today Dolly and I are going to the flea market to pick up a little surprise for you and the baby(That's all I can say without giving anything away). I love you Mama...be careful these next few weeks. The last picture you sent to us is hanging on the refrigerator. You look great...big stomach and all!

Love, little Flora

Flora read her daughter's letter again and then picked up the telephone to call Grama Fran. As the ringing signal rang in her ear she wondered what she was going to say. She almost hung up on the seventh ring. Then she heard Fran's voice.

"Hello... ."

It scared Flora at first to hear Fran's voice. But, she decided to face the music for little Flora's sake. Besides it had been a long time since she heard from Frances. They had been good friends before she and Jack broke up.

"Hi...Fran...this is Flora... ."

"Hi Flora," Fran said, matter-of-factly. Her salutation wreaked with a forced politeness.

"How are you and Pete...it's been a while since we've seen each other... ."

"It has been...," Fran said allowing her perturbed edge to cut through the telephone wire even more. "But we've been busy, too...Jack moved out a couple of weeks ago into his own place...and Pete's getting ready to go smelt fishing with him the end of April...I guess it has been a while...that's the way it goes when families break-up... ."

"Families haven't broken up...there is no war here Fran and you know that...Jack is doing fine...he sees the kids more now than he ever did...and his new job sounds great...he seems very happy... ."

"He *seems* happy...and what would you know about his feelings...it will never be the same...not that I want to alien-ate myself from you and the kids...but Pete will never budge from his vow never to see you again...I never thought things would end up like this...our oldest grand-daughter getting married half way around the world to some guy who barely support himself let alone a family...she had a perfectly good man right here at home...Dan was a gem...he loved her...he graduated from college and has a good job with his father...and you put some screwy idea in her head that that wasn't enough, just because you were going through some mid-life thing, did-n't mean you had to drag her down with you...I blame you for this whole big mess, Flora...you and your mixed up professor friend who filled your head with jumble...she made you desert your husband...you were perfectly happy before your Florence trip...perfectly happy." Fran took a deep breath. Flora jumped into Fran's discourse.

"Mom...Dolly, never made me do anything," Flora said very sure of herself, but making sure not to sound disrespectful. "Dolly never filled my head with anything...you know the funny thing is, that if you knew her...you'd like her...she's alot like you Fran... ." Flora didn't want to even get on the subject of happiness.

"Fran...I hope you'll try and change Pete's mind about going to the wedding. Little Flora just sent me a letter and asked me to call you...I hope you'll think about it...for her...that would be the best wedding present you could ever give her...you are two of her favorite people on this earth...and she's told Giacamo so much about you...please think about it."

There was a lull in the conversation. Flora didn't want to rush Fran so she comfortably went on.

"And...you always did want to see Rome...you'd have the best time...and Jack's coming... ."

"I didn't know Jack was going?...he didn't say anything about going to the wedding... ." Fran sounded completely surprised.

"Sure he's going...little Flora asked him to walk her down the aisle... ."

"I thought he couldn't get any time off from work...he just started his job...I can't imagine the company giving him any time off now."

"Maybe he's trying to work something out...we'll be happy with whatever arrangements he makes...but somehow he'll make it there... ." Flora wished she hadn't brought up Jack's going to Florence.

"Sure he'll work something out," Fran said in a huff, "...he'd feel terrible if he couldn't give little Flora away...he's her *father*...who else would give her away...Paolo?"

It would have been easy to snap at Fran with her last insensitive remark but Flora was tired of explaining things.

"Paolo is still in Bosnia with his son...but we're all hoping he makes it back for the wedding... ."

"I'd worry more about him coming home period...coming home to make an honest woman out of you...to give the baby his name...aren't you worried about that...what kind of example are you for the kids...no wonder little Flora is so mixed up."

"Sometimes I think little Flora is the only one who has her head on straight," Flora said defense of her daughter. "She fell in love and she followed her heart...I'm proud of her...you know Fran, I couldn't have hoped for a nicer life for her...Giacamo is a wonderful young man...and they are so much in love...isn't that the most we could want for her...isn't that everything we could want for all of our kids?"

"Since you're being philosophical here, let me toss in my two cents worth...I'm not saying this to hurt you, you know I love you so much...but, you're still dreaming Flora...I thought with everything you're going through...you'd be more realistic about life...but you're still candy-coating everything that comes your way...I'm getting nauseated by it all, especially when so many people are suffering for it...I'm not condemning you, I think what you're going through most women go through...but it will pass and you'll go on with your life with Jack and you two will be very happy...you have to grow up and accept things the way they are...there was a time when I looked at Pete and wondered about his cranky disposition...but then I looked at the kids and made a decision to weather out his moods...you can't have it all in life...you just can't have it all...but to each his own...you'll wake up one day...I hope you'll have no regrets...you are giving up so much... ."

"I hope none of us has any regrets...I do love Jack...with

all my heart...but it was never enough for him...and now...it isn't enough for me." Flora paused for a moment. She waited for her mother-in-law to respond. Fran was silent. Flora listened to the silence. It hurt very much.

"Well...Fran...it's been nice talking to you...you know I love you very much... ." Flora paused for a moment hoping Fran would say something. Fran didn't...she couldn't, there were too many tears in her heart. Flora continued.

"I have a doctor's appointment this morning...I'll call you tonight to tell you how things went...and please think of little Flora and how much she wants you at her wedding... ." Flora hung on to the receiver waiting to hear Fran say good-bye. Fran didn't say a thing for a few moments, then, with a deep sigh of regret in her voice, Fran said a quick good-bye.

Flora hung up the phone and sat by the kitchen table. Her mom's small garden caught her attention. At first glance one might think of it as barren and fruitless, Flora thought as she smiled. Flora knew the things that were going on in secret. Last year's oak leaves hadn't been raked out yet and the late April rain made them shimmer. Spring was underneath the rusty mound of old wet leaves, somewhere. Flora felt the promise of Spring. It was almost ready to burst out...with great joy!

T. Stellini

Chapter
thirty

The Stars Again

Dear Bill,

I can't tell you how I felt as I said good-bye to the Statue of Liberty...I thought of my Great-grandparents and how wonderful the great Lady in the harbor must have looked to them when they entered her waters. Years pass so quickly. I'm looking at my Grandma's lace coverlet right now, hanging on Dolly's rocker. She's alot like my Grandma. I know Grandma sees all of us and everything that's going on. She must be loving every minute of it. I wish I could hug her.

Our crossing the Atlantic was wonderful. When our cab pulled up to the docks on the Hudson River and we saw the Queen Elizabeth looking like a big elephant sitting on a thimble, we couldn't stop laughing. It is humongous, to say the least! The magnificence of it's presence took away half my fear of crossing the Atlantic. (The other half stayed in my bones till we docked in Southampton, thinking "fear in the bones will help a body float better!")

The ocean was relatively smooth, moderate swells. But at night in bed, you really feel the motion of the sea. A steady rhythm, like it was breathing calmly, trying to make me feel comfortable and at home in it's arms. One morning I managed to make it up to the deck on time to see the sun come up. How the water glistened! Like aquamarine gems.

The lovely British Captain made his daily report to the passengers over the public address system. His voice was strong and comforting. Day two, "WE ARE NOW IN THE WATERS WHERE THE TITANIC SANK". How sweet of him to mention that. That made me feel so much more at home on the sea. And then his announcement on day three, "TODAY WE WILL PASS OVER THE HIGHEST MOUNTAINS IN THE WORLD, THE MID ATLANTIC RIDGE, BUT NOT TO WORRY...THE HIGHEST PEAK IS A GOOD MILE BELOW THE SHIP!" That made me feel better! Lots of nice facts like that came from our charming Captain!

Young Jack, Joe, Jimmy, Emily, Angelo, Tommy, Danny, Donny and Tim kept all of us busy checking out every room on the entire ship. The girls relaxed and basked in the sun. They graced us with their presence at the dinner buffet.(Yes, the food on board ship is "too": TOO much...TOO good...TOO often!) The trip was good for everyone. Even Jack took back his negative words about cruise ships!

A few days before we left Union Lake, Jimmy was watching a video tape about the Kennedy years, he had to finish his report for history. Anyway, I was packing on the couch and couldn't help listening to the television. Needless to say, I stopped what I was doing and sat down on top of Emily's pile of clean cloths to watch the tape with Jimmy.(She needed her cloths pressed anyway!)

It was during the 1964 Democratic convention when Robert Kennedy addressed a nationwide audience. It was the first one since his brother John's assassination. We already knew the ticket went to Lyndon Johnson...and Robert was taking the opportunity to rally(?) for LBJ, and to offer a few words of encouragement to the American people. That was June of '64. I remember watching that coverage on T.V., I was fifteen. But now, seeing it again...I heard a different message...one from a brother's heart that had mourned intensely. It wasn't about loosing a President...he lost his brother...we lost a brother. Robert Kennedy opened his address with a quote from Shakespeare...it was beautiful. The emotion in his voice made tears come to my eyes...I felt like it was yesterday. I ran over to my book of plays with the idea that it had to have been from

Romeo and Juliet, where else would such words of love be written?

So, eager to find the four or five lines he spoke, I flipped from chapter to chapter until it popped out at me...

> "Give me my Romeo, and when I shall die
> Take him and cut him out in little stars,
> And he will make the face of heaven so fine
> That all the world will be in love with night
> And pay no worship to the garish sun."

Bill...who could go back to folding cloths after that? Well, I sat for a while and thought of the big trip that was ahead of me..I looked at Jimmy who was deeply into the video and his term paper...then I looked around at my room. For a few seconds, I wondered about my life and the 'up in the sky' philosophy I had adopted. Jack was a good person...I could have lived the rest of my life with him...but then, how could I have looked at the night sky and not believed what it said to me so many times. I could have lived with Jack...I could have gone on pretending he loved me...but I could not have pretended forever, not after Paolo. Then, I found myself going over things in my head...realizing that there is a portion of guilt that only time will help me understand. Anyway, enough! On with the trip.

Dolly was at the train station to greet us once again...only this time there were more of us. Dolly cried when she held little Paolo. The angel took the cruise well...almost as good as Grandpa Bubba and Grandma Flora. The five days on the ship seemed like one constant reunion...a big party...between shopping sprees and midnight buffets. The beeper should have beeped a long time ago on all of our credit cards.

My mother, Irene, and Rose...are going berserk over the kitchen in the pensione...I knew they would. Mama made Grandma's ravioli recipe tonight. Vince loved them...and Bubba loved Vince's cousin Gianni's homemade zinfandel. Hey...they loved the whole ding dang pensione!

There are so many things I have to tell you Bill, after the wedding though...when I'll be able to sit and think straight. But I want you to know that I plan on staying here for the summer, and maybe for the Fall. Br. Georgio wants me to do some work at the orphanage and Dolly lined up a lucrative job for me in town. The offer was..."too good to refuse", it seems I can never say NO to an Italian! Seriously, it's a great opportunity for me. Little Flora being here helped sway me, too, not to mention the salary for this project will pay for this grand excursion.

So, good friend, take care...remember, you will always have a room here, one with a view. I'll keep you in my prayers, keep me in yours. Love, Flora.

P.S.

Keep Paolo and Roberto and Alfredo in your special intentions. It's very bad over there right now and we haven't heard too much from them (hoping no news is good news). And,...pray that it's sunny on the fourteenth of June. We don't need the clouds crying on the bride!

It was a chilly day for the month of June in Florence, especially for Tracey and Christina who donned lavender silk chiffon sleeveless gowns for little Flora's wedding. The sun beaming through their bedroom window was a special blessing that morning. It gave the room an air of the mystical...befitting the big event that was about to take place. The girls thought it made the moon in little Flora's mural seem real. Little Flora's inspiration was felt by everyone who looked into it.

"Gosh...it's like the moon is real...it's like the moon wants to shine on little Flora's special day...huh Christina...I think there's going to be a fingernail moon tonight...last night it was barely a sliver, the clouds cleared for about ten minutes...just enough time for me and Stefano to say hello to it... it looked like a smile in the sky...Stefano said it was the sky laughing at us." Tracey hopped on her bed and touched the moon on the painting on the wall.

"It was laughing at all of us Tracey," Christina said giddily. "Imagine, in a while...little Flora will be married!...and then in a couple of months it will be *our* turn...Tracey, you and I will be sister-in-laws...like being cousins wasn't close enough."

"I always prayed that we'd stay as close as sisters," Christina said seriously, "...you and me and little Flora...and we will." She stopped putting on her make-up and joined Tracey on the bed. Little Flora walked in and joined them. As she sat down next to them she noticed their watery eyes.

"Right now...stop that...quit being such big babies, this is suppose to be the happiest day of my life...don't worry about anything except having fun at my wedding...nothing will ever come between us...I'll make sure of that." Little Flora grabbed a tissue from her dresser and blotted away the overflow of tears from each of their cheeks.

"Little Flora...you look...wonderful...you look like you stepped out of your mural and into a fairytale...," Tracey said with genuine awe.

"Really...little Flora...you look...you look...," Christina had a hard time completing her compliment. She sniffled in her tissue. "You look...BELLA BELLA."

"Gosh...," little Flora said with just as much feeling,"...you two look beautiful...too beautiful for words...I wish...I hope...I hope you'll never forget me." Flora closed her eyes as if that would hold back her tears. "Look, now I'm crying."

Christina tried to turn the tear faucet off with some harsh words. "What a good example you are...you were suppose to wait for us...we were all suppose to get married together." A big smile spread across Christina's face. She began laughing at her silly statement. And, like an epidemic, it spread to all of them.

"Little Flora...what if you *postponed* the wedding...and told everyone you had to wait till September for your cousins to get married with you...can you imagine what Giacamo would say...?" Christina made them all laugh some more.

"I think he'd handle his disappointment with great courage...and understanding...but...could I really wait...or *want* to wait that long to marry him? Little Flora had a dreamy smile on her face.

"You bragger...go easy on us," Tracey said seriously, "...we have to wait the summer...I don't know about you Christina...but it's really getting difficult for *me* to say good-night."

"That's why we are going *home* for the summer...no one could go through a Florentine summer without compromising her virtue...it would be impossible...even here...with crosses everywhere you turn and all the paintings of the Virgin Mary."

Christina didn't mean to sound sacrilegious...but her facial expression made Tracey and little Flora laugh till tears came rolling down their cheeks once again.

"You know...we're sick...really sick...what are we laughing at...we better sober up FAST," little Flora said hoping to snap them out of their giddiness. She looked at her watch. "OH GOD...check out the time...we're really gonna be late!"

"SO...what's new?", Christina said flippantly as she hopped up from the bed still laughing.

"Don't even look in the mirror girls...our make-up is shot to hell...", Tracey said warning the girls about the effect their giddiness had on their mascara. "Did you ever notice how much we swear when we're nervous?"

"What the HELL are you talking about, Tracey...?"Christina said as she took a concerned look in the mirror. "Oh my gosh...I do look like shit...my eyes are all red and puffy!"

"Sshhhh...," Tracey said as she pointed in the direction

of the doorway. "I think we have a special visitor...hello Miss Emily... ."

"EMILY...you look like an angel...I am so proud to have you in my wedding." Little Flora hugged her sister. "Here...I have a little floral wreath for your hair...let me put it on your head... ."

All the girls took their turns *ooohing* and *ahhhing* Emily while little Flora fussed with Emily's headpiece. Emily basked in their compliments.

"Mama said the same thing...but do you *really* think I look pretty?"

"You look more than pretty...," little Flora said as she brought Emily to the full length mirror. "See...you're *molto bella*...very beautiful." Emily's face blushed even more pink than the blush Aunt Irene brushed on her peaches and cream cheeks earlier that morning.

"I used to think that *molto bella* was a kind of cheese or a salami...," Emily said turning into her sister's arms and hugging her. "You too, Tracey and Christina...thanks for making me feel so pretty."

"You're welcome Em, " Tracey said sincerely.

"I *love* these dresses," Emily said giddily, "...but they're all the same color...when I get married...I'm gonna have a *rainbow wedding,* you know with all the bridesmaids in a different color...I saw one in little Flora's Bride magazine...yeah, that's what I'm gonna have...and I want at least *ten* bridesmaids...and...," Emily paused for a moment and looked into little Flora's face. "I *don't* have a *boyfriend* or anything yet...but I know that I want to have a rainbow wedding...and all of you I hope will be bridesmaids for me...oh...and I almost forgot...Aunt Irene told me to tell you that they're ready."

"*They're ready*?", Tracey said as if in a panic, "...and we're not......we'll wait for them to come and get us...I don't even know where my shoes are...look under that bed for me, Em?"

"Don't rush," Emily said as if everything were under control, "...little Paolo made a big *poo-poo* and Mama wants to give him a bath before we leave...he's so *cute*...I love his fat cheeks...Zia Antoinette keeps pinching them...that's what probably gave him the *diarrhea*...that's what Aunt Rose told me in my ear... ." Emily smiled at all the girls and then looked diligently for Tracey's shoes.

It wasn't until Flora, Rose and Irene went up into their room before some semblance of order came about. The mothers were far from a giggling mood...not to say that one silly word wouldn't have brought all of them to their knees in laughter. The drive to the church was quiet, not to many words spoken, lots of eye talk and brave smiles.

Despite the nervous hustle before the late morning Mass and the familial affectations delivered by the huge family that had gathered for the celebration, Flora couldn't shake her chill.

The boys choir from San Miniato, Giuseppe's cherub-like solo of the AVE MARIA, Brother Georgio's inspirational words, and Bubba and Grandma Flora sitting like the proud grandparents that they were...sent double reinforcements of goosebumps down Flora's spine. Seeing little Flora walking to the altar with Jack...and young Jack and Joe and Jimmy as ushers, and Emily as flower girl, put a huge lump in Flora's throat.

The ceremony was beautiful. *Bella, bella, bella.*

Then, the organ began to play the recessional song. Flora took a deep breath as Joe extended his arm to her. It was time for her to walk back down the aisle. Jack stood on her left. He held her hand.

"She looks beautiful...," Jack said in a loud whisper, "...just like you Flora...and little Emily looked so...grown-up." Jack squeezed Flora's hand.

"She did...and you look very handsome yourself, Jack." Flora answered back politely. "Do you have a way to the orphanage...if not...you can drive down with us."

"I'll hop in with young Jack...your car is full...the ceremony was beautiful...I can't stay too long at the reception...my flight leaves tonight so I'll have to catch the 9:40 train to Rome...I told little Flora that I'd be back next Spring for a month, and that I'd bring Pete and Fran, even if I have to carry Pete."

"At least you made it here...little Flora will never forget that...you know you will always be welcome here...Mom and Dad, too... ."

"I know...and I wouldn't have missed walking little Flora down the aisle for anything...she and Giacamo make a good looking couple." Jack kissed Flora on her forehead and walked away.

Flora watched him get into young Jack's car. He turned and motioned to Flora that Emily would be going with them. Flora acknowledged his sign language with a nod.

It wasn't until Flora had a glass of Vince's heartwarming zinfandel at the wedding reception, before the chill left her touch...and the tears left her heart.

"Well...to a great beginning...to the luckiest guy in Fiesole...who married the most beautiful girl in America." Brother Georgio said as he clinked his glass to Flora's.

"To *one* of the most beautiful girls in America...there are so many beautiful relatives here... ."

"There are many beautiful girls here...but the most beautiful girl at any wedding is the bride."

"You're right, Georgio, little Flora looks so beautiful and the ceremony was perfect," Flora smiled at Georgio, "...and your homily, Georgio, was very personal...they'll always remember it." Flora took Georgio's hand and squeezed it hard. She smiled at him. He thanked her with his eyes.

"I had to throw in a little humor...Giacamo's face was beginning to look as green as his tuxedo." Georgio laughed as he turned to watch the young kids on the dancefloor.

"I think we all felt a little green...the easy part is over...now it's *che sera, sera*."

"What will be, will be...," Georgio said as he brought his attention back to Flora. "And...you're okay...with every-thing...Jack seems to be doing fine."

"He is...I'm glad he made the trip with us."

Georgio worried about Flora, especially after Roberto joined Paolo in January. Paolo's absence had been longer than even Georgio had anticipated.

Things were horrible in Bosnia...Paolo and Roberto were in the middle of it all. Georgio looked directly into Flora's eyes. Flora looked into his knowing she couldn't hide some of the worry that was deep in her heart.

"I'm okay Georgio...really...little Paolo keeps me busy and full of hope...I can't wait for Paolo to see him." Flora cherished Georgio's friendship and appreciated his corre-spondences to her while she was back in the States...espe-cially that past winter when her separation from Jack and the preparation for the new baby turned her life complete-ly upside down.

Lucia pulled Br. Georgio onto the dancefloor. As Flora watched the celebration she thought back to her own wed-ding and the promises she made to herself and to Jack.

She wondered what little Flora was thinking dancing to the new song that was playing in her heart. She wondered if it was even a new song or maybe it was the same song she heard twenty three years ago. Flora thought how some things never change...and how other things change so much. Her life had changed and taken a direction she could have never imagined. Paolo led her to places in her heart she never knew existed.

When the music stopped, Georgio came back to Flora who seemed to be far away with thought.

"I worry about you Flora...and Paolo...I thought he'd make it here somehow for the wedding...I know our mes-sages eventually get to him...I'm worried about him...in my gut...I thought he'd be here for sure...I wanted him to be here...you know...well, I know one thing for sure...the next time I see him, I'm going to beat the...the you know what out of him...but they should have been here...Paolo and Roberto are putting us through the mill...listen to me, I sound as if they're on some tropical island on some big picnic...you know what I mean." Georgio looked at Flora, hoping to see the things she was thinking. "You know, Flora...if we don't hear from them soon, I'm going to go after them."

"I'd love to see you bop Paolo," Flora said as she smiled at Georgio with a devil's night grin of mischief. After a few somber moments, she continued.

"There are times I wish he were away on some big picnic...at least we'd know he was safe or having a good time...he should have been back here by now." Flora felt Georgio's sentiment exactly. Flora knew Paolo was wishing he was home. That thought made many dreaded thoughts come back to her.

If there had been any way at all for Paolo to come...he'd have been there, for sure. If there had been any way to send Roberto...he'd have at least sent him back with word. But, there was no messenger...no word. That's what worried her. That's what scared her, especially nights when the stars hid behind innocent clouds. Flora shared her anxious thoughts with Georgio.

"It's been over nine months since we've seen Paolo...and six since Roberto left...what if something is wrong...and we are just waiting here like idiots, even the United States is sending in more troops...I think things are going to get worse before they get better...we've got to go find him, Georgio." Flora looked to Br. Georgio again. This time she saw more concern than answers in his eyes.

"Flora...this waiting thing is difficult for all of us...and I'm not going to sit back much longer...Paolo has a new son...I know he's going to be flabbergasted when he finds out...he's going to feel bad when he realizes you had to go through this all alone."

"Georgio...wait a minute...*all alone?* I had all of my family with me...and *you* with me...Paolo's the one who's going through the rough time...don't worry about me and the baby, we're doing fine."

"I know, Flora...but seeing little Paolo and holding him...I don't want Paolo to miss these days...I talked with Fr. Cellini this afternoon and he gave me the go ahead to go and check things out...he's worried about Alfredo, too...the last time he heard from Alfredo, he sounded very tired...anyway, it's time to get on with the show."

"I think it's time."

"You'll have to fill in for a few of my classes...little Paolo will enjoy the boys...it's the only way it could work...with Paolo gone. Things have been piling up as it is...and the kids love you."

Flora knew Georgio had everything figured out for the best. "I'll do whatever I have to do...thanks Georgio...let's get going soon on this!"

"Trust me...we will." Georgio gave Flora a big hug and told her not to worry about a thing. Flora promised him she wouldn't...until tomorrow.

Donny whizzed by Flora and passed along a message from Irene and Rose. They needed help with cutting and wrapping the cake.

"I'll see you later...Georgio...let's keep our fingers crossed...the night isn't over yet." Flora crossed her fingers and kissed Br. Georgio on his cheek. He smiled at his friend Flora, and hoped they wouldn't be disappointed.

"Flora...," Jack said as he gently grabbed Flora's elbow, "I said all of my ARRIVERDERCHI's but this one." Jack gave Flora a quick kiss on her cheek. "Flora...I've got to go...but I will be back...I understand how all of you feel about this place...and...I hope everything works out for you and Paolo...take care of that new little baby." Jack hugged Flora hard.

"Thanks Jack...remember, you are always welcome here." Flora squeezed Jack with all of her strength...she wanted him to feel her words were true.

"I know." Jack looked at Flora and then walked toward the door. Flora lost him in the crowd but saw the door swing open. She said good-bye to him again in her heart.

"*Wasn't it beautiful,*" Dolly said when she bumped into Flora in the lady's room. "*Nothing* could top this event...wasn't the bride *bellissima*...and the groom, *bella figura*...the American girls, they are so *loud*...and...isn't the food *delizioso*...and what about the great band...is it a relative of Glen Miller?...are they *all* going to live here?...and what about the *baby?*" Dolly mimicked the voices that she had heard floating around in the banquet room. Flora laughed at Dolly's near perfect rendition of the elder relatives and their comments.

"Dolly...sshhhhh...be good...," Flora said as she pointed to the closed doors of the toilet stalls. She silently moved her lips and motioned to Dolly to read what she was saying.

"SOMEONE MIGHT BE IN THERE!"

"*No one will understand us...,*" Dolly said in a loud whisper, "...we can gossip in *pig latin.*" She continued brushing her hair while she spoke to Flora.

"I-a alled-ca ia-Za," Dolly said as she combed through her hair, "and-na he-sa old-ta e-ma...what the hey!...that little Paolo drank all of his bottle and is sleeping like an angel...I never was good at that stuff."

"E-ma either-na... ." Flora said laughingly.

"Zia is an angel," Dolly said sincerely. " She's one of the few women in this family who doesn't gossip for a living...seriously though, I imagine caring for little Paolo brings her great pleasure...holding her nephew's son the way she used to hold him...anyway, Flora...relax...the night is young...'AND I'M SO AMOROUS', da da dee, la la la...oh well, I can't remember the rest of the lyrics...but...try to enjoy this night." Dolly put her brush down and looked at Flora.

"You know...I love Vince's family,"Dolly said sincerely, "...but I'm still not used to all the *chit-chat* that goes on in this family...I guess I'm not a woman's woman...if you know what I mean...I can't get all worked up about who sits where and what color the bride's mother should wear...every other woman is dressed in black...I know it's out of respect...but come on...it gets a bit dreary, and you know, Flora, if they like wearing it so much, why don't they make it one of Italy's national colors? Seriously!" Dolly began adjusting her drooping pantyhose. She continued more mellow.

"All in all...the wedding was a smash...and little Flora is happy...that's the only thing that matters to me."

Flora watched as Dolly yanked her pink dress back down over her generous hips.

"Me too Dolly, and everyone is happy...and everything was beautiful...Mama and Irene and Rose were in heaven this week...you were our guardian angel...my mother would love to stay another week...I'm trying to talk her and Bubba into it." Flora spoke to Dolly through the mirror where Dolly was applying a fresh coat of her famous bright poppyrose lipstick. Flora smiled as she watched Dolly over emphasize her thin upper lip into a voluptuous Marilyn Monroe pucker. Dolly looked like Dolly again. Her lipstick always revived more than her lip color.

"Flora, this is what life is all about, when you get right down to it, babies, weddings, celebrations...and meetings in the *woman's restroom*...I think some of the most dramatic decisions in the world are made in these places...and some of the keenest observations are shared...oh well...we've got some more dancing to do...and don't worry about little Paolo...he's fine...or his Daddy...I still believe he'll be here." Dolly pinched Flora's cheek. She took one more quick look in the mirror. Her reflection pleased her.

"Flora...remember there are two things you need in life to get attention after fifty-five...a nice set of hips...and some *red shiny lips.*" Dolly winked at Flora from the mirror. Then, she turned around and shook her hips. "Let's shake this pispot and roll." Dolly shimmied out of the door like a pudgy flapper from the twenties.

Dolly tore up the carpet dancing...at least for a few measures of the twist. Flora was bounced back and forth between the young and old and the familiar and the strange...until the bridal dance came. Then Flora watched everyone scurry to partners.

Flora always told the kids that dancing was making love...set to music. Those were the lyrics to a song her mom used to sing in the kitchen; they definitely made sense to Flora. She watched the couples dance...and love. She felt like a sore thumb being the only one in the entire room not dancing, except for great *Nona* Teresa who was ninety-seven and had a broken ankle. Flora smiled as she watched her parents foxtrott by her to I KNOW WHY. Jack never enjoyed dancing. Flora sighed and made a wish for the newlyweds.

Young Jack saw his mother standing alone. He excused himself from Adrianna and went up to Flora and asked her to dance.

"Jack...I'm okay...you didn't have to interrupt your dance with Adrianna...she's really nice...," Flora said seriously. She displayed a hint of motherly inquisition in her raised eyebrow. Young Jack looked at his mother and smiled his boyish grin. Flora held a grand young man in her arms, tightly.

"God, mom...this week was great...I think I'm going to visit Flora quite often...she has a sharp sister-in law...maybe we'll keep this *thing* all in the family...Joe has his eyes on Adrianna's sister...and I don't want to miss little Paolo growing up!" Jack twirled his mother around again.

"That's what I keep telling you...you're more than welcome to come and stay at the pensione...you better keep close to your family...little Paolo's going to need his big brothers."

"I know Mom...," young Jack said in an affectionate tone, "...you know...I'm a pretty good dancer...or maybe it's the *gal* I'm dancing with." Young Jack smiled at his mother and spun her in a double twirl as the dance came to an end.

"You're a great dancer...I just followed your lead." Flora hugged her son for all the reasons a mother would.

The night continued with many toasts to the bride and groom...bouquet's being thrown...girl's crying...mother's crying...garters flung into the high ceiling with hungry guys reaching and diving for their dreams...cakes and desserts passed around like eating would be out of style the next morning...and special songs played for special people...soft lights and candles that burnt low.

Between greetings from newly acquired family...and dancing with her own...Flora found a space in the night...a space on the dancefloor where she politely edged her way to the gymnasium's back door exit. She took advantage of the opportunity to duck out of the celebration. Flora wanted to gather her thoughts. She couldn't wait to get back to the pensione and hold little Paolo. Zia Antoinette insisted the baby stay home and sleep in peace away from all the noise and smoke. Little Paolo was in heavenly hands.

Flora slid out of the back door like a thief and stole some quiet from the hills of San Miniato. She looked around at the orphanage that love had built...that Paolo built. She wished on many stars that he had been home for little Paolo's birth and for little Flora's wedding. Idle talk that past week gave rise to new hope of his arrival. That hope lifted Flora's spirits to the clouds. They had also been in abundance that week. Every night she looked for the stars...she looked for him...but neither were there.

His absence at the church for the ceremony kept Flora anxious...a part of her believed he'd be there. Flora thought herself to be silly for actually believing in the friendly gossip that echoed through the pensione...the orphanage...the marketplace that past week. It wasn't as if the rumors had been stamped and sealed in wax...but, such a big part of her believed, for whatever reasons, that Paolo would be there. She not only believed that...she felt it in her heart as real as her love for him.

Flora walked up to the chapel. As she opened the heavy wood carved door, a flood of fragrance rushed out to greet her. The scent was strong and took her back to that morning when Lucia, Giacamo's Godmother, personally attached a fresh floral bouquet to every other pew...all the way to the altar...it was a tradition in their family and her responsibility since Giacamo's mother passed away that past winter.

Before Flora walked inside, she looked back to the gymnasium. She smiled as she thought of Paolo's face and what his expression would have been if he had seen the simple gym and how little Flora, Giacamo and the orphanage boys had transformed it into a shangri-la. With MOONLIGHT SERENADE heard faintly in the distance, Flora walked inside the chapel. It was very dark, and when the door creaked closed, it became very quiet.

She headed for the tiny flames on the Blessed Mother's altar then knelt down in the first pew in front of it. Flora clasped her hands in front of her face and took a deep breath. Her fingers were cold again from her thoughts...and the night air. Her hands touching her face made chills domino up and down her spine; they marched in repeated order till finally her teeth even began to chatter.

Flora knelt back into the pew and stared at the flickering flames in front of her. She felt a warm tear fall down her cheek. She felt it roll down...like a friend's gentle touch of affection...till it dropped off her face and onto her folded hands, she kissed it. By then, it was cold like the path it drizzled down her cheek.

Flora focused her attention on her tear's journey; that strangely relaxed her. She looked at the statue of her

Blessed Mother and all of a sudden felt silly.

"What the heck am I crying about...you went through the worst pain...and you didn't deserve it...you were pure and good...and I'm...not so pure and not so good." Flora looked around the altar hoping her mind would get off the guilt trip Mother Mary's statue triggered. She went back to the life size figure of Mary and continued her thoughts.

"Really...I know what I want...I am sure about what I want and what I need...which probably makes it worse...I have no excuses for going against my Church, except, that what I believe right now, is good...I know it is good." Flora was a sinner according to all the laws of her Church, but she also believed in the power of love and the forgiveness of God.

"I ask your Son...my Brother...for forgiveness...so many things seem jumbled when I tried to analyze them...like love...like commitment...and forever. I love you dear Mary...I love your Son and our God...I still love Jack, as a person,...and the kids and my family...then I came to Florence and I fell in love with Paolo...I fell in love with a man I could have never imagined...you must know how much I love him...I wish he were here now...that wonderful man came into my life and brought a new definition of love...I know he's good for me and that I am good for him...talk about being afraid...I'm so afraid right now...sometimes I feel like I'm never going to see Paolo again...that would be the most terrible thing." Flora paused for a moment staring at the statue of our Blessed Mother as if it were real. Her mind went back to prayer.

"Please don't let anything happen to Paolo...not for my sake...but for little Paolo's...if it means I'd have to give up ever seeing Paolo again...I'll do that...but, please keep him safe...for years I worried about the commitment to my marriage vows...I believed that even if love leaves a relationship the commitment to it is still there...the couple is still bound to their wedding promise...but *commitment without love* is an empty thing...faith without love or...or hope without love...they're nothing." Tears accumulated to the brink of overflowing. They tripled her vision of the candles which brought her to the end of her prayer.

"Keep him safe...'Oh Mother of the Word Incarnate...despise not my petition...but in your mercy...hear and answer me, amen'."

Flora felt relief as she spoke her words to God and His mother. He would understand her; she would intercede. Flora knew all things were possible with God.

Flora had her Faith and her family...and her painting to get her through the difficult times in her life. Flora had been given the sun and the moon and the stars to keep her close to the man she would forever love.

Flora sat back onto the cold wood bench. Her prayer was finished, but a waterfall of thoughts kept her tired mind busy.

Jack made it to the wedding and despite their break-up, he was finally a content person. Everyone noticed that. Flora understood his contentment, she had found it, too.

Flora thought of the old oak leaves in May...how stubborn they are. How stubborn she had been in her life. Flora remembered how afraid she had been even at the thought of one day being alone...with no one to share simple things with...with no one to care for...or to care about her. Paolo made her brave...courageous. He made her see her life the way it was...and the way it could be. Clingy leaves in May are okay. It would be alright to hang on for the winter, but only for the right intentions...like for color on dreary winter days.

She smiled inside her heart at her late night thoughts and knew that her life was good. She always tried to do what was right. That didn't mean everyone would be happy. Flora slowly came to realize that she wasn't responsible for the world's unhappiness. She knew if she could keep her heart full of love and see things in that good light, the world would have to be a better place because she would be a better person.

Flora stood up and walked to the end of the pew. Her cheeks were still damp from her tears. She humbly genuflected and walked out of the chapel alone, yet not alone...somewhat relieved, yet scared of her promise that echoed in her heart. She knew those words had to be said. Now she had to get on with her life...and Paolo would be kept out of harms way.

Flora sat on the steps of the little church and visualized a watercolor of that night. Van Gogh's STARRY NIGHT came into her mind. That made her scan the countryside and appreciate the wonders God placed in everyone's life, even if everyone didn't always see them. The lighted windows in the distance and the soft music playing made her heart feel settled and confident that God always takes care of things...she knew He was taking care of her...and Paolo...everyone.

Her life had seen some dramatic changes, her visits to talk with her God had stayed the same. In her faith, she found great comfort and strength.

Tears filled Flora's eyes once again as thoughts of Paolo filled her mind. She wondered about love and how complicated it is if one tries to figure it with her head. Paolo's eyes had invited her into his home...into his world. He made her see again with her heart. Flora smiled with her thoughts of Paolo. How she missed that man who loved her. The crickets seemed to miss him, too.

An odd noise from the shrubs caught Flora's attention. It was probably a little rabbit, she thought. Flora started walking faster down the path, maybe the rabbit was more than a rabbit...maybe it was a *wolf*. Flora's imagination grabbed the serenity from the night and filled it with suspicion...and apprehension. She began walking even faster, almost jogging in her dressy garb. Her high heel snagged her long skirt making her trip. She fell a slow motion fall and landed flat on the ground.

She lifted her head that kissed the dry dirt and suddenly felt the effects of her grand-slam fall to the earth. She hadn't fallen that hard since she was a kid. Even though every muscle in her body felt as if it had been thrown down a flight of stairs...she had to laugh at herself and the picture in her mind of such a crazy scene.

Slowly rolling on her side and half dazed from the unexpected pounce to the ground, Flora began spitting out the rough grit that stuck to her lips. Flora's twisted skirt made her feel like she was caught in a giant Chinese handcuff. She tried to unzip her zipper, but tore it instead with her persistence. Little by little, she unwound her skirt; the way she had to unwind her winter flannel nightgown on nights she went to bed on flannel sheets. Between her grunts and groans...she heard another noise...only this time a little closer from the field.

"Need any help?" A voice asked in the near surroundings.

"Who's there?" Flora said wondering if the kids decided to prank her. "Who's there...answer me or I'll...I'll... ." I'll do what, scream and wake up the dead, Flora thought allowing her imagination to work overtime once again. It was probably the kids...just the kids hoping to scare her.

"What'll you do, Flora...," the voice teasingly chided. Flora suddenly heard through the soft disguise...her heart started beating like a run away train. Flora kicked off her other heel and pulled off her torn skirt...that set her free to finally stand. She ran in the opposite direction of the deep voice. He followed her, gaining the distance Flora desperately tried to set between them.

With his outstretched arm, he firmly yanked her to an abrupt stop. Flora didn't want to turn around. He walked around to the front of her. They could have been face to face...but, Flora wouldn't look up to see her night intruder...her night visitor.

"Flora...look at me." The voice was his own now and Flora wanted to look up, but like a little girl, she stubbornly refused his invitation for a moment longer...until her heart got the best of her. Then, Flora's eyes carefully climbed the stitches in his tattered wool sweater as far as his neck where the cable ended abruptly into worn threads. Paolo's heavy sweater had covered much of the past months hardship; his neck made her see it all too plainly.

As she placed her hands softly on his shoulders Flora felt his growing heavier on her own. With that encouragement she went carefully to his wonderful eyes. Affectionately but with much curiosity, she looked at him.

His eyes were the same as she remembered them. They sparkled. This was the man she fell deeply in love with. Even in the dim night light Paolo's eyes were bright and full of everything Flora needed to see. It was like Christmas and seeing the first bright lights of the season. As their eyes met, Flora remembered all the reasons why she loved Paolo so much. Her mind flashed back to Paolo's visit to the north where precious promises had been made. Time dissolved into nothing. His absence vanished from Flora's heart.

Paolo drew Flora closer to himself and they embraced. As Flora felt his back she realized how much his large frame had melted. As her fingers gently massaged his shoulders she bit her lip trying to hold back her tears. She didn't want to let go of Paolo, but she did. She wanted to see his face again. He was really, finally there.

"Paolo...you're back," Flora said trying to act as if she wasn't shocked by his physical differences, "...and...look how I look...if I knew you were coming...I'd have baked a cake...or put on a nicer dress." Paolo heard through Flora's humorous attempt at being courageous. He didn't allow her time for one more question or comment. Paolo held her tightly and then looked seriously into her face.

"No cake?" Paolo paused for a moment with a big smile.

"No cake here...but over there...," Flora said as she pointed in the direction of the gym. Paolo interrupted Flora and took her into his arms.

"Everything I want is right here... ." Paolo kissed Flora...she kissed him back tenderly.

"Paolo...do you know how much I missed you...," Flora whispered to Paolo, barely able to get the words out in one breath. Flora held him tightly.

"About as much as I missed you... ." Paolo held Flora even tighter. They were content to be in each others arms.

Suddenly, remembering Roberto, Flora asked where he was and if he was safe.

"Roberto is fine...he's okay, don't worry...but he had to stay back for a while longer...he's doing fine...he's tough like me." Flora knew Paolo was sparing her the complete truth. For the time being, she'd trust his discretion.

"Paolo...I'm sorry for everything you had to go through...I'm so glad you're back...I have to tell you something wonderful." Flora couldn't say anything else. Flora hugged him not ever wanting to let go. Paolo felt her emotion and found it difficult keeping back his tears of joy. After being together for a few moments Paolo broke his strong embrace. He placed his hands on her shoulders and looked directly into her eyes. He saw so much of what he needed to see.

"Flora...I've imagined being right here, a thousand times...I missed you Flora...there's alot I have to tell you...about everything...," he kissed her again. "Let's walk back up to the chapel." Paolo took Flora's hand noticing her feet were bare.

"You're gonna be alright?...with your barefoot feet?...I'll give you my shoes if you want them... ."

Flora looked down at her snagged nylons and bare feet.

"I'm not worried about my feet...but I wouldn't mind borrowing your jacket... ." Paolo took off his sport coat and wrapped it around Flora's shoulders; she slid it down to her waist hoping it would cover most of her flimsy slip. She tied the arms of the jacket around her waist like a belt. Flora smiled at Paolo. He wrapped his arm around her shoulder. He led Flora back to the chapel. "We have to talk."

"Let's go by the light...it smells like fresh flowers in here... ." Paolo led Flora up the aisle and scooted her in the front pew. He went over to the votive candles and lit at least five or six of them. "Remind me to drop some money into the donation box tomorrow." Paolo pulled the lining of his pockets inside out. Flora loved his sense of humor and timing. Paolo walked back to Flora. He sat down next to her.

"This feels good...and you look fantastic in the candle-light." Paolo looked into Flora's eyes. Flora kissed his lips. She felt his nervous jitters through their tender touching.

"You don't have to say anything, Paolo...let's just sit...it's been a long day." Flora looked ahead at the candles burn-ing like her heart. Paolo took her hand and kissed it. He sat back into the pew and took a deep breath. Flora heard anguish in his deep breathing.

"Paolo...everything is going to be alright...you're home." Flora hoped to relax him.

"It's always going to be something Paolo...and that's okay...you are like Alfredo...you are a lover of mankind and a generous person...you feel the sadness in the world...you'll be here and there...but...I'll always be here when you need me...and I hope you need me alot." Flora ended her words and sat quietly with Paolo even though there were a million other things she wanted to say and a thousand things she wanted to ask him. They sat in silence for a good while. Then Paolo cleared his throat. Flora jumped. He laughed at her reaction and then apologized for scaring her.

"I'm sorry, Flora...that's the second time tonight I star-tled you." Paolo smiled a big smile at Flora. He took her hand and squeezed it hard. Flora squeezed Paolo's hand back.

"And you love it, Paolo...but I'm keeping track...I owe you one...and *trust* me...I'll get to *startle* you," Flora said teasingly. For a moment Paolo looked more relaxed. Then, the anxious look came back on his face.

"Paolo, can you tell me about it?" Flora asked softly. Paolo looked for a moment into Flora's eyes. Her eyes were saying so much to him. He carefully began his story.

"Flora...the past few months have been heaven and hell... there were those heavenly days when Alfredo and I could feed the kids more than a cup of oatmeal...heavenly days when we were strong enough to take care of the countless others who were way worse off than we were...and then just when it seemed we saw a tiny ray of light in the dark sky that hangs so heavy over Bosnia, a *hell* day would come...a day when I felt no one understood what was really going on, days when you knew no one around had the strength to care...Flora...I never knew how difficult it was to get people to listen to plain common sense...anything I ever ventured before seemed to go so smoothly...but the redtape...and the lame excuses we'd get from people who supposedly *cared*...you know, adults say it's the kids who believe in fairytales...I say it's the adults who are living in the fantasy world with their excuses and countless reasons for moving slowly...their bellies are full at night, they have wood to heat the stoves and warm their aching bones...kids believe things can change, that one day things will be better...Alfredo was laughed at...even spat upon by his own people who had already given up...we were fighting more than one battle over there...it's never just one battle anywhere... ." Paolo stood up and walked around to the front of Flora's bench. He was very nervous. He went on.

"Flora...Alfredo died...a week ago." Paolo put his hands on his head and then ran his fingers through his hair as if to straighten out the details in his mind. Flora couldn't believe the good man was dead. She didn't say anything, she couldn't. She waited for Paolo to go on.

"He died from complications...from AIDS...can you imagine that...? I tried not to think about Alfredo...they burned his body...as if he had the bubonic plague...as if the saint was a leper...the man gave his life to everyone... ." Paolo walked away from Flora for a minute to gather his composure.

Flora couldn't believe the horror story Paolo and Roberto had lived through. As he kept on and on about the work that was done...and the work that still had to be done...she wanted only to go up to him and put her hand over his lips...he had gone through enough agony.

"I'm going to go back, Flora...Alfredo didn't die in vain...he knew for quite some time that his days were numbered...I remember the day I arrived there...I waited on the docks for him...I was early or he was late...finally he showed up. We made some stops on our journey to the orphanage and delivered food to some families that had been literally starving for months...old people to weak to stand, too cold to smile...babies with no *hope* in their eyes...like why were they even born...I can't forget what I saw...I won't forget...I've got to finish setting up the foundation...Roberto won't come back here, not until things are better...he sees himself in all the children...Flora, I know you understand... ." She didn't want to...but she did.

"I do." Flora said as she walked over to Paolo. He reached out to her and they embraced. She felt the great burden he was carrying. She tried to comfort him by simply being there. Paolo sat down on the Communion rail.

"Flora...so much has happened since we've seen each other...I've seen things that I can't pretend I never saw...I've felt things that I thought I was incapable of feeling...I felt RAGE to the point of wanting to kill...I felt *hate*...enough hate that I didn't want to believe in love...for a time I couldn't remember what love meant. Then, Alfredo died in my arms. This big, tough guy reduced to a thin, frail, wisp of a man...he became so weak giving away every ounce of himself...he was love...he was hope...the last words that came out of his mouth were about love.

"The night Alfredo died, I dreamt about you...about us, and in that dream I loved you more than all the rage and hatred...we loved each other in spite of all the anguish...Alfredo made me promise to come back here and see you...he told me that we were what life was all about...love was what life is all about. I love you Flora...we'll always have each other."

"I love you, Paolo...," Flora said as she walked up to the Communion rail toward Paolo. He took her hand. Paolo hesitated for a moment then began his explanation.

"Flora...I'm here illegally...they wouldn't give me permission to come back...I have to be tested in three months for AIDS...anyone who works in the public healthcare, in any way...has to be tested before leaving the country...Alfredo's death doubly enforced that law for me...Alfredo knew they would make it almost impossible for me to come home...he set everything up for this trip before he died."

"This all sounds so unreal."

"It's hard sorting out the real from the unreal...all I know...is that I love you...Vince doesn't even know I'm here, I'll see him tonight... ."

"Not hearing from you and Roberto has really upset his ulcer...he's going to be so surprised...and Dolly...she knew you'd come today... ."

"I can't wait to see Vince and Dolly, I've missed them so much...," Paolo said with controlled excitement in his voice. "And, I want to see the newlyweds before they go on their honeymoon... ." Paolo looked at Flora...he smiled at her, content to be near her. His smile made Flora smile. For the next few moments, they tossed back and forth sentiments that were best expressed silently.

"Well...how is everything with you...?" Paolo took both of Flora's hands and held them tightly as if to squeeze in the answer he wanted to hear.

"Everything is fine now." Flora said, squeezing Paolo's hands back. "But, this year was tough...for everyone...we all made it though...and...alot of new beginnings."

"Alot of new beginnings." Paolo let go of Flora's hands and whisked her in his arms. He held her close and tenderly. There was silence for a few moments.

"Flora...you had some good news for me?"

"Paolo...some very good news...are you ready?" Flora held both of his hands.

"Ready!"

"I don't know how to say it...Paolo... ."

"Flora...just say it...good news is good news."

"Okay...Paolo." Flora hesitated for a moment looking deeply into Paolo's eyes. She brought his hands up to her mouth and kissed them. Looking back into his eyes she continued.

"Paolo...you have...a little son." Tears filled her eyes but she continued. "He's seven weeks old today...he weighed seven pounds at birth and now he's eleven pounds and has alot of curly dark hair...and he looks like you...and me...good news?"

Paolo squeezed Flora's hands and looked into her eyes with great emotion. Flora looked back into his; their silence speaking to each other more than a million words could say. Finally, Paolo spoke.

"I'm a father...I have a son?...seven weeks old?...and he looks like me?...Flora... ." Paolo took Flora into his arms.

"Flora...it's a crazy wonderful world sometimes isn't it...thank you...for everything."

Flora dreamt of that moment for months...now she enjoyed the comfort and security of Paolo's embrace.

"Wait!" Paolo said as he abruptly let go of Flora.

"*Little Paolo*?...that's what you want to call him?" Paolo

squinted his eyes and wrinkled his nose as if tasting something sour in his mouth.

"Paolo is his middle name...I wanted you to name him."

"No, no, *Paolo* is good," Paolo said sounding not to sure of himself. "You like it...and I...like it...but...I was thinking... you know... ."

"You were thinking," Flora quickly interjected, "...that you'd like to name him something else...I kind of thought that...go ahead...he's your son." Paolo smiled at Flora and without delay he quickly announced his choice of names.

"How about...Alfredo Vincenzo Paolo...and we could call him... Freddy?"

"Sounds wonderful...," Flora said proudly. "I can't wait for you to see little *Freddy*."

"Flora...wait a minute...with all this excitement I almost forgot... ." Paolo unbuttoned his shirt. He opened it up, and looked down to his chest, "Flora...it's my treat for coffee."

Flora noticed her pendant hanging around Paolo's neck. She laughed at his wearing her ornate charm. He began defending himself for his fine taste in jewelry.

"You know, earrings were in last year...but now it's pendants...at least in Bosnia...looks pretty good...huh?" Paolo buttoned his shirt back up and reached into his pocket. "Here 's another popular item." Paolo reached for Flora's hand. He placed a diamond ring on her finger. Flora didn't know what to say.

"Paolo...it's beautiful...I...gosh...it's beautiful." Flora looked at her hand and then at Paolo. She was speechless. Paolo kissed her hand.

"It was my mother's wedding ring...Vince gave it to her on their third anniversary...I want you to have it...with one condition...promise me you'll never hock it for a cup of coffee."

"Not even cappuccino...with praline sprinkles?" Flora teased Paolo, then became very serious. "I'll never take it off, Paolo, not for all the coffee in Brazil or...all the tea in

China...*unless we're really thirsty.*"

Paolo kept his eyes fixed on Flora's. He smiled at her with a terrific tenderness in his heart. "We have a son." Paolo took a deep breath, "...a tiny, little baby... ."

Paolo looked at Flora like she was his most cherished treasure. He slowly wrapped his arms around her holding her carefully...as if he had snatched her from some grand dream. Flora hugged Paolo back with as much feeling. With her face nestled securely in his embrace she peeked up into the dark night sky so full of stars. In their company, Flora smiled and whispered a prayer for her and Paolo.

"Look," Paolo said excitedly. He twirled Flora from his arms and directed her eyes up into the sky.

"See that star...the bright one with all the little ones around it...it's Alfredo."

Flora nodded to Paolo.

"That is him...look how he's twinkling, Paolo."

"Twinkling...like *he knows what I'm thinking... .*"

"Like he knows what we're *both* thinking... ."

"Well...what are we smartfolks waiting for...the sky to fall on us? Flora, we have lots to celebrate...let's go."

"Let's go!"

Paolo and Flora headed back to the wedding celebration hearing the music that was playing from the gymnasium...hearing the wisdom from the stars.

"Love...wonderful love...it's the only thing that ever really matters."

About the Author

T. Stellini lives in a small town in Michigan with her big family, oak trees, little lakes and lots of stars.

She began her writing career at the age of six. She'd help her brothers and sisters and the neighbor kids design letters that would for *surely catch Santa's eye.* The little ones didn't care so much about the frilly red and green construction paper envelopes trimmed with paperlace, but they truly appreciated having someone who could very eloquently verbalize their wish lists.

And with age came bits of wisdom and grace, a few college term papers, love letters, grocery lists, school absent notes for her five children...and articles in THE FAMILY magazine. Then, letters galore to publishers inviting them to take a peek at her first novel.

One fortunately did.

T. Stellini is now at work on her second novel that will once again take us to Italy...to a small town on the Adriatic where much is happening over the eastern horizon.